FALSE FINDINGS

*This book is dedicated to my
mother, Jane Hutchison. Through
God's grace and pure determination,
you are the true definition of a fighter
and I am blessed to be your daughter.
I love you, Mom.*

ACKNOWLEDGMENTS

Cover Art & Formatting: Heather Payne, Payne-Design.com

Author Photo: Ethan Fuller, E.L.F. Photography

Thank you to my Beta Readers for your
insight, information, and encouragement!

Cheryl Corbin, Anna Fernandez, Wanda Fuller,
Heather Garent, Roberta Goodboy, Sandra Harvey,
Bob Hutchison, Heather Payne, Jeannine Russell,
Laurel Sorenson, Kathy Tripp, and Mary Westfall.

FALSE FINDINGS

A ROCKFISH ISLAND MYSTERY BOOK III

BY J.C. FULLER

CHAPTER 1

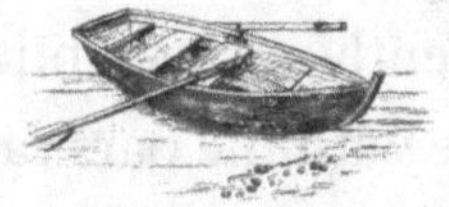

A full moon, unveiled from its dark castings, shimmered down upon the salted waters and the old dock jetting from the island's shore. The dock itself, beaten and worn, bore the white peaking waves of a riled ocean, its encrusted pilings standing firm against the tumultuous tide. Beside it, held captive by a rusty cleat, was its lone companion, a rowboat, the wooden counterpart, pulling and surging against the old dock, much like an undecided lover.

Hollow and thudding footsteps, sudden upon the pier, resonated, the hour past midnight, pounding heavily upon the wooden slats, the dock no longer abandoned. The white rowboat at once sinking further into the water under the unexpected weight of a passenger.

Quick, deft hands, unburdened from their heavy load, untied the small skiff from its slip, hastily throwing into the bow its weather-worn line, the rope, landing haphazardly against the cargo lying limp on the timber floor.

Pushed away from the dock's fender, the rowboat, oars dipping in and out of the sea-foamed waves, slipped silently away while grunts of exertion, marking time with the oars rattling inside their rings, sounded above the splash of the blades being driven into the dark.

The rower, eyeing the distance from the pier, abruptly lifted the poles from the ocean, the waves crashing against the small boat, bitter cold water slopping over the side.

Was this far enough out? Or rather, deep enough?

The oars were pulled in.

Time was a factor.

Visible from the secluded pier under the moon's spotlight, the rowboat now buoyed over the tempestuous water, swaying precariously, side to side, struggling to carry the load. At its stern was a large man, whose dark outline stood stark against the lit horizon, hesitation clearly visible in his stance, a wooden oar held high above his head.

As if sensing the delay, impatient waves splashed against the gunwales sloshing up and over the side, daring him to continue. The moment of indecision passed and the oar came crashing down, the blade cutting into flesh and bone.

Overhead, reaching and stretching, grasping sky in mass momentum, dark clouds moved steadily with the wind, touching the moon and overcoming its brilliance, its glorious radiance engulfed and swallowed whole. The absence leaving the dark deeds upon the water hidden from view.

The crunch of bone was sickening.

The man tugged on the oar, the wooden blade causing an unpleasant sound as he wrenched it free from the corpse at his feet. With a deep breath, he brandished the oar into the air once more, bringing it down hard, a loud THACK sounding across the water.

The oar was brought down again.

With more effort on each descent, he wielded the weapon into the air, a cascading spray of red following the arch of the upward blade before the downward fall, each sinking hit sounding denser and wetter than the prior.

He was going to be sick.

With a final pitch, the oar broke in his hand, the blade fastening tight into the bloody mass. It was more than he could take. He lurched to the edge of the boat and fell hard on his knees, heaving over the side.

His stomach emptied.

Pushing back, his labored breaths visible vapor upon the winter air, he sagged down onto the wooden seat, exhausted, the small rowboat, in return, rocking dangerously, threatening to topple him over.

Instinctively, he grabbed the sides to steady his balance, leaving bloody handprints on the gunnels, stark against the aged whiteboards.

The exertion of driving the oar down with all his force and trying to keep his balance in the small boat had worn him out, not to mention the deed of killing itself.

There was still so much more to do.

Wearily climbing to his feet, he worked the oar free, tossing the cracked pole to the floor. He then reached down and began to undress the body, his hands untying the worn winter boots, wrenching them off, thick woolen socks with them, shakily dropping the pair to the floor. He then lumbered to the waist, undoing the button and zipper, tiredly tugging and pulling each leg free. He moved up to the chest, lucky the shirt was a button-down, a heavy flannel, and paused at the last item, deciding to leave the underwear on.

There had to be some decency in death.

He laboriously sat the body up, hefting it onto the bow seat, and clumsily tied the small boat anchor around the waist. Then cinching the ratty rope tight, he said a short prayer, an apology of sorts, and pushed the body over the starboard side, the splash much louder than he had anticipated.

As if coming out of himself, he glanced up and nervously surveyed the nearby waters, shooting an anxious look towards the old wooden dock.

All was still and silent.

He needed to hurry.

Grabbing the rope tied to the bow of the boat, he jerked it free of its rusted ring, casting it down onto the floor. He then knotted the laces of the heavy disregarded boots together, hastily stuffing the socks into the toe, dropping the boots down onto the bow seat. He then snatched the rope from the floor, his heart pounding in his ears.

Had he gotten everything?

Staggering a step back, he took inventory, his eyes wide.

There was so much blood.

Panicked, he grabbed the flannel shirt and sloshed it into the cold water. Pulling the sopping mass out, he used it to smear his bloody prints off the gunnels and wipe the oar handles clean. He then tied the shirt arms to the old rope and snatched up the jeans legs to do the same.

Picking up the bundle of clothes, he threaded the corded rope through the tied laces of the heavy boots, knotting them together, a makeshift anchor of sorts.

About to toss the mass over the side, he suddenly realized he had forgotten something, and hurled everything down, quickly rummaging the jeans pockets.

He'd almost made a terrible mistake.

With trembling hands, he pulled a leather wallet free. Correcting his error, he stuffed the wallet back before hunting through the remaining pockets, finding them empty.

Satisfied, he then took the boots, carefully dunking them into the freezing water, letting the ocean fill the space, and pull the bloody bundle under.

That deed done, he stood up, his knees feeling weak, and tiredly reached behind his neck, grasping his own bloody t-shirt, pulling it over his head before grabbing the handgun stuffed in his waistband, yanking it free. He swayed with the little boat, his stomach churning and his skin goose-pimpled, waiting to see if anything would resurface.

The waters stayed dark.

Good.

Taking a deep breath, he wrapped the t-shirt around the muzzle of the handgun, doing his best to muffle the sound, then pulled the trigger, sending four bullets into the bottom of the wooden vessel, seawater beginning to seep in. He pulled the trigger again, hearing a hollow click.

That was it. It was empty.

Tossing the .22 into the water, a splash announcing its descent, he gauged the distance to the awaiting dock, a regret coming to mind.

If he was a stronger swimmer, he could have rowed further out.

It probably would have been wiser.

Well, there was nothing for it now.

His heart pounding in his ears, he plunged himself over the side and into the dark waves, desperately clawing for the surface, an irrational fear taking hold as an imagined hand, reaching from the depths, stretched out to touch him, the fingertips of revenge a hairsbreadth away.

Bobbing up like a cork, he gasped for air, his arms slapping down upon the rough waves.

He was safe.

Nothing could touch him now. He only needed to make it to shore.

The hard part was over.

CHAPTER 2

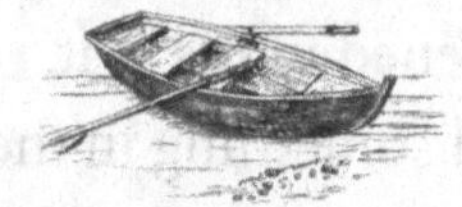

Squinting through his frost-covered windshield in annoyance, Park Ranger, Philip Russell, roughly closed the truck's glove box with an impatient swat.

The ice scraper was missing.

He shook his head, a half-smile on his lips. Kody, his younger counterpart, must have swiped it and forgotten to put it back. Typical kid.

Punching the defrost button, Philip sat back heavily in his seat, forced to wait. His whole morning had been like this. He had slept through his alarm, cut himself shaving... twice, and managed to burn his toast beyond recognition. But not before knocking over his coffee into his own lap, ...and now, he was going to be late.

"Phil, ya there? Over?" Kody's voice crackled

through the two-way radio.

Philip snatched up the handset and practically growled, "Here."

"You at the office?"

"Nah, I'm running late. What's up?"

"I found something out here, and I... I don't know what to make of it." Kody clicked off.

Philip straightened in his seat.

He once found something in the forest.

"What is it?"

"A rowboat."

Philip relaxed.

"Probably broke loose from the docks during the big wind storm last Friday. Is there a name on it?"

"There is, but I don't recognize it, and it's hard to see. It's got... it's got..." Kody broke off, and Philip wondered for a second if his radio had gone out.

"Kody, ya still there?"

"You're gonna need to come see for yourself, Phil. I'm out at Driftwood Beach, by the outlet. Something is not right," Kody's voice was unsteady.

It was clear to Philip that the young ranger was alarmed. "Okay, kid. On my way. Over and out." Philip clipped the two-way back onto the dash and hit the wipers again, this time, the black blades sliding easily as chunks of ice jockeyed back and forth across the windshield.

Almost mesmerized, Philip's mind flew back in

time to another cold morning, driving down the range road. He'd stumbled across a black bear and her cubs, fresh blood on the sow's muzzle. He'd thought nothing of it at the time, supposing the bears had taken a fawn for breakfast.

Deciding to move the remains away from the range road and deter the bears from coming back, he had gone in search of the deserted carcass. What he had found instead had been life-altering. A woman's mangled body, her throat slit from ear to ear.

The authorities had been quickly called in, the island's new sheriff coming to the rescue.

However, unfamiliar with the small community, it was apparent the new addition would need help with the tight-lipped locals. Thus, Philip had found himself assisting in a murder investigation, one with a tragic end.

Refusing to let his thoughts wander any further, Philip shook himself free and pointed the forest truck in the direction of Driftwood Beach and his young ranger.

"Alright, then. Let's see what the kid has found."

CHAPTER 3

Sheriff Lane's cell phone went off, and she risked a glimpse, the phone sitting in the cupholder. She recognized the name on the caller ID and sighed in exasperation, pulling her vehicle over to the side.

"Martha, what have I told you about calling me on my cell phone while I'm driving?" Lane lightly reprimanded, having left the sheriff's office only five minutes prior.

"I was hoping you were already out of the car," Martha Barnes said flatly. "It only takes five minutes to get anywhere on the island. You should drive faster."

Lane's mouth twitched.

Martha had been her idea.

Most people would have had trepidations about hiring the town's gossip as a dispatcher. Rightly concerned, the gossipmonger might be unable to hold her tongue when the occasional "newsworthy" report came in.

Lane, though, had sought the woman out and offered her the job.

She had her reasons.

The most obvious being the very advantageous upper hand of having someone on the staff who knew everything about everyone... whether they liked it or not.

Martha being in her late fifties and prone to half-whisper most of her sentences, had readily accepted the part-time position, thrilled at the prospect.

Too thrilled, Lane noticed.

So, with the greatest of coincidences, the sheriff "happened" to stumble across a cuddling couple in the back seat of a parked silver Mercedes-Benz the next evening. The supposedly serendipitous find promised to guarantee Martha's sealed lips and successfully put Lane's suspicious concerns to rest.

One could consider the arrangement dangerously close to blackmail.

Lane would argue it was more like insurance.

The locating and discovery of the very married Mrs. Martha Barnes in the company of the town's semi-retired and highly respected attorney, Mike Allister, had gone according to plan. However, Lane's flashlight landing on the lawyer with his pants down to his ankles had done little to improve the relations between them.

After all, it had been Lane who had accused his grandson, last summer, of being a murderer. In her defense, the young man had been the last person to see the victim alive.

He was bound to be considered a suspect. Though it didn't help matters, at the advice of his pompous and grandstanding grandfather, the young man had refused to cooperate fully and withheld pertinent information.

This still angered Lane.

Things could have gone a lot differently if the young man had been able to speak freely.

"Martha, I don't understand why you don't like to use the two-way."

"Sheriff, people listen in on scanners." There was a long pause. "I should know. I've got one at home."

"Martha," Lane started.

"Can I tell you why I'm calling now, or would you rather I waited till you got back to the office?"

"Might as well. Want me to pick up something from Hattie's General?" Lane started to dig out her notepad, ready to write down a list of office needs.

"No. Well... we could use some cookies upfront, but this will have to come first. Glen Sorenson says he's found a *floater*," Martha whispered the last word.

"A floater? As in..."

Lane wasn't quite sure if "floater" meant what she thought it did or if it was island lingo for a dead, bloated seal.

"A *dead body*, Sheriff. Snagged it on a crab pot, right off his private dock."

CHAPTER 4

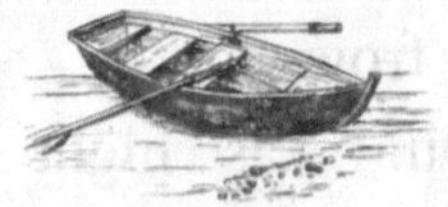

G len Sorenson, his shaking hands stuffed deep into his coat pockets, stood at the end of his private road, waiting.

It had been ten minutes since he'd phoned into the sheriff's office, greatly disappointed at hearing Martha's voice on the other end. She had a quick tongue, Martha, and no doubt, his news was probably already all over town.

Crestfallen, Glen sighed heavily, his shoulders rising and slumping with the breath.

What a shame.

He had a grand vision of sitting at the picnic table at Hattie's general store, regaling everyone with his find. Their eyes riveted on him, hanging on his every word, their earnest attention, wholly consumed, fascinated, and appalled. The small crowd, curious to know what he pulled from the cold deep, demanding morbid details only he could give with relish.

Even Dub, his best buddy, would have been forced to listen, pictured sitting there tongue-tied for once, unable to debate against his claim. That is, as far as Glen knew, Dub had never pulled a dead body from the sea. He might finally be one up on him.

Glen suddenly frowned.

Where was Dub? Last night he'd promised to help him check his crab pots in the morning though Dub didn't like doing so. He was funny about stuff like that. Just because crabs were out of season and technically it was considered poaching, Dub got all worrisome, giving him long rambling speeches, lecturing on how illegal it was and how detrimental it could be to the crustacean population.

Glen dismissed Dub's long-winded blatherings. After all, he only took enough for himself, a crab or two for his buddy in thanks, and then the couple dozen or so, he sold to The Royal Fork restaurant every day. A minuscule fraction compared to the amount of crab out in the deep Puget Sound as a whole.

But Dub still complained, all the same, even jawed on about it as he ate his corn and crab chowder at the restaurant last night.

Ol' coot of a hypocrite.

Truth be told, Glen knew Dub didn't like getting

up so early in the morning. But still, he had agreed and promised to be there before daybreak, and he wasn't.

Sleeping in! That's what he was doing! It would be just like him too.

The thought irked Glen to no end.

Dub knew full well how helpful it was having a rowboat to haul up the pots, not to mention, an extra hand. Especially with Glen's own boat being out of commission.

Where was he?

Maybe Dub's arthritis had flared up on him again? Strange he didn't call, though. Could it be the old codger got the jump on him? Had he already heard the news from quick tongue Martha?

There was more than a good chance.

Glen ground his teeth, the few he had.

That was probably it. Dub was making his way down to Hattie's right now, intent on telling everyone all about it! Likely telling the story as if he'd been here!

Damn that Martha!

The sound of gravel under tires caught Glen's ear, and he pulled his hands out of his jacket, splaying his fingers wide, his large hands still trembling. He stuffed them back into his pockets and took a halting step into the road to see who was coming.

Crawling down the drive was the sheriff's patrol truck.

Glen was more than relieved to see the sheriff hadn't come across town with lights flaring and sirens full board. That kind of commotion on a tiny island of their size would have brought the whole town's attention upon them. She was pretty smart for a greenhorn islander. Maybe he'd still have a story to tell at the picnic table after all?

Glen gave the small, blonde sheriff a nod of the head as she parked the truck a few feet in front of him. He walked to the driver's door.

"Mornin', Sheriff." Glen took a step back as the truck door swung open. "I take it, Martha got a hold of you?"

"Morning, Mr. Sorenson. She sure did. You, okay?"

Sheriff Lane, her foot braced against the front door, pinning it open, was leaned over the passenger side, digging for something underneath the seat. She popped up, a large roll of yellow police tape in hand.

Glen lightly tapped his veteran's cap. "Sure, I'm good. Not the first time I've seen a dead body."

Lane hopped down from the truck, giving the big, elderly man her full attention.

"I'd imagine not. Thank you for your service, Glen."

"My honor." Glen cleared his throat, always slightly abashed when thanked for his time and efforts in the war. "Got everything you need?"

"Almost." She leaned back into the truck, pulling an aluminum case from behind the driver's seat, setting it on the ground. "I've called the coroner, and he's on the way. Is the body secure?" Lane asked, unwinding the yellow tape and walking over to a wooden post, tying the end. "It's not going to float away, is it?"

She passed the roll to Glen, nodding for him to carry it to the far side of the driveway, blocking off the scene.

"No... no, it's hooked pretty well." Glen walked to the opposite side and tied his end. "Where's your deputy?" He handed the roll back.

"On his way. It's supposed to be his day off."

"I see. Well, um. Should we wait, or do you want to look at it now?"

Glen peered down at the short and petite sheriff standing next to him.

Though he'd lost an inch or so with age, he still towered over the young woman. With her hair pulled back in a tight bun, pink earmuffs, and a matching scarf cuffed around her neck, she stood there looking up at him. Her uniform pressed precisely, practically hidden under an oversized winter jacket, with knee-high galosh boots on her feet, not looking all that intimidating to him. But then again, Glen knew she had already handled two major cases since she'd been on the island, and it hadn't been quite a full year. The still considered "new" female sheriff had earned a lot of respect and a few loud-mouthed critics among the town folk in the small amount of time she'd been on the island.

"Not just yet." Lane reached behind and pulled out a notepad from her back pocket, clicking her pen as she flipped the leather flap over. "Tell me how you found the body? I am assuming you didn't recognize the person as you didn't mention a name to Martha."

"No, you're right. I didn't recognize the body."

"Clothing or anything like that look familiar?"

"No..." Glen shook his head in the negative. "Not one bit. Though, if I did recognize 'em, I'm not quite sure I would have told Martha, regardless." Glen's mouth twitched.

Lane shot him a look of understanding and nodded her head for him to go on.

He started jerkily, "Well... um. I'd decided to do a little fishing this morning on my dock. Thought a bit of fish for lunch sounded nice. Walked myself down with my poles and saw someone's crab pot line tied to a piling."

Lane's eyebrow arched.

Like most of the island residents, she knew exactly where The Royal Fork restaurant got its daily fresh crab supply.

"I bet you were surprised to find it there," Lane

said flatly.

"Sure, was! It's illegal this time of year, you know." Glen shuffled side to side, suddenly feeling uncomfortable under the small sheriff's gaze and surprised by it. He hurried on, "So, I went to make sure there weren't any crabs sitting inside. Didn't want them to go to waste if I cut the line. They can't crawl out if you do that, ya know." He nervously adjusted his cap. "Started to haul it in, and the line felt like it was snagged on something. Gave it a hard tug and up popped the body like a top!"

"And that's when you called—"

Rumbling tires sounded behind them, and despite the frost covering the ground, Lane could see a cloud of dust stirred up, heading in their direction. Deputy Caleb Pickens had arrived on the scene. Though he had obeyed her instructions not to use his strobe or siren, he apparently hadn't been able to control his lead foot. Even a speeding vehicle through town could catch someone's eye and pique unwanted interest. Then again, maybe something else was wrong?

The patrol car stopped short, gravel flying at their feet.

"Sheriff?" Caleb jumped out of the patrol car, giving a brief and hurried nod in Glen's direction. "I need to speak with you."

Lane flipped her leather pad closed with a snap,

having already started her advance towards the vehicle.

"What's up?" she asked briskly, noting Caleb's uniform was wrinkled, probably having been snatched off his bedroom floor.

"Have you ID'd the body yet?" Caleb reached into the patrol car, popping the trunk.

"Not yet. Why?" Lane followed him to the back, the deputy grabbing the small stack of tire-tracked traffic cones.

"Martha got a call from the Harbor Master's office. Mike Allister's boat has been reported missing from its slip at the Seattle Marina, and no one can reach him." He shot a look over Lane's shoulder, Glen having wandered a few paces closer. Caleb lowered his voice so he wouldn't be overheard. "I also found his Mercedes at the ferry's Park and Ride lot. All four tires slashed, Sheriff."

"You sure it was Allister's?"

Caleb nodded his head.

"He's got those stupid vanity plates. Couldn't miss it."

"Stolen boat, slashed tires..."

Caleb interrupted Lane, nodding his head with more force.

"Exactly, Sheriff. It got me wondering. Could the floater be Mike Allister?"

CHAPTER 5

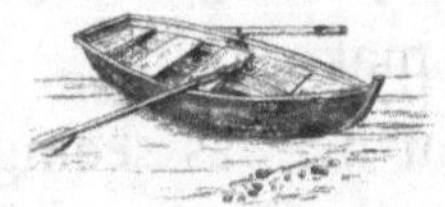

Philip took another walk around the moored boat, his feet sinking into the pebbled sand, shallow water splashing over his boots. It was his third rotation, and he was still taking it all in.

Quite the story had been unfolding on the surface of the beached boat. A bloodied oar blade, sticking up in the air, had been the first thing to catch his attention, the second being the four bullet holes peppering the hull.

On his next rotation, he noticed what appeared to be someone's attempt at wiping off bloody handprints from the side of the boat.

He circled around again.

Whoever had been in the small vessel had either failed miserably or had not bothered trying to erase the speckled, bloody aftermath covering most of the sea-worn wood inside.

He stopped, keeping his hands clear of the gunnels, and peered down. There was a black ski mask floating atop the shallow water at the bottom of the rowboat. His eyes roamed to the bow. He could see at least two bullet casings. He then turned his attention to the stern, spotting something underneath the seat, unable to make it out.

Not liking what he was seeing and not daring to reach for the unidentified object, he took several steps back. His young ranger had been right.

This was a crime scene.

"Did you touch anything, Kody?" Philip trudged his way back to solid shore, his thigh paining him slightly. Though his limp had virtually disappeared, he still suffered phantom aches and pains around his old gunshot wound.

"Just the bow, to haul her in," Kody called from the shore, his voice tense. "I grabbed it by the cleat on top."

"Okay. We'll need to make sure to let the authorities know. Don't want them finding your prints and thinking anything nefarious." He faced forward towards the boat, his hands on his hips and his face pensive, magnetic curiosity pulling his attention back to the abandoned dinghy once again. "Water Crest. A fancy name for a little boat." Philip absently scratched his head, his brow furrowed. "Sounds familiar, though." He shook his head in mild frustration, trying to jar his memory.

Kody's voice carried from behind him.

"So, with something like this... Do we call the coast guard or the sheriff's office?"

Philip turned at the waist and looked back at the young ranger a few feet behind him.

"You know, that's a good question. I suppose if it were found afloat out at sea, that would make it a coast guard issue. However, since it was found on island ground..." Philip's words trailed off.

"Sheriff Lane would kill you if you turned this over to the coast guard." Kody managed a small smile.

"That she would. Though I doubt she'll be pleased with me after I cancel our lunch date and drag her out here instead." Philip turned his back on the boat and signaled Kody to start heading up the incline to their awaiting rigs. "Who am I kidding? She'll be tickled pink! I'm gonna run in town and grab her. Why don't you head back to the office, gather the barricades, and quietly rope this area off? I doubt anyone is going to stumble across the boat while we're gone. In fact, I'm surprised you did!"

Kody pointed to the two overstuffed plastic garbage bags squished in the back of his jeep.

"Was picking up wind debris like you told me when I thought I better check the water's edge. This outlet always gets odd things beached on its shore from the mainland."

"This being the strangest by far," Philip agreed, clapping his hand on Kody's shoulder, using him as leverage to get up the embankment. "You know, I can't shake the feeling I know who that boat belongs to."

"Maybe the sheriff will recognize it?"

"Doubt it. She's not out and about at the docks all that much."

"Harry knows a lot of people. You could ask..." Kody stopped, seeing a dawned expression on Philip's face. "What? What did I say?"

"I know exactly whose boat that is!" Philip briskly started towards his truck, leaving his fellow, but bewildered, young ranger behind.

"Whose?" Kody followed after Philip, hot on his heels.

"Dub Granger, Glen's buddy. You know, the two geezers who gab it up with Harry over at Hattie's! It's Dub's boat!"

CHAPTER 6

"Well, Ralph?" Sheriff Lane's arm was pressed hard across her nose, her question to the coroner sounding slightly nasal.

At their feet, crabs still clinging to the discolored flesh, laid the bloated corpse of a man.

It had taken almost an hour, with the help of Deputy Pickens and George Barnes, the funeral director, the last having arrived with the funeral hearse upon the coroner's request, to untangle the swollen body and clumsily heave it face down onto the wooden planks.

The body was completely naked, except for a pair of white underwear briefs, the elastic band torn in the back, a corded and tattered rope still cinched tightly around the hips, the ends frayed and unraveled.

Spread around it, amongst the deserting crab,

were several yellow plastic numbered triangles marking key areas of interest, the sheriff's forensic case sitting open a few feet away.

"Is this anybody we know?" The question Lane really wanted to ask was, "Is this Mike Allister?" But since they were in mixed company, she refrained.

"Hard to say." The thin coroner stooped over the dead man, his fur-lined hood flopping forward over his head, giving the impression of a grim reaper.

"Can you at least tell how old he is?" Lane edged a little closer, peering down, noticing the dead man's peppered grey hair, a bald spot visible on the back-side of his head. "Forties, fifties, sixties... older?"

Coroner Ames shook his hooded head and mumbled, distracted, "Try there, Deputy. Careful." He pointed to the dead man's ankle and a portion of the snagged rope still attached to the crab pot. "Work your fingers between those two lines. That should give Glen enough slack to cut the leg free."

"We got it," Caleb said as Glen cut, the deputy hauling in the crab pot, tossing it to the side and out of the way.

"Think this is ferry related?" Glen took a step back, carefully closing his pocket knife, hands still trembling.

Caleb shot the old man a curious look before bending down to pick up the camera he had hastily placed on the dock's planks.

"You mean, like falling or jumping off the ferry?"

"Why sure!" George Barnes piped up, his all-black funeral attire stark against the ocean background. "Happens from time to time." He puffed out his chest, looping his fingers through his belt. "Suicides, mostly. Though you've got the occasional clumsy person leaning over the edge too far."

"But, he's basically naked." Caleb snapped a picture and then lowered the camera. "That wouldn't make any sense."

"Well... waves probably did that. Looks as if he's been out there for a few days. Wouldn't you say so, Ralph?" George didn't wait for the coroner to agree. "If it wasn't for the rope around his hips, I doubt he'd even have the underwear still on." George squatted down, flicking away a tiny crab sitting on the dead man's arm. "The rope, though..."

Glen pointed to the corded line. "Maybe he tied himself to his sailboat and still got tossed into the sea for all his trouble?"

"Nonsense! A person wouldn't be out sailing this time of year." George Barnes scoffed at the idea. "Winds are too high!"

"Oh, I wouldn't be so sure about that, George!" True to Glen's personality, he had to argue the point. "If you've got good ground tackle, there's no reason why you can't. Why, I know a guy who—"

Lane interrupted, slightly raising her voice.

"Ralph, what DO we have here?"

"Hard to say," the coroner repeated his answer, his attention focused on the dead man's hands. "See how it appears he's wearing latex gloves? Ones, which have split at the tips of his fingers? See that? In the trade, we call these washerwoman's hands." The coroner turned the palm over, indicating for Caleb to take a photo, and then lightly pulled off a strip of skin. "It's actually skin shuffling off the fingers. Reminds me of a shedding snake."

"Yeah, interesting." Lane tilted her head away, reluctant to look any longer. "Ralph, does that mean fingerprint identification is out of the question?"

"No, not necessarily."

Coroner Ames scooted around the body, picking up the other hand.

"Lots of grime and dirt under the nails," he continued, more to himself than the small group. "Here. Look at the palms. It's as if they're coated in some type of grease or oil." He looked up at Lane, pointing out the slick residue eagerly. "Interesting, don't you think?"

Lane, doing her best to focus on her notepad and not the smell, simply nodded her head in agreement.

"George, better go get the stretcher." The coroner gently laid the hand down and pushed his hood back, tugging a wool cap hidden underneath, further over his ears. "We need to get a move on."

"Sure thing. I'll get it and park the hearse right up to the dock." George's big boots stomped across the planks, the old wood squeaking under the pressure. "Gonna have to drive across your yard, Glen," George called over his shoulder, heading for the hearse. "Floaters don't last long out of water."

"He's right." Coroner Ames looked up, eyeing Lane. "I'll need to do an examination immediately. I won't be taking this one to the mainland."

Lane nodded her understanding and then slowly swallowed before answering, "That's fine."

She hated having a weak stomach.

Coroner Ames stood up, pointing down at the corpse.

"Okay, Deputy Pickens. Let's flip him right side up and see if you can put a name to the face."

The thin coroner stooped over and grasped the shoulders, indicating with a nod, for Caleb to help pull at the waist and Glen at the feet. Together, they manhandled the corpse onto its back.

Caleb lurched away, startled.

"Whoa! What in the world happened to his face?" He turned aside, completely repulsed. "Did... did the crabs do that?"

"Some of it," the coroner answered, hunching over, his head tilted in interest.

Lane too, inched closer, stunned.

"It looks as if... it's all bashed in."

The nose, or rather what might have once resembled a nose, was smashed flat, obviously broken. The eyes, a large gouge between them, were gone— the surrounding skin, black and purple. Long disfiguring gashes, running from the cheek to the forehead's crest, showed white bone, while the mouth, gaping open, was a black hole— the front teeth missing, a jagged piece of incisor hanging stubbornly to the bloodless gum.

"I wasn't fibbin' when I said I couldn't recognize 'em." Glen tugged hard on his cap, spitting into the sea. "Still can't make the features out."

"I don't think anyone could, Mr. Sorenson." Lane placed her hand on the old man's arm, then caught Caleb's eye, insisting in an apologetic tone, "I'll need you to take a few close-ups."

She turned her attention toward the coroner.

"Is this a boating accident?"

The coroner, seemingly unphased by the gruesome lump of flesh, crouched down for a better look.

"Not likely. This doesn't appear to be propeller related."

"Well, could waves have done this?" Caleb took a few shots, quickly dropping the camera from his line of sight. "I mean, could the waves bashing him against the dock pilings do this kind of damage?"

The small coroner shook his head, his latex-gloved finger sliding into a large gash in the forehead.

"I doubt it. These are deep cuts."

Lane's eyes roamed over the corpse's chest, the pale canvas devoid of tattoos, piercings, large scars, or healed surgery incisions. She scribbled down on her notepad. "No identifying marks." before slapping the leather cover shut and pointing to the man's left hand.

"I don't see any jewelry, not even a wedding ring. I wonder who he is, or rather, who he was?"

Sympathy for the deceased stranger was clearly etched on her face.

"Maybe he isn't married?" Caleb piped up, returning the camera to the forensic case, her young deputy slyly referencing the over sixty, single lawyer, Mike Allister.

She ignored him.

"Ralph, you think this guy was killed before hitting the water?" Lane looked down at the coroner, looking for some insight.

He hadn't seemed to hear her.

"Not a knife blade," he muttered, busily examining another gouging cut. "Nothing so sharp."

His attention moved to the corpse's chest.

"There are superficial cuts all over, but nothing matching these deep lacerations around here." His gloved hand circled the man's head. "The damage is completely isolated to the skull."

"So...the guy was bludgeoned to death?" Caleb

looked at the thin coroner, curious. "But with what?"

"Don't know yet. Definitely bludgeoned, but that's not necessarily what killed him." The coroner's hands moved down, lightly touching the base of the neck. "There's bruising around the throat consistent with strangulation."

"The waves definitely didn't do that." Caleb shook his head, his face stern.

"No, they didn't." Lane tapped the notepad against her leg, her thoughts forming. "This is a homicide. Somebody purposely removed this man's identification and did their best to make him a John Doe by distorting his features and tossing his remains into the sea, where I'm sure, they hoped he would stay."

"I won't disagree, Sheriff." The coroner, his lips set in a thin line, prodded another cut and met her eye. "I think our John Doe was never meant to be found."

CHAPTER 7

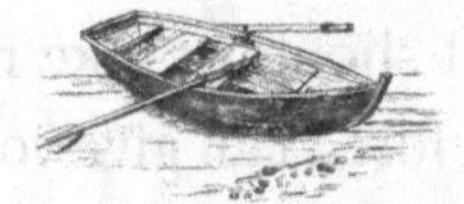

The hearse backed down the small hill leading to the dock, inching to a stop as the tires touched the wooden planks. The driver's door swung open, and the wind unexpectedly flung the door wide, forcing George to quickly lean out, snatching at the door handle while clumsily working his way from behind the steering wheel.

"Sheriff," George huffed, lumbering out of the vehicle, his long grey beard blowing beside him like a sail. "Your boyfriend is waiting by your truck. Told him I'd send you up." He jerked his head back the way he had come. "Said Martha told him where you were, and it's important, or he wouldn't be bothering you." George reached the back of the hearse and opened the extended tailgate.

"I'm sure it is important," Lane said stiffly, tucking her notepad into her back pocket, noticing their amused smiles. "And he's not my boyfriend," she suddenly insisted, unsure why she felt the need to deny it.

The coroner climbed to his feet, deftly changing the subject.

"I know you probably have a busy day ahead of you, Sheriff, but it shouldn't take me longer than a couple of hours before I can give you a better idea of what may have happened." He moved aside to make room for George and the stretcher. "We could go over my initial findings after lunch? Say, two this afternoon?"

Lane nodded and made a mental note. Lunch would need to be light.

"Thank you, Ralph. We'll talk more then."

She turned to Caleb, who had started packing up the small forensic case.

"Meet me at the station when you finish, Deputy."

"Will do, Sheriff." Caleb gave a quick nod as he snatched at the numbered forensic tabs, doing his best to collect them before George's big boots trampled them flat. "I'm right behind you."

"Ma'am?" Edging out of the stretcher's way, Glen stepped aside and asked, "Mind if I walk up with you? Dub was supposed to stop by this morning, and I'm guessing he's up there waiting along with Phil. Probably yammering his head off."

"Sure, Mr. Sorenson. We can talk as…"

"Dub isn't up there." George dropped the folded body bag to the dock with a heavy thud. "It's just Phil waitin'. Didn't see anybody else."

Glen frowned in concern.

"You sure?"

"Maybe he saw our rigs and the police tape? Might have made his way back home?" Lane suggested.

"Who, Dub? Nah! He would have plowed down here just to see what all the commotion was about!" George chuckled, waving Caleb out of his way.

Glen vigorously nodded his head.

"You're not wrong, George."

"Possibly Ranger Russell sent him home?" the coroner offered, pulling his large winter jacket closer around his thin frame before pulling his cap down tighter over his ears.

"I bet you, that's what he did. Why don't we go up and see?" Lane lightly grabbed Glen's arm, encouraging him to walk with her up the small incline. "Did you and Dub have a set time to meet today?" Lane let go once they reached the top of the small hill.

"Not exactly. He usually shows up before daybreak," Glen said, slightly winded.

"That's awful early."

Glen gave her a sidelong look.

"He likes my coffee."

Lane nodded, a smile forming.

"So, how long have you and Dub known each other?"

"Over sixty years."

"That's a long time. Did you serve together in the war?"

Glen shook his head, stuffing his hands further into his pockets.

"Married sisters. Lost my Ruth in seventy-six, and his Helen left us in eighty-eight."

"Left?"

Glen nodded his head. "Cancer. Both of them."

"Sorry to hear that."

"Part of life." Glen shrugged his shoulders, his steps slowing.

"So…you've got a private dock. I didn't see a boat, though. You keep it down at the local marina?" Lane decided to change the subject.

"It's sunk."

"What?" Lane gave Glen a surprised look.

"Yup. Right to the bottom." Glen took a deep breath. "That's why I'm suing the shop."

"Bobber's Boat Repair?" It was the only boat repair shop on the island she knew of.

"Crooked Bob is what I call him. Hired him to fix a few hoses which needed attention. Said he did, brought it home, and my boat sunk a week later. A cracked hose or broken hose clip is my guess. Either way. His fault." Glen's breathing was labored, trying to keep up with the sheriff.

Lane slowed her pace.

"Who is your lawyer, Mr. Sorenson? Mr. Allister?"

She doubted Glen would go farther than the island's shore to find an attorney. Maybe there was a connection?

"Mikey? Yeah. He's my guy."

Lane's step faltered.

"Mikey! I've never heard ANYBODY call him Mikey before."

A broad smile spread across Glen's wrinkled face.

"That's what his dad used to call him when he was a little boy. It's good to remind the stuffed shirt he was a regular somebody before he became a big shot attorney."

"And he agreed to take your case?"

Lane wondered, with the island being the size it was, if possibly suing fellow islanders might not actually be bad for business.

"Sure did. Dub and I were the first ones to join the lawsuit."

"Wait. Dub is suing the boat repair shop as well?"

"Yup. Took his trolling motor in for a tune-up and it went completely kaput a few days later. He was fit to be tied. His son had bought it for him for

Father's Day."

"Wow... and who are the others?"

"Mikey, for one. Got a faulty intake valve replaced. The replacement hose cracked worse than the old one, he says. Then Calvin Morton had a busted engine the shop couldn't seem to fix. I was told Mikey was working on Pastor Adams to join us. But the preacher said he didn't feel it was right to sue one of his parishioners." Glen shook his head, not seeing sense in it. "Preachers..."

"I'm surprised the boat shop is still in business?"

"Hard to put'em out of business when they're the only boat business around. Though, thinking about it, never had problems with them before last year."

"And was it your idea to sue?"

"Nah, Mikey's bright idea."

"So, when was the last time you saw... Mikey?"

Lane couldn't resist using the nickname.

"A week ago. Dropped off the last of my retainer fee." Glen's leg buckled a little, and Lane quickly grabbed his elbow to steady him. "Oh, I'm fine." He lightly shook his arm free and added, "Stupid gophers."

The two had finally reached the middle of the large yard. Here, the patrol vehicles and yellow police tape were in view, along with Philip, who was leaning up against his rig, his arms folded across his chest, his head bowed low into his coat. At the sight of him,

Lane smiled despite herself, happy to see him.

"And how much are you suing for, Glen?" She turned her attention back to the old man.

"What a... what time is it?" Glen ignored her question and pulled his hand free from his pocket, checking his wristwatch.

Lane noticed his trembling had worsened.

"Sheriff, it's time for me to take my medication. Want to come in for some coffee? Warm-up a bit?"

Philip, catching sight of the pair, straightened, and shouted to be heard above the wind, his voicing carrying across the yard.

"Sheriff, I need to talk to you!"

Lane dismissively waved her hand with a nod of acknowledgment before turning back to Glen.

"Thanks for the offer, Mr. Sorenson. But I better see what Ranger Russell needs."

Glen grunted in understanding, making for his front door.

"Sure, sure. Tell Phil I say, Howdy, and ask him if he's seen Dub."

CHAPTER 8

Philip watched as Lane parted ways with Glen Sorenson and started walking across the lawn. He nervously uncrossed his arms, his news about to burst from his chest.

"Sorry to barge in on you," Philip said as soon as she was close enough, obediently standing behind the police line. "I know you're working."

"It's alright." Lane bobbed under the yellow tape and tugged off her latex gloves, heading for the patrol truck. "George said you told him it was important." Philip was close on her heels. "So, it must be. What's up?"

She opened the truck door and gave him a quick smile.

"Found something you need to come see." Philip stepped aside, the door pushing him back. "It's a rowboat. Dub Granger's."

"That's concerning. Dub was supposed to meet with Glen today, and he didn't show. I was hoping you'd talked and sent him away." Lane threw the used gloves in a small trash bag hanging off the gear shift before turning back to Philip. "I take it, you haven't seen him?"

"I haven't. Could the floater be…"

"No… at least." Lane took a deep breath, exhaling slowly in thought. She was trying to remember if Dub had grey or white hair, the old man, always wearing a John Deer baseball cap. "Where in the park did you find the boat?"

"It washed ashore at the Driftwood outlet. Kody stumbled across it and had me come out and take a look." Philip put up a hand, arresting Lane's next question. "We didn't touch anything… except Kody grabbed a cleat to help haul it in."

Lane frowned.

He was unsure if she was irritated at Kody or him for being able to read her mind and hurried on, "Then I ran myself down to your office looking for you. It took some doing, but Martha finally told me where to find you and what Glen discovered."

"She shouldn't have said anything," Lane snapped irritably.

"If it helps, she swore me to secrecy."

By the stern look on Lane's face, Philip could tell,

it hadn't helped at all.

He continued, "And she knows you, and I are..." He paused, his eyebrows arched playfully, his smile slow. "Seeing each other."

Lane's lips tightened into a thin line, almost disappearing in displeasure, her facial features more annoyed than amused.

He was right. Martha knew. The whole town seemed to know! Though, if truth be told, the town hadn't needed Martha's loose lips to confirm what they already assumed. It seemed the budding romance between the sheriff and the park ranger had not gone entirely unnoticed by the townsfolk. Nor had it been hard for them to piece it all together. Especially with the small clues over the last four months... lunch dates, casual beers at the bowling alley, long hikes over the weekend, the ranger's truck parked at the backdoor of the sheriff's cottage... the early morning coffee runs. No, they weren't a secret. Most figuring, it was only a matter of time before the pretty, young sheriff took a liking to the handsome and roughish park ranger.

Predictable, really.

"What? What's with the frown?" Philip asked, leaning up against the patrol truck, lightly touching her scarf.

Lane sighed, untwirling the scarf from around her neck and pulling it from his touch.

"Martha still needs to follow protocol, regardless of who you are or what we might be."

Philip, stung, frowned.

"You know..." He stood up straight, facing her. "This is starting to be a sore spot between us. I don't think we should have to keep "US" a secret."

"Later, Phil." Lane hopped into her truck, quickly leaning over to give him a peck on the lips. "I need to stop by the office first. Follow me."

CHAPTER 9

As Lane and Philip walked through the front door of the Sheriff's office, Martha bolted up from her desk.

"Hold, please." She clutched the phone receiver to her chest, clasping her hand over the mouthpiece, and addressed Lane in a panicked, hissed whisper, "Well? Is it him?"

"Don't know." Lane closed the door behind them. "Coroner Ames is working on the identification now. The condition of the body made it impossible to ID on the spot."

"I was hoping—" Martha shook her head, not finishing the sentence, and sat herself down, reluctantly returning the phone to her ear. "Thank you for holding."

She scribbled a few sentences on a notepad, then

quickly said goodbye, slamming the handset down with irritation.

"Well, neither his answering service nor his daughter seems to know where he is, and he's still not answering his cell phone."

"Who? Dub?" Philip asked, making his way to the small coffee nook, intent on a warm cup of joe. "I didn't know he had a daughter."

"Dub? Dub Granger?" Martha shot Philip a confused look. "Does Dub know something?"

"No," Lane answered with a shake of her head, then tilted it in Philip's direction as if to say, "Don't pay him any mind."

"Oh. Well, here." Martha handed Lane a pink "while you were out" message slip, her attention lingering on Philip. "The marina wants a phone call back on his missing boat."

"Thanks. I'll have Caleb look into it as soon as he gets in. I have to go with Ranger Russ—"

"Marina?" Philip interrupted, plunking down the coffee carafe. "He doesn't keep it at the marina, and his boat isn't missing." He picked up four sugar packets, giving them a vigorous shake. "I found it this morning."

"You did!" Martha put a hand to her heart. "Where?"

"No." Lane lightly touched Martha's arm. "Not HIS boat. A different boat."

"Someone else is missing a boat?" Philip asked, surprised, adding powdered creamer.

"Mike Allister," Lane said, taking off her earmuffs. "I'll explain on our way to the rowboat."

She stuffed the muffs into her jacket pocket and pulled out a worn leather notepad.

"I might as well get this from you now, Martha, before things get hectic. When was the last time you saw or talked to Mr. Allister?"

Martha hesitated, glancing at Philip, who was now blowing on his coffee, peering eagerly over the rim as he made his way back.

"Well... um." Martha shrugged, her eyes roaming to the ceiling in recollection. "We spoke, I think—" She stopped, her eyes returning to Philip.

He gave her an encouraging smile as he sat down in the chair across from her desk and took a hesitant but loud sip of coffee, toasting his mug in her direction.

"Sorry, Martha. Go on. Don't mind me."

She gave him a weak, awkward smile and continued, "Um, I guess we spoke Thursday night?"

Lane watched Martha start to fiddle with the phone cord, clearly uncomfortable with Philip's presence.

"Martha, was that in-person or over the phone?" she asked, scribbling her pen against the notepad.

"In person. I had gone to his office to... to sign

some papers." Martha gave Lane a meaningful look and then shot a pleading glance towards Philip.

Lane gave Martha a quick nod of understanding. "Hey, Phil. Would you mind..."

"Geez, Martha!" Philip, his voice laced with honest concern, interrupted, "Are you and George having legal issues? Nothing with the funeral home, I hope."

Martha looked surprised and quickly shook her head, blushing to her roots.

"Heavens, no! Nothing like that!"

"Well, then..." Philip took a large sip and suddenly made a face. "Don't tell me Allister talked you two into joining the boat shop lawsuit?"

"Hold on." Lane held up her hand and turned towards Philip. "You know about the lawsuit?"

"Well, yeah. It's a small island. Besides, I think Mike Allister has hit up anybody and everybody who ever had their boat serviced there."

Lane, a questioning look on her face, turned to Martha, her curiosity piqued.

"Were you and George joining the lawsuit?"

Martha gave her head a firm shake, a hard crease across her forehead.

"No. George decided against it. Didn't like the idea of suing a neighbor."

"Well, then." Philip shrugged and leaned back into his chair. "What did you need to see a lawyer for?"

Martha gave him a light, dismissive shrug in return. "Personal reasons."

"Personal. Oh, PERSONAL." Philip put his mug down on the desk and stood up, turning his back on Martha, who shot Lane another pleading look as he returned to the coffee nook, seemingly aware of the affair between the married Martha and the town lawyer.

Lane decided to intervene.

"Listen, Phil." She picked up his mug from the desk and walked it over, a couple of extra sugar packets now in his hand. "Why don't you wait in my office?" She gently took his arm and guided him in the direction of her glass-paneled workspace. "I think I can handle the rest of the questioning from here."

"But I didn't mean to—" He shot Martha an apologetic look.

Lane nodded her head in a placating manner, cutting him off and steering him away from Martha, towards her office.

"I know, I know. You were just making conversation," Lane reassured, giving him a light push forward.

Philip, who knew the rest of the way, made for the door without Lane's escort and called over his shoulder as he grabbed the doorknob, "Mind if I make a phone call while waiting?"

"Yeah, go ahead."

Lane turned back to Martha and took the seat Philip had vacated.

"Okay, Martha. He's gone. You can speak freely."

The older woman, waiting until Philip had closed the door and taken a seat, turned to Lane with an expression of curiosity.

"Who do you think he's calling?" She turned back around, watching Philip pick up Lane's desk phone.

The park ranger, having made himself comfortable, was reclined in Lane's chair, taking a hurried sip of coffee before speaking into the receiver.

"Do you suppose it's Kody? He wouldn't be calling George for any reason, would he?" The married woman's tone had turned cautious.

"Martha..." Lane waved her hand, garnering the other woman's curious attention. "You were saying you saw Mr. Allister on Thursday?"

"Yes. But I hadn't gone over there to sign papers. I only said that for Phil. If word got out Mike Allister and I were having an affair, I'd hate to think what George would do." Martha's eyes widened in a sudden panic. "Not that George would do anything to Mike. It'd be ME he'd be upset with."

"You sure about that?"

Lane, having considered the strong possibility that the floater might be Mike Allister, had already started a suspect list.

George Barnes, being at the top.

Though Martha might hope her affair with the lawyer was still under wraps, much of the island had known or strongly guessed the two were lovers, and by now, Lane assumed, George had heard the rumors as well. He either was in denial, didn't care, or was willing to live with it. But maybe... maybe things had changed?

"Sheriff, I can see the wheels turning. Believe me, George may be a big man, but he's not violent." Martha lightly shook her head. "He lacks the passion for physical brutality."

Lane sighed heavily, lowering the notepad to her lap, plain curiosity taking over.

"Martha, if you're unhappy in your marriage, why don't you leave?"

"Who says I'm unhappy in my marriage?" Martha gasped, indignant, her hand to her heart. "I love George! He's the love of my life!"

"Then, why the affair?"

Martha blushed and gave a sheepish smile.

"I know. It doesn't make much sense, does it?" She ran her fingers through her silver-streaked hair, tucking a strand behind her ear. "You see, George and I are high school sweethearts. We fell in love very young. Too young, but despite that, we've managed in the last forty-plus years to raise a beautiful family and run a stable business." She suddenly sighed heavily, her smile dropping. "You know, you wouldn't think running a funeral home on a tiny island would take up so much of one's time. But George is constantly busy. Planning services, selling plots and urns, organizing viewings, writing up eulogies, embalming. He does it all! He's even trying to expand into pet funerals!" Martha shook her head side to side, almost disgusted. "As if he's got the time! I asked him to let one of the kids help run the business, but he's not ready to give up the reins, let alone think about retiring. Which I guess is understandable. None of our children are interested in taking over, not yet, too busy with their own careers on the mainland."

"So, you love him, but you feel neglected?"

"It's more than that, Sheriff. George... he's very set in his ways." She leaned in, putting her hand on Lane's arm. "Do you know we've not been on a vacation since the kids were in primary school? They're grown adults, now!" She nodded her head at Lane's surprised expression and continued, "Oh, it's not that he doesn't want to go! It's just he's completely petrified someone will drop dead, and he won't be here to deal with it. Makes it hard for him to leave the island for long periods of time. He is very reliable, George, is."

"You want excitement, then." Lane was starting to understand. "A thrill of some sort?"

"Childish, isn't it? At my age, sneaking off in the middle of the afternoon, squeezing in a mid-day phone call to hear sweet nothings whispered in my ear." Martha dropped her eyes. "I should make it clear, Sheriff. Mike Allister knows I'm not in love with him." She suddenly looked up with teary eyes, meeting Lane's. "That's not to say we don't care deeply for each other. It's just... we both know I'll never leave my husband."

"Don't you worry George will find out, though? You'd likely lose everything. Seems a considerable risk for a man you're not even in love with."

"No, you're right. But, that's part of the thrill, I guess." Martha shrugged her shoulders. "Being with Mike makes me feel alive and desired."

"Even if you have to do it in the backseat of a parked car?" Lane raised a questioning eyebrow.

Martha laughed, her face blushing.

"Makes me feel young too. Like I was a teenager again."

Lane, finding it all silly, decided to move on, bringing her notepad back up, front and center.

"So, I take it Mr. Allister didn't mention he was leaving town?" Lane underlined George's name, not entirely convinced, and looked up from her notepad, expectant of an answer.

"No. Not at all, and normally, Mike is really good about letting me know. It's odd his answering service doesn't know anything either. Said he last checked in on Friday afternoon."

"You said his daughter hadn't heard anything from her father as well?"

"Well, that's the thing. She doesn't quite care for me. Thinks I'm a gossip. She was tight-lipped, but she sounded surprised I was asking. I'm assuming she wasn't told he was leaving the island."

"Interesting." Lane's head turned at the sound of the front door chime.

Deputy Pickens entered, awkwardly making his way through the entrance, his arms full of equipment, a white deli bag hanging from his teeth.

Seeing him struggle, Lane quickly got up and took the camera bag and forensic case from his grasp.

"Thanks, Sheriff," Caleb mumbled, reaching up to remove the bag. "Anybody want a bagel? I picked them up on my way over." He tossed the white bag onto Martha's desk. "I was starving."

Both women declined the offer for separate reasons.

Martha, because she was worried sick, and Lane, because she thought it best to have an empty stomach when meeting the coroner later on in the afternoon.

"Suit yourself." Caleb opened the bag and pulled out a plain bagel, along with a handful of small cream cheese cups. "Anything new?"

"Possibly. I need to check out a rowboat found in

the park. Ranger Russell is going to take me to the location."

Lane tilted her head towards her office and Caleb followed her gaze, the deputy giving Philip a brief nod of acknowledgment and a smile.

Lane continued, "Might be where our mystery floater came from. And..." She took the pink message slip from her notepad, handing it over. "I'd like you to give the mainland marina a call. Let them know we'll be checking the public docks for Allister's missing boat, and assist in any way we can. Then I was hoping you could do a wellness check on Allister's residence. Finding his car with slashed tires should be reason enough. If he's not there, then head over to his daughter's place and see if she knows where he's at."

Lane addressed Martha, "Do we know how long his car was parked in the Park and Ride lot?"

Martha shook her head.

Caleb held up his hand, garnering Lane's attention.

"I noticed it coming off the ferry Friday night after the hockey game. My headlights bounced right across it," Caleb mumbled through a full mouth of bagel.

"What time was that?"

"It was the last ferry, so a little after ten. You think his car was sitting there all weekend?"

"It's a strong possibility, and it's somewhere to

start. See if you can find out what his plans were for Friday evening. Maybe he went to the game as well?"

Martha interjected, her tone somber, "No. He wouldn't have. He's not been to a hockey game since Brent... Well. It was something they used to do together. Besides, when I talked to him Thursday night, he made it sound like he'd be working in his office all weekend. Going through depositions." Martha suddenly brightened. "Maybe he needed to interview someone on the mainland?"

"That's an idea." Lane thoughtfully tapped the notepad against her chin. "Deputy, why don't you swing by Allister's office downtown on your way to his house. Double-check he's not there working on something, and while you're running around, why don't you stop off at Dub Granger's place."

Philip walked out of Lane's office, joining the group.

"I've got that covered," he announced, beaming at the trio. "I called Harry, and—" He paused, the Gelato Deli bag catching his eye. "Asked him to go over and check up on Dub since he knows where he keeps his spare key. I also tried Dub's place. There was no answer." Philip took a peek inside and gave Caleb a questioning glance, asking for permission before reaching in and grabbing a bagel. "So, Harry is on his way over to Dub's right now."

Lane wasn't surprised Philip had called Harry.

Besides being his best pal and sidekick, Harry was the store manager of the island's only grocery store, Hattie's General. Most locals referring to the one-stop shop as just plain Hattie's, after the shop's namesake, Harry's grandmother.

Hattie, still alive and kicking, was the island's pride and joy at the wise old age of one hundred and three. Though she could no longer manage the day-to-day operations of the store, it didn't mean she wasn't there every day.

In the mornings, white-haired and blue-eyed Hattie could be found sitting in her rocking chair, front and center to the main door, strategically placed next to the picnic table display.

Though the picnic table was technically for sale, locals used it as a coffee-fueled hearsay and gossip circle meeting ground, the daily tittle-tattle summits ruled by Hattie and her own two cronies, Dub and Glen.

It was a safe bet, Harry, if anybody, would know where to find Dub.

Philip bit into a poppy seed bagel, a pleased smile upon his face.

"Hope you don't mind, Sheriff."

"Actually, I do. But since we're a little short-handed, that's not a bad idea." Lane took a deep breath, stuffing her notepad into her back pocket. "Martha, you hold down the fort. Call me or use the two-way for the ranger's station if you need to get a hold of me. I'll be with Ranger Russell in his truck. Caleb, you do the same. I'll meet you at the funeral home at two if I don't see or hear from you before that."

Lane grabbed a bagel from the bag, having changed her mind.

It was going to be a long day, and it might be all the nourishment she'd get.

CHAPTER 10

Pulling his brown beast of a truck to the cabin's front steps, Harry gave the horn a light honk and waited for a sign of life.

A short twenty minutes before, Philip had given him a jingle at the store, asking if he'd seen Dub yet for the day. Finding it odd himself that neither Dub nor Glen had shown, the two having a standing coffee appointment with Hattie each morning around eight, Harry had told him, no. Not liking the answer, Philip had asked if he wouldn't mind swinging by and checking on the old man, you know, just in case.

Agreeing to do so, Harry had quickly shuffled Hattie into his office with a hot cocoa and asked Amy Holmes, his daytime cashier, to watch the store for a bit.

"Come on, Dub," Harry muttered under his

breath, expecting to see a figure, at any second, come to the door.

The front door remained closed.

Supposing the old man hadn't heard the first honk, the horn was held down again, a little longer this time.

Still, no one came to the door.

Surprised, Harry squinted through his windshield, trying to see past the squished bug smears and frost. He had been hoping Dub would at least come to the door or peek through the front window.

"Well, his rig is still here," he mused, spotting the hood of Dub's Ford poking out from behind the small cabin, the windshield still frosted over, a good sign the old man hadn't driven anywhere.

Perhaps his pickup wouldn't start, and Dub decided to walk down to the general store? As cold as it was, Harry thought it unlikely, and besides, wouldn't he have spotted Dub on the way?

Maybe he should go in?

Harry cupped his keys, still sitting in the ignition, and debated turning the engine off. The old brown beast was so temperamental in cold weather there was a good chance it might not start again. Thinking better of it, he withdrew his hand, deciding it best to leave the rumbling engine running while he snooped around.

Harry gave the horn one last tap before hopping

out of his truck and then walked up to the front of the house, cutting across the frosted grass.

The cabin, a small wooden log number, slightly unkempt on the outside, seemed deserted, the feeling enforced by the lack of smoke coming from the smokestack on the roof.

In a bound, Harry topped the porch steps and pounded heavily on the front door.

"Dub! It's Harry! Open up!"

He briskly rubbed his palms together for warmth and waited for a response.

There was none.

Taking a step down, Harry tried to peer through the front window, leaning precariously over the stoop railing.

"Probably doesn't have his hearing aids in," Harry grumbled, righting himself and stepping back onto the top step.

Not hearing any motion or scuffling inside, Harry made up his mind and leaped down the steps, heading over to a bright red birdhouse hanging in the tree, a large cedar, looming in the front yard. He stuck his fingers in and wiggled them around until he pulled out Dub's house key and then headed up the stairs again.

Sticking in the key, he gave the doorknob a good wrench and slowly opened the door.

"Knock, knock." Harry waited for a polite second

and stepped in. "Dub? Hattie was missing you this morning. You home?"

The small house was dark and quiet.

He flipped the light switch next to the door, lighting up a sparse living room with a tiny kitchen off to the right. The house looked empty of life. He shut the door behind him, and as he did, realized it was much colder inside than out.

"Brrr..."

He walked to the black wood stove against the wall and placed his hand on top.

"No wonder."

Harry bent over and opened the small cabinet door, peering inside.

"Fire has gone out."

He grabbed the fire poker from the stand next to the potbelly fireplace and stirred the grey ashes until he found red embers buried underneath.

"Better get this going again."

He put the poker back onto the stand and then chucked two big blocks of wood into the fireplace, worried if the house didn't get up to temperature, Dub's pipes might freeze.

Finished with the minor chore, Harry stood up, dusting black soot from his hands, mindlessly rubbing his palms on his work khakis. He frowned, his slightly balding forehead forming into a deep crease.

Something was off.

Even if Dub had left the island for some reason, he would have asked someone to house-sit for him.

In fact, didn't Dub have a cat?

Harry walked into the kitchen and spotted a small, empty food and water bowl on the floor.

Yeah, he thought he did.

Picking up the water bowl, he walked to the sink and filled it, placing the dish back on the floor.

"Here, kitty. Here kitty, kitty," Harry lightly called, starting to walk down the short hallway to the back of the cabin. "Dub, you back here?" he added, suddenly wondering if the old man was still asleep in bed, possibly sick with the flu or something, too weak to get up and feed the fire.

Harry stopped short, spotting a light under the bathroom door.

He leaned in, hearing running water, and knocked.

"Dub? You in there?"

There was no response.

"Probably the toilet running," Harry thought to himself, and then out loud, "Hope you're not in your skivvies because I'm coming in." He gently pushed the door open.

Lying on the floor, a calico cat curled on his back, was Dub. A pool of blood by his head, his skin pale, his lips slightly blue. Behind him, the shower ran freely, splashing water upon the floor, the small bathroom window above the toilet cracked open, cold air seeping in.

Shocked, Harry stepped back into the hall, his arm slamming the door wide with a bang. Dub didn't move, though the cat, surprised to see Harry as much as Harry was to see him, hissed and rushed between his legs, jetting out into the hall.

The exit startled Harry into motion and he quickly bent over, scrambling for Dub's limp wrist. He clutched it, his fingers pressed tight against the fragile thin skin, and waited, holding his breath before bolting up and swiping the folded towel lying on the sink, shaking it out.

Gently, he laid it over the naked old man much like a blanket and dug out his cell phone, dialing 9-1-1.

CHAPTER 11

Arriving at their destination, Lane slammed the passenger door and waited for Philip to make his way around.

"Come on, Phil! Get a move on."

Lane was more than impatient.

On the drive in, ignoring her persistent complaints, Philip had refused to exceed the posted fifteen miles-per-hour speed limit on the range road, lecturing to Lane's many protests the dangers of roaming wildlife and fast-moving vehicles.

"Coming." Philip rounded the headlights, still in mid-conversation, "I tell ya, deer can be dangerous. I've seen cars totaled, Lane, and when I say totaled, I mean completely—"

Lane cut him off, eager to change the subject.

"Hey, Phil? Kody was able to spot the rowboat

from up here? I can't even see the beach from where we're standing."

"Nope. Won't be able to see it until you've gone down the embankment." Philip zipped up his coat, pointing Lane to a small trail. "Winds this time of year wreak havoc, so I asked Kody to pick up any loose garbage or broken limbs littering the roadway. The kid said he'd finished the main road and decided to check the outlet. That's how he stumbled across it." Philip grabbed a limb from a nearby pine, using it to lower himself down the steep embankment. "This beach sees a lot of odd things wash ashore after a windstorm. The sea current funnels all sorts of junk in."

"Good to know."

Lane took a running stride down the embankment to the pebbled beach, stopping short of the water, and turned to Philip.

He nodded towards the rowboat, beached, its bloodied oar jetting out into the air.

"Well, there she is."

"Yeah, I'd say this is what we're looking for."

She took a cursory look and spotting a rotten stump, walked over and placed her forensic case atop, popping it open.

"Here. I'm gonna need your help." She handed Philip a pair of latex gloves, then turned towards the rowboat, snapping on her own. "Mind playing photographer?" She nodded towards a digital camera nestled inside the foam casing and grabbed a small hand recorder for herself.

"A voice recorder, huh? That's new," Philip said, gingerly lifting the camera out and making his way behind her. "Not gonna use your notepad?"

"Oh... this was Caleb's idea." Lane began to circle the rowboat and stopped short, fiddling with the small buttons. "I already don't like it."

"Here." Philip leaned over, pointing out a red dot on the side of the record button. "I think that's what you're looking for."

Lane nodded her thanks and mumbled, "I know," under her breath, then started to speak into the small device.

"Date is February, second. Time of day is eleven-thirty a.m. Location, Driftwood Beach outlet, located in the Rockfish Island National Park. Present, is myself, Sheriff Lane, and Park Ranger, Philip Russell." She clipped the recorder off, and quickly cleared her throat before punching it on again. "Following is the description of found rowboat, believed to belong to Dub Granger. The boat is approximately..." Lane walked the length of the boat counting. "Seventeen feet long, white, weather-worn, and blood speckled. Water Crest is hand-painted on the side in black." Lane suddenly stopped and clicked the recorder off, then stooped down, clicking it back on. "Appears there are four bullet holes in the base of the boat."

"The hull."

"On the right side."

"Starboard."

Lane shot Philip a confused look and stood up, beginning to walk around the boat again.

"Looking at the back of the boat..."

"The stern."

She clicked the recorder off giving Philip a frown.

"What are you doing?"

"Helping." Philip, on the opposite side, squatted down for a closer look himself.

"More like interrupting."

"Lane, when talking about boats, you need to use the correct terminology." He stood up, still looking down at the damaged hull. "I keep inviting you out on Mitchell's yacht, but you never want to come." He met her eyes. "If you ask nicely, I can teach you these things."

Lane, sighing heavily and dismissing his offer, started the recorder again before peering inside the boat. She waved Philip over, indicating she wanted a photo of the bullet casings.

"I count four... Twenty-two caliber casings, by the looks of them. However, I don't see a gun. There is also a broken oar, the handle snapped. Brain matter and blood on the blade. Another oar, lying on the left side..."

"Portside," Philip mumbled under his breath.

Lane ignored him and continued, "A black face mask is also floating on the water inside the boat. The water is a few inches deep towards the back of the boat... eh, the stern?"

She looked to Philip for confirmation, and he gave her a pleased smile.

Lane clicked off the recorder. "Whoever shot up the boat obviously meant to sink it."

"We're lucky they didn't use a bigger caliber gun. A forty-five would have done it." Philip bent down, snapping another shot of the peppered hull.

"If they had plugged enough holes in it, no matter the size, it would have sunk. Clearly, four holes wouldn't do much."

"Think they ran out of bullets?"

"Or they don't know much about boats."

"You mean, like you?" Philip cracked a smile, which Lane returned, admitting the fact.

"I should have said they didn't know much about guns," Lane corrected herself. "We may be looking at this wrong." She headed for the forensic case and rummaged around, tossing over her shoulder, "Could be those shots were fired during a struggle."

"Well, the bullet holes are pretty sporadic." Philip hunched down again, using his hand to measure the distance between the punctures. "I would have thought they'd be all clumped together." He stood up.

"I don't know. Either way, these holes weren't big enough to sink the boat before the ocean current got hold and dumped it onshore."

"Agreed." Lane, several plastic bags in hand, was making her way back to him. She stopped short, stuffing the bags under her arm, and bent over to pick up a twig.

"Bullets, broken oar, ...and a ski mask," Philip listed, his brows knitted together in concentration, as he stared down at the wool hood. "What the hell happened?"

"My guess? Kidnapping gone wrong," Lane casually speculated, plucking the remaining pine needles off the stick.

At the shocked expression on Philip's face, she expanded on her theory, "Seems to fit. Person or persons unknown snatch our victim, steal the rowboat to get off the island, probably trying to transport him to an awaiting getaway boat offshore." She made her way over to Philip, his face still unsure, and handed him an opened bag. "Obviously, something went awry. The victim is accidentally killed, and in an attempt to cover their tracks, they disfigure the body, dump it, and do their best to sink all remaining evidence."

"And did a lousy job of it."

Using the freshly stripped twig, Lane carefully lifted a bullet casing from the water, dropping the copper-colored cover into the awaiting evidence bag.

"Thankfully," she agreed. "Though, I wouldn't be surprised if the gun was sitting at the bottom of the ocean."

"So... the floater from this morning was shot? I thought he was bludgeoned to death?"

"Didn't see a gunshot wound," Lane said, distracted, fishing out another casing.

"That doesn't make any sense. If they held him by gunpoint to get him into the boat, why bludgeon him to death with an oar?"

"Actually, the coroner was leaning more towards strangulation."

"Throttle somebody when you can just shoot 'em?" Philip shook his head, not liking the idea. "Strangulation requires you to be in close proximity. Seems a pretty personal way to kill somebody."

"It is."

Lane lightly touched her own throat, a flash of memory causing it to tighten.

"Not to mention, how hard it would be to do in a boat of this size. They tip easy." Philip shook his head, stumped at the thought.

"Hmmm, that's a good point. Could be the victim fought back, kidnapper lost the gun in the struggle, and was forced to use their hands. May have meant to only knock the victim out and instead, accidentally killed him. Panicked, they did their best to cover up the crime." Lane shrugged her shoulders. "That is... if this is a kidnapping."

"Hold on. You're thinking the victim is Mike Allister, aren't you?"

"More likely to be him than Dub. He's got money, and he's not particularly liked. Also, his yacht is missing. Might have been where they were trying to take him." She leaned carefully over the side and into the boat. "There's a lot of blood. We should be able to get some latent prints, I would think."

"I don't know. You can see where they wiped their bloody handprints off the gunnels." Philip met Lane's eyes, a sly smile crossing his lips. "That means the upper sides of the boat."

"Keep it up, Ranger." Lane's blue eyes were not amused.

Philip quickly held his hand up in a placating manner. "Just trying to be helpful, Sheriff."

"No, really, keep it up." Lane lightly tapped her sidearm, a mischievous flicker in her blue eyes.

Philip's smile got wider.

Refocusing on the boat, Lane moved to the broken oar, giving the blade a closer look, and examining the shattered handle.

"Looks as if the oar was wiped down as well. I'll call in a forensic team from the mainland. Every inch of this boat needs to be—" She stopped. "Phil," her voice turned eager. "There's something under the seat in the back."

"Here, I'll get it." Philip snapped a quick shot and handed Lane the camera before stretching carefully over the gunnels, trying to reach the small brown object underneath the seat. Sucking in his gut, he managed to grip it by the fold, his fingers fumbling, and pulled out a man's wallet.

"Pay dirt." Philip smiled triumphantly, handing the brown wallet to Lane. "Let's see who it belongs to."

Taking the plain wallet gingerly from his hand, Lane stepped to the side, doing her best to avoid dripping water on the camera she had hastily placed on the pebbled beach. She eagerly, yet carefully, unfolded the leather.

"Not surprising," she said testily, checking the little side pockets and bill section, all documentation gone. "It's empty. Completely empty! Here."

Disappointed, she handed the wallet over, Philip opening it up himself, curious to see if she'd missed anything.

"Oh, come on! There has to be something inside! An old photo, a scribbled phone number, maybe a pawn ticket, or a dud scratch card? Some kind of clue."

"Only in cheesy detective novels, Ranger." Lane held a new, opened evidence bag, indicating for Philip to drop the wallet inside. "Put it in here, and help me fish out the ski mask."

Philip, wearing a disappointed frown, flopped

the leather wallet shut and dropped it into the awaiting bag.

"Why can't things ever be easy?"

"Life isn't easy. Why should death be?" Lane said primly, sealing the bag and placing it carefully aside.

Philip raised his eyebrows in consideration, then shrugged his shoulders and begrudgingly agreed. He then bent down and scooped up the ski mask.

"It's sopping wet." He handed her the black wool mass, water streaming down on her galoshes.

She held it up, trying to find the front side.

"Bet the kidnapper was the one wearing the ski mask." Lane carefully wiggled her gloved finger through the right eye socket. "In most abductions, if a mask or hood is used on the victim, the eye sockets are sewn closed." Lane wrung out the wet mask, the cold-water trickling into the boat. "This way, the kidnapper won't be identified, and the victim won't be able to see where they are taken. Less chance of them telling the authorities where they were held or who took them if they do happen to escape."

"But if the kidnapper was wearing the mask?"

"Means there is a good chance he was known to his victim."

"That's scary."

"It's only a guess. That is, if like I said before, this is even a kidnapping."

"What else could it be?"

Lane let her eyes sweep across the boat again.

"Just trying to keep an open mind, Ranger. You know, being objective."

Returning her attention to the mask in hand, Lane carefully began to turn it inside out, stopping short at the sight of long hairs stuck in the weave of the merino wool.

"Phil, grab the camera." Lane carefully eased one of the pinned evidence bags from under her arm and shook it open.

"What is it?" Philip snatched the camera up from the ground, his finger on the button.

"Two, long brown hairs."

"A woman?"

"Possibly."

"Female kidnapper?" Philip sounded skeptical.

"Or another victim."

"Oh, man. I hope not." Philip lowered the camera. "Definitely a lead, though."

"Definitely."

CHAPTER 12

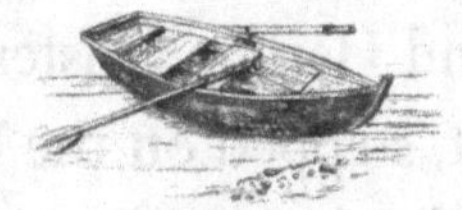

The seagulls above, squawking their welcome, didn't seem to mind the frigid air. The white and grey birds, fearlessly gliding across the gusting breeze, their wings spread wide, eyes keen on the men below, were spying for a bit of fish or an unwatched sandwich.

Hands stuffed deep in his pockets and his head tucked low, Caleb strode purposefully down the planks of the long fishing dock, blinking against the bitter wind, his eyes glued on his destination, a blue and white fishing boat at the end of the pier.

As he drew closer, ocean spray clung to his clothes and his hair, the chill penetrating through, sharp against his bare skin, a settling ache beginning to take root in his bones. Pulling his collar closer about his ears, Caleb perceived winter's bite was taking its pound of flesh, relishing every morsel, and though it didn't appear so, he imagined it was doing the same to the two men, one tall and one short, who stood on the deck waiting.

"Morning, Andy!" Caleb called, stopping short of the fishing boat.

"Morning! Cold enough for you, Deputy Pickens?" The Rockfish Island Harbor Master, his cheeks ruddy and eyes bright, stepped off the boat, his galoshes landing firmly on the dock with a thud.

"The wind isn't helping, that's for sure!" With a warm smile, Caleb pulled his hand from his pocket and offered it to the tall man, who took it in his own chapped hand, giving it a hardy pump.

"Record hot summer, and now a record cold winter? I'd say those scientists—"

"Martha called me. Said you found Mike Allister's lifeboat?" Caleb cut Andy off, knowing full well his ability for long-winded speeches on climate control.

"I called, but it wasn't me who found it." Andy turned and signaled for the younger and shorter man, still standing on the boat deck, to join them. "Len, here, did."

Caleb, not recognizing the stout man, watched as he disembarked, making his way towards them, dressed in a pair of well-used fishing overalls, a heavy jacket on top, and a wool cap crammed down over his ears.

"He called me early this morning. Said he thought—" Andy broke off and moved aside so Len could join the conversation, then made a hasty introduction, "Len, this is Deputy Pickens."

Len grunted in greeting but kept his hands inside his coat pockets, making no offer to shake Caleb's outstretched hand.

Somewhat relieved, as the man smelled heavily of fish, Caleb nodded in return and tucked his own clean hand back into his warm jacket.

Andy lightly nudged Len's arm. "Mind telling him what you told me this morning?"

"Sure. Uh, Saturday morning, after the huge wind storm we had, I came down to the dock. Wanted to check up on her." Len tilted his head back towards his fishing boat. "Noticed a rubber raft floating adrift not far from the dock." Len stopped and scratched his nose, then quickly stuffed his hand back into his pocket. "Managed to pull it in and tie it up. Figured it'd broke free in the storm, and someone would be along to claim it sooner or later." Len looked past Caleb's shoulder with a brief nod. "It's back there if you want to look at it. You walked right past it."

Caleb, distracted by the red scratches on Len's hands, slowly turned around to look behind, spotting the grey raft, which he had indeed walked right past. He returned his attention to the two men, his eyes falling on Len.

"What happened to your hand, Len?"

"Oh, this?" Len took his hands out, spreading the fingers wide, both covered in welted scrapes. "This is what you call working hands, sir," Len said, a lopsided smile on his lips. "Happens when you do actual hard work." He tucked his hands back in. "Suppose you've never seen that before."

"Len, stop being a smartass." Andy nudged the younger man again, this time with a warning frown, then shot Caleb an apologetic smile, pointing down the dock. "Come on. We'll show you. It's down here."

"Yeah, let's take a look." Giving Andy a short nod, Caleb stepped back, allowing the two men to lead the way.

The three paced down the dock, passing several slips, stopping short of a grey rubber raft, the words "Sue Happy" printed in bright yellow on the side, a small motor attached to the stern.

"There it is," Andy said lightly. "Allister's lifeboat."

"Was anything in it that's not in it now? I mean, it's been sitting out here for a few days, right?" Caleb cautiously leaned towards the lifeboat, trying his best to see inside.

"It was empty when I found it, except for the oars." Len pointed to the plastic poles, one assigned to each side of the tiny vessel.

"What made you decide to call Andy?" Caleb grabbed the rope and pulled the dinghy a little closer to the dock.

"When I found it, I hadn't thought anything of it. Wasn't until I heard people yapping about a Mercedes Benz with slit tires being towed at the park and ride that I put two and two together."

"Two and two?" Caleb asked, confused.

"The vanity plates on Allister's Mercedes," Andy explained. "Sue Happy."

"SUHAPY2... Yup, you're right. That's what his vanity plates say." Caleb bent down, examining the nylon rope tied to the dock cleat. It appeared new.

"Is this your rope?" He turned, addressing Len.

"No. Was already attached to the raft. It was floating free in the water."

"Well, the raft didn't break free from the dock because of a bad line."

Andy nodded, lightly kicking the dock cleat.

"Must have tied a lousy knot when they docked. Though, it was one heck of a wind storm. Crews are still pulling broken tree limbs off the roads."

"Yeah, even now, I hear they still have powerlines down on Mercer and Bainbridge Island." Caleb stood back up, surveying the rest of the boats lining the dock. "Well, thanks for calling this in. If you happen to see or hear anything about the actual yacht, will you give me a call?"

"Oh, I can do you one better than that, Caleb. I can tell you exactly where it is!" Andy beamed from ear to ear. "When Len called my office, I got to thinking. If someone used the raft to get to the dock, then the yacht can't be all that far away. Being those boats aren't made to travel long distances, more for short little jaunts to the shore or to keep you afloat until help arrives."

"You found it?" Caleb asked, shocked, pulling out his cell phone. "I need to get out there, and we'll need to call the Coast—"

"Hold on. I was getting to that. After Len found the raft, I called the Coast Guard and asked them to circle the island. They spotted her on the south side. I got the call a few minutes before you arrived. They tried to rouse her on the radio but didn't get a response, so they boarded her."

"Can you get me out there? Take me to it?" Caleb started to punch in Lane's phone number, sure she would want to know.

"Just listen." Andy put a firm hand on Caleb's arm, demanding his full attention. "After boarding, they gave her a quick search and found her empty with no signs of distress or foul play, except the engine key seems to be missing." Andy, this time, lightly kicked the side of the rubber raft with his booted foot. "They asked me what I thought happened. Told them I assumed whoever took Allister's boat from the Seattle Marina ended their joyride and is safely back on the island. No harm, no foul, I'd imagine."

He turned to Len, giving the fisherman a friendly wink. "They put the matter into my hands. I've got a commercial towing vessel hauling her to the Seattle Marina as we speak. Mystery solved."

"Andy, I still want to look at—"

A chirping melody exploded from Caleb's cell phone, drowning out his words.

"Sorry, thought I had it on vibrate." He went to hit the mute button but noticed the caller ID and added instead, "I need to take this. Excuse me."

Caleb stepped away, walking out of earshot further down the dock.

"Hey, Martha."

"So, any news?"

"Coast Guard found Allister's yacht on the south side of the island and are towing it back to the Seattle Marina."

"Towing it? Boating accident?"

"No. Missing engine key."

"And Mike?"

"No sign of him."

"What does that mean?"

"Don't know."

"Find anything at his office?"

"All dark and locked up. Same with the house. Talked to his daughter, though. She says she had a few missed phone calls around one in the morning on Sunday from her dad."

"Sunday? That's good news then."

"Yeah, probably, except he didn't leave a message. The daughter assumed it was a butt dial until you called this morning. She's trying other family members right now to see if they know where he might be."

Caleb hadn't said it, not wanting to worry Martha, but he thought it more likely someone had gotten a hold of Allister's cell phone. It might indeed be a butt dial, but not necessarily from Allister's keister.

"Well, that's more than I got out of her earlier today," Martha said sourly. "I've got some news of my own."

"Yeah?"

"Harry found Dub Granger unconscious on his bathroom floor. Apparently, Dub slipped coming out of his shower and hit the sink on his way down. Got himself a nasty gash on his head." Martha clucked. "The poor man about froze to death on his own bathroom floor! Left a window open to vent the room, and his fireplace burned out. Harry described it as an absolute icebox!"

Martha's gossipy tone had taken over.

"And you know that tiny place of his doesn't have a large water heater. He was probably lying there for hours with cold water raining down on him. Poor soul." Martha sighed heavily, seemingly annoyed by it all. "Anyway, they've got him at Doctor Hadley's office being stitched up now."

"So, he'll be okay?"

"Should be. Tough ol' bird. Though if you ask me, he's got no business living alone, especially since—"

"That's good news," Caleb cut Martha off while giving a wave to Andy and Len, motioning he'd be a minute more. "Any word from the Sheriff?"

"No. I tried her on the two-way, but no luck. She's probably still out in the park looking at Dub's rowboat. Now, what do you suppose that is about?"

"Haven't a clue. Listen, if you talk to her before I do, can you update her on—" Caleb was determined to stay on subject.

Martha wasn't having it.

"I don't see how Dub has anything to do with Mike missing, but Caleb, be honest with me. Do you think finding the yacht AND the lifeboat... means the body, in any way, could be—"

"Don't start jumping to conclusions, Martha," Caleb scolded, though his own thoughts had been on the same line of reasoning from the beginning.

"But it's so odd."

"Martha, we don't know enough. Mr. Allister's boat being found just means whoever took it on a joyride ditched it."

"And his car tires being slashed?"

"Punk kids up to no good would be my guess. Even you have to admit, he's not liked by everyone."

"Caleb! That's why I'm worried!"

CHAPTER 13

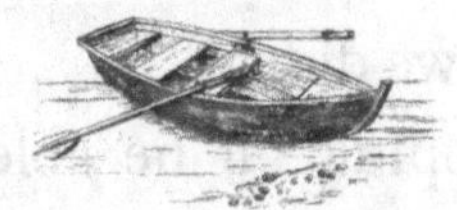

Lane, noting the 'Out to Lunch' sign posted upon the window, unlocked the front door of the Sheriff's office and ushered Philip in.

"We'll have to skip lunch. I've got a few phone calls to make before heading over to the funeral home. Mind putting those evidence bags on my desk for now? I'll take them over to the mainland after meeting with the coroner."

"Sure thing. I gotta get going anyway."

"Actually, Phil..." Lane locked the door behind them, leaving the lunch sign up. "I know you were wanting to stop off at Dr. Hadley's and look in on Dub before heading back to the ranger station. But..." She stopped short, spotting a pink message pad propped against Martha's monitor. She picked it up and gave it a quick read, adding in a louder voice so it would reach the back office, "But I'd like you to tag along if Kody can spare you."

"Tag along?" Philip stepped out of her office. "Is that a fancy way of saying you want my expertise on something?"

"Sort of." Lane gave him an apologetic smile. "You've known Mike Allister a long time. You might notice something we didn't."

"Ah, you're hoping I'll be able to identify the body." Philip pointed at her, leveling her with a knowing look. "Want a coffee?"

"Yes... and yes." Lane dropped the pink message pad flat on Martha's desk, the little notepad making a slapping sound against the wood. "Martha left a note. Says the Coast Guard found Allister's yacht deserted, and Caleb was able to track down the yacht's lifeboat to the main fishing dock on the island. No sign of Allister on either."

"Interesting. It's looking more and more like your idea of a kidnapping could be correct," Philip said over his shoulder, walking to the coffee stand and finding the carafe empty. "Though..." He pulled out the used coffee grounds and plunked them into the waste basket by the counter, then took the water pitcher, emptying it into the machine. "Why take Dub's rowboat when the lifeboat was waiting at the fishing dock?"

"Probably too many people around, and they

didn't want to risk being seen. Kidnappers were forced to find a different boat."

"Sounds plausible. But not logical." He placed a new filter in the slot and added two heaping mounds of fresh coffee grounds. "I mean, why bother to take the lifeboat to the fishing dock in the first place if they're worried about being spotted? Why not drive it straight to shore?"

Lane offered no answer, and he impatiently drummed his fingers against the counter, waiting for the carafe to fill. His fingers suddenly stopped and he turned to Lane.

"Where was the yacht found? Had to have been close?"

"Um." She pulled out Martha's chair, taking the seat, and referred to the discarded message pad.

"South side?"

"There's only parkland on that side of the island." Philip frowned, walking to the desk and placing a coffee mug down, scooting it closer. "Must be why they made for the fishing dock instead of landing straight onshore. Whoever it was would have had to hike hours before reaching Allister's place."

"Hours, huh?" Lane put her hand on the phone receiver, intending to make a call, but instead, peered down at the coffee mug, deep in thought. "Okay. So, the kidnappers steal Allister's boat from the marina on the mainland, sail it over, park it on the backside of the island to avoid being seen, then motor them-selves to land via the lifeboat."

Philip shook his head, disagreeing, and started back to the coffee nook.

"Lane, I'm having a hard time wrapping my head around a kidnapping. I mean, yes, Allister is one of the wealthier residents on the island, but he's not the richest by far."

"True. But I bet he's got an enemy or two. At least, I'd imagine with being a lawyer."

"Semi-retired, lawyer." Philip shook a finger. "Listen, I know you've got a bee in your bonnet for Allister." He raised his hand, asking to be heard. "And sure, he's a pretentious ass at times, but every-one goes to him if they need legal help."

"I do NOT have a bee in my bonnet about—," Lane started to protest.

"In fact," Philip spoke over her. "Most of his work is pro bono. Did you know that?" He raised an eye-brow, questioning if she did.

Lane shook her head in the negative, her hand still on the receiver.

"Didn't think so." He leveled her with a playful smirk. "Buzz, buzz."

Lane laughed despite herself. "Phil, that doesn't change the fact he's not everyone's cup of tea."

"Especially yours!" Philip countered with a chuckle, then waved his hand, indicating he was now being serious. "Okay, here's a theory that doesn't involve murderous villains."

He grabbed Caleb's chair and dragged it to Martha's desk, forgetting about his coffee.

"Suppose Allister, needing to go to Seattle, drives down to the lot and parks his car, taking the ferry over. Once he's on the mainland, he needs to get back to the island, for some unknown reason, but the ferries are down for the night. No problem, he's got a boat at the Seattle Marina. He takes his own yacht, and motors it over." Philip settled into the chair, his hands gripping the armrests. "And let's say something goes wrong. Engine goes kaput on him or runs out of gas. Knowing he's on the wrong side of the island, he takes off in the lifeboat, making for the fishing pier. But... it's too windy."

"Why didn't he radio the Coast Guard?" Lane asked, finding it highly unlikely the man wouldn't have called for help.

Philip impatiently shooed her valid question away, continuing to speculate, "NOW, due to the wind storm, the waves are huge, ginormous. Way too big for the small lifeboat."

"Another thing! Seattle doesn't face the south side? Why would he have motored to the backside of the island?" Lane was still stuck on the first part of the theory.

Philip plunged on, ignoring her, his vivid imagination taking hold. "The boat, unable to handle the huge waves, capsizes!"

Lane tilted her head to the side in consideration and mumbled to herself, "I guess the boat could have drifted if the engine was dead."

"Tossed over the side, poor, old Allister, struggling in the waves, unable to reach the shore is..."

"Drowned," Lane finished for him and then gave a skeptical shake of her head. "So, you think Allister's stolen yacht, missing lifeboat, and slashed tires have NOTHING to do with the floater and Dub's bloodied and shot up rowboat?"

"I don't know. Just trying to have an objective point of view."

Any counter comment was interrupted by Martha's desk phone, the receiver already in Lane's hand.

She answered it mid-ring. "Rockfish Island Sheriff's Department, Sheriff Lane speaking."

"What the HELL is going on over there, Sheriff?" A booming voice echoed down the line, the tone firm and full of authority.

Lane recognized it instantly.

"I've just landed in Florida to find my cell phone inundated with urgent voicemails and text messages."

"Mike?" Lane asked, awed, looking up at Philip, her eyes wide in surprise. "Mike Allister?"

"Sheriff, I've never considered us to be on a first-name basis. But yes, this is Mike Allister. Is it true my yacht has been stolen and my –?"

"Yes, I'm sorry, MR. Allister," Lane emphasized the mister. "I'm afraid to say, it was. We were notified—"

"If you would let me finish my question!"

Lane's lips pursed into a thin line, and her knuckles turned white, her grip on the phone tightening.

Mike Allister continued, not waiting for a response, "AND my Mercedes has been vandalized, as well? How is my house? Is my business still standing? It's not been burned to the ground, has it?" Mr. Allister's voice was heavy with sarcasm and thick-tongued. It was apparent he'd had a few drinks on the plane.

"No, sir. Your house and business seem to be untouched."

"Well, thank God for THAT!"

"Did you say you're down in Florida?" Lane ripped off the first page of the pink message pad and tossed it aside, then grabbed a pen, hovering it over the pad. "We've been trying to get a hold of you all morning."

"That's apparent by the many, and I do mean, many messages on my phone. I only landed a few minutes ago. Hold on."

Lane could hear him wrestling with something, the sound of a loudspeaker in the background accompanied by several other voices milling around. It indeed, sounded very much like a busy airport.

Coming back onto the line, Allister huffed into the phone, obviously walking at a brisk pace.

"I've had a family emergency. My brother has suffered a major heart attack, and my sister-in-law has asked me to come down for his emergency by-pass surgery."

"But your daughter didn't know anyth—"

"I tried calling her when I got the news, but she didn't answer. I figured I'd call her when I landed. Now she's all in a tizzy!"

"And your answering service?"

"I didn't have time! I had to catch a flight at the last minute." Mr. Allister whispered a quick, "Pardon me," before barking into the phone, "I've been stuck in the air for over six hours, Sheriff!"

"I'm confused. What day did you leave the island?"

"What day did I leave? ...Sheriff, I don't have time for this."

"It's for the insurance report on your slashed tires," Lane fibbed.

"Oh, well... On Friday."

"And how did you get to the mainland?"

"Are you seriously this inept? I took the FERRY!"

"I realize that. What I'm asking you is, did you take your vehicle over the ferry or simply walk on?"

There was always the possibility it wasn't only Allister's yacht that had been stolen from the mainland and brought back to the island.

"I was to be met at the Seattle ferry dock, so I walked on."

"Met by who?" Lane touched her pen to the pink sheet.

"That is not important, and it has NOTHING to do with my vandalized property!"

"I'm only trying to establish a timeline," Lane pointed out and then leaned into the phone, annoyed. "And, you know, it actually might. Possibly whoever knew you were suddenly leaving town decided to—"

"Sheriff, I assure you, THAT is not the case. The person who met me is also here with me in Florida."

"Oh." Lane paused, suddenly very curious as to who Mike Allister had taken along on his trip. "So, just to get this straight. You got the phone call about your brother while you were on the island. You then drove down—"

Mike Allister, his patience already blown, said loud and slowly, as if talking to a two-year-old, "I... was... already... on... the... mainland... when... I... got... the... call."

Lane visibly bristled and gripped the phone handle tighter, her knuckles cracking.

"I see." Her chest heaved as she took a deep breath, doing her best to rein in her temper. "Sorry. I misunderstood." She took another deep breath and continued, "You left for Seattle via the ferry, leaving your vehicle behind on the island, Friday evening. You then received a phone call about your brother and left Washington state on a plane sometime Sunday morning, and you are now safely in Florida, in the same company as the person who picked you up from the dock on the mainland, Friday night."

"Yes!" Allister's tone was dripping sweet sarcasm. "Now, are we done with the interrogation? Can I finally get some answers to my OWN questions?"

Lane could hear a woman's soft voice on the other end, anxiously telling the lawyer not to lose his patience. He instead snapped, "What about my yacht?"

"Your yacht has been located and towed back to the Seattle Marina. Coast Guard reported no damage to your vessel, except the engine key is missing."

"No damage! You call that no damage? Do you know HOW EXPENSIVE it will be to get a new key?"

"As for your vehicle, it was towed from the ferry's Park and Ride lot with four slashed tires and is currently safely stored at the Rowles's Towing yard."

"Safely? If you were better at your JOB, my car—"

"Mr. Allister," Lane cut him off. "We were very concerned for your wellbeing, so I'm glad to hear you are safe and sound."

"Oh, I bet you are, Sheriff. I bet you're thrilled to death," he drew out the last word, slightly slurred.

Ignoring his jab, a wild flash of regret passed

across Lane's thoughts, her assumptions obviously incorrect on the floater's identity.

Shaking the regret gone, she continued, "Do you know who may have been responsible for—"

"No, I don't!" Mike Allister's voice dripped with disdain. "I don't know who would want to do anything to harm me in any way. This is insane... OH, hold on!"

Once more, Lane could hear wrestling and talking on the other side. Abruptly, his voice came back on the line. "My niece is here to greet me and take us to the hospital. I need to go." And with that, the line went dead.

Lane, clearly relieved, slowly lowered the receiver, hanging up the phone.

"Allister is alive and well, I take it?" Philip surmised, an almost apologetic smile on his face.

"Very much so." Lane inhaled deeply through her nose, giving her head a slight shake of disbelief, and then exhaled, "He's in Florida."

"Well, Martha will be happy!" Philip tried to lighten the mood. "That's good news."

"I suppose." Lane stood up and pushed in the desk chair. "But who the hell is our floater?"

CHAPTER 14

The heavy steps of George Barnes thundered as the trio descended the narrow stairway to the morgue, his voice booming ahead, echoing down the short, dimly lit hallway.

"Your deputy is already here, Sheriff. He's been busy making all sorts of phone calls."

He suddenly stopped in the middle of the stairs, giving his belly a good scratch through his long beard.

"And he told us all about Dub! Close thing, that."

George started the steep stairs again, his boots clunking down the cramped stairway.

"Though, I suppose we can expect more of the same. Our island isn't exactly youth's paradise when it comes to residents."

The big man suddenly shook his head sadly, and Lane imagined he was contemplating the amount of work that was potentially coming his way as funeral director in the coming months or years.

His industrial musings passing, George suddenly perked up, his somber thoughts alighting on something new. "Anyway, the coroner says he's got some good news for you."

"Already? What is it?" Lane turned, curious to his reply, having reached the last step. She inched her way across the landing, making room for Philip to step down, then George, the latter squeezing by, his broad shoulders pushing her flat against the wall, working his way ahead of them, to the morgue door, oblivious to Lane.

"Don't know, exactly. Come on in."

Shouldering the door open, George held it wide with his arm, doing his best to suck in his gut, allowing Lane and Philip to squeeze by, and added, in an informative tone, "It's a toasty thirty-six degrees in here compared to outside."

He followed in behind Philip and addressed the thin man sitting by the door, including him in their conversation. "Quite the cold snap we're having this week, ain't it, Ralph?"

Sitting at a small card table, bundled for the Antarctic, was Coroner Ames, his face hidden behind a clipboard. Beside him was an open box of gingersnaps and a steaming cup of coffee.

"Couldn't say, really. It's always cold to me, George."

Picking up a gingersnap and giving it a good dunk, the distracted coroner popped the soggy remains into his mouth and lowered the clipboard, the new guests coming into view.

"Well, hello again, Sheriff." Coroner Ames hastily stood up, brushing cookie crumbs from his lap. "Ranger Russell, good to see you!" He extended his hand.

"Likewise, Ralph." Philip gave the older man a warm smile and a hearty shake, slightly jarring his bony frame. "Hope you don't mind me tagging along. The sheriff thought I might be able to help ID the body."

"Oh, no need for that. I've already done it!" The coroner pushed his coffee aside and picked up the clipboard, tucking it under his arm with a pleased smile, gesturing to the card table's contents. "Go ahead, get gloved up."

Looking down, Philip noted a small jar of ointment and a box of latex gloves sitting by the coroner's coffee and the opened box of gingersnaps, already half empty.

"Will do." Philip dutifully tugged a pair of gloves from the box, eyeing the cookies.

"And make sure to get some ointment under your nose." The coroner suddenly shook a wise finger. "You'll regret it if you don't."

"That, I don't doubt," Philip said, dipping his

finger in and then passing the small jar to Lane before smearing a good portion of ointment under his own nose.

"I have to admit..." Coroner Ames plucked a cookie from the box. "I'm a bit excited about this one." He continued mumbling through a full mouth, "So many things going on. We've got a lot to cover!"

"Well, let's begin then." Lane, who had immediately grabbed a pair of gloves upon stepping into the room, called out to her deputy as she pulled out her notepad, "We're starting, Caleb."

Tethered to a mounted phone next to the gurney elevator, Caleb appeared to be engaged in an animated conversation, unaware of their presence. Hearing his name, he stopped and curtly nodded, then turned his back on the group, once again speaking fiercely into the handset.

"Wrap it up, Deputy," Lane persisted, unfairly supposing he was chatting it up with Martha, or more likely, his girlfriend, Amy Holmes. The young deputy having stolen the desired girl's affections from the young ranger, Kody, over Christmas.

A sudden and loud bang came from the mortuary cabinet, the metal refrigerated door swinging shut.

"Sorry, folks!" George called over his shoulder, shoving aside an empty gurney with a stiff arm, making room to push past. "Just moving some stuff around. I'll have him to you in a jiffy," he promised, the gurney wheels squeaking as he passed by Deputy Pickens with the white-sheeted corpse.

Caleb, his conversation over, hung up the phone with a slam and followed behind the funeral director, his face red.

"What's wrong?" Lane held out a pair of gloves, keeping her voice low. "Woman problems?"

"No, Allister problems. Coast Guard says since they found the stolen boat, it's now their investigation, and they're being tight ass—"

"Tight-lipped, I am sure, is what you were going to say?" Lane gave him a small smile and an even look. "We'll have to take a step back for the time being on Allister's boat." She then gave him a motherly pat on the arm. "We've got something bigger to focus on right now, Deputy."

Caleb, nodding his head in forced agreement, took the offered gloves, his disappointment still evident.

"Okay, Ralph. I think we're ready." Lane turned her attention to the sheeted corpse, making her way to the gurney, her deputy and the coroner a step behind. "How were you able to make the identification? Dental records?"

"Hold on!" Philip, still standing by the card table, swiped a gingersnap and brought it up for a bite, then thinking better of it, placed it back and quickly joined the group, asking, "Dental records? I thought all of his teeth were punched out?"

The coroner slowly nodded his head, moving aside for Philip.

"Only the front, all the way back to the second bicuspid. Granted, even with most of those missing, I could have matched up the molars, but there was actually no need. I lifted his fingerprints."

"How?" Lane, her voice awed, looked down at the corpse's hand.

The entire skin surface, pruned like a raisin, was white and peeling, layers of tissue still hanging loose from the pale and bloated fingers.

"This side, Sheriff," the coroner beckoned her to the left edge of the gurney. "I think you'll find this interesting. You see, I inject saline solution into the fingertip, here."

The coroner pointed to a small pinprick on the pad of the index finger.

"The saline acts as a filler and plumps the wrinkles, reversing the pruning and allowing the prints to be lifted. Still... seawater is hell on fingerprints. But I'm pleased to say, the prints I lifted were good enough to match up with a concealed weapons permit." The coroner withdrew the clipboard from under his arm, scanning down the sheet. "Issued... four months ago to a..."

Philip casually leaned against Lane and whispered in her ear, "A concealed weapons permit means he had a pistol. Wonder if it was a .22?"

"Here it is!" Coroner Ames looked up with a bright smile. "Issued to a Robert E. Allen."

Philip recognized the name and took a halting step away from the gurney.

The coroner continued, "Mr. Allen, fifty-two years old, resident of Rockfish Island for the last ten years..."

"Hold on. You're talking about Bob Allen! Bobber's Boat Repair, Bob, right?" Philip shot a look at George for confirmation.

"That's him," George affirmed, nodding his head, his arms folded across his barrel chest. "Shame, that. He was on your bowling team, wasn't he, Phil?"

The coroner quickly scribbled a note on the top page of his clipboard and mumbled to himself, "Boat repair? That explains the oil and engine grease under the fingernails."

"I gotta see." Philip went to lift the white sheet away from the corpse's face, but Lane gently arrested his hand, shaking her head no, advising against it.

"You won't recognize him," she whispered, her eyes holding his with meaning.

Caleb joined in, "He's the kind of hippie dude, right?" He motioned to the back of his own head. "With a ponytail? Always wearing shorts and Birkenstocks, no matter the weather? And usually has a slogan t-shirt on, like, 'Save the Spotted Owl' and

'Give a Hoot, Don't Pollute'. That type of thing?"

"I'd say he was more of a conservationist than a hippie," Lane interjected.

"And he's married to a hottie, isn't he? She's like, what, fifteen years younger than him?"

"Try twenty-three years," Lane corrected.

Caleb's mouth dropped open.

"A hot babe in her late twenties and he in his fifties? Hmmm... I'd have thought she was WAY out of his league."

"She was," Philip said quietly.

Lane turned to catch the coroner's eye.

"You sure it's Bob, Ralph?" She pointed to the sheeted corpse. "This guy has short hair, no ponytail."

"Ah, you noticed. I'll get to that in a minute, Sheriff. Now, brace yourself, Phil." The coroner gave him a stern look, his face serious. "This isn't going to be pretty."

Philip gave a nodded jerk, signaling he was ready, and watched the coroner pull the white sheet down to the dead man's waist, revealing a long, sewn Y incision.

Eyeing Philip cautiously, the coroner began, "Now, taking into consideration the length of time the body was in the water, Mr. Allen was most likely killed last Friday, sometime in the evening, or possibly late afternoon. Hard to gauge which, by the stomach contents, his last meal being a hamburger and fries. Though I can tell you, he died roughly two hours after he ate."

The coroner flipped to the next page.

"As for toxicology, I'm still waiting on the results." He tapped the clipboard with his pen and then made a hasty check-mark. "I didn't see any signs of alcoholism or drug abuse, and according to the lungs, the man wasn't a smoker." He looked up, making eye contact with Lane. "Though, in all fairness, I won't rule out poison or heavy sedation just yet, considering how the body was treated."

"When will you find out?" Lane asked, regretting her bagel from earlier in the day.

"Oh, sometime tomorrow." The coroner flipped a few more pages referring to his written notes and continued, "As for the rest of him... he appears to have been a healthy man for his age, though his cholesterol was over the moon. Might have given him some trouble down the road if he'd continued living." The coroner slid his pen into the clip of the clipboard. "Anyway, as you can guess, Sheriff, Mr. Allen did not die of natural causes."

"What WAS the cause of death?"

"That... is much more interesting. To start, there was no water in his lungs. He was dead long before being tossed in the sea."

"He was strangled, then?" Lane began to note "strangulation" on her notepad.

"Actually, it was a gunshot to the side of the head, a few inches back from the temple."

The coroner gently lifted and tilted the skull to the left, displaying a shaved section, the small hole blatantly obvious. "As you can see, the gunshot hole is small, .22 caliber. I was able to remove the bullet intact and will be sending it to ballistics for you."

"Appreciate that," Lane said, scratching out "strangulation."

"There is clear stippling, here," the coroner continued, his gloved finger pointing to the dark speckled marks circling the wound. "This direct powder tattooing against the skull means the gun was held tight against the head." He carefully turned the skull back, setting it gently onto the block. "Between the small entry wound, the matted hair, and the seawater washing away the blood, I'd neglected to spot it on the dock this morning."

"Gunshot wound, no strangulation." Lane wrote the words down as she said them, placing them below her previous scribbled notation.

"Sorry, but..." Caleb shook his head, giving an apologetic wave for the interruption. "I thought you said on the dock, he was strangled? He wasn't now?"

"No, you're right. That was my original finding." The coroner paused and quickly scribbled on the top page of his clipboard, "False Findings Case" and then proceeded, Lane smiling at the notation. "And I was correct. Look at this." The coroner's tone had turned eager, pointing to a set of crescent shape marks embedded in the pale skin just below the Adam's apple. "The initial grip was made, here, and... see these scratches, there? Those were from the victim trying to grip the attacker's hands."

Several deep and superficial scratches could be seen, distinctly visible through the bruising.

"Clearly a desperate attempt to pull away the killer's hands. I've taken fingernail scrapings, the good they will do us. And here..." He moved his hand down to the base of the neck. "If you look closely, you can see the purple outline of fingers. Large hands by the look of it. They started low and then gripped higher." Tucking the clipboard under his arm again, Coroner Ames positioned his gloved hands above the finger-sized bruises.

It did not escape the group's notice that the marks were far too large to be from a woman.

"It was a brutal strangulation as well. An extreme amount of pressure was used." Coroner Ames took his hands back and indicated the incision below the jawline. "Normally, I'd have looked for petechiae hemorrhages in the whites of the eyes for signs of strangulation and left it at that, but since his eyes were missing, I had to take a deeper look. His hyoid bone has been fractured, which goes to show the severity of the throttling."

"Shot, strangled, and then bludgeoned." Philip stepped around Lane, looking closely at the base of the neck, lining his own hands above the bruises. They were close in size.

"Well, not in that order." The coroner lightly-moved Philip aside, indicating key areas around the chest cavity. "It appears he also took a few heavy blows to the ribs and stomach area, and I would assume, to the face as well." He stepped back, returning his attention to the upper half of the body. "Though, the actual bludgeoning which disfigured the features wasn't done by hand. The object used was wooden. I found splinters in the—"

"It was a boat oar," Lane confirmed, her voice thin. "The Park Rangers found a rowboat washed ashore this morning. The oar was bloody and damaged. Forensics is going over it now."

"Ah, an oar. Yes, that would line up with these marks here." The coroner's finger hovered above the crater-like lacerations. "And, of course, the nose being smashed flat."

"This obviously was not a random attack," Lane said out loud, but mostly to herself. "He was targeted. Somebody worked him over."

"You mean, like a shakedown? Someone trying to collect gambling debts... or a loan shark?" Caleb's voice sounded eager, the idea thrilling.

"The Mob," George Barnes said decidedly. "Seen

this type of thing in the movies." He rocked back on his heels, his fingers finding his belt loops, his chest swelling full of hot air. "I bet you Bob was part of a witness protection program, and they tracked him down." George nodded, sure of himself. "Found him, beat him up for being a snitch, and then fed him to the fishes, so to speak. I bet if I asked around..."

"For goodness sakes," Lane muttered, flipping her leather notepad closed with a snap. "George!" She leveled the big man with her best steel-eyed gaze. "I want to make something clear. Come here."

"Sheriff?" George suddenly dropped his arms to his side and walked over, looking like a wounded child.

"George... As you know, with your wife being a part of our office, she, like the rest of us in the Sheriff's Department, is obligated not to share information on an open case with the public. This, in a VERY big way, also extends to you, as her husband and, of course, the funeral director. You are privy to a lot of information in this town, and it does not serve the community well nor the Sheriff's Department, to theorize on possible reasons this poor man was killed and act on those theories, conducting your own investigation. That's the job of law enforcement."

Lane put a firm hand on his arm, her blue eyes serious. "Now. I'm sure I don't have to really ask this, but I will. As Martha has already sworn for herself,

I need you to promise me that you will not discuss this case with anyone outside of this room. No sharing theories, no speculating to your curious neighbors, no asking around, and for heaven's sakes, NO visits to the gossip-circle picnic table at Hattie's. Understood?"

The big man jerkily nodded his head in the affirmative, his large hands shoved deep into his pockets.

"Yes, ma'am."

"Wonderful." Lane's voice suddenly sweetened and dripped honey, "You're in the inner circle now, George. Don't let me down."

"Inner circle, huh?" George's smile widened and his stance relaxed.

Her play on his ego had been successful.

"I suppose..." George's hands found his beard, giving it a good stroke. "That goes for Phil, as well?" He gave Philip a stern look. "Loose lips, sink ships, ya know."

Philip nodded, furrowing his forehead in agreement, having been at one time, on the other end of that lecture. "For sure. Not a peep from me."

"Good. Glad that's settled." Lane put her hand on George's big arm and gave it a firm squeeze, drawing his eye. "Because I would have hated arresting you for interfering in an investigation." She smiled sweetly again, offering the bogus threat.

"If, uh..." Philip walked his way back to the card

table, plopping down into the metal chair, the coldness of the room seeping into his stiff leg. "If George doesn't mind, I'd like to share my own speculations with the... inner circle." He stretched his leg out, his thigh paining him. "I'm wondering if we aren't dealing with someone less formidable. I mean, if your job, as Caleb put it, is to shake people down. You'd use a different gun than the low caliber .22. Anybody familiar was firearms knows a .22 won't do much."

Philip held his hand up, warding off the coroner's protest. "Well, obviously, if you put the gun up to someone's head, it'll do the trick. What I mean, is you gotta be RIGHT up there. I would think a professional would prefer a little distance and use something a bit more powerful. At least a 9mm."

"I agree with Phil," Caleb said, nodding his head. "But I think the killer used the victim's own gun. Maybe the bad guy was roughing him up, and Bob pulled his concealed weapon? The perp manages to get the gun away from him in a struggle and then ends up popping him off with his own weapon."

"Popping... him off?" Lane questioned with disdain. "I think we need to move past the movie clichés."

"Well, if I'm allowed to throw my hat in the ring?" The coroner looked for permission and continued, "I find it odd you've not received a phone call from a worried spouse. After all, the man has been dead for over forty-eight hours."

"That's a good point." Caleb hitched his thumb towards the mounted phone. "Should I call Martha and see if—?"

"I was going to add." The coroner gave an apologetic smile. "One reason you may not have received a call is the man was kidnapped, and his wife, I would assume, has been informed of the fact and told not to contact the authorities."

"Why would anyone want to kidnap Bob?" George gaffed. "If it were Mike Allister or Mitchell Wilson... or even Sue Carter, I'd agree. I mean, they've all got lots of money! Bob... well, so Martha has told me, is in debt up to his eyeballs."

"Ah, so much for my idea." The coroner looked crestfallen. "Circling back around to your earlier question, Sheriff. About the lack of a ponytail?"

"Yeah, what about that?" Philip sat up straight, curious.

"They snipped it off." Coroner Ames made a cutting motion with his fingers, imitating scissors. "I'm assuming this was one more step taken to hide Mr. Allen's identity."

"The killer was buying for time," Lane said, marking her notepad. "They were, I am sure, hoping the body would never surface, but on the off chance it did, they assumed it would take us a while to find out the identity. Precious time they could use to drum up an alibi or get out of town." Lane shook her head, irritated at the notion, and mumbled under her breath, "Probably to Florida."

Hearing the muttered comment and knowing Lane was referring to Mike Allister, Philip smiled and said loudly, "Buzz, buzz."

Coroner Ames gave Philip a surprised look, placing his clipboard on the card table.

"I'm sorry, did you say something?"

"Nothing."

Lane shot Philip a dirty look, tucking her notepad into her back pocket.

The thin coroner, noting the exchange between the two, smiled.

"Oh, well, then, I agree with what you were saying, Sheriff." He returned to the gurney and picked up the white sheet, giving the corpse one final analysis, his tone distracted, "The removing of the clothes, the cutting of the hair, the distorting of the face, and the disposal of the body. They were all stalling tactics and probably not wasted."

He paused, pulling the white sheet across the length of the dead man, covering the head, and turned back to the small group.

"If you ask me, there's a good chance your killer is miles away by now. That is. If they have any sense."

CHAPTER 15

"So, what's the plan?" Caleb tossed the last of the evidence bags into Lane's patrol truck and climbed into the passenger seat.

"Well." Lane waited until he fastened his seat belt before putting the vehicle into reverse and backing out onto the main street. "There is the unpleasant duty of informing Kristen Allen her husband is dead. Let's hope she can shed some light on his final hours. Then, I'll drop you back at the station, so you can enjoy what's left of your day off, and I'll run those over to the mainland to the forensic lab." Lane nodded towards the small pile of brown evidence bags at Caleb's feet.

"Thanks, Sheriff. But my plans are already shot for today, plus they'll be a ton of paperwork. I might as well finish the day out." Caleb pulled the seat belt down and away from his chest, Lane braking hard for a stray cat. "Besides, the overtime won't hurt." He suddenly shook his head. "But man, do I hate doing death notifications. It's my least favorite part of the job."

"Agreed." Lane pushed down on the turn signal, taking a left, leaving downtown.

The cab was silent for a moment.

"So, do you know Kristen very well?" Caleb angled the heating vents on the dash, settling into his seat.

"Not really. I sometimes sit with her and a couple of others during Phil's league nights. Though, we don't do much more than polite chit-chat. Between the thundering bowling balls crashing into the pins and the rock 'n' roll blaring over the speakers, and everyone cheering, it's impossible to do much more."

"Any idea how long they'd been married?"

"Seven years, I believe?" Lane tilted her head to the side, thinking it over. "Or around that. She jokes a lot about Bob having the seven-year itch and leaving her for an even younger woman."

Caleb looked out the window, the forest-lined road whizzing past.

"She can't truly be worried? She's gorgeous."

"I said, she joked. Not complained," Lane clarified.

"I wonder how he landed her?"

"No clue."

"Or maybe, she landed him? Could have a father complex? That, or she's a gold digger."

"Caleb!" Lane shot him a severe look.

"What? You did say there was over twenty years difference between them!"

"Yes, but did you ever think they might have connected on an intellectual level? Not everything is physical."

Caleb shook his head, greatly doubting it.

"No offense, but she doesn't strike me as the intellectual type."

"No. Me either," Lane admitted.

"Besides, it's not like the guy was a professor or a Pulitzer Prize winner." Caleb suddenly shrugged. "He owned a tiny boat shop, and he—"

Lane cut in, "Alright, alright. You obviously don't believe in true love." She gave him a studious glance before returning her eyes to the road. "I suppose you think Kristen wanted her husband dead because she couldn't have possibly married him for love?"

"You know, as well as I do, the rule is, when investigating a homicide, you always look at those who were the closest to the victim."

"Except our victim was killed by a man."

"Murder for hire. Paid someone to bump him off."

"Bump... him... off?" Lane gave her deputy a sideways glance, chuckling, annoyed, and amused at the same time. "Yes, we'll have to rule that out. It is indeed one of MANY theories you and the others have floated about today."

"Okay, then." Caleb gave Lane a big smile, turning to face her. "I see you think we're full of it. So, let me ask you this. IF Kristen Allen can indeed rule out for us, her husband wasn't a compulsive gambler, who owed money to the mob, having turned state's evidence, and escaped by joining the witness protection program, but tragically was found and kidnapped in a futile attempt to ransom the monies owed from his gambling debts..." Caleb, himself, scoffed at the long-winded assumption. "Why else would somebody want to kill him?"

"Hmmm, why else?" Lane slowed down, braking lightly. A small cluster of driveways had come into view, and she peered closely at the mailbox numbers. "Glen Sorenson mentioned this morning, he and several others on the island are suing Bobber's Boat Repair."

"For what?"

"Faulty repair work. Services paid for, but not rendered properly." Lane sped up, seeing they still had a little ways to go. "With a pending lawsuit, there's the possibility someone hadn't wanted to wait for their day in court and decided to take their frustrations out on Bob directly, resulting in his death."

"I like the idea of a crime boss somewhere in Chicago better than a local." Caleb's smile had dropped, his face serious.

"Me too." Lane applied the brakes and peered

through the passenger window at a short, graveled driveway. "Here we are."

"Two vehicles in the drive," Caleb noted as Lane pulled in, slightly blocking a new Range Rover, the dealer sticker still in the back window.

An older, white Prius, was parked beside it.

Lane opened her door and stepped out of the rig, looking up at the modern Alpine home. It was one of the fancier cabins on the island with its towering windows reaching up to a steepled roof, stone masonry elegantly crafted between blonde logs, and a wraparound porch at the base.

Shutting the passenger door, Caleb said under his breath, "Well, I can see why they might be up to their eyeballs in debt."

"No joke." Lane tilted her head towards the Range Rover, taking the small path up to the stoned archway. "Wonder who the new car belongs to?"

As they approached, Lane could hear music and laughter coming from inside, along with the distinct sound of a blender.

With a firm nod, she indicated for Caleb to knock, and the two waited.

Inside, the loud music and laughter continued, and Caleb rapped heavily upon the door again, doing his best to time his poundings between blender whirls.

Minutes passed before they could hear someone on the other side, the doorknob suddenly rattling and the door, itself, shuttering in its frame, remaining closed. A flurry of muttered curses floated through the wood, heard above the sound of the deadbolt turning.

The door finally opened.

"Oh! Sheriff! Are we being too loud?"

Kristen Allen, her dark brown hair in a ponytail, wearing a plunging blouse with jeans, smiled upon them, an over-sized margarita glass in hand.

"Did the neighbors call you? I didn't think the music was THAT loud." She swiftly turned, wobbling as she did so, and called into the house.

Seeming to hear a reply, she returned her attention to the new guests and, in the process, spilled half her drink onto her shoes.

"OH..." Kristen sighed and then broke out into a lighthearted laugh, giving a slight shrug. "Oopsie."

From inside, someone obligingly lowered the volume.

"Sorry about that." Kristen began to shut the door slowly, concentrating hard on not spilling another drop. "We'll keep it down. Promise."

"Kristen." Lane placed her booted foot inside the door, blocking the action, and exchanged a knowing glance with her deputy before addressing the obviously intoxicated Mrs. Allen. "Kristen, we're not here about a noise complaint. Could we come in for a minute?" Lane gave her best-disarming smile, at the same time, forcefully pushing the front door open, taking pressure off her foot.

Kristen stepped back, a confused frown lining her forehead.

"Uh, yeah. Sure, Sher... Lane." She opened the door wider, taking an unsteady step back, her drink, despite her best efforts, sloping over the side. "Go on through to the living room. It's on the right."

"Can I ask who is here with you?" Lane kept her tone conversational, nodding for Caleb to enter first, and encouraged Kristen to walk between them down the hall, shutting the front door behind them.

"Only my son, Chad." Kristen turned to Lane, stopping dead in her tracks, breaking into a confidential tone, "He's not really. I mean, I didn't have him." She placed a hand on Lane's arm, bringing the salt-rimmed glass to her lips and then back down, continuing, "He's actually my stepson. That's our little joke. He's older than me, but he still calls me mom. Isn't that sweet?"

Not waiting to see if Lane thought it sweet or not, Kristen promptly started to follow Deputy Pickens again, doing her best not to dribble on the floor.

Lane gauged the level of Kristen's inebriation and concluded the woman was a little more than mildly tipsy.

"Would you mind if I asked him to join us?" Lane looked past Kristen's shoulder into the kitchen area. "Is he in there?"

"Yeah, he's making another batch of these!" Kristen exuberantly lifted her glass into the air. "We're celebrating!"

"Oh?" Lane encouraged her to keep moving down the hall.

"He landed a commercial!"

"He's an actor?"

"Aspiring." Kristen halted again, bringing her glass back down, salt crystals flying. "And he's waiting to hear back on a play. If it goes well, he can quit his bartending job!" She went to drink, and frowned, her lip stuck out in a pout. "Sort of a shame because he's such a great bartender."

"Looks like it," Lane muttered as she left Kristen in Caleb's hands and ventured off alone in search of the kitchen, it easy enough to find, the sound of grinding ice in the blender guiding her way.

There, behind a large kitchen island, swaying to pop music, barely heard over the blender, stood Chad Allen.

Upon seeing Lane, he lifted his finger from the button, the grinding noise coming to a halt.

"Hello!" he greeted, giving Lane a generous look up and down, his smile widening. "You weren't who I was expecting to see! Come to join our little soiree?" He gestured to the blender and the awaiting margarita glasses.

"Are you expecting more people?" Lane noticed

there was a total of three glasses still on the table, discounting the one in Kristen's hand.

"We were, but he just canceled." He turned and lowered the volume on the radio to light background noise. "Which is a drag. More the merrier, I say. Sure you don't want me to blend you up something?" Chad's voice sounded hopeful. "I make a killer peach daiquiri."

"Actually, would you mind stepping into the living room with me? I need to speak with you and your stepmother about something important."

Chad's smile dropped, and his happy-go-lucky countenance disappeared.

"Has something happened?"

By his sober response, Lane deduced Chad wasn't as tipsy as his stepmother and considered this to be a good thing.

"Let's join my deputy in the other room, and we can get started." Lane stepped aside, allowing Chad to maneuver around the counter and make his way down the hall to the living room.

Following close behind, she realized Chad was approximately the same height as Philip's six-four, though Lane put his age at around hers, a man in his mid-thirties. He was good-looking, muscular, and well-toned, just as an aspiring actor would be.

The two entered the living room together, Kristen and Caleb awaiting their arrival.

Lane was pleased to see Caleb had separated Kristen from her drink, placing the margarita glass on a side table, out of reach.

Kristen, herself, looked much more composed. Though her fingers worked nervously in her pony-tail as her hazel eyes searched Chad's expression, his face now somber.

He sat next to his stepmother on the couch with his hands resting on his knees and looked at Lane expectantly.

"This isn't good news, is it?" he suddenly asked, his fingers nervously tapping.

"I'm afraid not." Lane did her best to meet his eyes and then turned her full attention upon Kristen.

"I regret to tell you, Mrs. Allen, your husband, Bob, was found deceased this morning. His body was discovered in the ocean, caught on a private dock, here on the island. The coroner believes he died sometime Friday evening."

Kristen, her hand flying to her heart, looked, at first, stunned and then, to Lane's utter surprise, greatly relieved.

"Oh! I think you've made a mistake, Sheriff." Kristen suddenly chuckled and smiled at Chad as if sharing a private joke. "Bob is in Seattle! At a boat show!" She turned back to Sheriff Lane, her eyes wide, eagerly adding, "He called me from his hotel room, Friday night."

Chad joined in, leaning forward, looking relieved as well. "And I got a text from him Saturday morning." He started to dig his cell phone out of his jeans. "There must be a mix-up. It's a pretty common name."

He punched in a quick code and brought up a text message. "See." He handed Lane the phone. "You must have the wrong Bob Allen."

CHAPTER 16

Squeezing his forest truck between Glen Sorenson's Rubicon and Harry's brown clunker, Philip peered through the driver's side window, skeptical he'd left himself enough room to climb out.

There hadn't been much choice in parking spots, Jerry Holmes's double cabbed pickup already parked on the lawn, and Doctor Hadley's Bronco bumper to bumper behind it. He would have parked at the entrance, but Martha's Ford Explorer was already stationed at the end of the drive, blocking the mailbox.

Putting the truck in park, Philip snatched a black mini-mart bag from the passenger seat and took a deep breath, doing his best to wiggle out.

Exhaling, he slammed the door shut and inched himself forward between the vehicles, smiling at the buzzing beehive of activity inside Dub's house.

The cabin's drapes now open, Martha could be seen bent over Dub, the latter, comfortably layered in blankets, tucked into his La-Z-Boy recliner.

She looked to be offering a steaming bowl of soup, and upon acceptance, stuffed numerous napkins under Dub's chin in motherly affection.

Dub, in turn, suffered her attentions, an annoyed look on his face while she continued to hover, fluffing a pillow and placing it gently behind his bandaged head before moving to his blanket, tugging and pulling at it tenderly.

Dub, seeming to have finally lost his temper, waved the well-meaning Martha away, continuing to glare after her as she bustled into the kitchen.

Philip's eyes followed her and found Jerry, the town veterinarian, giving Dub's cat plenty of attention at the breakfast nook, chatting it up with Harry, who looked busy unpacking groceries.

Jerry spotted Philip through the kitchen window and waved Philip in.

He returned the wave and began to head for the door when the sound of splitting wood and the distinct clunk of an ax arrested him, the sound coming from the backside of the house.

Curious to know who was cutting wood, he rounded the corner, surprised to find Glen, an ax held high above his head, his arms steady.

With a grunt, the old man swung the steelhead

down, the blade biting hard into a large tree stump, split wood littered all around.

"You've got quite the arm there, Glen!" Philip called in welcome.

"I should." Glen stooped down with a groan and grabbed the freshly cut kindling. "Was a logger most of my life."

"Here, load me up!" Philip marched over, holding out his arms, the convenience store bag dangling from his fingers.

"Whatcha got there?" Glen nodded towards the bag, placing the cut wood in the crook of Philip's arms.

"A six-pack of beer and a canister of chew for Dub."

"Oh, he'll like that."

"I figured."

"Any... uh..." Glen bent down, grabbing two more pieces. "Any word on the floater from this morning? Spotted your rig at the funeral home on my way over."

"Yeah, but I can't tell you. Sheriff Lane needs to notify the relatives first." Philip gave an apologetic smile, moving a little closer, Glen's trembling hands dropping another heavy piece into his arms.

"Suppose you can't tell me who it isn't?" Glen gave him a broad smile and a wink.

Philip laughed and shook his head. "Sorry, Glen. Mums the word until Sheriff Lane says so."

"Fine, fine." Glen started picking up the lighter kindling, tucking small pieces under his arm.

"How's Dub?" Philip jostled the wood, adjusting the load.

"Grouchy as usual."

"Glad to hear it!"

"Me too." Glen took a deep breath and squinted over at the back door. "Thinking about asking Dub to move in with me. We're both getting up in age. If Harry hadn't found him..." Glen shook his head, words failing him.

"Yeah, scary to think it, huh?" Philip lightly nudged Glen, silently asking him to open the door.

The older man nodded and swung the back door open, a chorus of voices coming to life.

"Come on in, Phil. You can dump that wood right by the fireplace. I'll stack it up."

Glen led the way, and Philip followed behind, the back door opening into the kitchen.

"Hiya, Phil!" Jerry got up from the table and slid past Harry, who bounced from cupboard to cupboard, still putting away groceries. "Let me take some of the weight off you."

Jerry unhooked the black plastic bag from Philip's fingers with a devilish smile, his curled mustache adding to his mischievous appearance.

"Gee, Jerry, thanks." Philip chuckled, shouldering past him and into the living room, making for the fireplace. He gave the elderly man, reclined in the armchair, a warm smile. "Hey, Dub, how you feelin'?"

Dub, swaddled in blankets and a gauze head-wrap, gave Philip a peeved look.

"Alive," he grumbled, sounding regretful.

Philip lowered his arms to the ground, letting the wood roll out, and glanced over his shoulder to give Dub a big smile.

"Well, don't sound so happy about it," he teased, dusting his hands off and moving aside so Glen could stack the wood.

"Here, Phil." Jerry settled one of the kitchen chairs next to Dub's La-Z-Boy, nodding for Philip to take the seat, and handed back the plastic bag.

"Thanks, Jer." Philip sat himself down and placed the bag gently into Dub's lap.

"Brought you something."

"Everybody is being so damn nice," Dub said, his voice hoarse, not meeting Philip's eye.

"I can see that." Philip smiled, taking in the room.

By the look of it, Martha had done some dusting before heading home, a casserole dish sitting on the kitchen counter for later, and by Dub's elbow, on the little table, was a stockpile of medication and gauze courteous of Dr. Hadley.

In accord, Harry had shown up with two weeks' worth of groceries. While Glen had set to work on replenishing the woodpile, and Jerry had shown up with cat food and kitty litter, along with several feathered cat toys, already sprawled across the room.

"Makes a man feel helpless," Dub grumbled, pulling the top blanket up under his chin and shooting Philip a side glance. "All these people, waiting on you hand and foot, just because you slipped in the shower." He suddenly leaned forward, lowering his voice. "The soap squirted right out of my hand, Phil. One minute I'm standing there, the next I'm on the cold tile." He leaned back, shaking his head. "It's downright embarrassing. You'd think I'd almost died."

"On the contrary, Dub. You almost DID die."

"Pffft." Dub waved his words away and leaned forward again, his face turning red. "Do you know Martha took it upon herself to call my boy in Idaho? Says he's coming up to stay with me for a week! Oh, and on top of that..." He settled back into his chair, his voice rising with irritation. "Martha plans on swinging by to see me before and after she gets off work every day until he can get here!"

"She's only trying to be kind, Dub."

"Kind? Oh, don't fool yourself, Phil. Her kindness is paid in full with gossip! She'll be running all around town, telling folks how black and blue I am and how she's seen it with her own two eyes! By the end of the week, she'll have everyone convinced I'm on my deathbed, and then the whole damn town will come in droves to wish me well!"

Philip did his best to hide an amused smile and shook his head, commiserating with Dub.

"I'm sorry you have to put up with us well-wishers, Dub." Philip patted his arm and then leaned back. "But I've got some bad news for you that might cheer you up."

"Oh?" Dub's frown turned up at the corners, his interest piqued.

"Did you know your rowboat was missing?"

"No. Not surprised if she is, though."

Philip, taken aback by the comment, scooted his chair closer.

"Why do you say that?"

"Friday night, that huge wind storm? I couldn't sleep because the big cedar's limbs were banging up against the house." Dub idly pointed out to the front yard, to the looming tree. "It was a thunkin' and thackin' its heart out."

Dub's cat suddenly jumped into his lap, and he ran his gnarled hand down the feline's back, its tail flickering left to right.

"I was wide awake when I heard a car drive by after midnight, heading for my dock. By the time I got out of bed, it was out of sight."

The cat settled down, snuggling into his lap, its purr abundantly loud.

"Assumed it was a couple of teenagers looking for a place to drink and neck."

"Did you happen to see the car coming back?" Philip, his voice eager, inched closer.

"Sure. Couldn't sleep anyway. Around two, it came zooming up from the dock drive."

"Recognize who it was?" Philip was on the edge of his seat.

"Nah, too dark to see the driver and passenger. But it looked to be a green car, one of those fancy-dancy electric vehicles." Dub started snapping his fingers, trying to recall the name. "Starts with a P. Prous? Prenus?"

"A Prius?"

"That's it! A green one."

CHAPTER 17

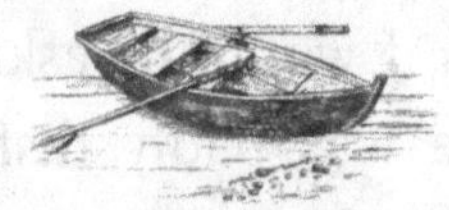

"I'm so sorry, Chad. The body that was recovered." Lane paused and handed the cell phone back, her voice sympathetically firm as she continued, "It is your father. The body's identification was made by fingerprint analysis."

Chad took the phone from her hand, shaking his head in disbelief, and persisted, "Sheriff, how could my father die on Friday and still be texting us over the weekend?"

"I know... that seems odd. The coroner could very well have the time and day of death wrong. The body was in water for several days and—"

Chad shook his head stubbornly, interrupting, "How can that be? He was in downtown Seattle! Are you sure—"

Kristen leaned in, cutting Chad off.

"So, you've seen him... Bob?" Kristen was still teetering on doubt. "Maybe I need to go with you and identify the body? Double-check sure it's my Bob. Why don't we go now an—"

Lane put a gentle hand on Kristen's knee, shaking her head against the suggestion, cutting short any further insistence.

"Normally, yes, I would be asking you to do so. However, his face was badly disfigured when we found him, and I'm afraid there would be no point."

"No point?" Chad stood up aghast and then sat back down, his arms flailing to his side in exasperation.

Lane turned to her deputy. "Caleb? Would you mind grabbing the evidence bag with the—"

Caleb gave a curt nod and left the room. He knew exactly what she wanted.

"Sheriff..." Kristen had sobered entirely. "What about a wedding ring? Maybe I could see that?"

Lane simply shook her head no to the question.

"I don't understand this!" Chad's voice was mystified, imbued with anger. "Why can't she see the body?"

"Let's back up a step." Lane turned to Kristen and removed her hand, pulling out her leather notepad. "When was the last time either of you talked to Bob?"

Looking to Kristen for direction, Chad spoke first, his tone impatient, "I texted dad on Saturday. Told him I wanted to come over for a visit and Dad said he was out of town for a week, but I should head over anyway." Chad started scrolling through his phone and suddenly stopped, reaching over and taking Kristen's hand in his.

"And you, Kristen?" Lane prompted.

"I, uh... I talked to him Friday night. He let me know he'd made it to his hotel room. Then I think," she paused, Lane, interrupting with a question.

"Where was he staying?"

"The Four Seasons. I have an email confirming his reservation if you'd like to see it."

Lane shook her head, noting for someone rumored to be in debt and engaged in a pending lawsuit, Bob had picked a spendy place to stay.

"Did you speak with him again after Friday, Kristen?"

"I texted him Saturday morning to see how he slept. He texted back, saying fine. Then texted again about thirty minutes later. Said he was heading over to the convention to set up the booth. I told him to call me when he had time and that I wouldn't bother him. I knew he had several meetings planned for the next day." Kristen's face turned eager. "Should I get my phone?"

"Yes, I'd like to see it, but for the moment, neither of you have tried to text or call him since Saturday?"

Kristen's attention was drawn to Caleb, who had entered with a paper bag.

"No, like I said, I didn't want to bother him. He

gets annoyed if I text or call too much."

"Dad's not the best phone person," Chad explained, inching to the edge of the couch, his eyes on Caleb.

"I see." Lane put her notepad down and turned to her deputy.

"Here, Sheriff." Caleb opened the paper sack and removed a clear plastic bag, handing it to Lane.

"Thanks, Deputy Pickens." Lane turned to Kristen. "I'd like to show you something."

Lane held out the bag containing the wallet retrieved from the rowboat.

"Does this look familiar to you?"

Kristen let out a moan, her hand clapping over her mouth, and softly wailed, "Bob's wallet!"

Wanting a closer look, Chad took the bag from Lane, flipping it over, examining all sides, shaking his head.

"Kristen, stop being dramatic! Dad's wallet was leather worked." He looked at Lane, adding to the description. "It had his initials pressed-in. This is just a plain leather wallet."

"But Chad..." Kristen put her hand on his knee, her voice cracking, "Your dad lost his old wallet a few months ago." She took the bag from him, petting the plastic. "I bought this one myself to replace it. I picked it up especially. He wanted something more refined... basic. It's a Bvlgari." She gave the bag back to Lane, tearfully adding, "It cost over five-hundred dollars."

"You're sure?" Lane asked, her blue eyes firm.

Kristen gave a sudden jerk of the head and sagged against Chad's shoulder, bursting into tears, her stepson quickly wrapping his arm around her, looking bewildered.

"I'm so sorry for your loss," Lane said softly, handing off the wallet to Caleb, who quickly placed it inside the brown evidence bag.

"We... we need to call Uncle Roger," Chad said weakly, pushing back from Kristen, running his hands through his hair and picking his phone up, starting to dial. "He has to know."

"Was he the other person you were expecting to-night?" Lane asked, recalling Chad had stated one other person was supposed to join their party.

"No, he's Bob's older brother." Kristen's voice hard-ened. "And I'd rather not." She caught Lane's eyes, and then her tone softened, "I think we should wait, Chad. I can see the Sheriff has more to tell us." Kristen put her hand on Chad's phone, lightly pushing it away, her eager eyes searching Lane's face. "I take it Bob drowned? Was it a boating accident of some kind?"

Lane took a deep breath and steeled herself.

"No, no accident, and I'm afraid, he was dead be-fore hitting the water." Lane took the widow's hand, holding it tight. "Kristen, Bob was beaten and then shot in the head. Whoever did this, threw his body into the ocean where it was discovered this morning.

He was pulled ashore, here on the island, next to Glen Sorenson's dock."

Mystified, Kristen pulled her hand back and wrapped her arms about her waist, gripping her stomach.

"Oh, Bob!" she whispered, her voice cracking. "Poor Bob."

"I'm so sorry." Lane turned to Chad. "Truly sorry."

Chad, his face red, nodded an acknowledgment to her comment, his hand on Kristen's back as she rocked back and forth.

"Sheriff, when can we... when can we see him."

"Like I alluded to earlier, I wouldn't advise it, Chad. It'll need to be a closed casket." Lane looked back and over at her deputy, his eyes steadily watching the scene.

"Closed casket? What the hell!" He suddenly stood up, his face red, his hands balled into fists. "What is going on? Who would do this to my dad?"

"That's a good question." Lane shot an appraising look towards Chad before tapping Kristen's knee, catching her eye. She almost hated herself for asking, "Did Bob have gambling debts or owe anybody any money?" Lane paused, debating on the next question. "You didn't receive any ransom notes, did you, Kristen? Bob wasn't kidnapped, was he?"

"Kidnapped!" Chad's voice raised even higher. "Are you nuts?"

"Kristen?" Lane noticed at the word debt, the young

woman's eyes had widened, her face flushing red.

"Is there something you need to tell us?"

"No!" She shook her head vehemently, pulling Caleb down, asking him silently to sit down beside her, back on the couch. "No, I'm just in shock, is all. How... how did his body end up back on the island?"

"We'll be investigating that," Lane promised, not entirely convinced the young woman was speaking freely. "Kristen, do you have guns in the house? I know Bob had a concealed weapons permit."

"Guns?" Kristen looked up, her eyes wide, and then quickly shook her head. "We have just the... the one gun. But..." She looked towards her stepson, almost confused. "It's not kept at the house. It's in the safe at the shop."

"Do you know the caliber of the gun?" Lane's eye fell on Chad.

He leaned in, wanting to break into the conversation, nodding his head. "It's a .22. He kept it there in case someone tried to rob the shop."

Kristen nodded her head in agreement, letting Chad explain, and then added, "I never liked the idea. A robbery on our little island? So dumb. But he said Roger insisted he get it. I..." Kristen's hand covered her heart. "I didn't want it. But whatever my brother-in-law wants..." She left the sentence unfinished, her tone disgusted.

Chad, clearly disagreeing with Kristen's comment, shook his head and sat back on the couch, not responding in return.

Lane addressed Kristen, "Well, we'd like to look at that gun, if possible."

The young widow shrugged and said, "Sure. Like I said, it's at the shop."

"Would it be possible to go—"

"I just lost my husband!" Kristen shook her head, her face mystified. "I'd rather not leave my home right now." She quickly grabbed Chad's hand, indicating she wouldn't be okay being left alone if Lane asked Chad to go instead.

"I understand. Could we meet there in the morning?"

"I guess." Kristen wiped at her eyes.

Chad suddenly sat forward.

"Does she... will she need a lawyer? I mean, do you advise she have one?"

"She's not a suspect, but she can ask her lawyer along if she wants. Right now, everything is voluntary, and any cooperation given by you both is greatly appreciated. If she or you chose to do so no longer, then if needed, I could get a warrant easily enough. We're still trying to establish where the crime took place."

Unbeknownst to them, Lane was planning on requesting a warrant for the residence and business, regardless of Kristen's promised cooperation. She wouldn't risk the widow having a sudden bout of regret in the morning and ceremoniously shutting the door in their face, stalling the investigation.

Lane would come prepared, warrant in hand, just in case.

"No. A warrant won't be necessary," Kristen's voice was firm. "There's no need for a lawyer either. I..." Kristen squeezed Chad's hand again and then let go. "WE have nothing to hide. We both loved Bob."

Lane gave her a grateful smile and slowly nodded her understanding.

"Kristen, can you think of anybody wanting to do your husband any harm?"

"Of course, she can't!" Chad turned on Lane, his voice incredulous, "He had no enemies! My dad was the most laid back, easy-going, kind—"

"Yes," Kristen spoke over him, her tone biting. "I'm sorry, but yes, there is. His brother Roger. He'd love to kill him."

CHAPTER 18

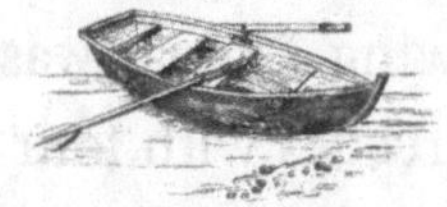

With the end of the day approaching, Philip returned to the ranger station, giving the horn a double-tap before hopping out and heading for the front door. The courtesy honk was a fair warning to Kody, who enjoyed sitting with his feet up in Philip's chair, to be back at his own desk and looking busy by the time Philip walked in.

"Hey, Phil! I didn't expect you back today!" Kody said out of breath, sliding behind his cramped desk in the nick of time, trying to sound casual. "Figured you'd be heading home."

"Hiya, kid," Philip greeted, pretending as well, that he didn't notice Kody's mad dash. "I wanted to check in and see how the forensic team was doing." He slid out of his winter coat and draped it over his chair, tossing his baseball cap onto the desk as he sat down. "Looks like they've already cut out. What time did they take off?"

"Oh, about forty-five minutes ago. They had Rowles Towing come out and load the boat up. He's hauling it over to the mainland." Kody stretched, doing nothing to stifle a yawn. "OH!" He suddenly sat up, his face eager, recalling something at the mention of Rowles Towing. "Edgar was saying he towed Mike Allister's Mercedes with four slashed tires this morning. Allister wasn't the floater, was he?"

"No. He's alive and well in Florida at the moment. Over there for a family emergency."

"Dang." Kody eyed Philip, his curiosity heightened. "I wonder who it was then?"

Philip, not volunteering a name, began going through a small stack of mail sitting on his desk.

Kody frowned, realizing he wasn't going to get an answer.

"Well, how's Dub? He gonna survive?"

"He's still kicking and not particularly happy about it." Philip chuckled, picking up an envelope of interest. "Doing his best to pretend he doesn't love all the attention he's getting." He ran his finger through the top of the envelope and ripped it open.

"He's damn lucky to be alive, the way Martha tells it." Kody plopped his feet up onto his desk, clumps of dirt falling from the bottom of his boots.

Philip gave his young ranger a frown of silent rebuke and pulled the letter from the envelope.

Kody obediently dropped his feet to the floor.

"She's not wrong." Philip ran his eyes down the paper. "Hypothermia in your eighties is nothing to scoff at." He crinkled the paper into a wadded ball, it being nothing more than junk mail. "Kody, do you know anybody who drives a Prius in town?"

Slightly taken aback at the change of subject, Kody nodded as he swept the mud droppings into a pile, contemplating the question.

"A couple of people. Leslie, the waitress over at Piper's place drives a silver one, and the new girl at the bank."

"Mollie? The one Harry is sweet on?"

"Yeah!" Kody's face brightened. "A red one." He finished sweeping the muddy pile into the wastebasket, his voice curious, "Harry likes her, huh? I don't suppose he's ever going to actually ask her out?"

"He's working up to it," Philip admonished, feeling slightly defensive on Harry's behalf, though he'd been ribbing Harry about it just the other day.

"What's he so worried about? I think she's super nice."

"Oh, I don't think it's her he's concerned about. It's her brother, Len. He's pretty protective of his little sister."

"Oh, Len!" Kody rolled his eyes, leaning back in his chair, his hands behind his head. "The guy acts like nobody knows the meaning of hard work unless they're a fisherman. I just ignore him."

"He does seem to have a chip on his shoulder, that's for sure," Philip agreed.

Kody stretched again, this time, giving an exaggerated look towards the clock on the wall.

"Well, brother or no brother, Harry better get a move on. He can't make a touchdown if he's not even on the field."

Philip chose to not comment, though he didn't disagree.

"It's getting late, Kody. Why don't you head home? I'll do the final run-through for the night, kid."

Kody, already up and out of his seat, headed for his coat on the wall. "Sweet! Thanks, Phil!"

"You got plans?" Philip, somewhat surprised at Kody's eagerness, slowly got up from his chair, his leg stiff.

"Sort of." Kody's hand was on the doorknob, his face mischievous, his tone playful. "I'm taking Mollie to the movies tonight."

CHAPTER 19

"Thanks for waiting." Chad walked back into the living room, taking a seat on the couch, his attitude calm and collected, a startling contrast to twenty minutes before.

"Not a problem." Lane looked up from her notepad with a polite smile. "Kristen, okay?"

"Alright, I guess. Still in shock, but she's resting now." He distractedly patted his jean pockets and pulled out a crumpled pack of cigarettes. "I... uh, I asked you to stay because I wanted to clear the air in regards to my uncle. Kristen shouldn't have said what she did." He gave a weak smile. "Uncle Roger will be devastated."

"Hmm, she didn't seem to think so." Lane's tone was still conversational.

"Well!" Chad threw his hands in the air in an

aimless gesture. "That's because they don't like each other all that much. Never have."

"Why is that?" Caleb, this time, asked the question, taking a seat on the couch beside Chad.

"Because..." Chad pulled out a cigarette and fumbled the pack back into his pocket. "Uncle Roger has always considered Kristen a gold digger, and she considers him a miserly business partner, sucking up all the profit."

"So, your uncle is co-owner of the repair shop?"

Chad nodded his head, his thumb flicking the filter of his unlit cigarette.

"He gave dad the startup money. Sort of a silent partner." Chad caught Lane's eye and added, "His wife died several years ago in a bad car accident. He ended up getting a major settlement from the car manufacturer and used the funds to invest in some very lucrative stock. He's ridiculously rich."

"The repair shop being another investment?"

"I guess, on top of helping out his brother."

Lane gave a casual look around the house.

"Well, the business must be doing well. This is a gorgeous house filled with beautiful things."

"Kristen likes to spend money."

"And your dad?"

"He likes... liked to make her happy."

"Were they happy? Kristen and your dad?" Caleb asked, his tone curious.

Chad leaned to the side and reached into his back pocket, pulling out a lighter.

"As much as any married couple, I suppose."

Lane decided to change the focus.

"It's nice to see you and Kristen get along well." She flipped the pages of her notepad, not looking up to ask her next question. "You never took issue with your father marrying someone so much younger?"

Bringing the cigarette up to his lips, Chad stopped, his shoulders tensing.

"I did, at first. I mean, I'm a year older than her." He continued to fiddle with the unlit cigarette. "But after hanging out with her a few times, I found out she could be a lot of fun, besides being easy on the eyes. Plus, Dad seemed happy. I decided to just roll with it and let them live their lives."

"And your uncle? He didn't like her from the start?"

Chad shook his head, a rude smile on his lips.

"No, not one bit. Uncle Roger told Dad he must be going through a mid-life crisis. Suggested he should buy a new car, pick up a prostitute, and work it out of his system. About blew a gasket when Dad called and told him they got married in Vegas."

"Hmm... I would imagine." Lane sat up straighter. "There's no love lost between them. Even so, why would Kristen think your uncle might be involved?"

"I'm telling you. She's exaggerating," Chad insisted, annoyed. "She's reaching for straws."

"Possibly the straw which broke the camel's back?" Lane pushed.

Chad shook his head side to side, irritated, and sighed heavily.

"I suppose it's because Dad and Uncle Roger have been fighting a lot over the business lately. Uncle Roger wants to be bought out of his share."

"And your father didn't want to be sole proprietor?"

"Well, I think that was always the plan. You know, make enough to pay back Uncle Roger's seed money and turn it into a family business." Chad idly flicked the lighter. "Except, I'm not interested, and according to Kristen, Uncle Roger is asking an exuberant amount in order to be bought out. She thinks he's trying to take advantage of them." Chad looked at Lane. "Which is silly. He's a fair man." He resettled on the couch, scooting back into the cushion. "I think it's because Dad had a new side venture. That, probably more than anything, drove the small wedge between them recently. Uncle Roger not liking Kristen has been old news."

"Side venture?"

"Yeah, he and a new business partner have developed a promotional deal with an anti-freeze company. Instead of using plain ethylene glycol for anti-freeze, this company uses propylene glycol instead. I'm sure you know how my dad felt about animals and the environment? Well, the normal stuff is super harmful to both and extremely toxic. This new stuff, it's a bit more expensive, but much better for the world all around. He and his partner have worked out a deal to sell it for a certain cost and promote it as an environmentally safe option over the generic stuff. It's why he was at the boat show. They'd rented a booth."

"What's this partner's name?" Lane's pen hovered over her pad.

"Ryan Jennings. I suppose I'll need to call him too." Chad ran his hands through his hair, agitated.

"We'd rather speak to him first." Lane looked up, catching his eye.

"Oh." Chad's shoulders slumped. "I guess so. I keep forgetting Dad was murdered."

"As far as you know, were things going well with..." Lane referred to her notepad. "Mr. Jennings?"

"Dad never said otherwise."

"Did you ever meet this Mr. Jennings? Do you know where he lives?"

"Never set eyes on him. Dad just talked about him a lot. And he lives in Seattle. Queen Anne area. I don't know the exact address."

Lane nodded her head, making a note.

"And Kristen, was she part of this new venture?"

"Don't think so."

"But she owns interests in the repair shop?"

"Hell, no." Chad lightly chuckled. "Uncle Roger put his foot down there. She works in the office, but only as the bookkeeper. And even that, Uncle Roger complains about. He's accused her a time or two of doctoring the books and taking work under the table for Jason."

"Jason?"

"Jason Powell."

"And he is?"

"The shop mechanic. Uncle Roger thinks the two pocket the extra money." Chad shook his head, thinking it ridiculous. "Regardless of whether it's true or not, he made sure Kristen had no legal claims to the business."

"And now?" Caleb, his tone eager, caught Lane's eye. "Could she?"

Lane frowned and quickly added, "What he means is, will Kristen be alright financially? How about you? Will you take over the business?"

Chad looked at them, the thought dawning.

"I didn't even think about that. I guess my mind hasn't gotten that far. I'm still..." He shook his head from side to side.

"It's a lot to take in," Lane's tone was sincere.

Chad quickly nodded, his shoulders straightening.

"Yeah, um, no. I won't be taking over the business." He peered down at his feet, contemplating. "I guess, if he did leave it to me. I'll sell it. It's gotta be worth a pretty penny being shorefront property, right?"

Lane, her eyes riveted on Chad, shut her notepad.

"Very much so," she confirmed, her tone deceptively light as she leaned forward. "So, you don't know the details of your father's will? I'm assuming he had one?"

"I suppose he does." Chad suddenly stood up. "I'll have to ask Uncle Roger."

He started for the front hallway, his arm extended out as an invitation for them to leave, the unlit cigarette still between his fingers.

"I better give him a call." He flicked the cigarette in the door's direction. "Oh, and to answer your question. I'm sure Kristen will be fine financially. There's always the life insurance if nothing else." He gave them a dazzling, Broadway smile. "Let us know when you find out more."

CHAPTER 20

At the sound of boots stomping up the cottage steps, Philip quickly made his way across the kitchen, struggling with the apron's strings as he went and swung the back door open, the smell of garlic wafting into the night.

"Perfect timing!" he called through the screen door, leaving the main door open and returning to the stove.

"Is it? I barely caught the ferry. What smells so—"

Lane stopped short and stared, the screen door slamming shut behind her, her head cocked to the side.

"Is that my favorite apron?" She took a step closer. "With red sauce stains down the front?"

Philip gave an apologetic smile and bent down for a kiss. Once received, he pulled the apron over his head and explained, "Yeah. Small incident with an exploding jar. Sorry."

Lane took the soiled apron and gave the stains a hard look, shaking her head before discarding it over the back of a kitchen chair, her good mood returning.

"It smells delicious in here. Did you stop and get takeout from the Gelato Deli?" She began to shrug out of her heavy down jacket.

"Take out?" Philip practically gasped, grabbing her coat collar and pulling down, tugging her limbs free. "Oh, Lane..." He leaned in, his voice hushed in excitement, "You're in for a real treat!" He stood back and flung his arm wide towards the stove. "I've made my world-famous spaghetti!"

Lane, though starved, sounded less than enthused, "Is it better than your world-famous Sloppy Joes?"

"Hey!" Philip gave her a wounded look and stubbornly continued, "Listen, I make three things really good."

"That's debatable." Lane laughed, taking her jacket from him, and hanging it on a hook by the door.

"My Sloppy Joes. As you already know."

Lane nodded, unclipping her duty belt, hanging it up as well. "Yes. Very sloppy, indeed."

"They're supposed to be! Thank you very much," Philip chided, rubbing his hands together and heading for the stove. "And then there is my Fahrenheit Chili."

"Oh, so dangerously hot!" Lane exclaimed, shaking her head in awe, recalling the days of heartburn that had followed, her anxiety mounting. "Ghost peppers, wasn't it?"

Philip nodded happily with a mischievous grin and lifted the lid of the large pot sitting on the stove, a rich tomato aroma filling the room.

He leaned in and inhaled deeply, his hand wavering over the pot in a circular motion, the savory smell floating towards him. He then stuck a large spoon into the noodles and turned back towards Lane, carrying the meal to the kitchen table, triumphant.

"And last, but not least, my spaghetti with special meatballs!" Philip plopped the large pot onto the middle of the table and quickly sat himself down. "Even made some garlic bread." He nodded towards a napkin-covered basket. "Dig in."

"If I must," Lane teased and apprehensively held out her plate.

Philip piled it high.

"So, what's so special about the meatballs?" she asked curiously, setting the plate down and stabbing one with her fork.

"They're super spicy! I use extra red pepper and garlic!" Philip's smile widened and he plopped two more meatballs onto her plate. "Hope you have some Tums in the house."

Lane cautiously put her fork down and reached for the garlic bread. She took a piece, and passed the basket to Philip, then curiously leaned over and looked down to the floor, underneath the table, between the legs.

"Where's the fluffball? she asked, sitting back up and taking a bite of bread. "Napping by the fire?"

Lane was referring to her pet, or rather, her landlord's pet. The small creature, which had come with the cottage, allowing for a considerable discount in rent, belonged to Philip's uncle. The eccentric, who moved to the mainland to live with his daughter, had not been able to bring along his beloved pet... a skunk named Stinker.

Chomping down on a meatball, unable to answer, Philip shook his head side to side.

"He's not outside, is he?" Lane asked, alarmed. "Is he in the front yard?" She started to get up.

"No, no. He's is in your room with a new toy. A gift from Jerry." Philip twirled his fork in the sauce-covered noodles. "Happy as a clam."

"Good." She sat back down. "It's too cold for him outside anyway."

"Stinker has grown on you, hasn't he?" Philip chuckled, remembering her extreme hesitation, let alone her anger with him for only mentioning the skunk a few weeks after she had moved in and fallen in love with the place. He hadn't done it on purpose. Life and a few court dates had gotten in the way and in his defense, she had mentioned she wanted a cat.

"A little." Lane avoided his eyes, nibbling cautiously on a meatball.

Stubborn as she was, she wouldn't give him the satisfaction of knowing she adored the old skunk or reveal the fact, Stinker was spoiled rotten with daily cuddles and special homemade treats.

"Yeah. A little, means a whole heck of a lot." Philip laughed. "You're not fooling me."

Lane gave her shoulders a careless shrug, playfully refusing to confirm or deny Philip's conclusion, and changed the subject, "How is Dub? Did you get a chance to see him after all?"

"Yes!" Philip straightened and pointed his fork at her. "And he gave me a lead!"

"A lead? On who took his rowboat?"

Philip nodded and scooted his chair closer, eagerly placing his elbows on the table. "Dub told me he wasn't able to sleep Friday night. Around one in the morning, he heard a car drive past his place, down to his dock."

"Heard? Didn't, see?"

Philip nodded his head.

"Said he got a good look at it."

"Did he get a license plate?" Lane put her fork down and reached for her notepad, it stuffed in her back pocket.

"Well, not that good of a look," Philip admitted. "But he did say the car was down there for about an hour before it came tearing out of his lane, back out onto the main road."

"A car? Not a truck or an SUV?"

"A Toyota Prius."

"Prius?" Lane, her tone eager, looked up. "Was it white?"

"No, green. Or at least, a dark color like that."

"Hmmmm. There was an older white Prius parked outside of Bob and Kristen's house. Thought it might be a connection."

"Could be Dub got the color wrong?"

"Hard to mistake green for a white car," Lane sounded doubtful.

"Well, it was the middle of the night, and Dub's an old man. Maybe his eyesight isn't the greatest."

"If you take that line of reasoning, Phil, then you have to discount if he even saw a Prius to begin with. Maybe it was a completely different car?"

"I see your point," Philip relinquished, and swirled his bread, sopping up the last bits of sauce from his plate. "How did Kristen take it? She alright?"

"She was hard to read, to be honest. She was obviously upset..."

Lane paused and began to play with her food, aimlessly rolling meatballs back and forth, deep in thought. "But she didn't strike me as devastated. Not truly." Lane suddenly shrugged. "Then again, Kristen was a little drunk. Her stepson was there playing bartender."

"Chad?"

"Yeah, they were celebrating. Chad is the new face for an anti-itch cream."

"Oh! That's a big break for him!" Philip pushed his plate aside and rubbed his stomach happily. "I guess, he's got a part in a play he's supposed to hear back on soon as well."

"Are you close with Chad?" Lane asked, surprised Philip was in the know.

"No, not at all. I mean, I've met him a couple of times, here and there." Philip grabbed the discarded white napkin and tossed it into the empty bread basket. "Bob is always talking... I mean, talked about him quite a bit."

"They got along?"

"Thick as thieves, from what I could tell." He pushed his chair back. "I got the feeling he wished Chad had gone into business with him, but he still seemed to support his dream of being an actor."

"When you say support, do you mean financially?"

"That I couldn't tell you." Philip stood up, picking up the large pot and placing it back on the stove. "But it wouldn't surprise me if he gave his kid a handout here or there."

"Kid? He's, my age!" Lane scoffed. "What about Kristen? I noticed a new Ranger Rover in the driveway and her Louie Vuitton purse in the hallway. She's got expensive tastes."

Philip shrugged. "She was out of his league in

more than one way."

"You think she loved him?" Lane watched Philip's face closely.

"They always seemed happy."

"No rumors about an affair?"

Philip slowly shook his head no, his eyes focused on the wall, thinking the thought through.

"None that I ever heard. Though Bob joked he'd leave her for a younger woman when she started to droop and wrinkle." Philip chuckled and then stopped, Lane not finding humor in the joke.

He decided to move the conversation along another line. "Were either Kristen or Chad able to shed any light on what happened to Bob?"

"Far from it." Lane adjusted the napkin in her lap. "To start, both spoke to him via text message on Saturday."

"Saturday? Coroner said he died on Friday."

"And I think he's right. I told them we might have the exact day of death wrong due to the body being in the water, but in reality, I think someone..."

"You mean the killer?"

Lane gave a hasty nod. "Was texting from Bob's phone to give the illusion he was still alive. I looked at both Chad and Kristen's messages, and the text responses were lengthy compared to Bob's normal one-worded answers a few weeks prior. I'm surprised that alone didn't make them a little suspicious themselves." Lane handed Philip her plate, giving him a warm smile of thanks, the spicy meatballs rolling across the dinner plate untouched, the noodles all gone.

"Lane, not everyone has a mind like you, thoroughly cynical," Philip said, stuffing a leftover meatball in his mouth before putting the dishes in the sink, the silverware clattering against the sides.

"It also makes you wonder how well the killer knew Bob? You would think they would have tried to mimic his short answers." Lane shook her head, dismissing that particular train of thought. "Which makes me think about his new business partner."

"New business partner?"

"Yeah, apparently, Bob and this new partner were working on a promotional business together. That's why Bob went to the mainland. They've got a booth at the boat show."

"Wait. The anti-freeze thing?" Philip asked, surprised.

"Bob talked about it?"

"Mentioned it a few times. Was looking for investors."

"Interesting. Seems he was trying to fund this business venture without his brother's help." Lane got up and opened a cupboard, reaching for a large bowl. "What can you tell me about his brother?"

"Didn't know he had a brother," Philip admitted,

filling the sink with hot water and way too much dish soap. "Bob was more Harry's friend than mine. We'd visit and joke around, especially on league night, but other than a few poker games over at Harry's..."

"Poker?" Lane interrupted, pondering the word as she Saran wrapped the leftover spaghetti. "What kind of poker player was he? Bet high? Bluff a lot? Owe money?"

"The cheap kind and always folding." Philip put a cleaned plate on the dry rack. "I think he was there more for the social interaction than actually trying to win any money off us."

"Hmmm... so, I guess the wild gambler on the run from his debts theory is a no go?"

"It seems unlikely."

Lane placed the leftovers into the fridge and then walked over to the sink, picking up a tea towel.

"You liked him, though?" she asked, picking up the silverware from the drying rack, giving a quick polish with the towel.

"Sure!" Philip turned off the hot water and placed the big pot into the sink for a soak. "He had a good sense of humor, not easily offended."

"Big nature lover too," Lane added, trying to recall what she could of Bob.

She hadn't spent any quality time with him, only the occasional run-ins while downtown and minor polite chit-chats across the grocery aisle from time to time, but he had seemed nice.

"Yup! Save this animal, save that tree, save the environment." Philip began to roll up his sleeves. "I guess that's how he met Kristen. They were at a silent auction to raise funds for..." Philip plunged his arms into the water, wrestling with the pot. "Killer whales or something like that. She was a masseuse and had donated a package of massages. I guess he had bid up to kingdom come and won... then eventually, won her over as well." Philip shot his hip over, knocking Lane to the side with a stuttered step. "If you know what I mean."

"Yeah." Lane gave Philip a return hip-shot, a little harder than he'd given her. "I know what you mean."

"Why were you asking about his brother?" Philip smiled down at Lane, threatening to splash her with sudsy water.

Lane's stern face promised retribution.

"Is he a suspect?" Philip wisely started to drain the water from the sink, not liking his chances.

"I don't know if suspect is the right word, but he's another lead besides the new business partner." Lane closed the silverware drawer. "Kristen stated she thought his brother, Roger, had something to do with Bob's death. But Chad quickly jumped to his uncle's defense. Apparently, Roger and Kristen don't see eye to eye on how the shop should be run and he's accused Kristen a time or two of cooking the books which could account for her own accusation."

"The business?" Philip took the tea towel from Lane, drying his hands and tossing it lightly on the counter. "What does the brother have to do with Bob's business?"

"According to Chad, Roger is a silent partner. Let's Bob run the shop but provides the extra funds when needed and takes a good portion of the profit for doing so."

"Maybe the brother is taking advantage? Sort of like a loan shark?" Philip suggested, excited. "Could be the business was failing..."

"It was failing. Or it soon would be, with the pending lawsuit Mike Allister was stirring up."

"Okay, okay." Philip nodded his head and reached into the fridge, pulling out two beers. "That fits. The silent partner, not so silent anymore, starts demanding more money. Bob can't pay him, so his brother—"

"You know, Phil. You might actually be on to something. It's not an uncommon practice for business partners to carry life insurance claims against each other."

"Key holder insurance?"

"Exactly."

"What about Kristen? I can't imagine Bob, him being so much older, not having life insurance in place for her as well." Philip twisted both caps and handed one of the bottles to Lane. "I know all the evidence points to a man, but..."

"Not all the evidence points to a man!" Lane gave him a pointed look, interrupting. "Don't forget the long brown hairs in the ski mask. Kristen has long brown hair."

"True, but I can't really picture her pulling the trigger on her husband." Philip sat down. "But then again, if this is a murder for hire, maybe she decided to take part? Pretty cold hearted."

A slow smile spread across Lane's lips. "You know..." She leaned forward, her voice growing husky. "You're kinda sexy when conjecturing motives for murder."

Philip arched an eyebrow. "OH, yeah?"

"Yeah, but... No, you've made a good point." Lane straightened, putting her beer on the table and quickly picking up her notepad. She flipped a few pages to the desired spot. "Money is always a good motive."

"And everybody wants money. So, everyone has a motive?"

Lane nodded, starting a list.

"So far, we've got a new business and a partner, who we don't know much about. A small group trying to sue the victim for money. Along with a wife, who will most likely profit at his death, alongside his brother, slash old business partner, and his beloved son, who should stand to profit as well."

"The business would still be worth a good deal.

If not the boat repair shop, the land and the building itself. Especially at its location by the docks." Philip took a swig of his beer and then brought the bottle down, a dawning expression on his face. "You don't think someone would try to break into the shop, do you? Like, if the business is related in some way? From either the pending lawsuit or bad books or who knows what?"

"Already thought of that. When I was at the King County Sheriff's station tonight, I ran into an old friend who happens to be off duty for the next two days. It cost me a pretty please and a six-pack of beer, but he's already parked down there, keeping an eye on the place. He can't stop anybody from going in, but he can let us know, and of course, observe any comings and goings at night."

"You know..." Philip scooted his chair a little closer. "You're kinda sexy when..."

Lane laughed, giving his chest a playful push, forcing him back.

"ALSO, I've got an appointment to meet Kristen first thing in the morning at the repair shop. We're meeting at seven."

"I suppose your Deputy will be in tow?" Philip took another swig of his beer, starting to fiddle with the label.

"No. I'm sending him to the mainland to question the new business partner and hotel staff, see if Bob actually did check-in, and try to track down his last movements. We still don't know how he got back to the island."

"That is if he even left. Might have said he was going over and then didn't."

"No, he left for sure. Kristen said she rode with him to the docks and then walked back to the shop. Said she watched him drive the car onto the ferry." Lane took a sip herself. "Hard to jump ship and abandon your vehicle without a lot of commotion."

"Especially if he was driving his Tesla, electric-doo-hickey car."

"Tesla? How much money does this guy make from operating a simple boat repair shop?" Lane asked, miffed.

"I think Harry said he had money in stocks at one point? Anyway, he must have come back over on a later ferry. Maybe he forgot something at home or the shop?"

Philip took a quick swig, a thought coming to mind, and brought the beer down, the bottle clinking hard against the table. "What if he came back to the shop for something and interrupted a robbery?" Philip leaned forward, excited. "Things go from bad to worse, and they kill him."

Lane scrunched up her face, giving the theory serious consideration.

"Possible. But I would have thought Kristen or

their mechanic would have reported a robbery."

"Oh, yeah."

"No, I'm of the opinion he was probably lured back to the island. Maybe someone called him and said Kristen was hurt?" Lane casually extended her hand, palm up, towards Philip. "Or, kind of like what you were thinking, told him the shop was being robbed or on fire, so he jumped on the next ferry back to the island."

"Oh, that's devious." Philip shook his head. "Anybody could have done that. A stranger, a friend, a family member. Anybody!"

"I know. If we can find out which ferry he returned on, it'll help to either establish or break an alibi."

"Okay, then. With Caleb on the mainland, do you need a volunteer to watch the ferry tapes?"

Lane smiled, Philip's eagerness to be involved readily apparent.

"No, I'll have Martha do that. Believe me, if Bob or someone else is on that ferry who's not supposed to be, Martha will sniff it out."

"Well, what about Bob's car? If he came back in his own vehicle, shouldn't it be on the island somewhere?"

Lane, her smile dropping, suddenly smacked her notepad against the table. "Dang it!"

"What?"

"I should have thought of that, Phil." She shook

her head, side to side, clearly disgusted with herself. "So, help me! If that car is sitting in Rowles Towing yard, and Edgar hasn't notified us. I will absolutely lose my—"

"Whoa, whoa." Philip put a gentle hand on her arm. "Why don't I swing by on my way home tonight and take a quick peek in his tow yard? Save you the trip and Edgar the beat down?"

Lane, only half-amused, nodded her head, agreeing. "Okay. Thanks." She took another sip. "If it's not there, tomorrow morning, would you ask Kody to check the jeep roads in the park and make sure the car hasn't been dumped somewhere?"

"Sure." Philip finished his beer, getting up to toss it into the bin. "Well, it sounds like you've got everything covered and all the help you need."

"Yup, think I do." Lane took another sip, smiling behind the bottle. "By the way, thank you for dinner."

Distracted, Philip paced back to the table and asked, "You sure, there's nothing else I can do to help?"

"Nope. Don't think so."

"Good, good. I'm glad." Philip nodded his head, a thoughtful expression on his face. "Well, I better get going. I'll head over to Rowles's Towing now." He wandered over to the door, grabbing his coat. "You, uh, you wouldn't mind if I stopped by the boat shop tomorrow morning and gave the widow my condolences?" He watched Lane from the corner of his eye and added, "Would you?"

"I don't see why not." Lane closed her notepad with a snap and gave him a Cheshire smile. "It's as good of an excuse, as any, for you to tag along."

CHAPTER 21

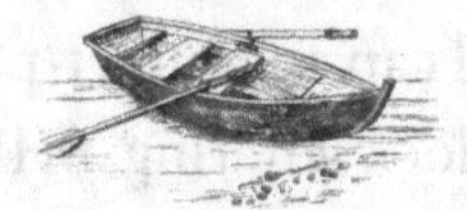

"Welcome to the Four Seasons." The hotel manager, middle-aged, balding, with a face etched in pained politeness, spoke in a hurried hush. He had practically skipped across the polished floor, buttoning his blue blazer as he approached, a mixture of curiosity and concern visible in his stride as he hurried to reach the uniformed officer loitering in his lobby.

"I'm the Hotel Manager, Miles Hursh." He gave a nervous tug on his tie before graciously offering his hand to Caleb, his eyes darting to the guests around him, a fairly fake smile plastered upon his lips. "Is there..." He paused as a large group of guests, voices raised in farewells, passed by, their suitcase wheels clacking loudly across the marble floor, heading for the lobby desk. "Is there something I can help you with?" His eyes raked Caleb in a subtle examination, reading the name on his vest. "Er... Deputy Pickens?"

"Mr. Hursh." Caleb returned the smile, his genuine. "I'm with the Sheriff's Department..."

The statement was unnecessary.

In his professional regalia, the young deputy stuck out like a sore thumb, his badge visible for all to see, his baseball cap and bullet-proof vest, stating, in bright yellow block lettering, SHERIFF.

His appearance was intimidating yet reassuring to those with a clear conscience, frightening to those without.

"I'm here in regards to a guest." Caleb took the manager's offered hand and stepped towards him, closing the distance between them, doing his best to match his hushed tone. "Is there somewhere we could speak privately?"

The hotel manager's gracious smile faltered, and his manner became protectively stiff.

"Of course! Please. This way." He stepped to the side, inviting Caleb to walk beside him. "I hope, whatever the issue is, it can be attended to quietly?" He gave Caleb a meaningful look and turned on his heels, leading the way past the white lobby desk filled with blue-blazered clerks, each greeting and dismissing hotel guests in their turn.

The two made for a short corridor, taking the first door on the right.

"This is my office. Please have a seat." Miles opened the door and then stepped aside with his arm extended in an invitation to enter. "I'm afraid I don't have much time to offer you. I have a very important, high-status guest checking-in later this evening, and I still have several things to attend to before their arrival."

"I'll try not to take up too much of your time." Caleb spied a modern, uncomfortable-looking chair, and walked in, taking the offered seat.

"Now," Miles, his tone more annoyed than polite, closed the door behind him and unbuttoned his blazer, heading for his desk. "What is this about?"

Caleb waited until he was seated.

"Unfortunately, a death. One of your guests by the name of Bob Allen was found deceased yesterday. I'm here to establish his last hours."

"I see. Very tragic." Miles straightened his desk calendar, his attention distracted. "If his family wants access to his things, I'll have my cleaning service pack everything up for you." He folded his arms, sitting back, unphased, admiring the organized desktop. "And for their convenience, we'll bill the credit card on file instead of sending an invoice." He finally looked up, his tone mildly curious, "I suppose it was a heart attack or something like that?"

Caleb, unimpressed with the manager's haughty and callous attitude, shook his head in the negative, offering no further information.

"A car accident, then?"

"No." Caleb leaned forward, his tone professional and stern. "Mr. Hursh, I'd like to ask you a few questions and then take a look at your surveillance tapes. I'm looking for..."

"Surveillance?" The manager leaned forward, surprised. "I hope you're not suggesting that whatever happened to this poor man had anything to do with the hotel directly." He gave his keyboard a strike, the monitor lighting up. "We take excellent care of our guests here at the Four Seasons. Their safety is paramount."

"I didn't mean to suggest otherwise."

"I would hope not."

Perturbed, the manager hovered his hands over the keyboard and asked, impatiently, "What was the guest's name again?"

"Bob Allen."

Swift fingers clicked across the keyboard.

"Well, I don't see a—"

"I have a confirmation number if you need it. The reservation dates were for the fifth through the twelfth."

"Ahh, yes. Here it is. Robert Allen." The hotel manager leaned into the screen, squinting. "Checked in at two in the afternoon last Friday, the second." He suddenly frowned, nervously grabbing his tie, running his hands down the length. "He appears to be one of our Elite guests."

"Elite?"

Miles looked up from the screen, his tone condescending, "A status we give to those who express loyalty and a healthy spending habit while staying at the Four Seasons."

"In other words. A high roller." Caleb smiled.

"The term is Elite," Miles corrected, his tone offended.

"Got it." Caleb took a deep calming breath, and then scooted closer, motioning to the monitor. "Mr. Hursh, can you tell me what day Mr. Allen checked out?"

"I don't show he has." Miles returned his attention to the screen. "It looks as if room service was ordered Friday night, but I don't show a check-out."

He turned the monitor so Caleb could see as well. "And I don't show the room having been serviced or cleaned since check-in. There must be a 'Do not disturb sign on the door. Though, why he was on that floor of rooms is..." The manager suddenly looked up, meeting Caleb's eye. "Oh. I think I understand now," he lowered his voice to just above a whisper, though it was only the two of them in the room. "Mr. Allen committed suicide?"

"Far from it."

The Four Season's manager frowned, displeased

with the tight-lipped deputy.

"Well then, what did happen?"

"Do you show any interaction with the room since Friday? Wake-up calls or anything like that?"

Miles hit two keys, a window popping up on the screen. "The key card was used Saturday morning, a little before eleven a.m."

"Saturday? You're sure?"

"It's right here." Miles pushed back from the desk. "I can print it out if you'd like."

"Thank you. What about Mr. Allen himself? Did he seem—"

"I didn't know the man. But..." Miles held up his finger and raised the desk phone handset to his ear, hitting three numbers. "Let me get our Elite Guest Services manager on the phone." He then spoke into the receiver, "Taylor? Can you send Bailee to my office? Yes, now, please. Thank you." He placed the receiver down and turned his eyes back to Caleb. "I've asked for the individual who handled the recent transaction with Mr. Allen to join us."

"Great, but I'd really like to look at the room as soon as possible. Any way you can give me access?"

"Depends. I'd still like to know exactly what happened to Mr. Allen and why it concerns the Four Seasons."

"I'd rather not say," Caleb answered honestly.

"I'd rather you did."

Caleb stood up, eager, intent on seeing the hotel room. "Mr. Hursh, I can come back with a warrant, if necessary."

Miles stood up with him. "I dare say you can." He tapped the monitor off. "But there is probably no need." He straightened his shoulders, running his hands down his tie. "Though you must understand, I can't guarantee corporate's assistance with little to no details. If my staff or our guests are in danger, we will, of course, give any assistance we can. But if this is just a minor issue of a pickpocket gone wrong or something of a sexual nature, such as a call girl or prostitute, then I'm afraid..."

"I'm working a homicide investigation." Caleb finally relented, irritated at the cold-hearted curiosity of the manager. "I believe his room could be a crime scene."

"Yes. Well, that changes things considerably." Miles buttoned his blazer, his smile dropping, the idea distasteful. "Can I have your assurance this investigation will be handled with the utmost discretion? As you can imagine, bad press would not be appreciated."

"You have it. Can I expect the same from you and your employees?" Caleb asked in return, fearful hotel staff's tongues would wag at the news of a homicide.

"I'm surprised you feel the need to ask. This, as I seem to keep having to remind you, is the Four

Seasons. Not a Motel 6." The manager carefully tucked his tie into his buttoned blazer and added, "Now, I'll need to make a phone call to my corporate legal department, but if you wouldn't mind waiting here, I'll…"

There was a light tap, and the office door suddenly opened, revealing a tall blonde, her hair generously piled high in a braided twist, a pair of dark rimmed glasses perched on her up-turned nose.

"Ah, Bailee! Come in." His tone an octave higher in apparent relief, Miles beckoned the young woman in with a wave of his hand.

"This is Deputy Pickens. He has some questions regarding an Elite guest of ours and I need to step out for a moment to make a call. If you wouldn't mind helping him?" He offered his seat behind the desk and then gave Caleb a curt nod before stepping out of the room, assuming correctly, her cooperation.

"Of course, sir."

Dressed in a blue blazer with a matching pencil skirt, the attractive young woman slowly sat down, a warm, practiced smile on her face.

"Hello, Deputy Pickens. I'm Bailee." She lightly tapped the golden name tag on her blazer, an action borne out of habit, and continued, "I'm happy to be of assistance or at least hope I can be!" Her smile widened, becoming genuine, her voice upbeat and friendly, at the same time curious, as her attention moved from the handsome deputy to the monitor. "Let's see. Who do we have here?" She quickly scanned the screen, taking in the information listed.

"Oh!" Bailee's friendly smile vanished and her tone turned cautious, "Has something happened to Bobby Allen?

"Bobby?" Caleb was surprised at the familiarity.

Bailee nodded her head, visibly troubled, her eyebrows coming together. "That's what Mr. Allen asks that we call him. He stays here quite a bit." She looked back towards the monitor. "He's not wanted for something illegal, is he?"

Caleb shook his head in the negative and Bailee's smile returned, relaxed.

"Well, good. You had me worried there for a minute—"

"He's actually deceased."

She stared at him, blinking. "I am sorry to hear that." The customer service comment came automatically.

Caleb nodded, his tone matter-a-fact, "I'm here investigating his homicide."

"His homicide?" Bailee practically whispered the words, clearly shaken by the news.

"Yeah. We pulled him out of the ocean yesterday—"

Caleb suddenly leaned forward, the young woman's face abruptly draining of all color.

"Miss, are you okay?"

Bailee, her hands placed flat on the desk to brace herself, didn't seem to hear his question.

"Miss?"

"I'm sorry. You said, homicide?" A tone of disbelief was embedded in her question.

"I did. Gunshot victim." Caleb inched closer, placing a steady hand on her arm, keeping her in place. "Would you like a water or something?"

"Do you know who killed him?" Tears had sprung to her eyes, her color remaining pale.

"No. At least, not yet. That's why I'm here."

Struggling with her emotions, Bailee nodded quickly, registering she understood.

"Would you like a tissue?" Caleb asked, scanning the desk for a Kleenex box, not finding one. "I could go get you some," he offered and then added lamely, "Are you sure you're, okay?"

"I'm fine." She gently pulled her arm free, giving him an unsteady smile. "It just surprised me. I only saw him a few days ago. That is, when I checked him in."

Her disbelief was evident.

"Yes, can you tell me about that? How did he…"

Bailee suddenly looked up at the ceiling, doing her best to keep her brimming tears from rolling down her cheeks.

"Sorry to be so emotional," she apologized. "Working in Elite services, our guests, they start to feel like extended family, and he was... was a very nice man." She finally looked down, using her knuckle to dab under her eye, attempting to keep her eyeliner in place. "I liked him a lot. He was... he was..." Bailee shook her head, her voice dying away, words failing her.

"I understand." Caleb took out his cell phone, placing it on the desk, eager to finish before the manager came back. "Mind if I record our conversation, Bailee?" He didn't wait for a response and hit the record button, asking, "How did he seem, when you saw him? I understand Mr. Allen checked-in at two p.m. on Friday last week. How was his mood? Did anything seem irregular?"

Bailee straightened in her seat and sniffled, regaining her composure.

"No, not in the least." She lightly patted her eyes again, adding, "In fact, he was in a very good mood. Even asked me to meet him in the lobby for a drink, which he knows is not allowed. He liked to tease like that." She turned her attention to the monitor. "I believe he was in town for the boat show if I remember correctly." She suddenly nodded her head as if confirming the fact with herself. "Yeah, um... he said he wasn't going out when I asked if he needed a dinner reservation or a taxi. Said he was probably going to order room service and head to bed early because he had plans to be at the convention center to set up his booth in the morning." She leaned in, making sure her voice was reaching Caleb's phone recorder. "I guess his business partner wouldn't be there until Monday, so he had to do the set up by himself. But he didn't seem upset about it."

"What time did he end up ordering room service?"

"Right before the 9 p.m. cut-off for the dinner menu. It's only late-night appetizers after that."

"And what did he order?" Caleb suddenly remembered the coroner's statement regarding the dead man's last meal and ventured a guess, "Hamburger and fries?"

"No," Bailee answered, hitting two buttons on the keyboard and peering at the screen. "Grilled beef tenderloin with a side of broccolini and mashed potatoes."

"Are you sure?"

"Pretty sure. That's what he was to be invoiced for." She blinked at the screen. "He also ordered a piece of vanilla cheesecake for dessert."

"Do we know if he actually ate any of it?"

"The food here is excellent. Why wouldn't he?"

"That's not what I meant. Those are slow digesting foods, and according to the coroner, his last meal was—"

The desk phone rang, interrupting Caleb.

"Excuse me." Bailee picked up the receiver, noting the internal line. "Mr. Hursh's office," she answered, smiling weakly at Caleb. "Oh, Mr. Hursh. Yes, he's still here... I understand... If I can be of assistance... No, I'm more than happy to help... Yes, I'll let him know. Good-bye."

She hung up the phone and straightened the keyboard, bringing her eyes back to Caleb.

"Mr. Hursh asked me to relay to you that he has spoken with the legal team at corporate, and they've permitted him to cooperate completely. However, he does send his apologies as he has other pressing matters to attend to this afternoon. In place of his assistance, he has authorized me to help in any way I can, including giving you access to the hotel room and our surveillance tapes. Which would you like to see first?"

CHAPTER 22

L ane walked up to the unmarked sedan discrete-ly parked across the street from the boat repair shop and rapped on the driver's side window. "Wake up, Bruce."

The tinted window, lightly covered in frost, immediately rolled down, revealing a tired and grizzly-looking older man, his face practically obscured by his bushy mustache and silver-laced eyebrows.

"Wasn't sleeping," he grumbled, his voice a deep baritone. "I was only..."

"Resting your eyes," Lane finished for him, passing a Gelato Deli bag through the window. "I brought you breakfast and a cup of joe."

He took the steaming cup gingerly from her hand, catching the name on the bag.

"Not a hoity-toity flavored coffee, I hope."

"No, I know better. Two sugars, no cream," she promised and then asked, "How's your back?"

"Stiff, sore, and still held together by six titanium screws." He grimaced and removed the plastic lid, casually tossing it onto the matted floor. "It's never been the same since surgery."

"Well, if you hadn't taken a bullet in the back," Lane pointed out in a light reprimanding tone.

"I know, I know." He studied her from underneath his bushy eyebrows, recognizing much of himself in the young sheriff. "Let it be a lesson to you, Lane. Always wait for backup. If you John Wayne it, you could end up like me or worse, stuck at a desk." He took a tentative sip and changed the subject, nodding towards the repair shop, a large, corrugated steel, depressing-looking building. "By the way, it was nice and quiet last night."

The building itself was in stark contrast to the two cartoon character billboards placed high on the roof, one facing towards the land, the other towards the docks. In bold print and bright colors, the signs depicted an old fisherman in a rowboat, dressed in yellow rain slicks and holding a fishing pole, the line cast over the words "Bobber's Boat Repair." A red and white fishing bobber dangling from the fisherman's pole, substituting the O in Bobber's.

"I hoped it would be." Lane peered across the street, the sparse parking lot still empty, except for her patrol truck. "That's a good sign."

"Good, but boring."

"True." She turned back, meeting his blue eyes. "I'll need you again tonight. That is. If you're up for it?"

Bruce tilted his head, his eyes slitting, his grey mustache hiding most of his smile. "Up to it? Listen, little lady, I may be old and stiff, but I was on stake-outs way before you were even born. By the way, how is Donnie?"

Donnie was an endearing reference to Lane's father, retired police chief, Donald Lane.

"Bored."

"Retirement will do that to you." Bruce sighed, "Is he still liking Montana?"

"Guess so." Lane shrugged. "He says it rains less there."

Bruce nodded. "And fewer memories, I bet." He placed the coffee into the cup holder and then grasped the steering wheel to pull himself up, stiffly straightening his position with a grunt. "Did you manage to get your warrant last night or do you have to head over this morning?"

"Nope. Got it right here." Lane tapped her breast pocket. "Judge Harris was kind enough to hear me out. I was lucky—"

"Pffft, lucky." Bruce shook his head. "You're a cute blonde. That's all the luck you need with Harris." He gave her a wink. "Well, anyway, thanks for breakfast." He twisted the keys in the ignition, the car engine coming to life with a soft purr, exhaust fumes funneling out in a long stream. "I'll be back tonight around five. Sound good?"

Lane nodded. "Thanks, Bruce."

"Nothing to it." He gave her a light wave and pulled out onto the street in the direction of the ferry, intent for the mainland, leaving her behind in his rear-view mirror.

Jaywalking back to her truck, across the street to the boat repair shop, Lane casually gauged the distance between her and an impending vehicle, a green car, speeding down the road. Though the fast-approaching vehicle wasn't a Toyota Prius, it appeared to have the same sloped distinctive shape, and it was heading in the shop's direction from the backside, away from the fishing docks.

Too far to glean a license plate number, Lane squinted in an attempt to make out the driver.

Perhaps it was Kristen or Chad behind the wheel, having arrived to meet her as planned?

If so...

Unable to make out the driver, the windshield, heavily frosted for the exception of a small scrapped circle for visibility, Lane headed for the back lot, the vehicle pulling directly into the fenced area, completely hidden from view.

She edged her way along the back of the building, finding a space between the sidewall and the wooden fence surrounding the back lot. Closing one eye, she peered through the small slat and focused on the green car, it now parked next to a dilapidated-looking Volkswagen Beetle, and watched as the driver's side door popped open and a young man, dressed in mechanic overalls, stepped out.

This, she assumed, must be the boat shop's mechanic, Jason Powell.

Good-looking and in his early twenties, the young mechanic walked towards the back of the vehicle and lifted the hatch, his head swiveling side to side as he did so.

The coast clear, the sheriff undetected, peeking through the fence, he lifted the trunk mat and retrieved a black object from within, casually tucking the item into his overalls, out of sight. He then slammed the hatch down and paced to the back door of the shop, a whistled tune upon his lips.

Already moving towards the front of the shop, determined to get in, Lane started ticking off boxes in her head.

Vehicle matching description?
Check.
Suspect known to victim?
Check.
Able-bodied?

Check.

Acting suspicious?

Check.

She definitely wanted to have a word with Jason Powell.

CHAPTER 23

Striding through the door of Hattie's General to pick up a few things before heading to the boat shop, Philip slowed to a halt, not entirely surprised to find the communal picnic table in its full gossip glory.

So much so, that no one even noticed him standing in the doorway.

Though the golden bell, sitting atop the door, had chimed, announcing his arrival, it had failed to break the visible spell in which the speaker had entranced the assembly, a handful of locals.

The tiny group, some standing, some sitting, but all holding cups of coffee, listened intently, their beverages, growing cold.

Even Hattie, in her rocking chair, hung on every word.

Indeed, all eyes were focused on Glen Sorenson,

and as he had previously imagined the morning before, the gossip circle was enraptured with his tale.

And the best part?

Dub, thankfully at home, safe and sound, wasn't around to contradict him.

Philip, with some struggle, withdrew his attention from the picnic table to Harry, found stationed by the register, bent over, both elbows resting on the countertop, watching the gathered group in mild amusement.

"Mornin' there, Phil."

"Mornin' Har." Philip approached the counter, his eyes still on the table, his voice low, "Glen looks pretty pleased with himself."

"Oh, he is." Harry stood up straight and turned his gaze on Philip, his eyes sad. "Glen says the body he pulled out was Bob Allen? That true?"

"Yeah." Philip reached over and squeezed Harry's shoulder. "Sorry to say, but it was." He gave his buddy a somber smile, then removed his hand, returning to face the small group, leaning his back against the counter. "Wonder how Glen found out? Lane wasn't going to release the name until later today."

"As Glen tells it, Bob's son, Chad, called the shop's mechanic, Jason, and told him the news. I guess he hadn't bothered to tell him not to tell anybody, because Jason went down to the bar last night and toasted a beer to Bob's memory."

"I bet that spread word like wildfire."

"It sure did." Harry sighed.

The two continued watching the small group, it quickly turning into a Q & A panel as Glen, almost giddy, answered questions tossed at him by the island's nosy neighbors.

"Think I should break it up? This is his fourth time telling the story." Harry began to dust the counter-top with a white rag, his eyes still on Glen. "Every time someone new wanders in, he starts all over again, and each time, the story grows. This last version, he said he knew it was Bob the second they pulled him... out of... the water," Harry's voice rumbled to a stop and Philip turned to see what or who had caught his attention.

Outside, on the sidewalk, stood Len Harrison, dressed in his fisherman overalls and a thick jacket. Beside him, her arm through the crook of his elbow, was his sister Mollie, her smile happy and contagious, her blonde hair curled across her forehead, her face framed by a fur-lined hood.

The brother and sister paused by the store entrance and said their goodbyes, and as Mollie turned to leave, her eyes scanned the large-window front, spotting Harry and Philip inside. She gave them a friendly wave as she parted, heading in the direction of the bank.

Catching the wave not directed at him, Len abruptly turned and opened the door to Hattie's, yanking it wide, the golden bell loudly ringing its welcome.

At the chime, all eyes immediately turned from Glen to see the new arrival, and the gossip circle, in one accord, stopped talking.

"Mornin', Len!" Harry called out, his voice overly friendly. "Can I help you find something?"

The fisherman turned from the picnic table of gathered gossips and looked at Harry, his eyes dull and uninterested.

"You got any bungee cords?"

"Sure do, sure do!" Harry beamed at him with a bright smile, then started to make his way around the counter. "If you want to follow me," he offered and then added, conversationally, "The... uh... weather seems to have warmed a bit today, don't you think?"

"Not down at the docks," Len, not budging, said, his tone condescending. "The wind chill knocks everything down a few degrees. You being indoors all day, nice and cozy, probably don't... notice." He suddenly paused, self-conscious, aware everyone was listening and faced away from the table, his voice gruff, "What aisle?"

"I'll show you!" Harry, unphased, tossed his dust rag down on the counter and waved for Len to follow along.

"That's okay. I'll find them on my own." Len walked past Harry, his eyes searching the printed signs hanging from the ceiling and over the corresponding aisle.

"Oh, fiddle faddle!" Hattie suddenly spoke up, wiggling her way to the front of her rocking chair, beaming a rosy cheek smile upon Len. "Help me up, young man."

She held out an arthritic hand, waving it lightly for Len to take, who hesitated for a moment before pulling his own welted and chapped hands from his pockets, a shy smile suddenly breaking across his face, his countenance changing completely.

"Yes, ma'am. Do you need your cane?" he asked concerned, taking Hattie's hand in his, bearing her full weight.

"No, no. I don't need a silly cane. Why should I?" She leaned heavily upon him, her bright blue eyes smiling. "I've got your arm! Now, let's head this way. I want to show you something first and then we'll get you, your bungee cords." Hattie took off, intent on their mission, while Len, surprised at her quickness, lurched with her, keeping pace, Hattie's hip sagging with every other step.

"Funny that!" Glen Sorenson pipped up, the pair out of earshot. "You talk about him and up he pops, just like the devil."

"What do you mean?" Philip asked, joining the group, wildly curious, as Harry returned behind the counter, somewhat crestfallen.

"Len!" Glen nodded towards the grocery aisles. "Showing up, just as I was talking about Bob Allen. I wouldn't be a bit surprised if it were him who done poor Bob in."

A chorus of shocked replies cascaded down upon the old man, their voices hushed and eyes watchful, focused on the grocery aisles, peeled for Len's return.

"Now, that's interesting!"... "You're not serious?"... "You think so?"... "Wouldn't surprise me."... "Why would he?"

Glen, pleased with the grand reaction, straightened his back, his smile as wide as a peacock's tail feather and explained, "Saw him and Bob toe to toe about a week ago." He nodded his head, declaring it so, his eyes scanning the small crowd. "Len was pushing him around a bit. Then stepped right up and got into his face, the two practically touching noses."

"Do you know what they were arguing about?" Philip asked, his voice carefully kept at a whisper, the group as a whole leaning in for the answer.

"Well, to be honest, the wind blew most of what they were saying out of earshot, but I caught bits here and there. Gathered they were arguing over his sister Mollie."

"Alright, everybody!" Harry threw his dust rag down on the counter, his voice raised in irritation. "Coffee hour is over! This is a grocery store, not Starbucks." He suddenly came around the counter, his face beat red, swiping up the thrown rag as he went. "Don't you people have stuff to do?"

Harry leveled his neighbors with a stern look, his hands on his hips.

"Glen, I'm pretty sure Dub wouldn't mind a visitor." He jerked his head in the direction of the door. "And Calvin, I think the firetruck needs a spit polish, don't you?" He turned towards Ernie Reames. "The ferry should be pulling in any second, Ernie. You better get your shop open for the day. Come on..." Harry waved his dust rag in the group's direction, shooing them towards the door. "Oh, and Alice!" His tone softened, "Don't forget your bag on the counter, and when you get to the clinic, can you tell Jerry I've got his soy milk on order?" He waved the rag in the direction of the front door again. "Now, come on, everybody, get going."

One by one, the gossip circle broke up, each guilty member quickly deserting the picnic table, tossing their coffee cups away as they sulked out the front door.

Worried he'd be booted out with the rest, Philip decided he better get his shopping done and headed for aisle six, Hattie and Len appearing at the entrance of the same aisle, Len holding a small paper bag and two bungee cords.

"Now, you take those, free of charge, and come see me next week, okay?" Hattie patted Len's arm, her runny blue eyes sparkling. "And you tell that pretty sister of yours to come see me. I'm in need of a good visit."

Len, docile and polite, walked Hattie to her rocking chair and gave a quiet but sincere "thank you," promising to relay the message to Mollie, and headed for the exit, firmly ignoring Harry's call to, "Have a good day, Len!"

Philip, seeing Hattie struggling to sit, quickly jogged over and helped ease her into the rocking chair, putting a soft hand upon her shoulder, giving it a gentle squeeze.

"What was in the bag you gave him?" he asked, his eyes on Len's back, the young man now on the sidewalk, the paper bag tucked under his arm, heading in the direction of the bank.

"Oh, a little concoction of my own. Hope it helps."

"Hope what helps?" Philip stepped back, giving her a questioning look, the contents of the bag still a mystery.

"Didn't you see his hands?" Hattie's white eyebrows were raised in surprise. "All chapped and welted?"

Philip, not paying attention at the time, thought back, realizing that indeed, the back of Len's hands had been covered with red, sore-looking scratches.

"Yeah, they looked painful." Philip frowned, the scratches bringing something else to mind.

"Don't they? I bet you it's why he's always got his

hands stuck in his pockets." Hattie wiggled in her chair, getting comfortable. "And why he's always making those snarky comments about working outside. He's embarrassed." Her voice turned hard, "Makes me mad. Being a hard worker is something someone should be proud of!" She shook her head as she pulled a folded tissue from her sleeve and dabbed her eyes. "My poor Earl use to have the same problem being a logger. Tough on the knuckles." She tucked the tissue back, straightening her sleeve. "So, I gave him a bit of the salve I use to make for Earl and a kind word."

"You like him, don't you?" Philip smiled down at her, knowing Len had been completely taken aback by her insistence to help.

"No reason not to."

"Noticed you mentioned Mollie should come over for a visit. You're not trying to pave the way for Harry to ask her out on a date, are you?" Philip teased, glancing down at his watch, noticing the time.

He needed to get going.

"She's a sweet girl and she's always got news to share," Hattie declared, avoiding his eyes.

"So, you're not playing matchmaker, then?" Philip's mouth quirked, trying to keep his face stern.

"Matchmaker?" Miss Hattie said innocently, blinking her blue eyes. "I don't know what you mean?"

Philip chuckled, shaking his head.

"Oh, yes you do, and you're not wrong. Harry needs all the help he can get!" Philip said it loud enough for Harry to overhear. "He's too chicken to ask her out on his own!"

"Am not!" Harry protested from behind the register, waving his dust rag in their direction, annoyed with their taunting. "I'm waiting for the right moment."

"So, you say," Philip countered, turning his attention back to Hattie, giving her shoulder another soft squeeze.

"Now, other than playing Cupid, have you been behaving yourself?"

"Not one bit!" Hattie patted Philip's hand, tilting her head back to give him a bright smile. "Hope you're not either!" She leaned back farther in the rocking chair. "Or is our lady Sheriff keeping you in line?"

Philip chuckled, nodding his head, admitting it was so.

"Shame." Hattie winked at him, giving his hand a final pat. "Now tell me, is it true about Bob Allen? Did Glen really fish him out of the ocean?" Her tone had turned from playful to serious, her smile dropping.

Philip moved to the bench of the picnic table, sitting to face her, his smile departing as well.

"Afraid so."

Hattie shook her head side to side, and then sighed deeply, "He seemed like a nice fella. Too bad he went that way."

"Yeah, it wasn't a pleasant way to die."

"No, I can't imagine it was." Hattie started to rock her chair, agitated. "I suppose, when surrounded by greed and jealousy, something like that is bound to happen."

Philip sat to attention.

Hattie, in her old age, had a knack of seeing things most people failed to notice and in turn, could hit the nail on the head, mysteriously explaining the unforeseen.

"You mean his family?" he prodded.

"Oh, I don't want to be unfair." She nodded towards her cup of cocoa on the table, silently asking Philip to pass it over, which he readily did, his curiosity piqued. "But a person can be too greedy in life, Phil. Wanting too much money, too much love, too much attention, too much everything, and not caring the cost." She sighed again, bringing the cup up to her lips, pausing. "Those kinds of people feel as if taking a life is worth the reward." She looked down at her cup, a disappointed pout upon her lips. "Ice cold."

"Murder always is."

"True," Hattie agreed, nodding, her eyes serious. "But so is my cocoa."

CHAPTER 24

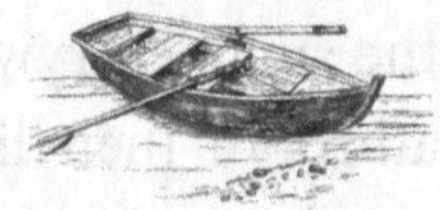

The lock for room 192 issued a brief mechanical whirl as the master key, shakily fumbled into the designated slot, gave way to a flashing green light, indicating the door would now open.

"There." Bailee pressed down hard on the door handle, causing the "Do not disturb" sign, slung over the doorknob, to swing violently back and forth with the motion. She lightly pushed the door ajar and quickly slid to the side, making room for Caleb to step forward, adding, "It's unlocked."

"Thanks," Caleb murmured, then rapped his knuckles hard against the door, announcing, "Sheriff's department!" The greeting, made as a small courtesy, in case there, indeed, happened to be someone inside.

There was no response.

Pushing the door wide, Caleb cautiously stuck his head in, zeroing in on a large mirror hung over an oak writing desk, reflecting most of the room, including a king-size bed.

"You stay here," he said over his shoulder and took a tentative step inside.

Bailee gave no protest.

Moving down the small entryway, Caleb ducked his head into the bathroom, then disappeared inside, the sound of clinking shower rings drifting from the room before he reappeared a few seconds later.

The bathroom empty, he stepped back out into the hall and peered into the open closet, his attention cascading down from the empty hangers to the floor and the black suitcase sitting inside. He then moved to the main area, checking the room's corners before bending down to look under the bed.

The room was indeed empty.

"Well?" Bailee asked from the doorway, her voice tense. "There's not anybody dead in there, is there?"

"No," he said, straightening. "No dead body. It's all clear."

Almost disappointed, he stood with his hands on his hips and took in the room as a whole.

The king-size bed, disheveled, had been slept-in with the TV remote control, left lying on top of the comforter, half-hidden under a discarded pillow.

Next to the alarm clock, on the nightstand, was

an old flip cell phone. Beside it, a key ring, car keys still attached, and in the corner of the room next to a large dresser, draped over the back of an oversized cushioned chair, was a pair of plaid pajama bottoms and a t-shirt.

"All looks pretty normal," he mumbled, pulling a pair of latex gloves from his duty belt, snapping them on, and gently tugging the comforter towards the end of the bed, revealing crinkled white sheets, unblemished.

He pulled the duvet back into place with a flourish and lifted the top mattress with a grunt. It was clean and unsoiled.

"So, everything is, okay?" Bailee inched out of the hallway and into the room.

"Yeah, it appears so." Caleb frowned, lowering the mattress, satisfied no one had flipped it over. "Unless..."

He began pacing the length of the room, focused on the carpet and molding, looking for pooled blood or splatter, not finding any.

Disappointed, he concluded, it was unlikely the hotel room was where the victim had met their end. He turned towards the door.

"Bailee? You can come in, but don't come any further than the hallway, okay?" He wandered over to the small writing desk, spotting a blank notepad and Bob's room key. He turned back towards the bed, his tone distracted, and added, "And don't touch anything."

"Okay, but where should I put this?"

Clutching Caleb's forensic case to her chest, Bailee entered, her eyes wide and searching.

"We can put it on here."

Caleb briskly moved to the closet and pulled out a suitcase stand, unfolding the metal legs, setting it up outside the bathroom door.

"Thanks." He stretched his arm out and took the case from her grasp, placing it down and popping the lid open. "Now, if you could move to the side, Bailee."

Bailee stood in place and scanned the room, her wide eyes lingering on the bed.

"Bailee?" he tried again.

"What?" She pulled her eyes away, focusing on the deputy.

"Nothing is going to jump out and bite you," Caleb reassured her, giving a crooked smile. "It's okay." He handed her a pair of latex gloves. "Here. Put these on, though. And would you mind closing the door for me, please?"

Blushing to her roots, Bailee walked to the door, stopping short, remembering to put the gloves on first, then shut it firmly, turning back to face the room, her eyes returning to the bed.

"Done," she said lamely, her hands close to her

side, afraid to touch anything.

Caleb took the digital camera from the case and followed her gaze to the disheveled bed.

"Does anything look out of place to you?" he wondered out loud.

"No. Not really." Bailee briefly peered into the bathroom, working her way past him. "I see a couple of towels on the bathroom floor. Typical." She skirted the edge of the bed, moving towards the oversized, cushioned chair in the corner. "And the bed has been slept in." She casually pointed towards the chair. "Clothes left out."

She bent down, looking under the writing desk at a small refrigerator.

"The mini-bar is still sealed." She stood up. "Pretty normal as far as a used hotel room goes."

"Except Bob seems to have left his room and car keys, along with his cell phone behind. I wonder if..." Caleb moved towards the bathroom. "Yeah, I don't see a toothbrush or shaver." He turned his attention to the suitcase in the closet, a small carry-on style with wheels. "Looks as if he never bothered to unpack."

"Most people don't." Bailee shrugged, dismissing his point. "He probably was too busy."

"But you said he didn't have plans to go out. Busy doing what?"

Bailee shrugged again, not having an answer.

Caleb frowned at her shrug, his eyes falling on

the nightstand.

"Makes me wonder if he got called down to the lobby to meet somebody?" He walked back into the main area, intent on the night table. "Might have gone down to the waiting area to greet them, expecting to return to his room, and was taken from there or the parking lot."

"Taken?" Bailee questioned, alarmed. "As in kidnapped?"

"Or something like that."

Caleb picked the cell phone up from the stand, flipping the lid open, pleased to not have to do battle with a passcode, or some other fancy security technology screening system, like face recognition or fingerprint ID.

"What do you mean, something like that? On the way up here, you said Bobby's body was washed up by his home." Bailee moved to Caleb's side, her tone somewhat demanding, trying to see the phone screen as well. "Why aren't you looking at his wife?"

"Who says we're not?" he countered, his tone distracted, engrossed with the phone's call log.

He toggled down the list, then reversed the action, verifying he'd hadn't missed anything.

"Hmm. Bob stopped answering phone calls a little after eight p.m. on Friday night."

Caleb turned his focus to Bob's text messages, finding the Saturday morning conversation Kristen had spoken of, surprised to see her number listed under "Ball & Chain." He also read Chad's text conversation, which was normal father and son stuff, plus two angry messages from an "RJ," which Caleb assumed was short for the new business partner, Ryan Jennings.

"Well, that's not odd." Bailee moved to the oversized chair, casually straightening the t-shirt draped over the back, giving her own theory to the lack of phone calls. "He probably went to bed early. He was over fifty."

"Please don't touch that," Caleb said, not bothering to look up from the phone screen.

Bailee clasped her hands together, close to her chest, and walked to the writing desk, her back facing the distracted deputy, and mumbled, "Sorry."

Caleb grunted his acceptance of her apology, then scrolled a bit more before shutting the flip phone with a snap, looking up.

"Bailee, can you do something for me?"

"Sure!" She turned around quickly, an eager, almost guilty expression on her face.

"I need you to get with hotel security and have them pull all the surveillance video from the lobby and the hallway outside of this room from Friday morning to Saturday midnight. How long do you think it will take them to put it all together for me?"

Bailee looked down at her watch, a half-smile

on her lips, the corners somewhat amused and answered, "A couple of hours?"

"Okay, and can you double-check the phone records to the room? See if there were any calls from the lobby?"

"Easy to do. Anything else?"

"Yes. I want to speak to the person who brought up his room service Friday night. I have a—"

"Oh, well, that might be a problem."

"Why?"

Bailee suddenly turned, heading for the door.

"Because they're finishing up the breakfast run and will be starting to prep lunch. We have several conferences this week. I just don't think they'll have time."

"They'll need to make time," Caleb said firmly, determined not to be put off. "Try to arrange something before lunch, say eleven?"

Bailee opened the door and gave a tight but accommodating smile.

"I'll see what I can do." She took her gloves off and rolled them into a ball, squeezing her fingers tight around them.

"You can give me those." Caleb held out his hand, offering to take the discarded gloves. "I'll toss them for you."

"It's okay," Bailee said lightly, stuffing them into her blue-blazer pocket. "I'll just throw them away when I get to my office. No biggie." She hiked a thumb in the direction of the hallway. "I'm heading to security now. Come find me when you're done. It's two doors down from the manager's office." She gave a light wave and exited the room.

Caleb followed after her, stopping short at the door, and watched as she greeted a hotel maid with a large cart of cleaning supplies.

The two turned a sharp corner, and Caleb followed, seeing them step into a large staff elevator, the cleaning trolley between them as they made polite chit-chat, the arrow above the sliding doors indicating the lift was heading down to the lobby.

Watching the elevator close, Caleb returned to the room and shut the door, grabbing an evidence bag from the case on his way, and walked over to the keycard, still sitting on the writing desk.

He placed it carefully in the bag.

She hadn't realized he'd seen.

In the large mirror above the desk, he had glimpsed Bailee picking up Bob's keycard, and aggressively wiping it against her thigh, covertly placing it back on the desktop when he had said her name.

Caleb found the action odd but not unexplainable.

Bailee, perhaps, out of some sense of loyalty to the hotel or Bobby, as she called him, had felt the need to wipe prints off the keycard. Possibly she had arranged for him a lady of the night? An expensive call girl?

He knew at other hotels, such things were done for extra money on the side, and it wasn't hard to imagine the expectation an Elite guest might have, in exchange for a hefty tip. Bailee had also mentioned that Bob had tried to pick her up. Maybe she knew he was lonely and arranged for him some company?

Could Bailee's actions have been in an attempt to protect her job?

Caleb crossed over to the clothing lying on the chair and peered down at the sleeve Bailee had felt the need to straighten.

Snagged on the collar of the t-shirt was a hair, blonde and long.

He quickly took a picture and then very carefully placed the hair into a separate bag. He then moved over to the bed, pulling the duvet and sheets back, closely examining them and the pillowcases.

He found two more, matching.

"You sly dog, Bob. You weren't alone."

CHAPTER 25

Philip pulled into the parking lot of the boat shop, surprised to find Lane, as cold as it was, out of her truck. The petite sheriff was coming from the backside of the building at a practical jog, her cell phone to her ear, her body language, determined.

Parking his rig next to hers, he leaned against the steering wheel, curious, as she reached the front door and impatiently gave the handle a good yank, finding it locked. She then began to pound on the store front's windowpane, and when there was no apparent response, doggedly smashed her face against it in a vain attempt to see inside the darkened storefront.

"Hey! Can't you see the closed sign?" Philip joked, jumping the curb of the sidewalk to join her.

"Phil! There you are!"

Lane dropped the cell phone from her ear and punched a button, ending the call.

"Sorry. I stopped by Hattie's and—"

"Not important. Kristen is a no-show, and she's not answering my calls." Lane jerked her head in the direction of the shop. "And there's somebody in there I want to talk to."

"Who?" Philip stepped to the glass window and cupped his face to peer inside, finding the storefront still dark and abandoned. "Doesn't look like there's anybody in there."

"I just saw them go through the back entrance."

"And you can't get past the fence?"

"Automatic gate. Locked tight."

Lane impatiently jarred the handle.

"Want me to scale it?" There was a boyish eagerness to his offer.

"Oh!" Lane gave him a sudden smile and then a quick peck on the cheek before shaking her head in the negative. "That would be trespassing, Ranger," she reminded and turned to pound on the glass once more.

"So, who's in there?" Philip tried the door himself and found it locked as well.

"My guess is the shop mechanic."

"Who, Jason?"

Lane gave a quick nod and punched re-dial.

"Think so. I saw him driving a green car, very Toyota Prius-like. He parked it in the back lot." She leaned into the window, hoping to see movement inside. "I was across the street when I spotted him, so by the time I got over here, all I could do was put my eye to the fence."

"And?"

"And he climbed out, walked to the trunk area of the vehicle, and pulled out a small, dark item. I saw him tuck whatever it was into his overalls, very suspicious like."

"Small, dark item? A gun?"

Philip's attention immediately heightened, and he took a step off the sidewalk, glancing towards the back fence.

"Um." Lane frowned, the phone still to her ear. "You jumped to that conclusion awfully quick. Is Jason known to carry a firearm?"

"No." Philip's face reddened. "Not that I'm aware of." He stuffed his hands in his pocket, embarrassed he'd jumped the gun, so to speak.

"That's good to know." Lane nodded slowly. Her face, serious. "Still, a concealed weapon is always a possibility."

Philip felt somewhat validated and wondered, out loud, "So, what did he do next?"

"Let himself in with a key."

"Hmmm. Well..." Philip removed his baseball cap

and gave the back of his head a good scratch.

"Well, what?"

"Well, if it wasn't a gun, then that doesn't seem all that odd." He put the cap back on and jerked the brim into position. "Could have been his lunch?"

"Inside his trunk?" Lane gave a heavy sigh and disconnected the unanswered call, stuffing the phone into her back pocket. "Whatever it was, he looked pretty furtive about it." She pounded on the storefront window, restless. "Which isn't the only odd thing. Kristen still isn't answering, and she should have been here already."

"Want me to run over to her place? I could—"

The front door suddenly cracked open, and Jason Powell, standing on the other side in mechanic's overalls, gave them an apologetic smile.

"Folks, we don't open for at least another half an hour. Thought I'd let you kno—"

"That's quite alright!" Lane grabbed the door and pulled it wide, making it clear she was coming inside, regardless. "We're here to meet with Kristen. Mind if we wait inside?"

"Um, I guess." Jason took a halting step back, forced to make room for the small and persistent sheriff. "Come on in."

"Thanks, man!" Philip shouldered in after Lane and gave the mechanic a guilty grin, rubbing his arms vigorously as he did, hoping to illustrate the drop in temperature outside. "It's pretty cold out there."

"Hey, Phil." Jason gave the park ranger a nod of welcome and a slight smile of familiarity as he held the door wider, cold air gusting into the shop.

"You've uh, you've met Sheriff Lane, haven't you, Jason?"

"No, not yet." The young mechanic scooted around Philip's broad shoulders and shut the door, locking it behind him. "But I've heard good things." He gave her a nod of acknowledgment, and his eyes quickly scanned from the crown of her head to the tips of her boots, his smile widening, becoming flirtatious. "Well, um. I, uh, I'll let you two wait here. I've got my breakfast in the back." Jason aimlessly pointed towards the workshop, showing his intent to let them wait for Kristen on their own.

"Breakfast, huh?" Philip gave Lane a meaningful glance. "Anything good?"

A bagged meal, as was suggested earlier, might be the explanation they were looking for.

"No, not really. I woke up late and grabbed a couple of breakfast burritos from the mini-mart. They taste like cardboard, but they'll get me through until lunch."

Lane gave a half-smile, unconvinced there would be any reason to covertly hide one's breakfast in what she felt was a suspicious manner, and watched as the young mechanic continued to inch towards the back shop, still beaming down upon her an over-friendly smile.

Aged in his mid-twenties, standing about six-two with a bright, white smile, green eyes, and light brown hair, worn short in the front and long in the back—she would never understand how mullets were coming back into style, Lane deemed Jason Powell to be a handsome young man.

Though immune to his good looks, her gaze lingered upon him with a suspect eye, and she, in return, brandished him with a cold-professional smile, taking note of his athletic stature, visibly muscular even under his oversized overalls.

Jason, feeling her stare, unconsciously zipped his overalls a little higher. The action drew Lane's eyes to his large hands, covered in tiny scratches, red cuts laced across swollen knuckles, his fingernails dirty with grime and grease, typical for someone who made their living as a mechanic.

But then again... Lane stepped in front of him, his escape halted.

"Jason, have you heard from Kristen this morning?"

"No. I didn't expect to, to be honest. Not with..."

"Then, you've heard?" Lane's blue eyes met his, intrigued.

"About Bob? Yeah, late last night. Chad called me."

"And did he tell you how it happened?"

"Some sort of boating accident? The guy sounded pretty broken up." Jason stuffed his hands into his overalls and shook his head in wonder. "He said Bob's body floated from Seattle to the island, which I didn't understand. Didn't think the current ran this direction and why would Bob be out on the ocean? He was at a boat show at a convention center. They don't actually take the boats out." Jason suddenly shrugged his large shoulders, none of it making sense to him. "Such a strange way to die."

Lane eyed the young man a second longer, not agreeing or disagreeing with his assumption of a tragic mishap.

"I see business is going on like normal?" She nodded towards the register till, a smattering of money inside, a blue bank deposit bag sitting next to it on the front counter.

Jason shrugged, color touching his cheeks.

"I guess. Roger said to open the shop, so here I am."

"Roger, the brother?" Philip leaned against the glass front door.

Jason nodded, explaining, "I talked with him last night, right after I got the call from Chad. Roger said to open up like usual, and he'd be here later today."

"He wasn't upset?" Lane asked, taking a curious look out into the parking lot, vacant for the exception of her and Philip's vehicles.

There was still no sign of Kristen.

The mechanic gave his head a light shake and his shoulders an equal shrug. "He's a stoic kind of guy. But, I mean, his brother died, so I'm sure he was."

"Of course," Philip chimed in, not really knowing but feeling it was the polite thing to say. "Bob was a good guy. Everyone will miss him."

"Yeah, I suppose. Well, my breakfast is getting cold. I'll leave you to it." Jason turned to leave towards the workshop to find Lane, leaned over the front counter, her attention focused on the door marked "office" just beyond it.

"I'm assuming it was you I saw pull-in this morning, in a green car? What kind of car is that?" Lane asked, arresting his second attempt at a departure.

"A Chevy Volt. Which reminds me." Jason pulled out a car key from his overall pocket, a custom Bobber's Boat Repair float keychain dangling from it, and casually, tossed it onto the counter. "I drive it when I run errands for parts. It belongs to the shop."

"It's electric, isn't it?"

Lane edged past the front counter, finding the office door locked, and ventured into the large workshop in the back, peering inside.

"Yeah, and nicer than my piece of junk." Jason turned to Philip, including him in the conversation. "My old Volkswagen. It's always breaking down on me."

"Is that why you were driving the shop's car this morning? Your Beetle is out of commission?" Philip asked, moving from the door and plopping down into one of the plastic lawn chairs reserved for customers, his thigh starting to throb. "You weren't already out and about running work errands this morning, were you?"

"Uh, not exactly." Jason shuffled his feet and gave Philip a crooked smile. "I ran to Seattle after work last night for a part, got stuck in traffic on my way back, and missed the damn ferry." He suddenly shrugged. "I decided to keep the car overnight." He turned from Philip and caught the sheriff's eye. "I'm not supposed to do that. So, if you wouldn't mention..."

"Mums the word," Lane promised as she came back to the small waiting room, reassured the shop was empty, except for them.

"SO..." Philip stretched his stiff leg out in front and crossed his arms, snuggling into the chair, finding a more comfortable position. "You've worked here, for what? A year now?"

"A little over."

"Like it?" Lane swung the door to the bathroom of the waiting room open, the one stall inside visibly empty. She turned her attention to Jason, her curiosity satisfied.

"Uh, love it. Listen, if you don't mind, I'll finish putting the till out, and then I'm gonna nuke my breakfast. You are welcome to wait—"

Lane cut him off, innocently blocking his path to the register.

"Out of curiosity, where were you last Friday evening?"

"Me?" Jason's voice turned cautious. "Last Friday?"

"Don't feel alarmed. We're asking everyone," Lane's tone was casual, her blue eyes dangerous.

"I was... home. Just home."

"You sure? You weren't out hot-rodding it around the island in the company car?"

Jason chuckled, clearly amused.

"Hot-rodding in a Chevy Volt? Uh, no."

"So, home. All night?" Lane did her best to corner him into an answer. Whether he was telling the truth or not, she could determine later.

"Yeah." Jason crossed his arms, his stature becoming somewhat defensive. "I mean, I did have a few beers at Piper's place, but then I headed home."

"In the green car?" Lane stepped closer. "And at what time?"

"I don't know. Nine? And, no! I left the Volt at the shop. You can check the back-lot security tapes if you don't believe me." Jason moved towards Lane, his friendly smile diminished, his tone accusatory, "I was in my own car and in bed by one a.m."

Lane let Jason stand toe to toe, her smile still professionally cool, her tone casually curious.

"Hmmm... Glad to know the shop has video. I'll be reviewing that."

"Oh." Jason took a halting step back, his expression a cross between surprise and... unease?

"And during the day, what were your movements?"

"Movements?"

"Did you go anywhere other than home and the shop?"

"Uh, yeah. I ran a broken part over to a shop in Seattle."

"What time?"

Jason shrugged. "Around four."

"And you got back to the island, when?"

"Eight? I stopped to have a beer with a buddy. I was off the clock at five."

"Uh, Jason?" Philip sat up, a thought dawning as he discarded a dog-eared boating magazine and re-united it with the rest of the waiting room literature. "Isn't it ladies' nights on Fridays? At Piper's?" Philip shot him a knowing smile. "Closed the place down, did ya?"

Jason's easy-going smile returned, and his stature relaxed. "You could say that."

"Ladies' night, huh?" Lane, her smile coy, stepped closer. "Did you leave Piper's place by yourself, Jason?" Her tone made it clear she didn't think he had. "Is there a "lady" who can vouch if you were, indeed, home?"

The insinuation clear, Jason looked down at the small sheriff, his flirtatious smile returning. "Hey, I'm not one to kiss and tell." He winked at her. "Besides, I don't see how it matters if I did or didn't."

"It matters because it wasn't a boating accident that killed your boss. He was shot in the head and then tossed in the ocean from here, on the island. And if I can be frank, you don't seem all that upset about your employer being deceased."

"Whoa, wait!" Jason put his hands in the air, incredulous, his eyes wide. "I liked Bob!" He turned towards Philip, almost as if the ranger would vouch for him. "I wouldn't have done anything to hurt him. I... I had no reason to hurt him!"

Lane stepped forward, taking advantage of the moment, her tone coaxing, "Any ideas who would?"

"No! Ehh—None." Jason's face turned red, Lane not finding him all that convincing.

"None, huh?" Lane's tone lightened and turned conversational, seeming to broach a different subject. "We heard Mike Allister was bringing a pretty sizable lawsuit to bear by some of the islanders. Bob wasn't worried?"

"What? That?" Jason let out a huff of air, almost relieved, his face turning from red to a light shade of pink. "Nah, just pissed."

"Not worried, huh? Why not?"

"Guess because they got an expensive lawyer from Seattle. The guy told'em Allister had no grounds and that, in fact, they could sue him back for libel. I don't think Bob even gave it another thought."

"But he was angry?"

"Wouldn't you be? If you might lose your business because people don't want to pay their shop bill? Yeah, he wasn't happy, not one bit."

"What about Roger? They were business partners, correct?"

"Yeah. Roger took it completely to heart. He wanted to settle, but Bob wouldn't have it."

"And you? What did you think of it?"

"I thought it was a bunch of bull!" His face grew red again. "I do good work, and I stand by it." Jason folded his arms across his chest, defiant.

"I'm sure you do," Philip interjected as he scooted to the edge of his chair, giving Jason an easy-going smile. "Though..." He held up a hand, silently asking for pardon. "Glen says his boat sunk because of bad repairs, and Dub, I guess, his trolling motor busted on him. Both were serviced here. Now, I know they tend to stretch the truth from time to time, exaggerate a bit, but I don't think they'd lie about something so big."

Jason let out a loud gaff and turned to face Philip, snorting, "You bet they would if money was involved!"

"Well..." Philip leaned back and caught Lane's eyes, shrugging his shoulders as if to say, "Fair enough."

"Besides, Dub had sugar in his trolling motor."

"Sugar?" Philip cocked an eyebrow. "That sounds like a bit of a malicious prank."

Jason gave a wicked smile and a nod.

"Or desperation. I think Dub wanted to join the lawsuit so bad that he damaged his own trolling motor." Jason suddenly shrugged. "That, or like you said, somebody doesn't like him."

Lane, intrigued by the suggestion and the stolen rowboat, wondered if Jason was onto something. She asked, "But what about Glen's boat?"

"Bogus insurance claim, plain and simple." Jason unfolded his arm, his stance relaxing. "No way there were bad parts. Len was a whiz with boats. I can tell you. Roger was furious when he quit."

Philip cut in, standing up from the chair with a grimace.

"Len? Len Harrison?"

"Yeah, he was the main mechanic." Jason's good nature was returning, and he smiled down at Lane. "Roughly when the lawsuit came about, he gave notice. Being Bob's right-hand guy, I guess he took it as an insult. Decided to strike it out on his own and bought himself a fishing boat."

Philip shot Lane a look, pleading to speak. "Pretty big money, buying a commercial fishing boat. Even one his size," Philip said, holding Lane's gaze.

Jason nodded. "Helps to have a sister who works at a bank, I guess."

Philip didn't doubt it.

Jason continued, "Anyway, I'm the lead mechanic now, which is a big deal. Bob hired me straight out of school. I hadn't even finished my apprenticeship."

"And Len?" Lane took out her notepad, making a quick note. "Did he leave on good terms?"

Jason scrunched up his face.

"Not really. He was supposed to finish out the month and show me the ropes, but he and Bob got into it one day and Bob sent him packing. Threw him out on his ear."

"Wow!" Philip feigned surprise. "Bob took offense, huh? He was such an easy-going guy. I would have thought he'd have sent Len along with his blessing."

Jason shook his head, negating the suggestion.

"Between you and me, I think the final straw had nothing to do with him giving two weeks. My guess, it was more... personal."

"Kristen and Len?" Philip's shock was evident.

Jason's smile turned into a laugh as he shook his head in the negative. "Hell, no! Kristen wouldn't have looked at him twice."

"Oh, then... Len's sister. Mollie?"

Jason gave a curt nod, his tummy growling. He absently patted his stomach and added, "Always seemed like every time she dropped by it was tense afterwards."

Philip tilted his head to the side in contemplation. "No surprise. We all know Len's protective nature, and Mollie is an attractive woman. Did she still come around after Len left?"

"Nope."

"So, maybe the tension really was about Len leaving?" Philip shrugged, meeting Lane's eyes, her pen still scribbling across the paper.

"Well, whatever it was, I'm taking my shot."

"What do you mean?" Lane looked up.

"I'm planning on asking Roger if I can buy out Bob's half of the business."

"That's a bit brash."

"Not today, obviously. But the doors need to stay open, and I want in."

"What if they sell the business completely?" Lane hinted, knowing if Chad had his way, it could very well happen.

"Then maybe Len's sister will give me a loan?" Jason's handsome face broke out in a broad smile, and Lane, not for the first time, thought him capable of abusing his good looks.

She smiled in return, hers not as genuine.

"Easy money, huh?"

Philip, reading the tension in Lane's shoulders, decided to intervene. "So, other than the lawsuit, everything around here ran smoothly? You never overheard arguments?"

"About?"

Philip shrugged. "I don't know, money issues?"

Jason suddenly looked nervous. "Hey man, I'm not a partner yet. You should wait to talk to Kristen. I don't want to get involved."

He moved towards the counter and register.

Lane blocked his way, her notepad held in front of her like a shield. "Non-involvement is not an option in a murder investigation. So, what have you overheard?"

The young mechanic suddenly crossed his arms and shrugged, his body language stubborn.

"Nothing. I'm always in the back of the shop working on stuff. Can't hear much."

Lane, her blue eyes serious, stepped even closer.

"Yeah, but I bet there is quite the echo in this place. I'd imagine words float across the building from time to time?"

Jason gave Lane a weak smile, and nodded his head, giving in.

"Alright. It's not really a secret anyway. Everyone knows things between Bob and Kristen were—" Jason paused, trying to find the right word. "Toxic."

"Toxic?" Lane wrote the word onto her notepad. "Explain that."

"They fought."

"Over?"

"Money, money spent. The shop, time spent at the shop. Chad, Roger, the lawsuit, the boat show—." Jason suddenly uncrossed his arms and flailed them in annoyance. "The color of the sky? Pretty much everything."

"So, things had grown sour between them?"

"You could say that. I mean, Kristen can be a real bitc—"

Jason's eyes flickered towards the front door, and he gave a quick start, his startled reaction drawing Lane and Philip's attention to the door as well.

A woman, her complexion ghostly pale against an all-black attire, stood in the open doorway, a wad of used tissues in hand, her keys still dangling from the lock, and her gaze fixed upon Jason.

Behind her, filling the doorway, was an older man, elegantly dressed in a suit, the color almost matching the grey at his temples and the silver of the five o'clock shadow lining his jaw.

Kristen had finally arrived and with an escort.

CHAPTER 26

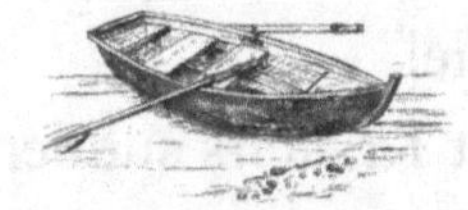

"Sorry, I'm late," Kristen halfheartedly apologized, jerking her keys out of the door and carelessly tossing them into the ebony Gucci purse slung over her arm. "It's, uh, it's been a rough morning."

The freshly minted widow, dressed in a heavy sweater worn over a pair of tight yoga pants, self-consciously dropped her eyes to the ground, her long black lashes fluttering. "I'm sure I look a complete mess." She reached up and ran her hand down a tight braid, her long brown tresses swept away conservatively from her face, the modest hairstyle exposing a blanched complexion and pale lips, free of colored lip-gloss.

"No! You look fine!" Jason pushed past Lane and put a comforting arm around Kristen's shoulders.

"Really!" He gave her a gentle squeeze. "How are you holding up, K?"

With a sob for an answer, the young widow unexpectedly flung herself against the even younger mechanic.

"Oh, Ja-Jason!" She burrowed her face into his chest, and her red nails gripped his overalls tight. "It's been so terrible!"

Taken aback at Kristen's sudden embrace, Jason gave a panicked look towards the older man, who shook his head in mild disgust and stepped forward.

"Excuse me?" the man addressed Lane, pushing past Kristen, shouldering her further into Jason, his hand extended in greeting. "I'm afraid it is my fault we're late. I'm Roger Allen. Bob Allen's brother."

"Sheriff Lane," she acknowledged the introduction, pleased as she had mistaken him for a lawyer, his leather driving glove smooth against her palm as he gave her a firm, respectful handshake.

"And you are?" Roger released his grip and turned his attention to Philip, presenting his hand to him as well.

"Ranger Philip Russell," Philip introduced himself and added, his voice sincere, "Sorry for your loss. I knew Bob. He'll be missed."

"By some," Roger said, slightly turning to peer over his shoulder, his eyes leering towards Kristen, who still clung to the sympathetic mechanic. He then faced forward again and addressed Lane, "I was checking in on my nephew, who is, understandably, upset." He cleared his throat and added, "As am I."

Roger turned back towards Philip, not quite sure if he should be including him in the discussion.

"And he, that is my nephew Chad, informed me of your meeting this morning with Kristen. I thought it best if I was here as well."

It was easy to spot the family resemblance between the Allen brothers, both good-looking men in their mid-to-late fifties with light blue eyes, sharing the same smile and a deep cleft chin.

In contrast, Bob had been much taller, by almost a foot, yet both appeared to have the same square shoulders. Roger's more noticeable by the expensive cut of his suit.

Their taste in clothes was another striking and drastic difference between them.

Bob lived mainly in t-shirts, shorts, and Birkenstocks, the loose attire not doing much for his physique, though his personality was what made him stand out. Friendly and outgoing, Bob never seemed to meet a stranger, while Roger came across as stiff, impersonal, and all-business. At least, that was Lane's first impression.

Roger Allen continued, "And I'd like to know the details of what happened to my brother." He suddenly tossed his head in Kristen's direction, his voice dripping with disdain. "Kristen wasn't able to tell me much. She's been complaining of a hangover."

Kristen broke away from Jason and put a wadded tissue to her unswollen eye.

"A headache, Roger. A headache!"

"Same thing," Roger countered, under his breath, but loud enough, Kristen still heard.

"It is not!" she exploded, her face reddening. "And you shouldn't even be here! You hated Bob! You wanted him... him to be... to be—"

At a loss for words, Kristen once again flung herself against Jason's chest, her sobs turning into a high pitch wail.

Roger gave his head a slow shake, his expression blank before catching Lane's eye, an amused smile blooming across his face.

"Oh, and apparently, I need to clear my name."

CHAPTER 27

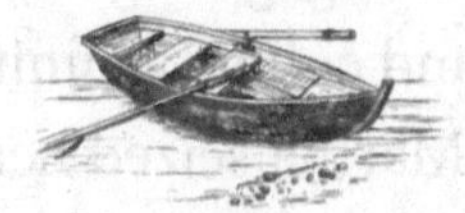

Martha clicked pause and tossed her glasses down next to the yellow legal pad on her desk. "I need a break!"

Left alone at the station, she had spent the entirety of her shift staring at the computer monitor. Watching hours of video, the comings and goings of strangers and friends as they departed or arrived on the island via the ferry.

This task, which she had eagerly accepted due to her desire to know the business of others, was more extensive than she had realized. Huddled over her desk, she had remained glued to her screen, fearful of missing a single second, struggling to take everything in at once, determined to find the minute details of recognition in every tiny pixelated face on the monitor.

Despite all her earnest effort, there had been no sign of Bob Allen returning to the island and the only consolation was the few golden nuggets of gossip scribbled down on her legal pad.

Martha extended her arms out, stretching, her shoulders popping with the motion, as she looked down at her coffee mug, giving way to a yawn.

"Yup, a break and coffee. Definitely, more coffee."

That decided, Martha seized her empty mug and headed towards the coffee nook, stopping halfway, her desk phone suddenly ringing, the shrill halting her actions.

Torn between her need for caffeine and her duty, she quickly lunged forward and grabbed the carafe from the stand, making a hasty return to her desk and plunking both the mug and carafe down at the same time before snatching up the phone and placing it to her ear.

"Rockfish Island Sheriff's office," she said, trying to catch her breath.

"Hiya, Martha. It's just me, checking in." Caleb's voice came over the line. "Sheriff Lane isn't around, is she?"

"No, she's over at Bobber's Boat Repair."

"Still meeting with Kristen and Chad?"

"I assume so, except Chad is with my George, or at least, was first thing this morning. They met at the funeral home to make arrangements for the burial." She suddenly spoke in a hush. "George says Chad is practically inconsolable. Cried and cried when George told him having an open-casket service wasn't an option."

"Really?" Caleb sounded surprised. "Sheriff Lane made it very clear the condition his father's body was found in, and when we broke the news to him last night, he seemed to be holding it together pretty well, considering."

Martha clucked, disagreeing, and added, "Well, that's to be expected, isn't it? Chad was probably in shock and was trying to keep himself together for Kristen's sake. Grief isn't always instantaneous."

Martha returned to their previous subject.

"Have you tried the sheriff's cell phone?"

"Yeah, my call went straight to voicemail."

"Want me to take a message?" Martha offered as she picked up and tossed down the legal pad, looking under it for her pen. "Give me a second to find something to write with."

"Eh, no need. I'll try her cell phone again in a bit."

"You sure?" Martha found her pen, the point to paper.

"It's not pressing. I wanted to let her know that I'll be staying on the mainland for the night."

"At the Four Seasons?" Martha doubted an expense of that kind would be prudent for the station's budget.

"Not unless they comp me a room." Caleb chuckled. "Don't worry. I'll find someplace cheap." He lowered his voice, the busy lobby behind him full of curious patrons and staff. "There's a couple of odd things I need to look into further. It's easier if I stay close."

Martha sat up straight, her ears perked. "What do you mean by odd things?"

"Odd in that, it appears Bob never left his room. Heck, I can't even find any video showing he left the building!"

"I don't understand. Is the hotel's video surveillance down?"

"Not at all. It so happens Bob's hotel room is located in a blind spot."

"Blind spot?"

Caleb grunted, a muted yes, continuing, "They put him at the end of a hall, around a corner. It was almost like the architect was doing his best to squeeze one more room into the place."

"Still. You'd think the hotel would have a camera shooting down the hall for security reasons?"

"They do," Caleb said, frustrated. "Unfortunately, it was off-kilter and pointed down towards the floor. The video was useless outside of the occasional pant leg or passing wheel from a food-service cart or cleaning trolley."

"But what about the lobby? He has to be on a camera there, I would think."

"Oh, he was. I watched him check-in, take the elevators to his floor, then get off the elevators. That's the last place I could find him."

"Well, maybe he didn't go to the room at all?"

"The key card report says otherwise, and his car was, and is, still parked at the hotel."

"What?" Martha threw her pen at the monitor, her own frustration mounting. "You're kidding me!"

"Nope. Forensics is coming for it later today. Hotel security found it parked directly under a light pole and within a perfect shot of the parking lot security cameras. His car didn't budge all night."

"Great! That makes my whole morning nothing but a waste of time!"

"Come again?"

"Caleb! I've been sitting here watching hours of video looking for his car!" She irritably rubbed her eyes, forgetful of her mascara and eyeliner. "Not to mention, taking note of every vehicle which has driven up or off those planks!" She half-heartedly lifted the top page of the legal pad as if to show him the tally of license plates written down, forgetting Caleb was miles away.

"Geez, Martha. I'm sorry. I should have called sooner."

"Oh, it's okay." She sighed, dismissing his apology. "It needed to be done regardless." She picked up the coffee carafe and tipped it over her mug, the steaming liquid rising to the brim. "It's strange, though." She put the carafe down and frowned.

"What is?"

"Him disappearing." She adjusted the monitor on her desk, pulling it closer, her other hand reaching for her spectacles. "I haven't been able to spot him either, that is, coming back. Not as a driver, a passenger, or even as a walk-on." She put the glasses on, the frames sliding down the bridge of her nose, and she pushed them back into place. "You know what I'm starting to wonder, Caleb." Martha paused, her voice dropping into a gossipy whisper, "Maybe it's because he came back in somebody's trunk."

CHAPTER 28

"Why don't we move this conversation to a more private setting?" Roger suggested, waving Lane along and lightly tapping Philip on the arm as he walked past towards the small office, his touch including Philip in the invitation. "Oh, and Jason?"

Roger turned on his heels, simultaneously digging out his keys, and addressed the young mechanic, whose arm still hung around Kristen's shoulders.

"Get this put away." He casually motioned at the register, the deposit bag still laid out on the front counter. "And flip the open sign over. I'm sure my brother would want us to carry on with business as usual."

He quickly turned his back on the group, oblivious of the daggers Kristen was staring into his back, and thrust a key into the lock, wrenching it over and flinging the door wide, beckoning for Lane to enter first. She obliged but paused at the entrance, curious to see if Kristen would be joining.

Jason's back to Lane, he was now facing Kristen, bent forward, his forehead resting on hers, his words soft and indistinguishable from where Lane stood.

Kristen responded with a quick jerk of her head and brought a crumpled tissue to her eye, it not entirely hiding her smile before Jason enveloped her in a hug, his arms practically swallowing her small frame. When he released her, he gave her a gentle push towards the office door, his fingertips lingering on her back.

Lane turned away from the intimate scene and caught Philip's eye, her eyebrow raised as if to say, "You catch that?"

Philip, in turn, gave a slight nod before smiling down at the small widow and taking a step back, his ingrained manners allowing the lady to go ahead of him, both making their way to Lane and the office.

"Sheriff, would you like the chair?" Roger offered, pulling out from a squat, unkempt desk, a leather chair, the wheels squeaking as they rolled across the floor.

Lane shook her head. "No, thank you, Mr. Allen. I'd prefer to stand."

"I would." Kristen stepped past Lane, intent on

the chair, and stopped short as Roger sat down, taking the seat for himself, ignoring her declaration with a cold smile.

"Roger!" Kristen unceremoniously slammed her purse down on the desk, the ebony bag tipping over and toppling out half its contents. "That's my chair!" She looked pleadingly between Lane and Philip as if needing to convince them, her face breaking into another sob. "This is my desk and my office! You can't come in here—"

"Enough with the crocodile tears, Kristen," Roger snapped, exasperated, his eyes meeting hers. "Enough."

The statement would have struck Lane as cruel if she had not suspected Kristen's mourning to be more by design than genuine sorrow, herself.

It appeared as if Kristen's pale pallor, achieved by copious amounts of powder, had remained flawless, tear-streak free after the sudden outburst in the waiting room, stark against her black designer-named attire, which clung to her thin frame. And though red, her eyelids had remained unswollen, enhanced by dark circles under her eyes, a tad too green in Lane's opinion, her mascara still securely in place.

To be fair, Lane knew firming creams, anti-puffing serums, and expensive make-up could hold back the tide of legitimate grief. That any woman, with all of these cosmetic wonders at hand, could simultaneously uphold her vanity and feel heartbreaking sorrow at the same time, especially with everything being waterproof these days.

"I need to give you this," Lane interrupted the shocked silence, her eyes darting over to Philip, who had opted to stand in the doorway, doing his best to remain inconspicuous, a fly on the wall.

She pulled out the folded warrant and handed it to Roger, but addressed Kristen, "I understand this is a difficult time, and I apologize for intruding upon your grief. Truly. But this is important." Lane turned, now speaking to Roger. "We're still unsure of the motive for Bob's murder, so we will be focusing on his last movements and collecting all the information we can about his associations." Lane purposely neglected to use the verbiage "family relations," not wanting to spark additional back and forth between the two in-laws. "To start, I'll need to confiscate all the bookkeeping records for the shop, along with any video surveillance of the property. Pretty much anything I find which might be helpful to the murder investigation."

"I don't understand?" Kristen suddenly leaned against the desk, bewildered, and it shuddered back against the wall, a loose lipstick dropping to the ground, it rolling across the floor. "Why our bookkeeping records?"

"Money," Roger said, barely above a whisper,

his eyes still scanning down the legal document. "Money is always a motive for murder." He turned his eyes to his sister-in-law, his lips in a thin smirk. "Nervous?"

"No! Of course not!" She stood up straighter, self-consciously pulling down on her sweater, meeting Lane's stare. "You don't seriously think the business has anything to do with his death?"

"Why shouldn't she?" Roger spoke up, his voice hard. "It's why you married Bob in the first place. For his money."

"That is not true!" She gave his shoulder a hard shove, pushing Roger forward with force, his smirk quickly turning into a scowl. "I married for love!" she insisted, then stepped closer to Lane, out of Roger's reach, though he had made no move to retaliate.

Lane put out a reassuring hand, nodding as she did. "Now, Kristen. This is all routine."

"Still, he can't say stuff like that!"

Lane ignored her and started looking about the room, craning to see below the desk, finally spotting a black burglary safe nestled between two short filing cabinets. She noted the safe door was open, and walked over, using her pen to pry the door wide.

"Is this where Bob kept his gun?" Lane craned her neck, her question addressed to Kristen.

"Yes. It's in a lockbox in the back." Kristen turned around and grabbed her purse, mumbling, "I have the key to the box in here somewhere."

"Why do you need my brother's gun?" Roger asked, his voice dumbfounded.

Lane ignored his question, asking one of her own, "Kristen? What's that?"

She stepped forward, her eyes fixated on a boat float keychain, the bright yellow object mixed among the other items which had tumbled out of Kristen's toppled purse.

"What?" Her head practically buried inside the Gucci bag, Kristen stopped what she was doing and looked over.

Lane picked up the keychain, the name "M. Allister" printed on one side in black and "Bobber's Boat Repair" in red font on the other.

"That?" Kristen shrugged, returning to her purse, digging down to the bottom. "Someone's boat key."

"I can see that. Mike Allister's key. What is his yacht key doing in your purse?"

Kristen stopped, and looked up again, her eyes confused. "It wasn't." She waved at the desktop, cluttered with various items, loose invoices, and un-opened mail. "It probably got tossed on my desk by accident. It should be hanging up on the key peg upfront."

"But why do you have it?" Lane pressed again. "I mean, here at the shop?"

Roger, his eyes asking for permission, reached for

the key chain, desiring to check the name for himself.

Lane released her grip and watched as Roger gave the keys a brief examination before saying, "Simple. He owes us money. We always hold keys as collateral." He returned the bright key float with a shrug. "Is that a problem, Sheriff?"

"No." Lane broke off, deciding that Mike Allister's boat being stolen with the motor key never being retrieved, most likely the spare, wasn't any of Roger Allen's business. "Speaking of keys." She glanced over at Philip, garnering his attention, and tossed her patrol keys. "Do you mind? Behind the passenger seat, silver case."

Philip shot her a smile as he palmed the keys, and said, "Be right back."

"Excuse me, Sheriff." Roger rotated in the chair, placing the warrant down on the desk, adding to a stack of invoices, and then twisted back to face her. "Putting the warrant aside, I'm still in the dark. What exactly happened?" He gestured his wrist in a circular motion, asking her to elaborate. "You still haven't told me how or why Bob was killed or even why you need his gun?"

Lane held up her finger, begging pardon, and stepped out of the office, dragging in a small stool, which was stationed behind the register, and placed it beside Kristen, giving her a curt nod, an instruction to take a seat.

"Mr. Allen, what I know for sure is your brother's body was found snagged on a crab pot next to a private dock here on the island. He was shot with a .22 pistol, and because that is the same caliber as the gun he owned, I need to verify he wasn't killed with his own weapon." Lane purposefully neglected to mention the strangulation, holding that nugget of information close to her chest. "The condition of the body when found at the dock was—"

"Whose dock?" Roger cut her off, his voice wobbling for the first time.

"Glen Sorenson. He's an elderly man—"

"Sorenson?" Roger shook his head, then looked at Kristen, as if searching for confirmation. "He's one of the plaintiffs in Allister's lawsuit, isn't he?"

Kristen nodded, wisely choosing to remain quiet.

"Well, mystery solved then, Sheriff!" Roger shook his head, his voice cutting. "I told Bob he needed to take that damn lawsuit seriously."

"Meaning? You thought he was in danger?" Lane had taken out her notepad, flipping three pages over.

Roger once again traded looks with Kristen, and she gave him a minute nod.

"Let's say there was... concern. Allister and his cronies had been making threats for a while. I wanted to settle out of court, but Bob was being stubborn about it." Roger looked back at Kristen, his chair swiveling. "You still got those letters?"

"They're in the safe."

"Good." He turned back to Lane. "We started getting threatening letters in the mail." He pointed to the small vault, inviting her to root around inside. "Bob threw the first couple away, but when we were served papers, I told him to hold onto the rest."

"Kristen? Why didn't you mention this last night?" Lane turned a quizzical eye on the widow, who shrugged, hapless.

"I don't know! I was in shock. It never dawned on me!"

Lane gave a frustrated sigh as she took a pair of latex gloves from her duty belt, Philip walking into the office at the same time, gently placing the forensic case on the ground beside her and returning to the doorway.

She snapped the gloves on and bent down, peering into the safe, pulling out a small stack of black bookkeeping ledgers, along with a large envelope of cash, a manila folder full of letters, and lastly the locked box.

"I'll be taking all of this," Lane declared, placing the ledgers, manila folder, and envelope of cash on the filing cabinet next to the safe, her full concentration on the small box, taking note of several scratches in the paint around the keyhole and the lock itself as if it had been jimmied.

She held out her hand to Kristen. "Key?"

Kristen placed a small silver key onto her palm and Lane squatted down with the box, carefully placing it on the floor, inserting the small key into the lock, it twisting easily.

She looked up and met Kristen's eyes, then Roger's, pausing before lifting the lid, a thought dawning.

"Have either of you ever touched this gun?"

Kristen shook her head, declaring she hadn't, and then looked to Roger, who paused before answering, "I have. Bob and I used to go target shooting." He cleared his throat. "It was actually my idea he get it. Brother bonding and all. But it's been months. Six months at least."

"And Kristen, when was the last time you physically saw the gun?" Lane's tone made it clear she expected to find the lockbox empty and the gun missing. To her, it was too much of a coincidence that Bob was shot with the same caliber of gun and thought it more likely he was killed with his own weapon, having been lured back to the island under unknown pretenses.

Kristen blinked a few times as if she was trying to remember, her eyes roaming to the ceiling.

"I told you I don't like guns. I always made Bob keep the damn thing in the box since ROGER..." Kristen eyed her brother-in-law sourly. "Insisted we kept it at the shop. If I had to guess, it probably was about the same time he was just talking about."

"I see." Lane lifted the lid and Philip craned his neck from where he stood, trying to see past her bent head and into the box. "Well..." Lane rocked back on her heels, the box in open view, a black .22 glock sitting inside with a box of ammo. "Looks like it's still here."

"You look surprised, Sheriff." Roger leaned back into the swivel chair, an amused expression on his face. "Was the gun supposed to be missing?"

CHAPTER 29

Instructed to wait for his number to be called, the fast-food restaurant busy, Caleb peered over the heads of the other hungry customers out into the parking lot and watched for Lane's patrol truck.

He was eager to sit down and share his findings, primarily the roadblocks he had come up against, the majority encountered at the Four Seasons. Well, all for one exception. The most damning blow of the day had come from his interview with Ryan Jennings, the previously described new business partner, an hour earlier.

What Mr. Jennings had told him hadn't made much sense, and Caleb was hopeful Sheriff Lane would be able to give him some insight and direction.

"Number one-eighty-one!" A female voice, the tone impartial, called out into the crowd, breaking into Caleb's thoughts.

"Here!" He held up his ticket, the employee behind the counter slamming two empty beverage cups down in front of his order. He said a polite thank you and gingerly took the plastic tray in hand, beginning to elbow his way to the beverage machine.

"Is one of those for me, Deputy?" Lane asked from behind. "Or should I get in line?"

"Hey!" Caleb shot her a big smile, handing her one of the empty cups. "I got you a number two." He nodded towards the serving tray lined with four hamburgers, three sets of fries, and two dessert pies. "Glad we could meet for dinner. Did you make it to ballistics, okay?"

Lane smiled back, having missed her deputy's company, despite him only being gone for the day, and pressed her cup against the pop fountain machine, carbonated liquid flowing down.

"Yup. Dropped the gun and the ammunition off for testing and left the bookkeeping ledgers with the Forensic Accounting Department." Lane snapped a plastic lid onto her beverage and then plucked a straw from the dispenser, scrunching the paper off and stabbing the straw through the designated hole.

"Is a window seat, okay?" Caleb asked, placing his drink on the tray and making his way to one of the few vacant tables.

"Sure." Lane followed, selecting the seat across

from him and slid along the plastic bench. "Did you remember to order mine without mustard?"

Caleb rolled his eyes, a smile cracking his handsome face, and handed her a yellow wrapped hamburger designated as "minus mustard" and a paper tray of hot fries.

Lane smiled her thanks.

"Martha tells me you've hit a few snags at the hotel." She lifted the top bun of the burger and frowned down at a large dollop of mustard, perfectly squirted in the middle.

"Not just the hotel. I went down to the convention center, to the boat show. I spoke with Ryan Jennings, the supposed new business partner."

"Supposed?" Lane looked up, the word catching her ear. "What do you mean by that? They have a falling out?"

"They never had a falling in." Caleb took a huge bite and quickly chewed, waiting until most of the food was down before speaking, his mouth only slightly full. "As Mr. Jennings tells it, he bumped into Bob a few months back. They used to work together at the same brokerage firm." Caleb took a slurp of his pop, swallowed, and continued, "They had exchanged niceties at the time, and Mr. Jennings mentioned he had opened his own business. He said that Bob was extremely interested and was even the one to suggest the idea of marketing to the boating community and not limiting his business to land transportation. Bob even offered to introduce Mr. Jennings to his connections in the boating world and hinted he might invest money into the project as well."

"Well, that sounds like being involved." Lane scrapped a fry across the top bun, doing her best to eradicate the yellow condiment from her meal.

"Except..." Caleb paused, waiting until Lane finished, the mustard-covered fry discarded onto the tray. "It never happened. He never heard from Bob again." The deputy snatched up the fry and popped it into his mouth. "That is, until about a week ago. Bob called him up out of the blue, said he was going to be at the boat show and he wanted to have lunch or dinner, talk about how things were progressing, maybe introduce Mr. Jennings to others at the convention."

"That's interesting. Did the two meet up? Is that who he—"

Caleb shook his head, quickly going on, "No. Mr. Jennings said he was booked out with potential clients for dinner, and he wouldn't be able to leave his booth for lunch, but he could manage a breakfast Saturday morning. Bob never showed." Caleb took another massive bite of his burger, not even chewing before adding, "There were two missed texts on Bob's cell and one very irritated voice message from Mr. Jennings about being stood up."

"Does our Mr. Jennings have an alibi for Friday night?" Lane put her hamburger back together and then grabbed a napkin, wiping her hands clean.

"Yes. Receipts from the mini-mart down the road from his hotel, a signed room service bill, AND his mistress, who was staying the night with him."

"Mistress, huh?" Lane shook her head. "Did he beg and plead for you not to tell his wife?"

"Yup, and offered me two free bottles of anti-freeze for my troubles." Caleb held up a hand, stopping Lane's next question. "And no, I didn't accept the bribe, as lame as it was."

"So, then no new business partner? Why would Bob lie about something like that? I mean, what did he get out it?"

"I've got a theory." Caleb reached for a second hamburger and began to unwrap it. "I found several long, blonde hairs in his hotel room. I think Bob, much like his friend Ryan Jennings, had a female visitor. He probably made up the excuse of a fake business, so he could sneak off for a week, without raising suspicions at home, and planned himself a week of x-rated pleasures."

"Blonde hair? How do you know it wasn't from the cleaning crew?"

"First, I found the hairs attached to his sleeping clothes and on his pillows and bedsheets. Second, I spoke with the cleaning lady that made up his room.

She has jet black hair. Third, he put out a "Do Not Disturb" sign on his door handle after he checked-in. Which would be natural if you had company and you paid them by the hour."

"Paid by the hour? You think it was a prostitute?"

"Well, he did check-in alone."

Lane paused in thought as she picked up a fry, then said, "Unless this lady friend was in another room under a different name?"

"I'm more apt to think the staff at the Four Seasons provided his entertainment." Caleb proceeded to describe how he saw Bailee, without her knowledge, wipe off the fingerprints from the room's keycard. "She also mentioned that Bobby—"

"Excuse me?" Lane's eyes grew big. "This Bailee referred to Bob as Bobby?"

"Weird, huh? I guess he insisted on it, and since he's part of their Elite program they accommodated him."

"Okay, go on."

"When she checked him in, he asked her out for a drink and when she declined, he said he'd call it an early night and stay in his room for the rest of the evening." Caleb took another quick sip of his soft drink, eagerly putting the beverage down. "I'm thinking "calling it an early night" was code for "arrange some company for me."

"Could be." Lane was pondering the suggestion, her own drink in hand, the straw resting on her bottom lip. "Did you confront her on it?"

"No, not yet. I wanted to get your thoughts first because Bailee is my hotel liaison. She's assigned to gather anything I request, be it security tapes, phone records, staff interviews, etc., and I don't want to burn a bridge until I've got everything I need. It'd be bad if she started blocking evidence because she thought it might get her in trouble."

Lane tilted her head to the side, considering, and then nodded, agreeing with his assessment. She then tapped the table, her mind moving past the hotel staff.

"You know, I can buy that Bob might have had a lady friend that evening and if so... could be, she was the one text messaging from his phone Saturday morning? We know it wasn't Bob."

Caleb's face lit up. "What about a third party? Like a pimp? Maybe Bob got rough with the girl and her pimp showed up? Things get out of hand, and he kills Bob. Then to buy time to get rid of the body, they send the text messages the next morning to throw authorities off the scent?"

Lane immediately disagreed. "A pimp killing a rich client is unlikely. He might charge him extra for making his product black and blue, but he won't kill him." She held up a finger. "But, if that was the case, they'd cut and run. No need for an elaborate ruse. And another thing, the idea that a call girl or prosti-tute spent the entire night in the hotel room? I don't know. It makes me feel as if this was a more intimate hook-up, rather than a quick sex transaction." Lane took a quick sip of her drink. "It's still more likely he was lured from his room, back to the island. For all we know, whoever persuaded him to leave, might have returned to the room the next morning, sent the text messages, then left again." Lane leaned forward, a light gleaming in her eyes. "Heck! It might all be the same person, our mysterious blonde."

"Too bad his wife is a brunette."

"Yeah..." Lane stared off into space, lost in thought, and Caleb could almost see the gears working. She suddenly shook her head, as if tossing away the mental notions. "What about the security tapes? You haven't mentioned those. No luck, I gather?"

Caleb gave a big sigh and shook his head.

"Yes and no. The hotel has Bob's arrival and check-in on video, along with his vehicle stationed in their parking lot for the whole stay. If he went anywhere, it was either on foot or in someone else's car."

"What about internal video? Shots of him entering and exiting his room? Have you been able to build up a timeline?"

"The hall camera was off-angle. You can't see anything but vague shadows, a random shoe now and then, or a trolley wheel. It's all but useless."

"That's unfortunate." Lane wadded up her burger wrapper and lightly tossed it onto the tray. "What about room service? Phone calls? Wake-up calls? Anyone else on the staff spot him?"

"No wake-up call was requested, and no calls directly from or to his room from the lobby or any other hotel room. But here's the thing," Caleb paused, his excitement palpable. "He did order room service."

"That would be the hamburger and fries found in his stomach?" Lane picked up one of the two dessert pies.

"No!" Caleb gave her a Cheshire cat smile. "It was grilled beef tenderloin, broccoli, and mashed potatoes."

"Really? Then it wasn't Bob who ate the meal. Those would take days to digest! Are you sure they had the right order for his room?"

"I've got his room receipt, right here!" Caleb started to dig into his shirt pocket, his smile widening. "I'm thinking Bob's visitor got hungry and ordered herself a fancy dinner."

"Maybe? Did you talk with the wait staff?" She took a quick sip. "Could be someone saw our mystery woman when they delivered the food to the room?"

"That's another dead end. It was a new employee named Lilli Adams." Caleb handed Lane the room service receipt. "Turns out she was a no-show the next night, so I asked Bailee for the address listed on her employee file. That led me to a rent-a-day hotel. The manager says he never heard of her."

"Was she blonde?" Lane asked, curious if maybe the missing Lilli was a link, they weren't aware of.

"I wish. Bailee described her as having bright red hair and freckles." He accepted the offered receipt and folded it, carefully placing it back in his shirt pocket.

"Dead end indeed." Lane slumped in the booth and looked at her deputy, mulling over what he said. "Caleb, I want you to go back to the hotel and talk to the food service staff." Lane suddenly straightened. "Ask around about this Lilli. Even though she was new and a no-show the next day, someone may remember her. Heck, maybe one of the staff knows where she disappeared to? I'd be curious to know how she got the job in the first place. Maybe a fellow employee recommended her? It's worth a try."

Caleb nodded his head, eager to please.

"I also have another assignment since you're staying here on the mainland. I want you to verify a couple of alibis for me."

"Who?"

"Chad Allen, for one. I took the liberty of calling the bar he works at. They said he was working Friday night until about nine. I guess it was a slow evening, so they let him off early. I want you to find out what he did afterward."

"That's a tall order. It's a big city."

"Check out his apartment complex for starters." She tore a page from her notepad and passed it across the table. "That's his address. See if anybody spotted him or noticed a white Prius parked on the block." Lane had made the natural presumption that of the two cars parked in front of Kristen Allen's house, the older, white Prius had belonged to Chad. "Then maybe hit the bar, ask around about him."

"I can do that, and the other alibi?"

"Roger Allen." Lane referred to her notepad, reciting, "Bob's brother said he was at home all night alone. No one to vouch for him." She looked up, meeting Caleb's eye. "I guess he's got a live-in maid, but she was out of the country at the time visiting relatives. I want you to knock on his neighbor's doors, see if anyone can verify if he was at home for sure."

"He a likely suspect?"

"Likely enough I'm not going to take his word for it that he was home all night. I want it verified. I've also got Martha checking for his vehicle on the ferry tapes for last Friday night. He drives a Mercedes S-class coupe. Red."

Caleb gave a low whistle of appreciation.

"That's a nice car!"

"And hopefully easy to spot on video." Lane flipped her notepad closed. "Think there is enough room in the trunk for a dead body?"

"Plenty."

CHAPTER 30

Philip looked up from his book, his readers perched on the tip of his nose, and found with some surprise the front door to the ranger station slowly opening, the bitter cold gusting in.

A green and tan bundled body came through the entrance, holding two coffees, with a donut box precariously balanced upon short arms.

"Lane!" Philip jumped up from his chair, recognizing the sheriff, and dropped his book, the spine splitting in two as it landed on the desk with a flop. "I didn't hear your truck outside. You should have honked. What are you doing here?"

"Bringing you breakfast!" She gave him a bright, cheery smile and kicked the door closed behind her.

"I can see that." Philip carefully took a coffee and the box of donuts from atop her outstretched arms and put them down on Kody's desk.

"Since I had to cancel our dinner plans last night, I thought I'd make up for it with breakfast." Lane began reaching into her coat pocket, stopped short by her bulky gloves. "Hold on. I got an energy drink for Kody." She plucked the gloves off and pulled out a tall can, placing it down on the desk with a loud metal clunk. "There. Is he around?"

"Nope. Out doing the morning run, but he's on his way back."

"Oh, too bad I miss—"

Philip swiftly reached out and grabbed Lane by the waist, pulling her close. "Too bad you missed me? Is that what you were going to say?" He peered down, his eyes locked on hers, giving her a coy, expectant smile before leaning in, his lips brushing against hers. "You did miss me last night, didn't you?"

Lane leaned into the kiss, enjoying the shiver up her spine, then pulled back, her voice teasing, "A little."

"Oh, only a little, huh?"

Philip went in for another kiss, but Lane playfully swatted his chest, stopping his progress.

"Won't Kody be back any second?"

"I can lock the door."

She laughed and stepped back, out of his reach, slipping past him and asked, "Want a maple bar?" She flipped the lid of the pastry box open. "Or a powered donut?"

"I'd rather nibble on you," he stepped towards her and leaned in, nuzzling her neck.

"Now, Ranger..." She pulled away, laughing, her voice warm but full of warning. "Save that enthusiasm for off-the-clock hours."

At her half-hearted rejection, Philip's shoulders slumped, and he nodded his head, resigned to behave himself, knowing Lane wouldn't risk Kody coming back and catching them being anything other than professional with each other.

"Alright, I'll keep my hands to myself." He circled his desk and sat down, his eyes still lingering on her, and asked, "How did things go last night with Caleb? Is he making any progress?"

"Despite the dead ends he keeps coming up against? I think so."

Lane brought over two donuts, each on a napkin, and dragged Kody's chair with her, sitting across from Philip.

Between bites of sweet pastry and sips of coffee, she shared her and Caleb's conversation from the night before, finishing with the instructions for her deputy to look into Chad and Roger's alibi and for him to question the kitchen staff directly.

"Gee, I guess we were wrong in thinking Bob and Kristen were happily married." Philip swiped at the dusting of sugar on his tie and then took another bite, the white powder coating the corners of his mouth. "Especially if he was fooling around on her."

Lane nodded her head, agreeing, "I hate to admit this, but I thought if anyone was stepping out on their marriage, it was Kristen."

"With who, Jason Powell?"

"Or Chad?"

"He's her stepson!"

"True, and yet, they're around the same age, both ridiculously good-looking and vain, and they like to hang out with each other. Maybe not an emotional affair, but I could see them having a physical one." Lane suddenly shrugged and pulled out her notepad, flipping to the first page. "But I think you're right. If she were having an affair with either of them, Jason seems more likely. He's handsome in his own right, and once again, around her same age. They also spend the majority of each day together at work and were pretty cozy back at the shop."

"Maybe she and Bob had an open marriage?"

"I think news of that kind, especially in this tight-knit community, would get around pretty fast, don't you?"

Philip didn't disagree, his attention drawn to Lane's open notepad, a list of names written in order by degree of guilt at the top of the sheet, and by each suspect, several additional lists titled: Motive, Physical Ability, Opportunity, and Alibi.

"That's a mighty long suspect list," Philip observed,

counting at least six names. "Who is leading the pack?"

"Jason. He's got plenty of motive."

"Which would be?"

"Kristen, the business, and consequently the money that comes with both." Lane continued down her list, ticking each column as she explained, "He's young and athletic. Keep in mind, whoever killed Bob had to have strength enough to load his body into Dub's rowboat, oar it out to sea, then inflict damage to distort the features, before swimming back to shore."

"During a wind storm, in the middle of the night, in below-freezing temperatures taboot."

Lane's pen now rested upon the "Opportunity" column. "Jason admits to driving a car very much like the one Dub described on his property the night of the murder. He also has no alibi for Friday night. Or at least, one he'll fess up to." Lane underlined Jason's name with force. "And most importantly, he had access to the shop's safe and Bob's gun." She tapped the notepad and looked up, meeting Philip's eyes. "I'm convinced that was the object he pulled from the car's trunk, then covertly hid in his overalls before going into the building. My guess is he was returning the weapon to the safe, expecting no one to realize it was missing."

Philip frowned and nodded towards the notepad and its litany of checkmarks. "Well, if he checks all the boxes, why haven't you brought him in for official questioning?"

"Because I'm not convinced he did it all on his own."

"He had an accomplice?" Philip's eyebrow hitched in surprise.

"Or he WAS the accomplice," Lane suggested, her head tilted to the side, her eyebrow matching his.

"Who, Kristen?"

"She or possibly a future business partner?"

"Roger, then."

Lane nodded and held up a finger, continuing, "OR it could be a son, willing to sell his share of the business?"

"Ah, Chad." Philip nodded, catching onto the idea.

"It would explain how Bob returned to the island without his car."

"What do you mean?"

"Well, it's been bugging me. Caleb said he found Bob's cell phone and keys in the hotel room, and his car never left the hotel parking lot. Now, if somebody called him, saying, for example, the shop was on fire or Kristen was hurt, any normal person would snatch up their keys and phone out of reflex before heading out the door to an emergency."

"Unless someone showed up at the door, telling them there was no time?"

"Possibly. The point is, Bob didn't drive himself to the island." Lane settled back into the chair and crossed her legs. "Then again, he might have taken his things, but whoever killed him returned them to the room by morning, making it appear as if he'd simply vanished."

"Vanished is a good word. I guess if his body hadn't been found, it would have been assumed he'd chosen to disappear or worse." Philip suddenly rapped his fist against his desk, startling Lane. "Which doesn't make sense. If their plan was to make it look like a suicide, they failed miserably."

"Not to mention, a missing body would cause everything to be dragged out. They'd have to wait at least seven years before officially declaring Bob dead through the courts and pushing forward with his will or any life insurance claims."

"So, then maybe that wasn't their plan? Maybe they conked him on the head, took him from the hotel, not realizing he'd left behind his cell phone and—"

Lane interrupted, "They would've had to devise some way of getting him out of the room without being seen. He was too big of a man to be squeezed into a suitcase."

Philip rubbed his temple, fighting off a headache.

"Fine. Bob left his hotel room on his own... and then what?"

"Well, since he didn't take his own car. I imagine he got into someone else's."

"And that person brought him back to the island?"

"Jason did say he was on the mainland Friday evening, plus, both Roger and Chad live in Seattle. Any one of them could have shown up at his hotel room and coaxed him into their car."

"Alright. Then once Bob got to the island, regardless of who brought him over, you think Jason killed him and then disposed of the body?" Philip sighed heavily, now rubbing both temples. "How does the blonde Caleb talked about fit in?"

Lane shrugged, tapping her notepad in thought.

"She might not, in the grand scheme of things."

"Meaning, wrong place, wrong time?"

"Something like that. Either way, I'd like to find her. She may know who came to his hotel or who he went out to meet?"

"My head hurts."

"I know. It's confusing, like a jigsaw puzzle." Lane took a deep breath. "And I feel like we're missing a few pieces."

"Or we're trying to fit a piece where it doesn't belong? Who's next on—" Philip looked back down at the list, curious to who else was suspected, and remarked on the next name, flabbergasted, "Glen Sorenson? You've got to be kidding!"

Lane shook her head, her face blank.

"He's like eighty years old!" Philip pointed out, tapping Lane's notepad.

"And he's a big man who is in great shape for his

age. Those crab pots he pulls out of the water each day, full of crab? Those aren't light. AND..." Lane hurried on, foreseeing Philip's rebuttal, "He told me once he used to be a logger."

"A logger? What does that have to do with anything?"

Lane gave Philip a flat look. "Hacking a body up with a boat oar strikes me a lot like someone chopping up a log."

Philip frowned, not liking the mental picture.

Lane continued, "Not to mention, he knows where Dub moors his rowboat, and Glen was home alone with no one to vouch for him either."

"Everybody on this island knows where Dub keeps his row—"

"And Glen sent the victim threatening letters, not to mention the body being found at his dock."

"That's ridiculous. He'd never—"

"For all we know, Glen shot Bob and decided to get rid of the body. Now, because his boat is sunk and at the bottom of the ocean, he takes Dub's rowboat. Once he gets out on the water, he tosses the body over the side, hoping it'd stay down, then swims for his dock, but not before, blasting holes into the rowboat, expecting it to sink."

"Lane, a couple of problems with that theory." Philip, adamant, shook his head, adding, "The ocean current wouldn't have taken Dub's rowboat from

Glen's house and dumped it at the Driftwood outlet. That boat had to have been at Dub's dock. If it were at Glen's, it probably would have been taken out to sea and stayed out there."

"Hmm. Okay, good to know." Lane quickly added a small notation by Glen's name.

"And you forget two big things. Glen doesn't own or drive a green Prius, and he didn't have access to Bob's gun!"

"I know you've known Glen a long time, Phil. But try to look at this objectively."

"Meaning the green Prius was only a pair of teenagers looking for a place to make out, and the gun at the repair shop wasn't the murder weapon?"

Lane smiled, it touching her eyes, and nodded. "Just because we think it, doesn't make it so."

Philip opened a desk drawer and pulled out a bottle of aspirin. "Regardless, I don't think Glen sending a few letters in the mail constitutes motive enough for murder, do you?" He shook out three tablets and then tilted the bottle, offering to share.

"To a sane person." Lane declined the aspirin and circled the question mark by Glen's name in the "motive" column. "But if someone feels as if they were severely wronged?" Lane let the insinuation hang in the air and underlined Mike Allister's name next on the list. "That's why I'm also examining the lawsuit. It's possible that Mike Allister was worried he was going to lose, and his ego couldn't take it."

"Buzz, buzz," Philip cautioned before taking a sip of his coffee, downing the aspirin, and adding, "Forget Allister. What about Len Harrison?"

"What about him?" Lane quickly looked up from her notes.

"He has motive... or I think he might. According to Glen, Len and Bob almost came to blows a few weeks ago, and after what Jason told us at the shop, well, maybe it's something worth looking into? Plus, his sister Mollie owns a red Prius, which could have looked green at night to Dub."

Lane flipped back through the pages on her notepad.

"Wasn't Len the one who found Mike Allister's lifeboat?"

"Well, yes, but he also works by the docks, so that's not surprising."

"Okay, so that's not a strike against him, then?"

Philip shrugged, unsure. "Nobody else seemed to notice it adrift. Also, have you seen his hands? He's got these long red marks running down the back-side." Philip was warming up to the subject. "Another thing. If Bob was hitting on Mollie, well, Len may have decided to put a stop to it one way or another?"

"But Jason made it sound as if Len had been successful in shooing Bob off. I think if he and Mollie had kept something romantic going on the side, she would have been seen around the shop."

"With his wife there?" Philip shook his head. "I think her excuses to be around would have dried out once Len had quit."

Lane frowned, adding Len's name to the list. "I don't know, Phil. I can't picture Mollie being interested in a married man."

"I can't either, but she's super friendly and outgoing. It's not hard to see how Bob might have seen encouragement where there was none." Philip shrugged. "But then again, Len might be overprotective for a reason. Maybe she has a history of getting mixed up with the wrong guy?"

"Has Harry asked her out yet?" Lane gave Philip a curious smile. "Maybe we could do a double date?"

"You mean, a cross-examination?" Philip laughed. "He's been too chicken."

"Well, maybe we can help push things along?" Lane flipped her notepad closed, symbolizing the decision had been made. "Try to make it happen for tonight if you can." She glanced down at her watch. "Oh, I better run."

"Lane, Harry might not appreciate—" Philip was interrupted by her cell phone.

"It's ballistics," she said quickly, sitting up straight in the chair and answering the call, "Sheriff Lane."

Philip did his best to eavesdrop, but the conversation was short and to the point.

"Understood. I'll be in before the lunch hour to pick it up. Thanks." Lane ended the call, her demeanor no longer cheerful.

"What is it? What's wrong?"

"Bob's gun." She stood up and grabbed her coat. "It's not the murder weapon."

CHAPTER 31

"Sorry, I'm late!" Martha came bustling through the doors of the Sheriff's station, slightly out of breath, her hands full. "Would you believe I hit every red light on my way over?"

Lane rolled her eyes at Martha's excuse. "There's only one stoplight on the whole island, Martha." Lane pointed out as she stepped out of her office and walked into the reception area.

"I know! And it takes five minutes for that damn light to change color!" the older woman complained, juggling a handful of mail and a grocery bag, her purse strap caught on her shoulder, a dirty casserole dish protruding from it. She clunked everything down in a crash upon her desk.

Spotting the brown grocery bag, Lane thought it more likely Martha had been sidetracked by the local gossip circle at Hattie's, an issue she knew she might run into when hiring the town gossip.

Lane sighed and said, "Listen, I've got to run over to the mainland. I got a call from —"

"And then that ol'bag of bones wouldn't stop fussin'! Has me waiting on him hand and foot! Thank the good Lord his son and daughter-in-law should arrive today!" Martha tugged off her winter jacket and hung it on the back of her chair.

Deciphering the not so affectionate term "ol'bag of bones" to be a description of Dub, Lane asked, "How is he feeling?"

"Besides ungrateful?" Martha snapped and then immediately apologized, "Sorry, Sheriff." She took a deep cleansing breath, her hands held at her side, her palms flat, then smiled weakly, amending her statement, "Dub is feeling much better." She opened her bottom desk drawer with a jerk and dropped her purse inside. "He must be if he can find the air to complain about how I cook and in the next breath ask me to make him a week's worth of frozen meals for his boy's visit." Martha's hand suddenly went to her heart. "Which I am more than happy to do. From what I understand, his daughter-in-law can't cook. She'd burn water, as Dub tells it."

"Well, it's been very nice of you to check in on him," Lane said, walking over to Martha's desk and peering into the brown paper sack, finding coffee and paper filters, a stack of notepaper tablets, and a tin of cookies. "Find out anything of particular value from the gossip circle this morning?"

Martha did her best to express innocence as she sat down and began sorting through the mail. "Oh, just the usual speculation." She looked up at Lane, her eyes earnest. "I, of course, only listened. I didn't participate." She suddenly leaned in. "Some of those people can't keep a secret to save their lives."

"So, what's the consensus?" Lane knew their little town was rife with opinionated citizens, and, though she tried, things didn't always stay secret.

Martha suddenly shrugged, a large envelope resting against her chest, her fingers sorting through the smaller letters and bills.

"Some say Len Harrison had it out for Bob, but that's only because Glen Sorenson has been shooting off his mouth. Others think it's the mob and—"

Lane could figure out where the "mob" theory had come from, despite her little chat with George Barnes about loose lips within the inner circle.

Martha continued, "Some folks believe it's got something to do with his wife. You know, a love triangle."

"Could there be any truth to that? Have you ever heard anything about an affair?"

"Not an affair, exactly." Martha started to rip open the large envelope. "It's only that Bob wasn't known for keeping his hands to himself." Her head bobbed up and down at Lane's surprised look. "A bit of a lech."

"What about Kristen?"

"I've always wondered myself, to be honest. Her being so much younger than him, and having a stepson the same age, and then that good-looking mechanic at their shop." She paused, pulling out the contents of the large folder. "I mean, no offense to the dead, but Bob, for being a handsome older man, he sure didn't do much with what he had." She shook her head. "Running around with a comb-over ponytail." Martha suddenly leaned forward with a wink, her voice lowered to a hush, "Cheaper than a toupee." She sat back. "Always dressed in a t-shirt and baggy shorts. I mean, a grown man strutting through life wearing socks with sandals!" She shook her head again. "I wouldn't have been surprised if a pretty young thing like her lost interest."

Lane wouldn't have either. She agreed with Martha that Bob was an attractive man, and now having met his older brother, Roger, who dressed to the nines and sported a sharp haircut (or possibly an expense toupee), she could see how attractive Bob could have been if he'd paid attention to his appearance.

Speaking of Roger...

"Any luck with the ferry tapes?" Lane changed the subject, scanning Martha's desk, taking note of the yellow legal pad, a catalog of license plates written down in precise, bold writing.

"A little, though I don't know how much it will help." Martha put the mail aside and picked up the yellow pad. "I saw only one green Prius, and it had Canadian plates. It came over Friday afternoon on the six p.m. ferry and returned on the first ferry out Saturday morning."

Lane perked up and took the legal pad from Martha's grasp, eagerly reading the page.

"Description of the driver? It wasn't a blonde female, was it?"

Martha shook her head, picking up the discarded envelope and unsealing the large flap.

"Hard to make the driver out at all, truth be told. Those cameras on the loading dock are not the best quality. They're supposed to email me the interior shots hopefully today." Martha pulled a stack of papers from the large folder, giving them a cursory look.

"Okay, did you run the plate?"

"No, I wanted to check with you first since it was out of the country. Could be a tourist?"

"You're probably right, but run it through anyway. That way, we can cross it off the list."

"Sheriff?" Martha's tone had changed, her voice curiously urgent, "I think this is the coast guard's report on Mike Allister's yacht." She handed Lane the papers pulled from the jumbo-sized envelope.

"Really? I asked them to send it via email."

Lane took the handed sheets and immediately flipped through the pages.

Knowing it would take the sheriff a minute or two to pour through the information, Martha picked up her dirty casserole dish and headed to the small kitchen in the back.

"Well, this is interesting," Lane said a few minutes later, her eyes still pinned to the report, Martha coming back, the glass pan gleaming clean. "The report says the cabin door to the yacht was pried open. The Coast Guard didn't notice at the initial boarding but they found pry marks during their follow-up investigation."

"Why is that odd?" Martha opened the bottom drawer of her desk, carefully laying the dish on top of her purse, and shut it with a slight bang. "I mean, the boat was obviously stolen."

"Well, it's odd, unless you can hot-wire a yacht, like a car." Lane took a deep breath, the report smacking against her knees, as she lowered her arm, thinking. "I'm assuming the thief or thieves had a key."

Martha shrugged, not knowing the answer herself. "Want me to ask Mike?" she offered, reaching for the phone.

Lane hesitated and bit her lip in consideration.

"Martha, have you talked to him since I found out he was in Florida?"

Martha nodded, a bashful smile spreading across

her face.

"This morning. He called and told me about the family emergency and apologized for not getting word to me sooner. He knows how I worry."

"Good." Lane stacked the report against Martha's desk, the pages disheveled after pouring through them. "Out of curiosity, who did he take with him?" Lane knew she probably shouldn't ask, but it still irritated her that Allister had refused to say.

"What do you mean?"

"Who was the woman that went with him, down to Florida? A family friend?"

"What woman?" Martha's tone turned sour, her eyes slitting in suspicion.

"I'm not sure... um, I." Lane stopped, realizing she'd outed the sleazy lawyer. "Oh, man! I'm late." Lane took a sweeping look at her watch and headed for the coat rack. "I gotta get over to ballistics. I'll see you later, Martha!"

Lane hit the door, not bothering to put her coat on, and heard Martha's voice behind her, loud and shrill, "Sheriff! What woman?"

CHAPTER 32

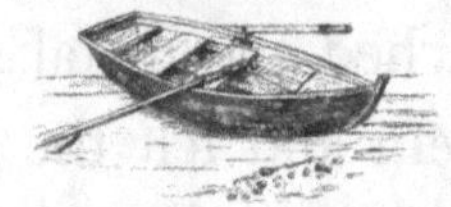

"What in the world is he doing?" Lane kept her eyes on the lone figure, the only passenger standing on the outside observation deck. She was confused as to why he had chosen to brave the freezing wind and pelting rain instead of joining his fellow travelers inside the warm, cavernous cabin of the ferry.

She had recognized him instantly, even from the back, and after a solid ten minutes, decided it was time to intervene, ignoring the notion he might not appreciate her intrusion.

She didn't care.

At best, he was frozen to the bone, and at the worst... Well, the words of George Barnes the day before regarding attempted suicides, echoed through her subconscious.

Propelled by this concerning thought, she hastened from the window booth, leaving behind her half-eaten lunch, and snatched up her winter coat, shrugging it on. She zipped the front with a jerk and walked towards the observation platform, feeling the eyes of curious and bored bystanders boring into her back.

When she reached the metal green doors, she leaned against them and felt the resistance of the wind as she pushed past and out onto the wet deck, ocean spray instantly whipping her hair loose from its tight bun.

"Chad?" Lane yelled, her call snatched up by the wind and flung to the sky. "Hello?"

He remained unmoving, giving no indication he'd heard his name, his full attention upon the sea.

Lane white-knuckled the metal railing and inched forward, careful to keep her balance. When she got close enough, she reached out with a trembling finger, the wind's chill factor in full effect, and roughly tapped his shoulder.

With a jerk, Chad whipped around, his hair plastered to his forehead, cheeks ruddy, and eyes wide, surprised at the unexpected touch.

"Can I have a word with you? Inside?" Lane jerked her head towards the cabin doors, hoping he could decipher the request, her words practically drowned out by the white-crested waves and squawking seagulls.

He gave her a quick nod of understanding, and Lane held out her arm, silently asking Chad to lead the way before following him inside, grateful to leave the freezing deck behind.

"Sit there." She pointed to the deserted booth, her lunch still on the table, and added, "I'll be right back." She made for the cafeteria section.

When she returned, Chad was seated, shivering, his wet jacket still on, water dripping from his hair down onto the table.

"You better dry off." Lane grabbed a wad of napkins from the dispenser and placed them next to the steaming cup of coffee she put before him. "And drink that."

Not meeting her eyes, Chad grunted his thanks and used the napkins to pat himself dry, then shrugged out of his wet jacket, carelessly tossing it aside.

He looked terrible.

The difference in the few days since she had seen him last was startling. It was apparent that Lane had mis-categorized Chad, mistaking him to be a pillar of strength, strong and unbending, when in truth, he was fractured, devastated by the loss of his father, covered in emotional sackcloth, mourning, and vulnerable. His denial, in their earlier meeting, now swallowed and digested, the arranging of his father's funeral plans combusting any hope in a misidentification.

"Thanks," Chad suddenly addressed Lane, his eyes falling on the pile of empty saltine wrappers and the half-eaten bowl of clam chowder. "The choppy water ruin your appetite?" he asked, conversationally as if he'd walked himself over and sat down, instead of Lane coaxing him inside.

The sudden and altering difference in tone and attitude rudely reminded Lane that Chad Allen was an actor whose grief could be, in fact, an act.

"A little," she matched his casual tone, and pulled her coffee close, the warmth seeping into her chilled palms. "I didn't know you were planning on leaving the island? Heading home?"

"Only for a change of clothes." His gaze moved to the window, peering through the rain-speckled pane. "Dad's funeral is in three days and I... well, I need something nicer than jeans, and t-shirt." His eyes left the window and settled on her. "I assume since I'm not a suspect, that is permissible?"

Lane gave a brief nod and avoided answering his question directly. She hoped if Chad considered himself above suspicion, he wouldn't do anything silly like make a run for it, and for the sake of his mental health, she wanted to avoid burdening him with an open accusation.

"Okay, then." He shrugged, almost annoyed. "What did you want to talk to me about, Sheriff? Is there an update on the case?"

"I need your help," she said simply. "I want your insight on your father's relationships. Primarily with your uncle and stepmother. How are they getting along, by the way? Any better?"

"Oil and Vinegar mix better than those two."

"Ah, that well, huh?"

"Worse, actually." He shook his head, disappointed. "Everyone should be coming together, and they've been nothing but at each other's throats."

"Over the boat shop?" Lane prompted, and Chad nodded, his eyes closing in frustration.

"Kristen is convinced Uncle Roger and Jason are trying to squeeze her out of the business, while Uncle Roger swears Kristen and Jason are scheming to sell and cash out." Chad shook his head, suddenly giving her a weak smile. "And the sad thing is, I don't think either one is necessarily wrong."

"Meaning you think Jason is playing them both?"

"It's obvious Jason is out for Jason." Chad began fiddling with the coffee sleeve around his cup, moving it up and down. "Whoever gives him what he wants..." Chad looked back out the window. "It's a mess, to be honest. As soon as Uncle Roger informed Jason I inherited thirty-five percent of dad's half of the business, he approached and asked me if he could buy my portion."

"How does your uncle know about the specifics of the will?"

Chad turned away from the window, his eyes wide, and answered, "He's the executor. I guess you haven't seen it yet? I know he asked the lawyer to send a copy to your office."

"No, not yet. Could you give me a brief summary?"

Chad nodded, leaning back into the booth, propping his arm along the top, relaxed.

"I get Dad's thirty-five percent. Kristen gets the rest, plus everything else, and we split the life insurance payout."

"What is the amount on that?" Lane gave an apologetic wince. "I realize that seems like a callous question."

"It is." Chad sighed, then answered, "Five hundred thousand each."

"And Roger?"

"Except for the keyholder insurance policy they had on each other? Nothing, I'd imagine. He already has plenty of money."

"And the amount on that policy?"

"No idea."

"And your father's wishes, regarding the business? Have you decided what you are going to do with your share?"

Chad nodded, though the practiced smile dropped from his face. "I'm gonna sell. It was never my dream."

"Who will be the lucky new owner then? Your

uncle or Jason?"

Chad began to once again fiddle with the coffee cup's sleeve, twisting it around the base.

"Neither. If Dad knew I was declining, I think he'd want Kristen to keep it running. Besides, if it hadn't been for my uncle putting his foot down, she probably would already be half owner." He suddenly shrugged. "And I think it'll keep her safe."

"Safe?" Lane was intrigued by the word.

"I... I, uh, only meant if she had a bigger piece of the pie, no one could cut her out."

Lane gave him a flat look. "Chad, I don't think that's what you meant at all."

"I suppose not," he suddenly confessed. "Kristen told me about the threatening letters surrounding the lawsuit."

Lane had read the so-called threatening letters, the poison-pen author's attempt at forcing a settlement out of court, and found, interestingly enough, the described threats directed more towards Bob's loved ones, Kristen in particular, than Bob himself. She theorized these letters had laid the groundwork, succeeding in luring Bob back to the island after being told the supposed warnings had become a reality.

"And you're concerned. What about—"

Chad cut her off, "Aren't you?" His tone was eager and he leaned in. "What about the couple of near accidents Kristen has had lately? They've not been all at once, but with Dad's death and the threatening letters, on top of the prank phone calls."

Lane leaned in as well and pulled her notepad from her back pocket.

"Wait, back up, Chad. What do you mean by near accidents? Like what?"

"A few weeks ago, Kristen mentioned her old car was acting up. Something with the accelerator. From what I understand, she was driving home late and it unexpectedly sped up on its own. She about wrapped it around a telephone pole."

Lane frowned, speculating Kristen probably hit the gas pedal by accident.

"What else?"

"Her prescription medicine was switched."

This earned a cocked eyebrow from Lane.

"She got a refill but noticed the pills, though the same size, were slightly a different shade of white. She took the bottle back to the pharmacy, but they wouldn't tell her what she had received by mistake." He gave Lane an expressive look, and when she didn't seem that upset, he hurriedly added, "It looks innocent enough, except she had a few days of medication left in her old bottle. Maybe someone switched the medicine before she opened the new bottle hoping she wouldn't notice?"

"Or the pharmacy made an honest mistake," Lane suggested, trying to be the voice of reason.

"Maybe." He shrugged and then sighed, "Probably."

"You said something about prank phone calls?"

"The day you told us... the day I was over mixing drinks? The house phone kept ringing, and every time I answered, the line went dead."

"And you don't think it was a wrong number?"

"Could have been."

"Did Kristen say these hang-up phone calls happen a lot?"

"No, not at all." Chad suddenly gave her a brilliant smile, and it was as if someone had pulled back the stage curtain. "You know what, forget I said anything, Sheriff." He chuckled, shaking his head, his grin widening. "Typical downfall of being an actor. Overactive imagination."

"Chad, I'm glad you told me. It's obvious that you care about her."

He didn't respond, so she prodded, "How do you think Roger will take the news of you selling to Kristen? I can't imagine he'll be pleased."

"No. It's not going to be a pleasant conversation." Chad's smile disappeared, and he changed the subject, "How is the investigation coming? Any progress?"

"We're still gathering information."

Lane was embarrassed to admit the inquiry was slowly coming to a stand-still.

The coroner's latest email had confirmed Bob's toxicology screen was clean, which meant he hadn't been drugged or under the influence when killed, making it more likely than not, Bob had been transported to the island under his own power. It was still unclear if he had returned himself or had been brought back and, for that matter, if he was still living or already deceased when he arrived.

Of course, not all hope was lost, she was simply being impatient.

There was still the forensic audit of the business and personal finances of the Allen's to be reviewed. Lane was optimistic the audit's findings would reveal a solid motive for Bob's murder. There was also the DNA forensics department. They were supposed to get back to her on the hair found in the ski mask and, hopefully, would successfully pull a fingerprint or identify blood DNA from the rowboat that wasn't from the deceased. Not to mention, who knew where things would lead once Caleb tracked down their missing blonde from the Four Seasons.

She hurried on, seeing his impatient frown.

"We are making progress, though." She took control of the conversation, "Chad, do you know if Kristen and your dad had an open relationship or... if either were unfaithful in the marriage?"

Chad cocked his head to the side, mystified.

"You want to know about my father's love life?"

"I know this may be awkward to talk about, but some questions have come up regarding the fidelity of their relationship."

"Are you telling me Kristen has been messing around?" Chad's voice, still imbued with awe, now carried a hint of anger.

"No. Not that I'm aware. It's actually the other way around." Lane tried a different tactic. "Your father. Would you imagine he was happy in his marital relations?"

"He never complained, if that's what you're asking."

"So, as far you know, they were still..." Lane raised an eyebrow, hoping the slight facial movement would convey her insinuated meaning. "Active?"

"I'm assuming." Chad leaned in and whispered, "I think Viagra is a pretty standard prescription for most men in their fifties." He then leaned back with a smirk and laughed, his face suddenly flushing. "Actually, what am I saying? I know they were."

"Oh?"

"This is embarrassing." Chad shifted in his seat. "I came over unannounced, right before Thanksgiving. Showed up on their doorstep and rang the bell. I thought I heard someone yell, telling me to come in, so I opened the door, not thinking I was walking into a little afternoon delight." Chad shook his head, his cheeks reddening at the memory. "Found Dad pulling up his boxers and the backside of Kristen, in a blonde wig, making a run for the bedroom."

"A blonde wig?"

"Yeah. Spicing things up, I guess."

"So, what happened next?" Lane kept her eyes on the notepad, trying to keep a professional, straight face. "Did you stay or go back home?"

"Dad whisked me out the door, and we went and had a beer. He thought it best if I returned to Seattle, and we all pretended like nothing happened. I was happy to oblige, and it never came up again, not even in teasing. Since then, I've always called or sent a text announcing my pending arrival."

"I can understand why." Lane allowed herself a small smile. "And your dad never mentioned any other women?"

Chad shook his head.

"What about a Mollie Harrison?" Lane prompted.

Chad frowned. "I have no idea who that is."

"Len Harrison's sister? He was the previous mechanic before Jason."

Chad shrugged and then added a nod, rethinking. "Oh, yeah. Now that you mention it, I think I do remember her. Pretty blonde, right?"

"Yes, very pretty."

CHAPTER 33

"Have a good day, Philip!" Mollie chirped, walking past him and out the bank's front door.

"You too!" Philip took a deep breath and made for the exit as well, quick to follow behind. "Oh, hey, Mollie? You got a second?"

Philip, internally, cringed at the audacity of his intentions, having spent the last fifteen minutes staring at a half-filled-out deposit slip, waiting for Mollie to walk past. He'd known her lunch break was roughly around this time and was taking a calculated risk he'd be able to speak with her alone.

"Sure!" Mollie, her smile friendly yet hesitant, stopped on the sidewalk and faced him. "I'm actually on lunch, but if it'll just be a second?"

"Oh, sorry! Listen, are you heading to the Gelato

Deli?" Philip nodded down the street. "Here, I'll walk with you and buy you a sandwich for your trouble." He moved up alongside her. "I'm on my lunch break too. Was planning on taking mine back to the station."

The two began walking in the direction of the sandwich shop.

"So, what can I help you with? Are you interested in a loan? Has Mitchell Wilson finally talked you into buying a boat?" Mollie wrapped her coat tighter around her neck, the February air biting.

"You guessed it," Philip slightly bent the truth, wanting a boat but not interested in actually purchasing one. He fibbed a bit more, "I was hoping to find out about interest rates, but with my hours being so much like the banks."

Mollie nodded, understanding his time crunch. "No problem. If you give me your email, I can send you all the information."

They arrived at the door, and Philip held it open, the smell of freshly baked bread and salami greeting them as they walked in.

Mollie looked up at Philip with a smile, elaborating, "In fact, we can do the whole loan over email, even the signing."

"Wow, email, huh?" Philip sagged a little. He hadn't counted on that. "Great! That'll be helpful. Thanks!" He mustered a smile and waved at the owner, Stefano, behind the counter. "Afternoon, Stef! Can I get my usual and whatever she orders?" He hiked a thumb in Mollie's direction.

"Really, Phil, you don't have to." Mollie suddenly looked suspicious, and Philip wondered if she thought he was hitting on her.

"Oh, come on now. Lane would kill me if I told her I bugged you on your break and then didn't even buy you lunch." He steadily ignored her as he pulled out his wallet, fishing inside for a twenty-dollar bill. "Speaking of my girlfriend. She was hoping you could join us for dinner tonight at the Royal Fork? I know it's late notice." Philip handed the bill to Stefano and took the offered wrapped salami sandwich in exchange.

"Oh! Um. I'll have the—" Mollie's attention was distracted, Stefano asking for her order.

Philip waited until she had finished speaking and added, "I'll be honest. She's trying to play matchmaker," he hurried on, his face reddening, finding the whole conversation way more awkward than he had anticipated. "Harry will be joining us as well. You know Harry, right? From the general store?"

Mollie laughed, a pretty shade of pink coloring her cheeks. "Of course, I know Harry. It's a small island, Phil."

"Right. Sorry." He leaned in a bit closer, his voice lowered, "I don't make the best Cupid, do I?" He suddenly straightened and shrugged, smiling down upon her. "But I can tell you. Harry is a super nice guy. He's got a heart of gold and is a "give the shirt off his back" kind of soul."

Philip moved to a white outdoor metal table, dragged inside for the winter season, and sat, forgetting his claim to return to the office for lunch, and slightly nodded at the opposite seat.

Mollie pulled the chair out with a smile of acceptance and sat down.

He continued, "I admit, he's not much to look at...

"Stop!" Mollie protested and unwrapped her sandwich, knowing Philip was giving her a hard time. "Harry has a nice smile, and he's funny! He reminds me of a big teddy bear." She started to play with the sandwich wrapping, her eyes playfully rolling up to the ceiling. "And I have to confess. I do find him cute."

"Cute?" Philip scrunched up his face, teasing. "Well, I don't see it." He took a huge bite, remembering to cover his mouth as he mumbled, "Anyway, that big teddy bear has been meaning to ask you out. Despite your brother discouraging him."

Mollie frowned and looked down at the table still playing with the paper, her voice apologetic, "I'm not surprised. About Len, that is. He means well." She sighed and gave a furtive look around, the deli practically empty with the exception of two indecisive teenagers scanning the gelato case. "I, uh, I haven't always made the best decisions in regards to my love life."

"Oh, boy. Can I relate." Philip shook his head, his memory involuntarily flashing a nightmarish scene of betrayal from his past. "Try not to be too hard on yourself. As they say, love is blind."

"And stupid." Mollie's shoulders slumped. "It breaks my heart because Len has spent most of his life trying to keep me safe, pulling me out of one disaster or another. Here."

Mollie offered Philip a napkin, pointing to a smear of mayo on his chin, and continued, "Len and I grew up with an abusive father and an alcoholic mother."

Philip hastily wiped his face and scrunched up the napkin, nodding his thanks.

"That must have been hard."

"It was and as soon as I turned eighteen, I bolted. Straight into the arms of a man exactly like our father." She shook her head, disgusted. "And much like my mother, I never left. I tried several times, but... then it was too late." She picked up her sandwich. "Poor Len. He had to drop everything to help me piece my life back together."

She saw Philip's confused expression and explained, "A year ago, my ex beat me so bad I was hospitalized for a month." She pointed to her right eye, where a faint crescent-shaped scar, barely visible, was half-hidden behind the blonde curls cupping her face. "He shattered my eye socket, broke four ribs, and threw me down a flight of stairs breaking my right hip. I was in a coma for two weeks."

"Mollie... that's... I don't even know..." Philip was taken aback, unaware she carried such physical and psychological scars. "I hope he's rotting in jail."

"For the next five years at least. He'll be eligible for parole after that." She shimmed her shoulders as if trying to shake the dreaded thought away. "Anyway, Len had moved to the island for a job and thought it best if I followed along. He's been my overprotective guard dog ever since. Barking at anyone who looks at me funny."

"His moving to the island? Was it to work for Bob Allen at the boat shop?"

Mollie nodded, quickly chewing and, when able, added, "He was there for a few years until he saved up enough for his fishing boat. Now he's the boss, if not a bit grouchy for it. I get worried about him spending so much time alone out there on the water. I keep telling him he needs to hire—"

"What made him decide to move into fishing? That's a pretty big jump from fixing boats." Philip inwardly winced, his question an excuse to change the subject and not really a huge leap at all.

"That would be my fault again," Molly confessed, then glanced at her watch before starting to wrap the remains of her meal. "His boss was hitting on me."

"Roger Allen?"

"The other one."

"Bob." Philip frowned.

When Lane had questioned the fidelity of the Allen's marriage, he had held out hope it was a misunderstanding. Bob hadn't struck him as a cheater. Now, hearing it straight from Mollie, there was no denying it.

"Surprising, huh?" Mollie unknowingly voiced Philip's thoughts. "We were working on an equity loan on the shop. It started as playful banter and the occasional leering stare at my chest, but I ignored him. Then he asked me out to lunch on the mainland to celebrate the loan going through." She put the wrapped hoagie in her purse. "I said something non-committal out of politeness, which he took to heart. Next thing I know, he's sending me inappropriate pictures via text and a reservation link to a hotel in Seattle."

She slung her purse over her shoulder and pushed back her chair.

Philip followed her lead and crumbled up his sandwich wrapper into a small ball, standing up with her.

"When I told him I wasn't interested, he became even more persistent. I finally had to say something to Len because it had gotten so bad."

"And Len set him straight?" Philip could suddenly picture the scene Glen Sorenson had described at the picnic table. Len, angry and protective, in Bob's face, telling him in no uncertain terms to leave his sister alone. Philip didn't blame him. Not one bit.

"Thankfully, it worked. Sort of. The text messages and pictures stopped, but Bob still made an effort to see me at the bank. I had to politely work into our last conversation that if he didn't stop, I'd be having a word with his wife." Mollie suddenly looked somber. "It was the last conversation we had. Hard to believe he's dead. Poor guy."

CHAPTER 34

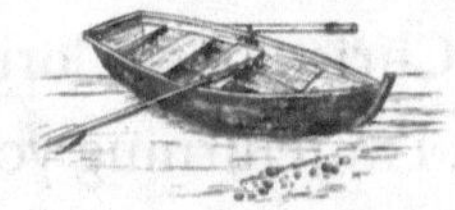

Pulling up to the boat shop, Lane stifled a yawn. It had been a long day with the trek over the ferry and the Seattle traffic, bouncing back and forth between the King County Sheriff's office and the Washington State Patrol's Crime Laboratory, followed by another choppy ferry ride back to the island. She still had to get home, check in on Stinker, and then get ready for the small dinner party at the Royal Fork.

She hopped out of her truck and pulled the evidence bag from the passenger seat, it containing the lockbox and gun she'd taken from the boat shop the day before. The plan was to drop it off, quickly update Kristen on the investigation, and then get herself home.

"Five minutes and then I'm off-duty," she promised herself, seconds before her cell phone exploded in chirps.

Lane gave an audible groan as she looked down at the caller ID stating, 'Possible Spam'.

"Sheriff Lane speaking," she answered, stepping onto the sidewalk, ready to dismiss an annoying telemarketer.

"Hello! This is Christopher Corbin with Colonial Square Assurance. I'm returning your phone call requesting information on Mr. Allen's life insurance claim."

"Oh, yes!" Lane placed the evidence bag down on the cement walk and began to pull out her notepad one-handed. "Thank you for giving me a call back."

"Of course." Christopher paused, the sound of papers shuffling, filling the void until he spoke again, "I think I've got everything you need here. I was able to confirm Mr. Bob Allen had a personal life insurance policy through us for one million with two beneficiaries. His wife, Kristen Allen, and his son, Chad Allen. Both will receive five-hundred thousand each."

"Got it," Lane mumbled, her pen in her mouth as she flipped to a new page.

Finding a blank spot, she snatched the pen from her lips and asked, "Were you able to check with the other agencies?"

"Yes, as far as I can see... Where did that go? That's not it." More papers were shuffled as Mr. Corbin mumbled under his breath, "Wow. We're lucky it wasn't Mrs. Allen." Then in a much louder voice, "Here it is. Looks as if Mr. Allen only had the one policy on him, with the exception of the key holder policy, those premiums being paid by Roger Allen, who looks to also be the sole beneficiary. I believe Roger Allen is also the brother, along with being the deceased's business partner? Is that correct?"

"Yes. How much is that policy for?"

"Well, that's the interesting thing. There are two policies, each on the other business partner, both originally for one million each. Looks as if two weeks ago, both had been increased to two-point-five million."

"Which partner requested the increase?"

"Appears as if both signed. I don't know who was the initiating party."

"Any reason given for the extension in coverage?"

She was briefly answered by more shuffling and a bit-off swear word. The latter in regards to a papercut.

"Sorry, none was noted," Christopher's words were muffled, likely from sucking on his injured finger. "That's all the information I seem to have, Sheriff."

"I understand, Mr. Corbin. Would you be able to send a copy of those to my office? Both the keyholder and personal insurance claims for the entire Allen family?"

"Sure. Is it alright if I have my assistant send them over tomorrow?"

"I would appreciate that, and thank you for your call. Have a good night." Lane hung up, sticking the pen behind her ear and her notepad back into her pocket.

She paused, noting both Kristen's new Land Rover and Roger's Mercedes-Benz were parked up-front. Wondering who else might be in the building, she walked to the backlot and peeked through the fence slat, spotting Jason's red Volkswagen parked by the backdoor. There was no sign of the green Chevrolet Volt.

Her curiosity sated, she made for the front door. The neon sign was unlit in the main window while the cardboard sign, dangling from the door, was posted as OPEN. Unsure if they were closed or not, Lane tried the door. It swung easily, and she stepped in.

From where she stood, she could see the front counter unoccupied and the back-office door wide open, the office itself empty.

"Hello! Anybody around?" Lane called, hearing voices coming from the shop area.

She stepped around the counter and peered in, about to raise her voice in welcome, but stopped when she realized the voices heard, those of Kristen and Roger, were raised in anger, loud and biting, echoing through the tin workshop.

"You backstabbing little whor—"

"Roger!" Kristen's voice, full of venom, cut him

off. "I'd be very careful with your next word."

"What? I'm calling it as I see it. To think, I actually thought—"

"You've lost your mind! You've got to stop this!"

"I'm— I'm the one who's crazy? Kristen! You can't go into business with the damn mechanic!"

"Well, WE can't go into business with each other. That's obvious!" Kristen was leaning against the workbench, her arms across her chest, her bosom heaving, angry eyes pinned on Roger dressed in another designer suit, grey in color, matching his driving gloves.

"What about Chad?" Roger roared, his face purpling.

"What about CHAD?" Kristen suddenly flung her arms in the air. "He's desperate for money and doesn't give a rat's ass about this place, and you know it! But I DO! And another thing? I'll do whatever I have to do to kee—"

"Listen... LISTEN!" Roger held a hand up, arresting her words. "He's, my nephew! There is no way he's going to sell to you! And this IDEA of yours is never going to work! I'm family!"

"Family! Get real, Roger! When was the last time you had him over for dinner? Or gave him a few extra bucks to spend? We both know you're swimming in money, and he's a starving actor. You could—"

"Oh, cut it out! He's got no future in acting. I love

him as if he was my own, but he can't act worth a damn! Even Bob knew it! I don't know why you continue to coddle him."

"You're looking at this all wrong, Roger! If you're not careful—" Kristen began to move towards him but stopped short, spotting Lane. "Sheriff?"

"Hello. Sorry to interrupt. I called out, but I guess no one heard me." Lane took a sheepish step in, finding herself caught red-handed, eavesdropping. "I wanted to return the gun and give an update—"

"I don't want it back," Kristen snapped, running her fingers through her hair and nervously dropping her hand to her chest, fiddling with the top button of her blouse, it unbuttoned so low Lane could see her bra. "Can't you keep it or destroy it?"

"I'm sorry, but—"

"Here, I'll take it for her." Roger strode forward with his hand held out.

Lane looked to Kristen, who gave a solid nod, and she relinquished the bag to Roger's care.

"I'll put it back in the safe before I leave," Roger said as he passed Kristen, walking to the workbench and placing the evidence bag down.

"Fine," Kristen huffed, then rolled her eyes before giving Lane an impatient frown.

Lane hurried on, "I thought I would also update you on the investigation. If, uh, if this is a good time?"

"Of course." Roger, his temper cooled, pulled out

a stool from the workbench and offered it to Lane.

"I'll stand, thank you." Lane gave him an acknowledging smile and then was surprised to see him offer the rejected seat to Kristen instead of taking it for himself.

"Have you arrested anyone?" Kristen asked as she took the seat. She turned her back away from Roger, and faced Lane with her legs crossed, her foot nervously jiggling up and down.

"No. We're still gathering information." Lane cleared her throat. "As I mentioned on the phone earlier today, Bob's gun was not the murder weapon, which is why I'm returning it. Also, the toxicology screen came back clean, indicating he wasn't drugged." Lane paused, expecting questions, but both continued to stare. "Also, my deputy is currently tracking down Bob's last know movements for Friday night."

"Wait a minute." Kristen's brow furrowed. "Why Friday night and not Saturday morning? If you recall, Bob sent me a text on Saturday. Even Chad got one!"

"Yes. We believe the texts were sent by someone else and that Bob was already deceased when you received those messages."

Roger stepped closer and put an arm around Kristen, who was too stunned to push it away.

"We're also investigating how Bob's body arrived back on the island. If he had returned by his own volition or was brought back against his will."

"I can't believe this has happened." Roger removed his arm, roughly running his hands through his grey hair, the action almost convincing Lane it was natural and not a toupee.

"I also spoke with the insurance company. They stated the key holder policy was increased a few weeks ago? Can I ask why, Mr. Allen?"

"What?" Kristen stood up from the stool, facing Roger, her mouth dropping open. "Roger? Why would you—"

"Oh, calm down, Kristen," Roger barked, annoyed at her accusatory tone. "I didn't want to increase it. Bob insisted."

"Why?" Lane got her question in before Kristen could.

"That's personal." Roger stiffened.

"I'm afraid, Mr. Allen, that in a homicide investigation, nothing is—." Lane was interrupted by the sound of the front door opening, Chad and Jason Powell strolling in, the latter holding a box of greasy motor parts.

"Sheriff? What are you doing here?" Chad's eyebrow was raised, his face suddenly concerned as he turned the corner and searched for his uncle and stepmother. "Is everything alright?"

"Of course, it is!" Roger spoke up, waving his nephew towards him. "The sheriff has only stopped by to give us a quick update. Nothing to be worried about." Roger suddenly looked down at his Rolex, and when he looked up, a stern frown was on his face, directed at Jason. "What took you so long? You should have been back an hour ago!"

"That was my fault," Chad volunteered, speaking before Jason could respond. "We bumped into each other on the ferry ride back." Chad caught Lane's eye, not mentioning their own little run-in on the trip over. "And we got to talking about cars. I suggested stopping off at Rowles Towing to see if maybe he had a few extra parts lying around for Jason's Volkswagen." Chad pointed at the box Jason was holding. "Turns out he did."

Jason finally spoke up, his tone hopeful, "I was hoping you'd let me borrow the shop's car until I can get mine running. It should only be for a day or two."

"Absolutely not!" Roger spoke over Chad, who had been about to agree. "That is a company car and only to be used for business. Not your personal loaner car."

Jason's smile dropped for a millisecond, and then he suddenly gave an easy-going grin, rivaling Chad's own debonair smile.

"Sure, Mr. Allen. I completely understand." He nodded, his eyes sweeping over to Kristen. "Then would it be alright if I pulled the Volkswagen inside the shop and worked on it tonight?"

Roger was about to reject this request as well, but Kristen spoke first and gave consent. If only to annoy her brother-in-law.

"Yes, that would be fine." She swung her eyes to Lane. "Was there anything else you needed, Sheriff? It's getting close to five and I've still got a million and one things to do."

Lane eyed Roger, his face almost pleading that she leave her questions unasked regarding the policy change for the keyholder insurance.

"No, that's it." She nodded towards Roger. "I have some paperwork I need you to sign. Can you be in my office first thing tomorrow morning?"

Relieved, Roger immediately nodded.

"I will be there bright and early, Sheriff." He gave her a brief nod as he walked past, grabbing Chad by the elbow, taking him along to the small office, and closing the door behind them.

When the door closed, Lane turned back around to find Kristen and Jason Powell heading towards the backdoor and outside without a word of farewell.

"Hmmm. Looks as if no one wants to stick around for more questions."

CHAPTER 35

From the table, exploded, "That can't be true! No way that's true!" Harry's face turned beet-red, the whole table enjoying a good-hearted laugh at his expense.

"Harry?" Mollie put a gentle hand on his arm, hiding a giggle behind her wine glass. "Did that really happen?"

He bowed his head and a sheepish smile crossed his lips verifying that yes, embarrassing as it was, the story Philip had shared was, indeed, true. He took a quick swig of his beer and then pointed it towards Philip, returning the taunt.

"You're gonna wish you hadn't brought that up, buddy ol' pal!" Harry ribbed, then leaned in, moving aside one of the two wine bottles on the table, that particular one, empty, and addressed Lane, his eyes darting between her and Philip. "Lane? Has Phil ever told you about his rock band in college?"

With a groan of protest, Philip placed his own bottle of beer down next to their empty plates with a loud clunk. "Man, you swore an oath to never bring that up!"

"It was a grunge band in his parent's garage!" Harry divulged with glee as Philip tossed his used napkin at his chest.

"Come on, Harr—"

"Shhh! I wanna hear this!" Lane playfully hit Philip's arm, her eyes still on Harry. "What was the name of the band?"

"Phil? Do you want to tell them, or should I?" Harry leaned back, a wise-crack smile on his face as Lane and Mollie turned their curious eyes upon Philip.

The tables had turned and Philip was now in the hot seat. Their days of misspent-youth and poor decision making, being a great source of entertainment for the small dinner party.

"Traitor," Philip teased, then sighed and shook his head good-naturedly. "To set the scene, it was the nineteen-nineties and grunge bands had off-the-wall names. Nirvana, Pearl Jam, Sound Garden, Alice in Chains, etcetera."

"Oh, and you should have seen him!" Harry interrupted, turning to Mollie. "Dressed in ripped jeans and flannel plaid shirts, long greasy hair, black eyeliner, strutting around like a deranged rooster!"

Philip glared across the table at his oldest friend, pretending to take offense.

"Hey! You're no one to talk!" He pointed at Harry. "Growing your hair out to look like Eddie Vedder! You looked more like a wrung-out mop!"

Harry gaffed, subconsciously rubbing his balding head. "Oh, man! Those were the days!"

Lane filled her wine glass and then Mollie's, the table still laughing.

"So, wait!" She looked over at Philip and tried her best to be serious. "I didn't know you could sing?"

"I can't," Philip admitted with a laugh. "That was our problem." He picked up his beer and clinked it against Lane's wine glass. "Now. Can we change the subject?"

"No, no, no." Lane shook her head, sharing a wink with Harry and Mollie, her tone mischievous. "The band's name? You didn't say!"

Mollie chimed in, "You gotta tell us!" She cuddled closer to Harry, whose smile widened at her touch.

"Come on, tell the girls, Philly boy!" Harry encouraged, determined not to let his buddy off the hook.

"Alright, alright." Philip gave in, holding up his hands. "Like I said, odd band names were popular. The one I came up with was supposed to be ironic."

"More like prophetic," Harry chided.

"Soooo! What was it?" Lane pressed and Philip sighed, his eyes closing in defeat.

"Destined Failure."

The table erupted with laughter, the foursome's amusement causing the neighboring couples to join in with their own smiles at their merry-making.

"Ooooo! That's hilarious." Lane finally caught her breath and wiped a tear from her eye, still giggling. "Oh, this has been a fun dinner!"

"It has!" Mollie concurred, pulling the cloth napkin from her lap and placing it on the table, the universal sign the evening was coming to an end. "And I hate to call it a night, but I do have work early in the morning."

"What time is it?" Harry looked down at his watch, his eyes widening. "That late! I've got to get going too! I'm meeting the butcher at five a.m." He looked over at Mollie. "Can I walk you to your car?"

She gave a shy nod and a smile, her eyes darting over to Lane and then Philip, the smile widening.

"I really had a good time. Thank you for inviting me." Mollie stood and Harry pulled back her chair.

"Glad you could make it! Let's do it again soon." Lane tilted her head and cheered her half-empty glass in Harry's direction. "You both get home safe."

"Night, Har." Philip nodded, giving Mollie a wave as the two left the table and headed for the front door.

"Well, I think that went well." Lane finished her wine with a pleased smile.

"It looked like it." Philip finished off his beer as well, clinking it down on the table. "At least, I sure hope it did for Harry's sake."

"What do you mean by that?"

"I didn't get a chance to tell you. Harry has competition. Kody took Mollie out to the movies the other night, and well, you know he's a bit younger than her."

"What does that have to do with anything?" Lane shook her head, her eyebrows arched. "I mean, what does it matter? He's what? Twenty-four, twenty-five?"

"Twenty-five. That makes her at least six or seven years older than him."

"And Harry is ten years and change, older than Mollie! Why don't you have a problem with that?"

"I didn't say I had a problem. I was only point—"

"Heck, Phil. You're five years older than me! And you know what? You sure didn't seem to have a problem with the age gap between Kristen and Bob Allen." Lane bristled. "But if the woman is OLDER than the man, suddenly you—"

Phil reached over and grabbed her hand, giving it a gentle squeeze. "Hey, hey." He caught her eye, bowing his head low. "I'm not taking issue with her age. At least, not in the way you're thinking." He squeezed her hand again. "Harry is a homebody, okay? Nowadays, a wild and crazy night for him is going bowling and night fishing. His life is taking care of Miss Hattie and running the general store. He might not be as appealing as Kody, who is full of vinegar, willing to kick up his heels and grab life by the throat. That's all I was saying."

Lane huffed and then suddenly smiled up at Philip, her eyes squinting at the corners. He was always surprising her.

She sighed, "Oh, I do like you."

"And I like you." Philip gave her a gentle kiss.

A small tray containing the bill and four chocolate mints slid onto the table, announcing their waitress, Lacey, who was busy refilling their water glasses, the ice clinking against the pitcher as she set it down.

"Aren't you two lovebirds cute!" Lacey gave them a bright smile and started to gather the empty plates left behind by Harry and Mollie, balancing them on her inner forearm. "How was the meal? Everything, okay?"

Lane straightened and physically distanced herself from Philip. Letting go of his hand, she tucked a strand of hair behind her ear and gave Lacey a half-smile with a hasty nod.

"Everything was great. Thanks," Philip answered, frowning, his eyes still on Lane, hurt that she'd pulled away.

"Great! It's been super busy, so when you're ready, you can pay up at the bar." She shot them a knowing smile as if she knew a secret and then bustled off to the kitchen.

"Well, we both have an early start tomorrow." Lane started to push back from the table, grabbing her jacket hanging from the back. "Better get going ourselves."

"Hold on." Philip was still staring, noting that she was doing her best not to meet his eyes. "We need to talk."

"I'm sure they'll want this table, Phil. We should leave so Lacey can finish clearing the dishes."

Lane started to stand and Philip reached out, gently grabbing her by the elbow and pulling her down.

"Lane, are you embarrassed to be dating me?" Philip watched her face, his eyes bouncing from her eyes, to her lips, to her eyes again, trying to translate what he was seeing.

"Phil."

"Because it seems like every time I try to be affectionate in public, you shut me down. I'm starting to feel like a dirty secret."

Lane looked away, her eyes glancing over the neighboring occupied tables, and leaned in closer, lowering her voice, "Can we talk about this back at my place?"

"No." Philip's tone was firm, the timber causing her to sit up, her eyes jerking to his. "Lane, I want to know. Are you? Because if you are, I don't see where—"

She sighed, her shoulders rising with the motion, and shook her head, answering, "Of course, I'm not embarrassed."

Philip gave her a pleased smile.

"But I would like to keep our relationship under wraps. At least for a few more months."

His smile disappeared, and she hurried on, "Phil, I'm the sheriff, and you're the hometown hero. The town folks... If we didn't work out and our relationship soured?" She took another quick glance around and lowered her voice, "I'd be the most hated woman on the island."

Philip's mouth quirked at the edges. "Why wouldn't we work out?" He took her hand, his tone curious.

Lane bit her lip and considered how to reply, then asked, "Have you ever considered, if Allister has his way, that I might not always be the sheriff? If that were to happen, I'd need to move to find another job. Would you be willing to leave the island?"

It was Lane's turn to watch Philip's face, the possible scenario never occurring to him before.

"Phil, this is my career, my chosen profession, and my passion." She tilted her head, seeing wrinkles of concern etch his forehead, and put her hand to her heart. "And I know being a park ranger is yours. You love this island and everyone on it, and I would never want to pull you away."

Philip took a deep breath, inhaling and exhaling out his nose as he nodded, seeing things from a perspective he'd never considered. He paused as he reflected on her words, his eyes looking off in the distance, contemplating.

Lane shook her head, her smile sad. "Maybe it's best we call this quits now?"

"Lane," Philip started, then watched as her eyes moved from his to over his shoulder, focusing on the front door, and then slowly tracking across the room. He turned in time to see Mike Allister casually strolling past the hostess stand to the bar, taking a seat on the first barstool.

"Look who is back from Florida?" Lane whispered under her breath, and Philip nodded, knowing full well, that the conversation about their relationship's future, for now, was over.

"He must be getting his food to go," Philip said, offhanded, placing his silverware on top of his empty plate, Lacey making her way back towards their table.

"Here." Lane pushed the small platter with their restaurant ticket in his direction. "Go up and pay our bill, and see if you can get any information on the lawsuit with Bob Allen."

Philip opened his mouth to object, but Lane had already stood and was saying, loudly, "I'll see you outside, Phil. Thanks, Lacey!" She quickly bent down and whispered in his ear, her eyes still on Mike Allister. "And don't forget to leave a tip."

CHAPTER 36

"That could have gone better." Philip pushed away from the table and muttered under his breath, "Much better."

He stood and snatched up the bill, along with the dinner mints, and stiffly meandered to the bar, intent on Mike Alister, the lawyer looking jet-lagged and impatient. He was staring up at the small flatscreen in the corner of the bar, his fingers impatiently drumming on the countertop, the bartender nowhere to be seen.

"Looks like you got a bit of sun, Mike," Philip pulled out his wallet and leaned against the hostess's stand, giving the lawyer a friendly smile.

Mike Allister, realizing he had been addressed, swiveled on the barstool and looked at Philip, then down at his own forearms, frowning.

"It's sunny in Florida," he said flatly.

"Heard you were down that way for a family emergency. Your brother, wasn't it?" Philip searched his open wallet, keeping eye contact with every other word, and pulled out his debit card. "He on the mend?"

The lawyer nodded, his fingers still tapping the bar top. "Heart attack on the golf course." Allister swiveled forward, ending the conversation with a clipped, "He's fine."

Philip ignored the subtle dismissal and said cheerfully, "Glad to hear it! I'm sure he'll be back on the greens before he knows it."

There was a crash of dishes from the kitchen, and Lacey whizzed by, her index finger held high as she zoomed past, tossing over her shoulder, "I'll be there in a minute, guys!" before approaching a table of twelve to take their order.

"I'm assuming you've already heard about Bob Allen?" Philip asked, now having the perfect excuse to continue their small talk.

Allister swiveled back, nodding his head, and sneered, "Couldn't have happened to a nicer guy, in my opinion."

Philip raised an eyebrow.

Though some considered the semi-retired lawyer a snob, rude, and arrogant, he was also known to be liberal with his time, knowledge, and charitable donations, especially with fellow islanders. For him to make such a statement, there had to be bad blood between them indeed.

"I had heard you were suing him. Guess you're out all that money?"

"Oh, no! Have no doubt. The lawsuit will continue."

Philip looked surprised. "Gonna nail him for every penny he's left behind, huh?"

Allister frowned, the comment seeming to unbend something in the older man.

"You know me better than that, Phil. I wouldn't leave his widow destitute. The poor woman has had a great loss, and I can relate." He shook his head slowly, looking to Philip as if he'd aged right there on the barstool by ten years. "But Roger Allen." His voice turned hard, "He's not off-limits."

"No sympathy for him? Really?"

"None, whatsoever."

"Isn't that a bit harsh? The man has lost a brother and a business partner."

"Business partner, indeed. More like hired-help." Allister slowly looked left to right, then beckoned Philip closer. "Normally, I wouldn't say anything, not wanting to be accused of slander, but since the man is dead and I know you won't say anything, unlike our big-mouthed sheriff—"

"What do you mean big-mouthed?" Philip stepped

closer, unwrapping a chocolate mint and popping it in his mouth, his tone amused.

Mike Allister ignored his question and continued on his original theme, "I hired a private detective for the lawsuit."

"Is that normal?"

Allister nodded impatiently. "Common practice. I felt there were underhanded dealings worth investigating beyond the shoddy workmanship." He tapped the bar countertop heavily, his eyes staring hard at Philip. "Has anyone ever told you what Bob did for a living before opening his shop or how Roger got his millions?"

"Um, Bob was a stockbroker, I believe. I'm assuming he handled Roger's finances?"

"You could say that." He waved Philip even closer, lowering his voice. "Roger Allen's wife died in a freak car accident. According to documentation, it was an electrical malfunction causing the vehicle to speed unexpectedly without the gas pedal being pushed down. The poor woman lost control and Roger, in his grief, sued the car manufacturer. Turns out, the vehicle had a recall for another large issue making waves in the news at the time, so the car company settled out of court."

Allister suddenly straightened, sitting upright on the stool, and swiveled left to right, making sure they weren't being overheard.

Satisfied, he continued, "Roger then gave his money to Bob to invest, making both him and his brother wealthy men. That is until Bob was accused of insider trading. It was only rumored at the time. No official charges were brought. But it must have been more truth than lie because Bob gave up his license. Sold his house and sunk every penny, plus a good deal of Roger's money into opening the repair shop and building the house on the island."

"Seems underhanded, but not villainous."

"I would agree if the detective hadn't also uncovered that Roger's wife was on the verge of leaving him before her accident. Did I mention he also cashed out on a large life insurance policy, additional funds paid out because it was an accidental death?"

Philip let out a long whistle. "You think the car accident was deliberate?"

"The court records were sealed. I have no actual evidence the vehicle had been tampered with. However, if someone had tinkered with the mechanics? My money would be on Bob."

"Are you saying Roger and Bob planned to murder Roger's wife?"

"I'm not "saying" anything," Allister skirted, then added, "But it is suspicious, along with the amount of money Bob was flashing around. He built that huge cabin with every luxury, drove fancy cars, and his wife dressed to the hilt in every expensive brand-name imaginable."

Allister's eyebrows raised, and he tilted his head down as if he were peering through imaginary glasses. "I couldn't possibly correlate how a small island repair shop with only one mechanic could possibly bring in enough income on its own to afford that level of riches. Not to mention the lousy workmanship, which was causing Bob and Roger to lose customers right and left. I was absolutely flabbergasted when he turned down the offer to settle out of court."

"Really? I heard Bob wasn't upset about the lawsuit at all. That he thought it would be thrown out of court."

"Not upset!" Mike Allister raised a silver eyebrow, it practically menacing his hairline. "The man, personally, threatened me! That unpleasant conversation was why I moved my boat to the Seattle Marina to be moored. The little good it did!"

"When was this?" Philip leaned against the bar. "What exactly did he say?"

Allister waved the questions aside but answered, "Before Thanksgiving. I'd mentioned I'd hired the private detective in an attempt to force the issue of settling out of court. The crook turned as white as snow when I mentioned I would be asking the judge to look into his business finances. If you ask me, Bob was up to no good. Possibly laundering money."

"You mean, like for the mob?" Philip asked,

shocked, wondering if George Barnes, after all, had been right."

"The mob? No. That's ridiculous!" Allister chuckled, giving Philip a rare smile. "Probably something related to stocks would be my guess. Anyway, Bob had some choice words for me. Vague threats. Nothing I could prove in a court of law. But I read between the lines. I had my boat towed to Seattle the next day."

Philip looked skeptical, once again, the picture being presented not matching up to his opinion of Bob Allen. "Maybe the shop was losing money, but Roger kept it afloat with his personal cash flow and savings? For the sake of his brother and their business venture?"

Mike Allister started to respond but stiffened, his eyes falling behind Philip.

The ranger turned to see who had caught his attention and saw Lane approaching, her face devoid of a smile.

"Hey? I've still got to pay the bill—," Philip greeted her, Lane stepping between the two men.

"Mr. Allister." She gave a curt nod to the lawyer, then faced Philip, the older man giving a huff of indignation as she turned her back, completely blocking him out of their conversation.

"A 9-1-1 call just came through," Lane whispered, leaning in even closer. "A body has been found at Bobber's Boat shop. We've got to go now."

CHAPTER 37

Climbing into the driver's seat, Caleb hit the dome light as he plucked a pen from his shirt pocket and reached for the metal clipboard sitting in the passenger seat, his thumb pressed against the plunger of the ballpoint, the repeated click unnoticed as he compressed multiple conversations into precise bullet points.

He'd spent the last hour canvassing Roger Allen's neighborhood, walking door to door or rather, traversing one large lawn to another, the houses separated by lavish, park-like grounds and greenery.

The consensus was the same for every door he knocked upon. Roger Allen, as far as his neighbors knew, was home Friday night, his Mercedes-Benz sitting in the driveway left parked in front of the garage, an oddity, it usually stationed inside.

Also, the house lights were on, exterior and interior, indicating someone was home. When asked what time the lights had gone out for the evening, no one could recall. Why would they? This was a safe and quiet neighborhood with no reason to spy upon one's neighbor. After all, why else have security cameras?

Caleb finished scribbling his notes and tossed the log back into the passenger seat, his stomach growling. He laid his head against the headrest, tired, having spent the majority of his day tracking down Chad Allen's alibi for Friday night.

He'd started by chatting up the pretty bar manager at Chad's job, confirming the want-to-be-actor had left work early at around nine p.m. He then made his way to Chad's apartment building, where according to a nosy landlord, he'd had company Friday night, a pretty blonde woman.

"Probably some floozy he picked up from work. He's always bringing strays home. Too bad they don't pay his rent." These had been the landlord's final words on the subject as she pinned an eviction notice on Chad's front door.

Taking her statement to heart, Caleb had gone back to the bar, where he managed to track down the blonde, a fellow actress and regular customer, who was unable to vouch for much of Chad's evening, having passed out on his couch upon arrival.

According to her, she'd been turned down for a part and had proceeded to get drunk in an effort to console her bruised ego.

Instead of getting behind the wheel, Chad had invited her back to his place, mentioning he was leaving to see family, and she'd have the run of the apartment. She had thought nothing of it the next day when she woke up around noon and found his apartment empty.

Another dead end.

The day virtually wasted, Caleb had decided to head over to Roger's neighborhood. Figuring most people would be returning from their corporate jobs or shopping, having the best chance of catching someone at home, the evening growing dark, the sun slipping below the horizon.

Now he was ready to grab dinner via a drive-thru and return to his hotel for an early night. He had plans to tackle the Four Season's food staff first thing in the morning and knew their day started before the sunrise.

A pair of headlights turned onto the street, catching Caleb's attention, the vehicle crawling down the road, the driver keeping to the posted twenty-miles-an-hour before suddenly pulling into Roger's Allen's driveway, the headlights briefly flooding the cruiser and blinding Caleb.

Surprised, he grasped the steering wheel and

blinked away the glare as a green, older Prius sat idle in Roger's driveway, the driver waiting for the third garage door to open.

"Must be the housemaid?" Caleb asked himself, the vehicle carefully entering the garage, the door lowering behind it, swallowing it in one gulp.

As if in answer to his query, lights started to sporadically pop on throughout the house, propelling Caleb to climb out of the cruiser and quickly head to the front door, giving the doorbell a solid push.

Minutes passed, and he wondered if anyone would answer when from inside, he heard a friendly, "Sorry! Just a second!"

The door suddenly opened to reveal a middle-aged woman, her dark hair pulled back in a French braid, with a warm smile that instantly dampened at the sight of Caleb.

"Evening, Ma'am. I'm with Rockfish Island Sheriff's Department. May I have a word?"

"Yes, of course! Um, come in." Without hesitation, the woman, dressed in what reminded him of surgery scrubs, pulled the door wide for him to step inside the foyer. "Is Mr. Allen, okay? Has something happened?" Her voice had a tremor, the tone itself, holding a slight accent he couldn't place.

"Thank you." Caleb gave her a disarming smile, fully aware that good news did not typically show up on one's doorstep in a sheriff's uniform. "Nothing to be concerned about, ma'am. As far as I know, he's fine. I'm only here to ask a few questions regarding his brother, Bob Allen? Are you aware—"

"OH, yes." The woman bobbed her head up and down, cutting him off. "It's so sad, isn't it?" She scooted around, closing the door. "I work for Mr. Allen, by the way."

"Nice to meet you..." Caleb gave her a prompting smile.

"Emma Girard." She returned his smile and beckoned for him to follow. "I was going to put the kettle on. Why don't you come into the kitchen and warm up a bit? That easterly wind is chilly tonight."

"Appreciate that." Caleb followed her down the hall, stopping now and then to peek into the rooms they passed on the way to the kitchen. "Beautiful house."

"Thank you. It's a full-time job to keep it clean!" Emma said, pleased, having taken the comment as recognition to the house's cleanliness versus the expensive items and décor it held. "And it's a good thing it does, or I'd be out of a job." She walked to the kitchen sink, snatching up a tea kettle from the stove on her way, turning on the faucet, and tucking the kettle underneath the running water. "Peppermint or Earl Grey?"

She shut off the flow and moved to the stove, turning a large knob on the stainless-steel top, a blue flame spurting to life.

"Earl Grey, please."

Caleb pulled out a stool from under the over-hanging counter and sat, watching Emma place two mugs onto the marble countertop before pushing a plate of shortbread cookies in his direction.

"Help yourself." She quickly picked up a hand towel and wiped her palms. "I suppose you know Roger is still on the island? I don't expect him back until after the funeral."

"I do. I believe it's in three days? Were you with Mr. Allen, when he found out about his brother's passing?"

"No. I wish I had been." Emma shook her head, plopping a tea bag in each mug. "I only got back into town yesterday." She used the hand towel to give the squeaky-clean counter an unnecessary polish.

"So, you weren't here last Friday?"

"No. I was visiting my new grandbaby. It was good to be home."

"At home? You don't reside, here, in the house?"

"Sorry." She lightly chuckled. "I should have explained that better. I do live here. I have ever since Mrs. Allen died. But I'm from Vancouver."

"I've got an aunt who lives there. It's a nice part of the state."

"No, not Washington. Vancouver, British Columbia." Emma snatched up the kettle whistling behind her and quickly pulled it off the stove, wrenching the large knob and turning off the gas.

"Ah, Canada." Caleb was finally able to place the light accent. "But you live here in the states year-round?"

Emma nodded and poured scalding water into the mugs, the tea bags floating lazily to the surface. "I do. With family in both countries, I have dual citizenship. Apart from working here, I have a special needs sister, and wanted to stay close. She's in a facility."

"And did you fly to Vancouver, B.C.?"

"I drove. It's only like a three-hour drive."

"Yeah, that's not far at all," Caleb acknowledged, disappointed, wishfully thinking he'd solved the mystery of the green Prius seen on the island. "How did you meet Mr. Allen and come to work here?"

"His wife, Laurel. We went to high school together. She was Canadian as well." Emma walked towards the pantry and reached in, pulling out a small honey pot. "I had told her I would be staying in the area, and we reconnected. After her passing, I offered to stop by once a week to clean and help Roger with this big, empty house. The next thing I knew, he was offering me a full-time job and a salary I couldn't refuse."

Caleb plopped a dollop of honey into his mug.

"Sounds like you two got along then." He stirred his tea. "I hope you don't find this question intrusive, but are you and Mr. Allen romantically involved?"

"Heavens no!" Emma laughed, her cheeks reddening. "I mean, he's handsome enough, and believe me, rich enough, but he has only ever seen me as Laurel's friend or the hired help. Besides..." She lifted her braid from her shoulder, grey strands glittering under the bright kitchen lights. "I'm not his type."

"Oh, has he dated much since his wife's passing?"

"A fair amount, but then again, it's been years now. Before her death, he and Laurel were going through a rough patch." She grabbed the string attached to the tea bag and dunked it up and down. "He lost her to a car accident."

Caleb, mid-swallow, nodded his sympathy, and she continued, "I think Roger was able to rebound quicker than most folks who lose a spouse in a tragedy of that kind." She blew on the tea before taking a quick sip. "I don't want you to get the wrong impression. He's not a cold-hearted man. He was devasted when Laurel passed and I know he'd hoped they could work things out."

"Did you think they would?"

Emma shrugged, shaking her head. "I don't know. It takes a strong person to forgive an affair."

CHAPTER 38

The red strobe light of the ambulance lit the backlot like a flare. Lane took a deep breath, her exhaled sigh pluming into the night air and exited the tin building. To her right stood four people, two huddled together, one standing apart, isolated, and Philip, his eyes glued to the trio like a shepherd watching over his frightened flock.

"Sheriff?" Ethan Richardson called to her as he exited the cab of the ambulance. "George Barnes is on his way with the hearse. Need us to stick around?" He slammed the back doors closed, the red strobe going dark.

"No, you guys head on home. Thanks for the assist."

"Night, Sheriff." Ethan turned and waved to Philip, then gave a solemn nod to the remaining three before jumping into the passenger seat, Calvin Morton at the wheel.

"Night, fellas."

The ambulance slowly pulled away, its absence plunging the lot into deep shadows, the overhead street lights barely illuminating the center of the yard, the corners remaining dark.

"What's the verdict?" Philip had wandered over, his eyes darting to the remaining three, his voice hushed.

"Nothing yet. He's examining it now."

The coroner had politely asked Lane to step outside, requesting time to assess the body and scene without distraction, the impatient sheriff peppering him with questions. Questions he did not have the answers to... yet.

Lane slightly nodded towards the three witnesses. "What's going on over there?"

Philip brought his hands to his mouth in a double fist and blew, the exhaled breath warming his skin, then spoke, his words purposely muffled so as not to carry across the yard. "They've been quiet. One smoking like a chimney, the other two, clinging together for warmth or support, I'm not quite sure."

"I can see that." Lane frowned, finding the dynamic surprising.

"Sheriff Lane?" Coroner Ames stuck his head out the backdoor, his eyes raking across the darkened backlot, finally falling on Lane and Philip. "I'm done with my examination."

"On my way in." Lane turned to Philip, her eyes darting past his shoulder, and whispered, "It's too cold out here to make them wait." She sighed, frustrated. "I don't want to release them yet. Can you bring them around front and stick them in the office? And keep the door shut? I don't need them overhearing anything."

"Can do." Philip lightly brushed the brim of his cap in salute before meandering away, while Lane, taking one last look at the odd sight, headed for the backdoor and the coroner.

Stepping inside, the large warehouse was virtually empty with the exception of Jason Powell's Volkswagen Beetle, the trunk open and motor exposed. Lying on the ground beside it, was a body covered with a white sheet, blood soaking the edges, the coroner standing beside it, waiting on her.

"So, is it what it looks like? A suicide?" Lane asked, stopping short of the beaded splatter on the floor.

"You tell me." Coroner Ames snapped on a fresh pair of gloves and cocked an eyebrow. "Ever heard of anybody shooting their brains out while trying to repair their car?"

"No, this would be a first."

"For me, as well. I put time of death around five to seven-thirty. When was the body discovered?"

"Nine."

"Ah, well. At least you know where the weapon came from." He nodded towards the evidence bag, still sitting on the workbench where Roger had left it, the brown bag now ripped open. Next to it, was the lockbox, opened, the .22 Glock missing. Not missing, exactly. The gun was on the floor, still clutched in Jason Powell's stiff hand, his index finger wrapped around the trigger.

The coroner cleared his throat as a silent apology, his comment unnecessary, and turned at the sound of shuffling from behind as Philip led a parade of three people into the small office, shutting the door behind him.

"Witnesses?"

"They found the deceased and called it in." She tugged on a pair of latex gloves and expounded, "They're also tied to the body pulled from the water earlier this week. This was his place. You just saw his wife, brother, and son." She pointed to the deceased man at their feet. "And employee."

"Intriguing. Suspects, then?"

"Absolutely."

"In that case." He bent down, flipping the white sheet back with a flourish. "We could try our luck with a GRS test and see if one of them has fired a gun lately?" He jerked his head towards the office and the awaiting group, the hood of his coat flopping off in the process.

"No point." Lane shook her head, clearly disappointed. "According to their statements, after I returned the gun and left, the two males departed around five-thirty p.m. and headed home, where they enjoyed a couple of beers while hot tubbing. Kristen arrived at the house with a pizza after coming from the gym at six-thirty and once dinner was over, she took a quick shower before she and Chad, he's the son, returned to the office."

"Wow. All three conveniently squeaky clean, then." The coroner pulled the coat hood back over his bald head. "Why'd they come back to the office?"

"The widow "accidentally" left her cell phone behind." Lane gestured with air quotes. "She supposedly realized it was missing when her stepson asked if she'd gotten his text. It was his idea to retrieve the phone instead of waiting until morning."

"Hmmm. Innocent discovery or planned?" Coroner Ames squatted down. "Speaking of a mobile device." He reached carefully into Jason's front pocket and tugged out a cell phone.

"It's probably locked," Lane predicted, irritated at modern technology.

"Probably." He jerked his head towards a small black camera in the corner of the shop before swiping left on the cell phone. "Think anything was caught on video?"

"Recorder was unplugged."

"Unlucky."

"More like suspicious," Lane countered.

"Or he may have not wanted his death record-ed." The coroner sighed and looked down at the pale body, his forehead crinkled. "Suicide IS plausible, Sheriff. He's holding the gun in his dominant hand." The coroner looked up with a smile, beating Lane to the punch, explaining, "His watch." He then pointed to Jason's left wrist and continued, "All three individuals left, forgetting to put the gun away, and Jason here, for whatever reason, decided to use it to take his life. Did anyone find a suicide letter?"

Lane shook her head.

"They don't always leave one, but still." He paused, then gave a grunt of discontent, handing Lane the cell phone, a plastic evidence bag already in hand. "Yup, you're right. Phone is locked."

"Excuse me! Sorry to interrupt!" Philip called from the office, closing the door behind him and stopping short at the entrance of the shop. In his hand, he held a cell phone sheathed in a glittery case. "I think you need to see this. Looks as if Jason sent Kristen a text confessing to Bob's murder."

"You're kidding me." Lane held out her hand, marching towards Philip, mindfully avoiding the splatter on the ground.

Philip handed the phone over and addressed the coroner, who now stood, eagerly curious himself.

"Jason admits to picking Bob up at the hotel under the pretense that there was a problem at the shop. Once he got him here, he killed him. He said he did it for—"

"Love." Lane sighed, looking back at the small office, three faces plastered against the small window, peering back at her. "And money."

She handed the phone to the coroner, who took it, reading out loud.

"It's all my fault."

"I was impatient."

The coroner scrolled as he read,

"I meant to have a man to man talk. To explain."

"I chickened out. Told him there was a problem at the shop."

"I thought I was helping you."

"Don't hate me. I know I've ruined everything."

"Forgive me. Please."

"Well, that seems pretty clear cut." The coroner returned the phone. "What does this, Kristen, say?"

Philip, feeling Lane's eyes on him as well, held up his hands, protesting innocence.

"When she found his texts on her phone she started spouting off before I could come get you."

"What'd she say?" Lane moved her attention back to the office window, Kristen still standing at the glass, a tissue to her eye, her face blotchy.

"Well, she admitted to making Jason a promise, when Bob was alive, that she'd convince Bob to sell his shares to Jason instead of Roger because she thought Roger was undercutting the value of the shop and giving Bob a raw deal."

"And Jason apparently got impatient?" Lane slowly scrolled through the messages again.

"Then tonight, she and Jason got into a fight before she left the shop for the day. It was why she was hesitant to come back to get her cell phone, she didn't want another confrontation."

"Confrontation over what?" The coroner pulled the sheet over Jason's body, Philip's eyes darting between it and the sheriff.

"Apparently, Jason was upset with the way Roger was treating him and growing concerned he wouldn't be allowed to buy into the business. He insinuated that Kristen could do more to persuade Roger's decision, which she did not take kindly. The conversation ended with a hint that Jason might want to start looking for a new job."

"Thus, the apology text." The coroner stood and dusted his knees before grabbing at the base of his wrist, removing his glove. "He's taken a life and with no payout. Reason enough."

"Officially a suicide, then?" Lane turned, her eyes searching his solemn face.

"Well, that depends." He stuffed the used glove into his coat pocket. "I've bagged the hands so I can run a gun residue test. Holding a gun is not the same as shooting one. But, if it's there... then yeah, I'll rule it a suicide." He looked at the sheriff, giving her an anemic smile. "On the bright side, sounds like case closed on the floater. Not a bad night, huh, Sheriff?"

CHAPTER 39

Caleb took a seat, his eyes roaming the office walls. As he did, a smile of appreciation spread upon his lips at the contrast between the upstairs hotel manager's pristine office and the one he sat in now.

This office, belonging to the kitchen manager, though clean and tidy, was busy and utilized. A huge whiteboard hung on the wall with a rainbow of pen marks etched on its front, marking dates, times, and scheduled events. There were files piled on the desktop, held down by a large paperweight, and a coffee mug full of hotel pens, sitting next to a bronze name plate, titled Lillian Adams - Kitchen Manager.

He was waiting for Ms. Adams, who was nice enough to take his appointment at the last minute, a call he had made on his own without Bailee's assistance, convinced she would have done her best to dissuade him from interrupting the flow of the hotel.

"Sorry, it's a madhouse today. I've got two servers out sick with head colds." She shut the door behind her and beamed at Caleb. "The nasty little bug is, unfortunately, making the rounds. I had four out yesterday." At this comment, Ms. Adams, dressed in an ill-fitted blue blazer and pencil skirt, produced a used tissue from her blazer pocket and quickly wiped at her running nose. She stuffed the tissue back and extended her hand with an eager smile. "It's nice to meet you."

Caleb stood and politely shook her hand, cringing inwardly, and then sat down, inconspicuously wiping his palm on his pants leg as he did so.

"Thank you for meeting with me. I'll try not to take up too much of your time."

"Oh, no worries. I could use the break." She waved a friendly hand in his direction and unbuttoned the blazer button as she sat down, her plump stomach pooching out. "You had a question about one of the wait staff?"

"Yes. I'm wondering about a Lilli that worked last Friday? Red hair, freckles? As I understand it, she had started that night and then no-showed the next day, Saturday?"

"Well, that doesn't sound familiar at all, but let me check." She stood up and walked over to a tall black filing cabinet. "What was the last name?"

"Oh, um." Caleb pulled the room service receipt Bailee had given him a few days before and read the bottom. "Adams."

"Well, you'd think I'd remember. That's my last name." She laughed as she pulled the top drawer open, her fingers rifling through the files. "No, that's what I thought. I don't see a file for a Lilli Adams. You sure it was Adams? I have a Lori Adan and a Lonnie Akers."

"Yeah, it's right here." Caleb stood up and walked over, pointing to the bottom of the receipt. "Adams, Lilli. L-I-L-L-I."

"Can I see that?" She took the receipt from his hand, and extended her other, inviting him to sit back down, returning to her seat as well. "Um..." She took a deep breath and let it out in a guff of laughter. "This is me!" She pointed to the receipt, her smile widening at Caleb's surprise, and then pointed at her bronze nameplate sitting on the desktop. "Lillian Adams."

He blinked at the small plaque and then looked up at the kitchen manager, confused.

"I don't understand."

"Well, the system uses the first five letters of the first and last name to identify the wait staff taking the order. I took this order. See. Adams - and then the first five letters of my first name, Lilli."

Caleb shook his head, his frown deepening. He had instantly comprehended the initial explanation, kicking himself that he hadn't put two and two together when he'd seen the nameplate upon arrival in the office. What he didn't understand was where the red hair and freckles came in, or the rent-a-day hotel. No wonder the motel manager hadn't recognized the name or description.

"Do you remember that food order? Were you the one to deliver it to the requesting room?"

"Well, I can't say off the top of my head, but let's look it up." Lillian Adams was enjoying herself, not bothering to query why the deputy was asking or why he was even in her office. She was accommodating in her customer service skills and had learned a long time ago to be obliging without asking undue questions.

She squinted down at the small receipt and punched a five-digit code into her computer, then turned her gaze to the large screen, her eyes widening back to normal.

"Oh, yes. I remember this! Mr. Allen." She was nodding her head. "An Elite guest." She said it almost in reverence, her voice lowered to a practical hush. "Very important."

"I'm familiar with the status. Who was the server that actually delivered the food cart to his room? Was it you?" Caleb leaned forward, wondering if maybe this was where the redhead had come into play? He may have had the name wrong, but the girl described actually existed.

"No, it wasn't me. Mr. Allen was... special." Lillian looked abashed and explained, "It's not uncommon for our Elite guest services to facilitate meals for their favorite members. In fact! It was our Elite Manager, Bailee. She came down and requested the meal to be expedited over other orders. I was able to accommodate and she took the cart up herself to Mr. Allen's room."

Caleb could feel the heat rising up his neck, and did his best to keep his voice level when he asked, "The cart. Did Bailee bring it back down after dropping off the meal?"

"No." Lillian, absent-mindedly, shook her head, still looking at the computer screen. "Looks as if it was found out in the staff parking lot the next morning." She suddenly leaned in, wiping her nose, and added, amused, "Our trollies pop up in the weirdest places. You'd be amazed at some of the stories I could tell!"

CHAPTER 40

"Man, I'm gonna be so late to work." Philip yawned and his boots tiredly stuttered to a stop as he peered down at his watch, seagulls circling above.

"The kid won't be happy with me. That's twice this week," he muttered to himself, remembering all the occasions he'd given Kody a hard time for being late to the office.

Accepting there wasn't much he could do about it, Philip turned his attention to the blue fishing boat anchored at the end of the pier, relieved to see Len Harrison standing on the deck. Praying Len wouldn't suddenly disappear into the bowels of his own ship, Philip tucked his chin into his coat, the early morning wind biting, and quickly paced to the end of the fishing pier, his boots thudding down the worn wooden timber.

"Ahoy, Captain!" Philip gave a friendly bellow as he worked his way up the loading plank. "Permission to board?" He abruptly stopped, his boot hovering inches above the platform, waiting patiently for approval before boarding.

In the midst of swabbing the deck, Len stopped and stared, the unfriendly scowl on his face an apparent answer to the question.

Reading the facial expression accurately, Philip cleared his throat and pulled from his jacket the excuse for visiting. "Mornin'! Hattie asked me to drop this off on my way to work." Philip dangled a small brown paper bag in the air.

At the mention of Hattie, Len's scowl of certainty turned uncertain.

Philip hurried on, "So, mind if I?" He nodded towards his extended, levitating foot, silently asking to step down onto the deck.

"Come on aboard," Len begrudgingly instructed as he relinquished his mop, propping it against the boat railing, and crossed the deck to Philip, his hand outstretched for the bag. "What is it?"

"She didn't say, and I didn't ask," Philip lied, knowing full well it was more of Hattie's hand salve, which by the look of it, was doing the trick. The grouchy fisherman's hands were no longer chapped or red, the long scratches healed.

"She's also invited you and Mollie to dinner next Friday at six."

At the invitation, Philip watched Len's face soften, even more, the hard exterior melting. Knowing what he knew about Len and Mollie's childhood, Philip could understand how the warmth of Hattie's generosity and kindness might soften a guarded heart, especially for someone in search of found family.

Philip continued, "I'm jealous. Hattie doesn't cook often, but she makes the best chicken pot pie around when she does. You must have made a good impression on her."

Len shyly avoided Philip's stare and peered inside the bag, a slim smile breaking through the seemingly permanent scowl. "She's a nice old lady." Len closed the bag. "Thanks for dropping this off."

"You were on my way, but you're welcome."

Philip gave a friendly smile and a wave before turning as if he would leave, suddenly pausing. "Oh, and dinner? Should I tell Hattie, yes?"

Len, for an answer, nodded, his cheeks reddening.

"Good. That'll make her day. Thanks, Len." Philip put his hand on the boat railing but didn't move, his face dampening. "I, uh, I'm assuming you've heard about Jason Powell?"

In the process of stuffing the brown bag into his slicker, Len stopped and looked up, mildly curious.

"I don't get much news out here."

Philip bowed his head, demonstrating he was about to deliver some bad news. "Well, I'm afraid he was found dead at the repair shop last night. Apparent suicide."

Len's scowl reappeared. "Suicide? He never struck me as the type." Len sat down on the edge of the deck and looked up at Philip. "Liked himself too much."

"Yeah? I know you used to work together. Did the two of you stay in touch?"

"Nah." Len shook his head, then said, in a practical whisper, "He was bad news."

"I'm sorry. Did you say, bad news?"

Len nodded, then shook his head in a fluid motion, his frown deepening. "Sticky fingers and a bad temper. You don't wanna get...," he stopped and amended, "Sorry, you DIDN'T want to get on his bad side. Ask Dub Granger. He could tell you."

Philip raised an eyebrow, intrigued. "Dub?" Philip gave him a coy smile. "I'm sure he would, but I don't have three hours to spare." He gave Len's arm a light punch, invoking a knowing nod and a shrug of the shoulders. "Think you can take pity and fill me in?"

"Yeah, he's an ol' windbag, that's for sure." Len seemed to relax, the two men finding common ground, and then added, "Well, it can't hurt to tell anyone now, I guess." He looked up at Philip, his face scowl free. "Right before I left the job, Dub complained to Bob about Jason's piss-poor attitude, and in retaliation, Jason put sugar in Dub's trawling motor."

"Sabotage?" Philip's tone made it clear he believed Len's story but was curious how he knew.

"Bragged about it over a beer. Even showed me the bag of sugar."

"And you didn't report him?"

"It wasn't any of my business. Not anymore. I'd given notice, and it was my last day of work. Besides, Bob Allen wouldn't have done anything about it."

"You could have talked to Roger? What with the lawsuit—."

"That's why I kept my mouth shut. I figured Dub would get his money back one way or another. Besides, I didn't owe Bob, or for that matter, Roger, any sense of loyalty."

"Not even Kristen? Or was it because she and Jason got along well together?" Philip let the tone of his question hint at something carnal between them.

"Those two? He wished!" Len scoffed. "Jason tried it on a few times, but she always shot him down."

"Because she was married?"

"No," Len answered, matter of fact. "It was because he didn't have any money. Don't get me wrong. She loved to flirt. Didn't matter if it was Jason, the customers, or even Roger. She'd bat those big blue eyes of hers and —"

"Hold up." Philip waved his hand in the air stopping Len. "Roger?" Philip was dumbfounded. "Those two hate each other! I can't picture Kristen batting Roger with anything other than a baseball bat!"

Len laughed, an actual smile breaking across his face. "That may be the case now. But don't think Roger didn't try his luck as well. If only for revenge."

"Revenge? Who did he want rev—?"

"His brother!" Len leaned forward, moving the brown paper bag from one hand to another. "Bob broke up Roger's marriage. He was having an affair with his brother's wife before her accident."

"Get out of here! Did Kristen know?"

Len shrugged, suddenly tossing the little bag up and catching it, his tone almost jovial. "Probably not. It was before they met and married. Even if she did, I don't think she'd have cared as long as she could treat the shop as a personal piggy bank. That woman loved to spend money."

Len rubbed his nose, the tip red from the crisp morning air. He continued, "There were some weeks the shop barely made payroll, business being so slow. If I'd been the bookkeeper, I'd have been pinching pennies. Not Kristen. She spent cash as fast as the government could print it."

Len suddenly snorted and spat over the side, using the back of his hand to wipe his mouth before speaking again.

"And then Bob had his grown-ass son coming around for handouts all the time." Len went from pleasant to bitter. "His kid had a job waiting for him at the shop, anytime he wanted it, but he couldn't bear to get his hands dirty." Len huffed, his resentment starting to boil at the memory. "Both Chad and Kristen acted as if Bob was a walking ATM."

"I would have thought the repair shop, being the only one on the island, would have been booming?" Philip inched closer.

"Yeah, well. At first, hand over fist." Len folded his arms across his chest. "Then Bob started stocking cheap parts, which caused more issues and for a while, repeat business to fix the unknown recurring problem. This was until customers started getting upset. When I complained we were backlogged with orders and needed his help, Bob hired Jason, and that's when things really started going downhill."

"Downhill, as in, the lawsuit?" Philip leaned against the railing and crossed his ankles.

"If he'd hired someone with some real mechanical knowledge and paid for good parts..."

"There wasn't anything underhanded going on, was there?"

Len looked surprised, then thoughtful. "Could have been. But if there was, I wasn't in on the cut. I kept my head low, did the job I was hired for, and put my money in the bank until I could buy my freedom." He unlocked his arms and patted the railing of his fishing boat, another rare smile crossing his lips.

"Then... Bob hitting on Mollie had no bearing on you quitting?"

Len straightened to attention, the question hitting a nerve, and sniped, "That Glen Sorenson sure has a big mouth!" He shook his head, disgusted. "Told you about Bob and I's shoving match, did he?"

Philip nodded and wisely kept silent.

Though Glen had mentioned the confrontation between employer and employee, it was Mollie who had shared the details of Bob's adulterous actions over lunch the day before.

Len turned rigid, the relaxed attitude of earlier gone. "Well, it's none of Glen's business."

"No, it's not, and it's none of mine either, but I hope you don't mind me saying I think it was a solid move to protect your sister." Philip slipped his hands into his coat pocket to keep warm and shrugged. "Sounds as if Bob wasn't the type of guy you'd want around any woman, let alone family."

"The guy was a pig!" Len snarled, then stood, stuffing the wrinkled bag into his slicker with force. "As far as I'm concerned, he had it comin'!"

"You're glad he's dead." Philip meant to say it as a question, but the words came out as a stern statement.

"Well, he's not around to harass my sister anymore, now, is he? Yeah, I'd say I'm glad."

CHAPTER 41

"What are you doing here so early?" Martha called from the front door as she shrugged out of her jacket and tossed it on the coat rack. "George didn't get home with the remains until well after midnight. I can't imagine you got home any sooner!" She walked straight to Lane's office and popped her head around the corner. "It's not even six a.m. yet!"

"I couldn't sleep," Lane admitted, a yawn suddenly breaking out, her following words a jumble.

"Say again?" Martha laughed and leaned against the door jamb, tugging off her gloves.

"I said," Lane covered her mouth to hide the gaping yawn. "I thought I'd rehash the evidence. By the way, found the forensic accounting report on the fax machine."

"They must have sent it over after I left." Martha hitched her purse over her shoulder and added, "My George says Jason left a confession suicide text?"

"How does George know about that?" Lane's tone was incredulous.

"You don't seem happy about it."

"I'm not! George shouldn't have known—"

"Not George! About the confession."

"Oh, well, you're right. I'm not. The confession text was vague and open to interpretation." Lane rubbed her forehead, her fingers trailing to her temples. "And until the coroner officially calls Jason's death a suicide, our office is going to keep investigating Bob's murder as an open case."

"Better safe than sorry." Martha, wanting to change the subject, suddenly moved to the chair by Lane's desk and cozied up, her voice lowering into a gossipy whisper, "Listen, Sheriff. Um, yesterday, about Mike Allister. You mentioned another woman—"

"Martha, would you be a dear and get me a coffee? I'm about to fall asleep right here at my desk," Lane asked sweetly, doing her best to stave off Martha's incoming questions about Allister and the mystery female.

"Sure. But uh, this... woman... she went with Mike to Florida?"

Lane quickly snatched a report from the pile on her desk and began to peruse it, adding casually, as if she hadn't heard Martha's question, "And can you put it in the biggest mug you can find?"

"Ohhhh!" Martha stood, her lips pursed in annoyance, and lightly slapped Lane's desk with her gloves. "I'll be back, but don't think I'm going to drop this."

"Believe me, I know," Lane muttered under her breath and turned her full attention to the form in hand. It was a fascinating read.

Not only had the accounting forensics department reported on Bob and Kristen's finances, but Roger and Chad's as well.

The married couple's finances had been no surprise at all, Lane recalling Martha's comment about Bob being in debt up to his eyeballs. Though, she was astounded, at the reason of accumulated debt.

Having assumed it was due to a failing business and pending lawsuit, her jaw dropped upon reading that Bob was playing the stock market and losing... badly. The margin calls so severe that he'd taken an equity loan on the repair shop and opened additional lines of credit under Roger's name.

The desperate man was committing fraud against his brother and their business in an attempt to keep up with the lifestyle he could no longer afford.

Lane scanned down to the life insurance amounts listed for the couple, suddenly understanding the insurance agent's comment regarding Kristen.

"He wasn't kidding. That's a lot of dough."

She flipped to the next page. Like father, like son, Chad too lived off of credit cards. At an alarming rate, the thirty-something was transferring balances to freshly opened accounts, then, in turn, racking up the zeroed-out credit cards while paying only the minimum required. It was clear this juggling act wouldn't work for long, and when the balls eventually dropped, he'd be in need of a considerable payout to escape his mounting debt.

Lane wondered where he thought that relief might come from, be it his acting career taking off or an upcoming inheritance?

The financial support he was receiving from his father had been dwindling, and according to her deputy's late-night text, Chad was soon to be evicted from his own apartment. Where did he plan on going? How serendipitous was his father's death?

As for Kristen, her spending habits never faltered, and she appeared to either be unaware of their dire financial situation, which seemed odd, as she was the bookkeeper, or she hadn't cared. Possibly, when all the money was gone, and everything had come to light, she would have left Bob for richer shores? Kristen didn't strike Lane as the type of woman to stick by a man's side through thick or thin and definitely not for richer or poorer.

On the other hand, Roger Allen had no financial worries, not counting the fraudulent accounts opened by his brother that Lane was fairly sure he knew nothing about. It appeared Roger was unaware of the embezzlement by his brother, which was surprising, as Roger struck her as a man who would notice such blaring signs. Had the shop lawsuit been that much of a distraction? Then again, Bob was not just his business partner but his only brother. One would hardly imagine being betrayed like that.

As if thinking of Roger had conjured him into being, Martha walked into Lane's office, holding, as requested, the biggest coffee mug she could find, along with Roger Allen in tow.

"There, Sheriff." Martha set the big mug down, coffee slopping over the rim in her haste. "Can I get you a cup, Mr. Allen?"

Dressed in a leather coat with matching driving gloves, a white t-shirt, and jeans, Roger Allen sat down in the vacant chair next to Lane's desk. The man looked exhausted, which wasn't surprising, considering the events of last night on top of the loss of his brother, the upheaval of the business, and its unknown future.

"No, no thank you. I'll only be a minute." Roger gave Martha a nod of dismissal as if it were his office and turned to Lane. "I wanted to come by as promised, but I'm assuming you have more important matters to attend to other than asking me frivolous questions, so I won't take up much of your time. I'd like a progress report. No one was able to tell us—."

"Frivolous?" Lane interrupted, her mouth quirking at Roger's statement. "Sorry to disagree, Mr. Allen, but I don't find increasing a life insurance policy months before the death of the signee exactly a waste of time?"

"I'm sure you wouldn't, normally. But in light of Jason's confession, don't you find it frivolous now? You did see the text messages on Kristen's phone?"

"I did. However, the coroner has not officially declared Jason's death a suicide, and there are still some unanswered questions."

"Such as?" Roger, annoyed, leaned forward, insistent. "I would think it's pretty clear, Sheriff. The young man wanted to step into my dead brother's shoes! He wanted his wife, his business, his home, his bank accounts, everything! It was bad enough he was treating my business like a loan department."

"What do you mean?"

"Oh, I caught him on tape taking money from the til and then paying it back on his paydays. Probably to pay for fixing that jalopy. If he hadn't done himself in, I was going to fire him."

Lane suddenly realized what Jason had hidden in his overalls the day she saw him in the back lot. He must have come into work early, intent on sneaking the stolen funds back into the shop's register.

"Speaking of money, Mr. Allen." Lane sorted through the papers on her desk and, finding what she wanted, placed it in front of him. "This is a forensic accounting report. I suggest you contact your financial advisor. It appears that, and I'm sorry to be the one to tell you this, Bob was embezzling funds from the repair shop."

Roger looked genuinely shocked.

"And, that's not the worst of it, I'm afraid. He also opened several lines of credit under your name. A clear case of identity theft."

"I don't understand." Roger gathered the report from the desk, his eyes running down the length of the page and onto the next. "But why did he need the money?"

"Excess margin calls."

"Caused by insider trading backfire, no doubt!" Roger spat. "Sorry, Sheriff, but my brother was always a sucker for a quick windfall." He shook his head, tossing the sheet onto her desk. "Thank you for letting me know. I'll... I'll take care of everything."

Lane nodded and shuffled the page back into the report, changing the subject, "Kristen experienced quite the shock last night. How is she this morning?"

"Still stunned." His earlier bravado gone, Roger leaned back into the chair and swiped at his grey mane. "As is Chad. He's waiting in the car. I really should be on my way."

"Speaking of your nephew, has he decided what he's going to do with his share of the business?"

Lane wasn't ready for Roger to leave.

"He's still undecided." Roger's tone was terse.

"Really? I mean, with Jason no longer being an option, it really comes down to selling to either you or Kristen, unless he's decided to keep the shares?" Lane took a quick sip of her coffee, holding the cup high enough to hide her mouth as she added, "Not that the shares mean much now."

Roger frowned, his face reddening.

"Sheriff, what exactly do you mean by that?"

Lane quickly shook her head, putting the cup down, her eyes wide and innocent. "I'm so sorry. That was insensitive of me. It's just that I know Chad is in great need of money, and with the lawsuit... I don't suppose he's told you he's about to be evicted from his apartment?"

"No, he hasn't." Roger gave an exasperated sigh and sat up, ready to stand. "But as executor of my brother's will, I'll see he gets enough funds to correct the issue."

"Not a personal loan?" Lane asked, her eyes wide with surprise. "He's your nephew. I'm surprised you'd make him wait until the will was out of probate."

"Of course, if he asks, I'll lend him whatever he needs. Now, I've got to get going." He suddenly reached behind him and pulled out a wallet. "Can I have you fax a copy of the accounting report to my financial advisor? I've got his card right here."

Roger pried open the leather pocket, a large amount of cash inside threatening to tumble out as he tugged a business card from a side slot.

"That's an interesting wallet." Lane's full attention was on the worked leather, initials stamped into the brown calfskin. "Are those your initials?"

Roger tilted the wallet to the side so she could see more clearly.

"They are." He cleared his throat and placed the card on her desk. "It was a Christmas gift."

"R.E.A," Lane quoted. "What does the "E" stand for?"

"Ernest." Roger sorted his cash, tucking it back inside the middle fold. "I was named after my maternal grandfather and Bob, our paternal. Grandpa Gene."

"B.G.A," Lane muttered to herself, scribbling the initials down on a post-it note before turning back to Roger, her eye drawn to the door, where Chad stood, his eyes glued to the cash sticking out of Roger's wallet.

"Hey." Chad licked his lips, his eyes still on the cash. "I got tired of waiting in the car."

"Sorry, your uncle and I were discussing initials." Lane pointed to the wallet. "What's your middle name, Chad?"

The nephew blinked, then frowned at Lane before answering. "Roger."

"Ah, that's nice." Lane gave him a warm smile. "Your uncle being your namesake.

Roger suddenly cleared his throat. "Yes, well, we need to be going." His brow furrowed as he returned the wallet to his jean pocket and stood. "I promised I'd bring Kristen back some breakfast."

"You two starting to get along?"

"Hope so." Roger headed for the door and slapped a hand on Chad's shoulder. "It's been a rough week and I'm tired of fighting. I think we all are." He squeezed Chad's shoulder and his expression shifted to mildly surprised. "You're tense, Son! I think a soak in the hot tub might do you wonders. Let's get back home."

Chad numbly nodded his head as Roger turned his attention back to Lane.

"If you need anything else, Sheriff, kindly contact us after the funeral tomorrow."

"I may need to—"

"Have a good day." Roger cut her off with a curt nod, then placed a firm hand on Chad's shoulder, practically pushing his nephew out the door.

CHAPTER 42

"Yes, Mrs. Oestreich, you are confirmed for Wednesday of next week. Yes, the sixteenth." Bailee's pen bounced against the calendar in annoyance, the ballpoint tattooing the appointment entry. "No, the fifteenth is a Tuesday. You said you wanted the sixteenth, which would be Wednesday. Wednesday is the sixteenth."

At the sound of the office door opening, Bailee straightened in her chair, and her voice suddenly dripped like sweet syrup into the phone, "Yes, I also booked your spa facial for the same day. Yes, Wednesday."

She held up a finger and beamed at the unknown guest, her thousand-watt smile flat-lining as soon as she recognized Deputy Pickens.

Caleb returned Bailee's initial smile, and took a

seat in one of the chairs positioned in front of her desk, and whispered, "Got a second?"

Bailee shook her head but said into the phone, "Yes, I'm still here. Of course, I understand and thank you for choosing the Four Seasons, Mrs. Oestreich. We look forward to seeing you on Tuesday." She frowned and quickly corrected herself, "Ah, I'm sorry, I meant Wednesday. Yes, Wednesday the sixteenth." Bailee hung up the phone and made a quick checkmark by the name Oestreich before addressing Caleb, her tone bordering on rudeness, "Deputy, I'm afraid I'm rather busy at the moment."

"Oh, I won't take long. I promise." Caleb held up a hand, begging pardon, and then plucked a folded paper from his shirt pocket. "I'm sure you have time for one question, don't you?"

He grinned as he unfolded and placed the wrinkled and well-worn receipt down on the desk, turning the fragile scrap of paper so Bailee could see it.

"Well, if it is important," Bailee, her smile tight, consented. "What's your question?"

"The Elite guests. I, uh..." He flashed her a hotel brochure and then explained, "I picked this up in your little mini lobby outside your office." He unfolded and scanned the page, his finger resting on the third paragraph down. "It says here, there are three floors dedicated to Elite members only." He flipped the brochure and pointed to a miniature map on the back. "And it looks as if those are close to all the amenities?"

"Yes. That is correct."

"So, here is my actual question." He tapped the receipt on the desk, his large finger looming over the room number printed at the top. "The room Bob was assigned. It wasn't on any of the Elite floors. Why was that?"

"Oh, I..." Bailee shrugged. "I must have hit the wrong key. It can happen sometimes when I'm in a hurry. Friday evenings are always busy with guests checking in for the weekend."

"Yeah. I thought about that," The deputy admitted with a slow nod. "Then I remembered Bob's hotel room being sandwiched between the ice and vending machines and the staff elevator." He suddenly leaned forward, his eyes earnest. "Now, I know Bob was pretty friendly. That he came across as an easy-going guy. But let me tell you, Bob..." Caleb suddenly shook his head and corrected himself, "Sorry, Bobby. Bobby loved to live life at its finest. I mean, you should see his cabin on the island, and the fancy car he drove. Way out of my price range. Oh, and his wife! Always dressed to the nines in some expensive designer outfit!" Caleb tapped the brochure against the edge of the desk and drew Bailee's eye.

"I tell you this because... Bobby, who is used to being placed in an Elite room, on the Elite floor, and living life high on the hog... Well, I'm pretty sure he would have taken one look at that room and made a straight beeline back down to the lobby to complain." Caleb raised his eyebrows and tilted his head down. "But he didn't. Why do you think that was?"

He didn't wait for her to respond, the young woman's deer in the headlight look, answer enough.

"Let me tell you my little theory, Bailee. And mind you, I had a nice visit with Lillian Adams, the hotel kitchen manager." He decided not to mention the hasty trip afterwards to the security room and instead, tapped the printed name listed at the bottom of the receipt. "My theory is that Bob did make it to his hotel room. But once inside, he was either knocked out or killed by your partner."

Bailee's eyes widened and she gave a small gasp, her hand flying to her heart.

Caleb continued, his voice steel, "Meanwhile, off-duty, you've rushed down to the kitchen demanding a meal. Your wish is granted and you wheel the large food trolley to Bob's room, where your partner stuffs the body under the white draped linen, and takes the staff elevator down to the lobby, with the hall camera conveniently not being a concern."

Bailee gave a feeble shake of her head, her blonde curls waving, words failing her.

"He, and I say he, because we've got him on video, then rolls the trolley out to the staff parking lot, where your vehicle is parked closest to the door. Does that sound about right?"

"No! It's, it's..." Bailee's professional demeanor was gone, her words coming out desperate. "It's not what you think! I was only—"

"I think!" Caleb lurched back, placing a large hand on his chest. "I think your job was to wait in the hotel room and make it look as if Bob never left. You had yourself some dinner, watched some TV, and when you got tired... climbed yourself into Bobby's pajamas, and fell asleep in his bed."

Caleb smirked at the memory of finding blonde hairs on the bedding and Bob's clothing.

He continued, his voice harsh, "Then morning came. You replied to a couple of text messages, before leaving the room key behind, with your fingerprints on top of his, which is why you tried to wipe them off. You then left the room as if nothing happened." Caleb, his eyes hard, bent forward. "Except something did happen, Bailee. A man was murdered, and his death is partially at your hand. That's called being an accessory to murder."

"Hold on!" Bailee bolted from her chair, her head swinging side to side, her eyes wide. "That's not what happened!"

"Bailee, the hotel's security tapes show the man on video getting into your car."

"Yes, they do!" Bailee began to urgently nod in

agreement. "You're seeing BOBBY! Bobby is the one on video! He's the driver!"

Caleb frowned in disbelief and directed her to sit.

The scared woman immediately plunged herself back into the chair and gripped the side of the desk, knuckles white. "Please, Deputy Pickens! You need to believe me! This has been such a nightmare."

"I don't know. It's hard to believe somebody who has done nothing but lie from the second I met her."

"I understand, but you see, Bobby... Bobby and I were... I didn't want to lose my job. This is so hard to explain! We were having an affair."

Caleb, unable to help himself, made a disgusted face.

"It wasn't tawdry, he was divorcing his wife." Bailee's back straightened, regaining some of her poshness.

"He told you he'd get a divorce?"

Caleb knew from their investigation into the boat shop owner, that neither Bob nor Kristen had a divorce attorney on retainer.

"Not would. WAS getting a divorce." Bailee took a deep breath and set her shoulders. "His selfish soon-to-be-ex has been dragging everything out, begging for more money. She even went so far as to hire a bunch of private detectives to follow him."

"Follow? Wait, did she suspect he was cheating on their marriage?"

"Yes, but you see, Bobby suspected her doing the same."

"Did he say with who?" Caleb's breath hitched, his body inching forward. "Did he give a name?"

Bailee pressed her lips together and nodded, answering, "An employee named Jason. Bobby was convinced if he left the island, the two would shack up together and he'd be able to get the proof he needed, so he'd have the upper hand in divorce court."

"So, you booked the room, bumped the hall camera, and waited for him to arrive?"

"I made sure to put him in a room with easy access to the staff elevator and parking. I did as you said. I got the food trolley and took it up to his room, and as I came in, he went out with his bag of tools hidden under the linen sheet."

Bailee suddenly broke into tears, her voice trembling, "He was supposed to come back in a few hours, but when he didn't, I... I don't know. I didn't want to mess anything up, so I spent the night. When morning came, he still wasn't back, and then his damn cell phone started blowing up and I had to respond to keep the illusion he was still in the hotel."

"Didn't want to be tracked."

"Excuse me?" Bailee shook her head, not understanding the statement.

"Bob. By his cell phone. He left it behind so he wouldn't be tracked. It would have been pinging off towers." Caleb took a deep breath, and then shook his head, an apology for interrupting. "Then what happened?"

"Well, then I left the room. I had to go to work! I changed out of his pajamas, threw them over the chair, and got dressed into my work clothes, leaving the hotel key behind. I figured once he was back, he'd come find me, and I could just issue him a new one."

"Hold on, I'm missing something." Caleb unconsciously tapped the brochure against the desk, his brow furrowed. "The parking lot video. You don't drive a green Prius. Where does that come in?"

"Prius? I don't know anything about a Prius. Maybe he got it at the marina?"

"Marina?" Caleb smacked the brochure down. "Allister's yacht!"

CHAPTER 43

"Knock, knock." Philip rapped on the door jamb of Lane's office and stepped in, plopping a white deli bag down. "You look as tired as I feel."

"That good, huh?" Lane scoffed as she pulled the white bag towards her and peered inside. "What's this?"

"Well, it was meant to be lunch, but by the look of you, I'm guessing breakfast." Philip sat and moved the bag aside, it blocking the view. "Getting anywhere?"

Lane's desk, normally organized and clear of chaos, was nothing but chaotic, the oak surface hidden under a litany of scattered papers, loose paperclips, and coffee-ringed manila folders, the latter speckled with random post-it notes riddled with Lane's scribbled thoughts.

"Not really." Lane pulled a bagel from the bag and set it between her teeth as she began to gather papers.

She handed the small selected pile to Philip and pulled the bagel away, chewing, then said, through a full mouth, "Read those. They're the financial statements and the analysis on the ski mask."

"I forgot about the ski mask!" Philip's eyes grazed the top of each page as he shuffled, searching for the DNA report. "The long brown hairs? Did they end up being Kristen's after all?"

"Nope."

"Well, then—" Philip stopped, finding the desired sheet, and quickly read through to the bottom of the page. "Bob! They were his hairs? Why would he be wearing—"

"If I knew Phil, I wouldn't be sitting here eating a bagel. I'd be out there arresting somebody." Lane tilted her half-eaten meal in his direction. "Thank you for breakfast, by the way."

"You're welcome." Philip was now scanning the financial reports, his brow puckered as he read down the page. "Wow. You think you kinda know a guy." Philip put the papers down, and pulled the deli bag closer, reaching inside. "I had a nice visit with Len Harrison this morning."

"Oh? How did that come about?" Lane arched an eyebrow.

"I was dropping something off for Hattie." He pointed his bagel in her direction. "And not because I was snooping."

"Fibber." Lane's mouth quirked, taking another bite. "What'd he have to say?"

"Plenty, actually. Jason wasn't only a bad mechanic; he was a spiteful one. He's the one that put sugar in Dub's motor." Philip nodded his head at Lane's shocked expression. "That's not the most interesting thing Len said either. Roger's late wife was having an affair with Bob AND..." Philip paused for dramatic effect. "Roger, in retaliation, tried to pull a few moves on Kristen, resulting in her rejection and I am assuming, their growing hatred for each other."

"Hmmm."

Philip was disappointed with Lane's reaction.

"Hmmm? That's all you have to say? I would have thought you'd be busting out of your seat and tracking Roger down. I mean, especially after this financial report!" Philip picked the papers back up and waved them in the air. "I mean, the guy has motive coming out of his ears!"

"I've already talked to Roger this morning." Lane gave a tired smile as Philip slowly lowered the papers down, frowning. "He seemed legitimately shocked that Bob was embezzling. I don't disagree he's got plenty of motive, I just don't feel it is money-driven, and as far as Kristen is concerned—"

Lane's desk phone beeped and Martha's voice floated through the intercom.

"Sorry to interrupt your lunch, Sheriff. But Mr. Allister is on line one. Again."

"What does he want?" Philip asked, turning to peer through the glass-paned office out into the front section, giving Martha a wave, who was peering back.

"An update on his car and boat being vandalized." Lane sighed, "Martha, I've already told him we've retrieved his boat keys from the boat shop. He can have them back when this investigation is over. Besides, he should know a murder case takes precedence. He's going to have to be patient." Lane suddenly frowned. "And when did you start calling him Mister?"

Martha, for a response, huffed over the phone and clicked off.

"Those two fighting?" Philip glanced at the desk phone, making sure the intercom light was dark.

"Yes, and it's most likely my fault." Lane took a deep breath and scrunched the empty white bag into a small ball and tossed it away. "Me and my big mouth."

Philip, bemused and curious, waited for Lane to explain and when she didn't, he changed the subject, his attention drawn to a post-it note stuck to her monitor.

"What's this about?" He peeled the post-it from the screen. "B.G.A. What does that stand for? Bad Guy Association?"

"No! Bob's initials. Bob Gene Allen." Lane took the post-it back and returned it to its location. "When Roger was here, we got to talking about family names. Found out Chad's middle name is Roger, which means, at some point Bob and Roger were close."

"Family names, huh? Did I ever tell you I'm named after my dad?" Philip leaned back and stuck his leg out, it growing stiff. "I'm number three."

"What? What does that mean?" Lane chuckled, giving him a confused smile.

"I'm the third, Philip T. Russell. My granddad was Philip, and my dad was Theodore because it was too confusing in their house to have two Philips, and then by the time I came around, Granddad was gone, so I got to be Philip. Though, everybody called my old man Teddy for short. What's your middle name? Lane?"

The sheriff held up her hand, silently begging for a moment, her mouth slightly open, her eyes set off into the distance.

The desk intercom beeped again and Martha's voice carried into the small room.

"Sorry, Sheriff. This time I've got—"

"Not now, Martha!" Lane shook her head, making eye contact with the other woman sitting at her desk.

"But it's Caleb! He says it's important!"

Lane frowned and gave a hurried nod in response. "Sorry. Put him through."

"Sheriff?" Caleb's voice, high-pitched with excitement, echoed through the speaker.

"I'm here. Whatcha got, Deputy?" Lane barked into the phone, pulling out her notepad and flipping it down hard onto the desk, her pen immediately etching out the flow of information in short-hand.

"Great work, Caleb." Lane bit her lower lip, her mind racing. "Now, get yourself back here pronto."

"Boarding the ferry now." Caleb clicked off and the phone line went dead.

"Sorry, Sheriff?" Martha stood in the doorway, a pink message pad in hand. "While you were on the phone, Mr. Allister called again and I have Coroner Ames on line two. He says..."

Lane snatched the pink message from Martha's hand, Philip sitting back to avoid being in the cross-fire, and scrunched it in her fist. "We gotta go! Phil, you're with me."

"Sheriff!" Martha whipped around as Lane marched past her with Philip, confused but following directions, only steps behind her. "Coroner Ames said it was important! Jason Powell didn't—"

Lane waved the older woman off and grabbed

her jacket from the coat rack, the stand threatening to topple over.

"I know!" Lane reached the front door and yanked it open, tossing over her shoulder as she stepped through."Jason didn't kill himself. But I know who did!"

CHAPTER 44

"You wanna catch me up to speed?" Philip leaped the curb and wrenched the passenger door open, climbing in beside Lane. "Where are we going?"

Lane didn't answer. Her attention focused on backing out onto the main road and avoiding traffic. She shifted the truck into drive and pressed down on the gas, her arm reaching across her chest, pulling the seat belt forward and down, clicking it into place one-handed.

"Lane? Where are we—"

"Kristen's! We're heading to Kristen's cabin." Her fingers drummed the steering wheel as she pressed harder on the gas pedal, the back of the truck bouncing in and out of potholes. "I'm praying we're not too late."

"Too late? Too late for what?" Philip gripped the dash, his knuckles white, and turned to face Lane, the seat belt halting his movements.

"Sorry!" Lane yelped, the truck bouncing over a curb, Lane making a hard right and narrowly avoiding taking out a fire hydrant.

"You, okay?" she asked and smiled at Philip's haggard expression, adding firmly, "You're okay."

"Who are you—Hey, there's a stop sign coming! Slow down—"

"Hold on." Lane flipped the siren and lights and blew past the red sign, cars skidding to a panicked stop. Zooming past, she clipped them off, mid-howl, and increased the speed, her eyes glued to the road.

"Listen, Phil," she started, still not answering his question. "When we get there, stay behind me, and keep your mouth shut." She shot him an apologetic grimace. "Hopefully, we're not too late, but if we are, I'm gonna need you to—Damn it!"

She slammed the brakes, a row of mailboxes flying past, and wrenched the wheel, the truck coming to a rumbling stop behind three parked cars.

They'd reached the cabin, and for the first time ever, Philip cursed living in a small town, it taking them less than a handful of minutes to barrel through to their destination.

"Let's go!" Lane unsnapped her seat belt. "Remember, stay behind me."

"Wait! Who are we here for?" Philip pressed against the passenger door and hesitated, his other hand grasping Lane's arm and arresting her progress. "Roger?"

Lane vehemently shook her head.

"No. For Chad! We're here for Chad."

CHAPTER 45

"Hello! There's a doorbell!" Kristen groused, wide-eyed, and alarmed as she swung the front door open, Philip practically pounding it off its hinges. "You don't need to knock like a crazy person!"

"We need to come in, Kristen." Lane moved forward, intent on entering, but the widow's small frame held in the doorway, forcing the eager sheriff to come up short.

"Now, wait a minute!" Kristen put her hand out, coming inches from touching Lane. "This isn't a good time. I've got a killer headache, and I don't feel like answering any more questions. You can come back after the funeral. You can't just hound—"

"Fine," Lane said through gritted teeth. "Is Chad home then? May I speak with him?"

"He went on a walk with Roger."

"A walk where?" Lane relaxed her stance, stopping short of sighing.

"The path behind the house to the beach." Kristen folded her arms and stubbornly jutted out her chin. "Why do you want to see Chad? He's had a bad enough day already."

At Lane's annoyed frown, Kristen expanded, "His agent called. They've scrapped the commercial for the anti-itch cream."

"That's too bad. How long ago since they left?"

"Um." Kristen, arms still folded across her chest, shrugged. "No idea. Maybe like, an hour ago? I can have him call you—"

There was a sound of bottles clinking and then a loud crash, glass shattering.

"Are you not home alone, Kristen?" Lane edged closer, bobbing to see past the homeowner and into the hall.

"Oh, the cat probably knocked something over." Kristen looked startled but stood firm, beginning to close the door. "I'll let Chad know—"

Philip stepped away from the front door and pointed to his right, already moving. "It sounds as if it came from this direction." He took off and followed the length of the wraparound porch, his ear picking up the sound of bottles rolling across concrete. "Is somebody back here, Kristen?"

Philip rounded the corner of the walkway and stopped short, jarred at the scene before him.

On the concrete patio, a sliding glass door leading to the master bedroom as a backdrop, was a bubbling hot tub, empty beer bottles lining the side, a few shattered and broken at the base, clearly knocked off by the dangling arm attached to Chad Allen, blood seeping from his wrists, his head lolled to the side, his eyes open, unseeing.

"Lane! Need an ambulance!" Philip bellowed, aware of her pounding footfalls seconds behind him as he crossed the patio, his arms diving into the hot water, reaching up and under Chad's armpits, pulling him from the tub and down to the ground.

"Watch the glass!" Lane warned, her cell phone pressed to her ear, her boot scrapping at the concrete, shoving away large shards of broken glass.

"Kind of hard to do!" Philip snapped, more bottles falling from the hot tub ledge and crashing down.

"Here!" Kristen whizzed past and jerked open the sliding glass door to the master bedroom, waving Philip over. "Here! Put him on the carpet!" She skirted around and grabbed Chad's legs, doing her best to help maneuver through the sliding glass door.

Inside, Philip eased Chad down as Kristen abruptly dropped his legs.

"I'll get a towel!" She stepped over the beet red body and made for the hallway, Lane giving clipped instructions to 9-1-1 behind her.

"Chad?" Philip shouted, pressing his fingers against the man's neck, searching for a pulse. "Chad, can you hear me?"

"He's not responsive," Lane reported to 9-1-1 and then asked Philip, "CPR?"

He lifted Chad's wrist, a clear cut visible, and shook his head.

Lane swore under her breath, then spoke into the phone, "We've got a DOA." She glanced around the room, spotting Kristen returning from the hall. "Keep the ambulance en route. Thanks."

Philip sat back on his heels, his face red. "He's long gone," he confirmed, then looked behind, spotting Kristen at the doorway. His voice low, he turned back to Lane, "When you said we were here for Chad, is this what you meant? Did you think he was going to hurt himself?"

Lane gave a slight shake of her head, putting a gentle hand on his shoulder, and then addressed Kristen, who stood a foot away, a large folded towel in her arms.

"Kristen, I thought you said Chad was with Roger on a walk? You didn't know he was out here?"

Kristen shook her head and slowly sat down on the bed. "No... but... Oh, I've been worried something like this might happen." Kristen pressed a trembling hand to her forehead. "He's been drinking so much."

She addressed the room as a whole, her words barely above a whisper as she placed the towel on top of the bedspread.

"And depressed. I should have kept a closer eye on him." She lowered her hand to her heart. "I honestly thought he was with Roger."

"It's not your fault," Philip began when the bedroom door abruptly banged open, and Roger burst in, his eyes darting from Kristen, sitting on the bed, to Philip standing inches away from the bedroom door.

"I knew it! I knew you were screwin' around—" Roger stopped short, seeing the sheriff, his expression comically confused until his eyes tracked to the floor. "What's happened?" Roger pushed his way past Philip as he dropped to his knees. "Chad?"

Roger lifted his nephew into his arms and shook him, Chad's head rolling to the side.

"Oh, no," Roger groaned and lifted Chad's arms, seeing his wrists. "Please, please, no."

Kristen stood and shot Lane a wide-eyed look, carefully approaching Roger, her hand held out. "We found him in the hot tub, Roger." Kristen, her voice cautious, edged to his side. "He was drinking and..."

She swallowed, pausing as Roger shook his head, gruffly clutching Chad to his chest.

"And he must have decided to..." Kristen clapped a hand to her mouth, taking a moment before letting it drop. "I had thought..." She paused again and

Roger bowed his head, his forehead resting against Chad's. "Roger, I had thought he'd gone with you on your walk. He must have gotten drunk and then cut his..." Kristen's words trailed off.

Roger suddenly sat up. "This isn't happening." He shook his head, his body rocking back and forth on his knees, his nephew still in his arms. "This is not happening."

Kristen placed a hand on his back, her eyes meeting Lane's, her words addressed to the sheriff and ranger. "We were waiting until after the funeral to talk to Chad about his drinking. Roger was going to offer to pay for rehab." She took a deep breath and squeezed Roger's shoulder. "Chad wasn't himself when he was drinking, was he, Roger? Even scary at times. And then he seemed to be so guilt-ridden."

Roger, at her words, stiffened, and he gently released Chad. "Don't, Kristen."

"I know it's hard to hear, Roger." She moved her hand to his shoulder and gave it a hard squeeze. "But I think the Sheriff needs to know. It might help with the investigation."

Roger lumbered to his feet, wobbly and weak-kneed, and Kristen held on, gripping his upper arm, her tone leading, "Between his depression and excessive drinking—"

"I'm warning you." Roger faced her, his head swaying side to side. "This is too far."

Sirens broke in the distance, the sorrowful wail cutting through the surrounding woods and breaching the cramped room.

Lane tilted her head and whispered to Philip directly behind her. "I need you to stall the ambulance, Phil."

"Stall them?"

Lane didn't bother to respond and moved swiftly, stepping in between Roger and Kristen, roughly grabbing Roger's hand and jerking it up into the air, revealing the red scratches lining his bare skin. It was the first time she'd seen Roger not wearing driving gloves, and the hidden scratches were now on full display.

Roger met the Sheriff's eyes, and he snatched his hand back.

"What's too far, Roger?" Lane poked a finger into his chest, her head tilted to the side, inquisitive. "The framing of your nephew for murder, is that FINALLY too far?"

"I... I don't know what you mean," Roger stuttered, his eyes darting to Kristen and then down, to the body at his feet. "I... I..."

Lane, her voice cutting, pressed, "You're actually going to let your nephew, your NAMESAKE, take the blame? Mar his memory with accusations of murder, when you know the truth?"

Roger shook his head, bewildered.

Kristen shook his arm. "Roger, explain to the Sheriff. Tell her about Chad," Kristen said forcefully, her head bobbing up and down, encouraging him to speak. "Go on."

Roger nodded and hurriedly said, "He... he did have a drink—"

"Oh, come on, Roger," Lane sneered, "Don't tarnish him to save her."

"Tell her!" Kristen insisted, her tone instructive, her eyes wide with meaning. "Tell Sheriff Lane what Chad confessed to you. Tell her what he TOLD you."

Roger shook his head.

"Roger!" Kristen stamped her foot. "Tell her!"

"No!" Roger roared, swiping his arms in a wide X and breaking free of Kristen's grasp. "I'm done listening to you!"

He paced towards the sliding glass door and then whirled, spit flying from his lips. "If we'd gone to the police in the beginning, none, NONE of this would have happened!" He suddenly reached up and grabbed the side of his hair, wrenching his toupee loose in the process, and swiveled towards Lane, practically yelling, "I wanted to call the police! But she..." He pointed at Kristen, his face red, "SHE said we couldn't!"

The siren wail of the arriving ambulance practically drowned out Roger's last words. The paramedics were on the scene.

Swearing, Philip darted into the hall as the front door crashed open and Lane put a firm hand on Roger's chest, drawing his eye.

"It was self-defense, wasn't it, Roger?" she asked, her voice coaxing. "Killing Bob."

Roger stared back at the small sheriff, stunned, and then eagerly nodded, his face lighting up, astonished. "Yes!" He suddenly looked past Lane and at Kristen, his finger pointing towards the sheriff. "See! I told you they'd understand! We should have—"

The siren's wail suddenly stopped, and the room went still, leaving only the sound of voices carrying from the front of the house and Philip's tread heading back towards the bedroom.

"We should have called for help." Roger stared down at his nephew's body, his face lost and confused. "How did we get here? If only I had pulled off the ski mask before..."

Kristen shook her head. "Roger, please. Wait for a lawyer," she pleaded as she backed away, her legs bumping against the bed.

He stubbornly shook his head and then appealed to Lane, his words coming in a rush, his soul needing to be purged. "Kristen and I. We're lovers." He gestured between himself and his sister-in-law. "When Bob headed to the mainland for a week last Friday, I rushed over to be with her. Time got away from us, and I missed the damn ferry going back, so

I had to stay over."

Roger's hand plowed into his hair, his fingers tugging the toupee further to the side. "I'd gotten up, having stomach issues, and stepped into the bathroom, not bothering to turn on the lights. I didn't want to wake her." He flipped a hand towards the master bath, the door open, the porcelain toilet centerstage. "I was still in there when I heard a voice, muffled from the other side of the door."

"Roger," Kristen tried again. "Please. This is salvageable."

He continued, determined to go on, "I cracked the door open. The moonlight was streaming down from the skylight, and I could see a man, in the middle of the bedroom, in a ski mask, holding Kristen at gunpoint. I didn't know what to do! It was clear he wasn't aware I was there, and when I tried to open the door all the way, I startled him." Roger's toupee flopped to the side as he turned his attention to Philip. "I didn't have time to think! I... I charged him like a bull, knocking him to the ground, and started throwing punches, trying to keep him from getting a shot off."

Roger looked down at his hands, his fingers splayed wide, his voice dropping low, "We were locked in grips, and I managed to get my hands around his throat. I... I thought I could knock him out if I could cut off his air supply. I never intended on killing him, just... wanted to stop him."

Roger's eyes shot to the bedroom entrance, Philip stepping into the doorway.

Lane held up her hand, cautioning the ranger not to come any closer.

"What happened next, Roger?" she prompted, her eyes leaving Philip and returning to the man in the middle of the room.

He shrugged, his hands flopping to his side in defeat. "It was complete chaos. I yelled for Kristen to call 9-1-1, and I heard her climb out of bed from behind me. I asked her what was taking so long, and she was suddenly beside me, my jeans in her hands. She'd snatched them up from the bedroom floor and I thought... I had thought she was getting my cell phone from the pocket." He gave an unexpected guff, his throat rough. "Then I... I started to sit up and tell her that I thought he was unconscious." He gave an involuntary shudder. "And she... she put the gun to his head and pulled the trigger." Roger put a hand to his heart. "She'd pulled my concealed gun from my jeans and just... just put the barrel to the side of his head. It happened so fast."

Lane watched as Kristen slowly sat down on the bed by the nightstand.

Roger suddenly pleaded, "You have to believe me, Sheriff. We didn't know who was under the mask and when we peeled it off and found Bob staring back at us." Roger shook his head, suddenly flinging a hand in Kristen's direction. "She said it would look bad for us!" His anger flared. "That people would think we'd orchestrated it because of the affair. That the best thing to do was to toss Bob's body in the ocean." His voice broke, "And God forgive me, I listened to her."

"Oh, Roger." Kristen cupped her face and groaned, "You've ruined everything."

"I've ruined? Me?" he exploded, turning on her. "You're the one that panicked! Killing the damn mechanic! For what?"

"For you," Lane answered for Kristen. "The key-holder life insurance policy on Bob? Kristen realized it could be construed as motive and wanted to remove suspicion from you and place it on someone else." Lane's blue eyes drilled into the widow. "And that's why she killed Chad. She felt he was dangerous. She was protecting you, Roger."

"Protecting me? From Chad?" He stumbled back, dumbfounded.

Philip quickly stepped behind Roger and placed a firm hand on his back.

"Yes." Lane's eyes remained glued on Kristen as she spoke to Roger, "This morning, when you were in my office, Chad saw your wallet. Or should I say, Bob's leather-worked wallet?" Lane pointed down at the body lying on the carpet. "Kristen had told Chad that Bob had lost it. Yet, there it was in your hands." She suddenly turned and squared herself with Roger. "Your nephew recognized his father's initials on the wallet. R.E.A. They stand for Robert Eugene Allen. You kept your brother's wallet, didn't you?"

Philip gripped Roger's shoulder, catching on, and said, with a smirk of amazement, "The middle name. Not Gene, but Eugene."

Lane nodded, her eyes still on Roger waiting for an answer.

Kristen suddenly huffed, her shoulders heaving.

"You sentimental, old fool," she whispered, shaking her head, her hand falling onto the nightstand. "You should have dumped it with everything else like I told you."

Roger whipped around, his eyes wide and furious. "What did you do to Chad?" Roger stepped forward, his voice demanding. "Kristen?"

"Nothing," Kristen sighed, sitting up straight, rubbing her forehead. "She's wrong." She dropped her hand and gestured towards Lane, adding, "Yes, Sheriff. Chad did confide in me. He had recognized the wallet and was convinced Roger had killed Bob for the insurance policy. I told him it was nonsense. That Roger didn't need the money." She slapped her thigh and shook her head at her lover. "He was fine, Roger. Chad believed me! So, there was no reason for me to harm him." She suddenly smiled, her eyes darting down at the still body. "Now, I really think you should stop talking, Roger, and let me call a lawyer."

Lane bit her lip, gauging Roger's body language, seeing his longing to believe. She spoke up, "But had Kristen convinced Chad? Completely?" Lane shook her head. "I don't think she was willing to risk him having second thoughts." Lane gestured towards the other woman. "And she'd do anything for you, or rather, for your money. Even murder."

Lane reached behind and grabbed her cuffs.

"You, Roger, might not have been able to make out the voice behind the bathroom door, but Kristen, here, she could. She recognized her husband's voice." Lane locked eyes with Kristen, her mouth quirking at the edges. "She may not have understood why Bob was there or even realized that he was planning on killing her for the life insurance policy, set at seven million."

Kristen's head rocked back, shocked at the dollar amount.

"But she knew it was him." Lane snapped one of the cuffs open and addressed the young widow, "Then again, Kristen... Maybe you did understand what Bob was doing there in a ski mask? Maybe it all clicked into place, and you suddenly realized that the mix-up with your medication and all the car troubles... weren't just a series of accidents, but intentional." Lane turned her head, catching Roger's eye. "It wouldn't have been the first time Bob arranged an accident, would it? He was the one to tamper with your wife's car, wasn't he, Roger?"

Roger wilted and took a step back, bumping into Philip's chest, making no attempt to deny the accusation.

Lane scoffed, "Did you both grow tired of Laurel and decide she was worth more dead than alive? Was it your idea or Bob's?"

Roger stood, unbending, and Philip gave him a rough push, trying to rouse him, resulting in Roger tugging off his toupee and simply shaking his bowed head for an answer.

"I see. It was Bob's idea."

Filled with contempt, Lane faced Kristen and continued, "I'm sure your husband, if he hadn't been interrupted by Roger's unexpected attack, would have killed you, and then ransacked the house. Making it look like a robbery-gone-bad before heading back to the mainland where he had a rock-solid alibi." Lane shook her head, Kristen still sitting on the bed. "But you were quick on your toes and saw an opportunity to be rid of Bob." Lane hitched a thumb back at Roger. "And you had to do it before Roger pulled the mask off, didn't you? So, you pulled the trigger and then convinced your lover to do your bidding to cover up the murder."

Kristen gave no defense, but sat silent, her fingers trailing the knob of the nightstand, her eyes shied away from Lane's piercing glare.

"And you thought you'd gotten away with it. Playing the part of the sorrowful widow. That was until Jason Powell started making a big stink about wanting to join the repair shop. I'm pretty sure he knew you and Roger were having an affair and I think, he made it very clear that he'd keep his mouth shut for a piece of the pie. Problem was, if the pie was arrested, a.k.a. Roger, then nobody got a slice."

"What a nightmare," Roger finally spoke, his throat gravel.

Lane turned slightly, pointing her hand in his direction. "When the key-holder insurance policy came to light, you became suspect number one, and Kristen knew it. She could see the writing on the wall, and the only way to keep you from being pulled from her clutches was to point that ever-waving finger of guilt at somebody else."

Lane turned back to Kristen. "You stayed behind at the shop with Jason, probably offering to help him with his car, or maybe, for some other carnal reason..." She glanced back at Roger. "I'm guessing your jealous streak is not unwarranted?" Lane smirked at Kristen, stressing the innuendo, and continued, holding her stare, "You'd gotten a hold of Jason's phone and dummied up the confession texts, and then, I am assuming, while his attention was on the car motor, you put the gun up to his head and pulled the trigger. Basically, a repeat of Bob's murder. Then you locked up the shop, purposely leaving your cell phone behind, and headed to the gym, making sure you were seen. The little side trip also giving you an excuse to shower and wash off the gunpowder. You then brought home dinner and started to bemoan the fact you'd left your cell phone at the office."

Lane twisted, half-facing Roger. "Kristen knew Chad looked upon her as a quasi-mother figure and would be willing to accompany her back to the shop, especially after explaining a made-up argument between her and Jason." Lane looked down at the sprawled body. "Poor Chad. He just wanted everyone to get along and be a family." Lane sighed, "And here you were, Kristen, starting to set him up to take the fall. A backup to your backup plan."

Lane looked up and shook her head, her blue eyes hard. "You must have really panicked when Roger went on his walk, and Chad came to you with his suspicions. He'd seen his father's wallet, the one you claimed Bob had lost, in his own uncle's hands. I'm sure you hoped you had convinced him otherwise, but Chad was an actor. How could you really trust that he believed your denial? You couldn't. So, you encouraged him to have a soak in the hot tub, something I know Roger had suggested earlier and probably again, once the two had arrived back home, putting the idea into your head."

"I can't hear this," Roger whispered.

Lane, her voice harsh, spoke louder, "You then brought Chad a six-pack of beer, the two of you being drinking buddies and all. But one of his beers was probably spiked. My guess, with a sleeping pill."

From behind Roger, Philip let out a low groan, having fallen prey to such a tactic himself once upon a time.

"And then you left Chad to boil in the hot tub like a lobster before slitting his wrists." Lane took a deep breath. "Kristen Allen, I am arresting you for the—"

Kristen's fingers tightened around the nightstand handle, and with a sudden jerk, she yanked the little drawer open, reaching in and pulling out a stubbed-nosed revolver, her thumb on the hammer, cocked back, her finger gripping the trigger.

In one fluid motion, Lane pulled her service weapon, leveling it at Kristen's chest.

"This is a no-win, Kristen!" Lane warned, her hand steady. "Put the gun down."

"Guess I should be thankful my stupid husband always kept a gun on his side of the bed," Kristen sniped, waving the weapon at Philip and then in Lane's direction, her deception apparent by how she held the gun. There was no fear of the firearm. "Now, you two back up."

Roger stood his ground as Philip inched away.

"Come on, Roger. This is nothing an expensive lawyer can't fix." Kristen edged around the bed, intent on the sliding glass door. "We'll go out this way and down to the beach."

"Okay, Kristen." Roger held out his hands. "I'll follow you and then we can—"

Without warning and much like he had described from that moonlit night, Roger suddenly charged, his arms outstretched for the gun, his voice raised in a courageous challenge as Philip lurched towards him, his fingers brushing the back of Roger's belt, failing to grip the leather, himself, falling to the ground.

Kristen pulled the trigger, a loud bang proceeding the action, a bullet flying from the weapon and embedding itself in Roger's forehead, her lover dropping like a stone, his chest landing across Chad's unmoving legs, dead.

There were two short clipped shots from Lane's weapon, and Kristen's shoulder flew back, her hand dropping the revolver to the floor, her body falling against the bed, and then ricocheting down to the carpet.

Lane kicked the revolver to the side and shouted, "Get the EMT, Phil!" and then holstered her gun. She put a knee in Kristen's back and yanked the woman's arms behind her, cuffing her wrists before applying pressure to her shoulder, blood soaking through the shirt and in between Lane's fingers.

CHAPTER 46

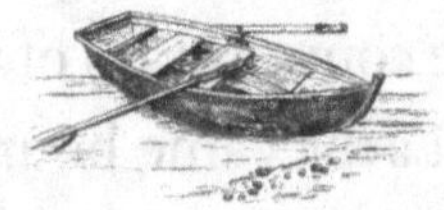

"Hey, Sheriff! You need an order to go, or would you like a table?"

"Evening, Lacey. A table for two, please. That is if you've got one." Lane peered into the main dining area of the Royal Fork, the eatery filled to capacity.

"We're pretty busy. It's our surf and turf special tonight," Lacey admitted and then leaned in. "Fresh crab and sirloin steak. Only fourteen-ninety-nine!"

"Count me in." Lane smiled, having a pretty strong guess on where and how the restaurant owner had gotten their hands on fresh crab during the off-season.

"Great! Um, let me see." Lacey stepped from behind the hostess stand and rubber-necked the room. "Oh, it looks like table fifteen is being bussed right now. Give me like five minutes, and then I can seat you?"

Lacey bustled off, weaving her way through tables, stopping now and then to nod and give a quick word about the menu.

Lane spotted two familiar faces at the first stop.

Harry and Mollie, the pair an official couple, a whole month into their budding relationship, were sitting with their heads bowed together. The lovebirds sharing an intimate conversation of whispers and giggles, that is, until Lacey came bounding by, the two suddenly sitting back with matching giddy grins.

Mollie's brother, who hadn't been thrilled with the idea of her dating a much older man, eventually bent to Hattie's will, the old woman softening Len's heart with frequent dinner invitations and a continuous supply of hand salve.

Harry caught sight of Lane and tried to wave her over to join them, but the sheriff gave a shake of her head and a warm smile, hitching her thumb towards the door, indicating she was waiting for someone.

Not far from Harry's table sat Martha and George, the funeral director shoveling butter-dipped crab in his mouth, the golden goodness dripping off the ends and soaking his beard. Martha, almost bemused, lovingly dabbed at the corners of George's mouth with a napkin, her eyes occasionally darting to the suited man, sitting at the bar, eating dinner alone.

Though Lane had never approved of Martha and Allister's affair, she couldn't help but feel a tiny bit guilty that Martha had ended their forbidden rela-tionship, the older woman suspicious the semi-re-tired lawyer had been seeing someone on the side.

As it turned out, the mystery woman who had flown with Mike Allister to Florida had actually been his sister arriving from Chicago for dinner and a few days of sightseeing. The two had met up as planned, and when they received word, that their sibling had suffered a heart attack down in the sunshine state, they'd hurriedly gotten on a plane to be by his side.

Mike Allister laid the death of the affair squarely at Lane's feet.

This was in conjunction with his numerous com-plaints to her supervisors, stating if she had made the investigation on the vandalization of his yacht and slashed tires a priority, she would have discov-ered the video of Bob Allen slashing the Mercedes-Benz's tires in the Park and Ride lot.

Lane, secretly kicking herself, had quickly point-ed out that she had been short on manpower with limited resources and rightly justified in focusing on the murder investigation and the subsequential suicide-homicide of Jason Powell.

Reasonably certain of and even sympathetic to-wards Bob's motives, she imagined that after sneak-ing out of the hotel and driving Bailee's car to the Seattle Marina, where he'd stolen Mike Allister's boat to traverse the waters back to the island, Bob had found himself unable to fight temptation. Slashing Allister's tires as he passed the Park & Ride lot on foot in the middle of the night, trekking his way to his own house, intent on killing his young wife for the insurance money.

Consequently, Allister's opinion of her plummeted to an all-new low, and unable to wreak revenge on a dead man, Allister turned his sights on Lane, seeking retribution where he could. The lawyer, actively declaring his concerns for the town's wellbeing — was asking his fellow islanders what would happen to people's property and safety if they kept Lane as sheriff in the next election? Could they be sure she'd be thorough in future investigations?

As if feeling Lane's eyes on his back, Mike Allister swiveled on his barstool and gave her a sneering half-smile followed by an indignant huff before turning back around to his meal for one.

"He'll get over it." Philip's voice sounded from behind her, his breath moving her hair. "I heard Sue Carter is taking him to Europe on one of her antique treasure trips to help him heal his wounded heart."

"Is that so?" Lane twisted around and smiled up at the ranger, his hand falling on her shoulder and lightly pushing forward, Lacey waving from table fifteen, indicating they could now be seated.

"Sorry, I'm late." Philip pulled out Lane's chair, smiling to himself as she took a deep breath, the chivalrous action always seeming to get under her skin. "How did things go with the state prosecutor today?"

"He's decided to let Bailee off with a plea deal and no jail time."

"Boy, is she lucky."

Lane had thought the same. Charged with multiple misdemeanors, one of which was purposely misleading the police, Bailee had managed to convince the prosecutor she was completely unaware of Bob's true intentions and if, she had been aware, would not have participated in the deception.

Lane wondered if Bob had successfully killed Kristen, returning to the hotel, his alibi secured... What would he have told Bailee? Knowing full well that Kristen's death would be reported in the news the next day?

Lane supposed upon his planned return, he would have told another wild story, one where he found Kristen murdered and the house burgled. Convincing Bailee to stay quiet and pointing out that it would be dangerous for him and her if the authorities knew he'd been to the island, let alone inside the house.

If Bailee would have been able to see through the ruse and genuinely have a conscience, that would never be known.

"And what about Kristen?" Philip waved at Harry and Mollie, both standing and getting ready to leave the restaurant.

"She's claiming self-defense for Bob and Roger and then, a plea of innocent for the charges of Jason and Chad's homicides. She's insisting both deaths were, in fact, suicides."

"Will she get away with it?"

"Not a chance in hell."

"Good."

Harry, holding Mollie's hand, stopped at their table. "Hey, you two! We still on for bowling next Friday?" Harry clapped his free hand down on Philip's shoulder, "Or are you tired of losing?"

"Never tired of losing. Looking at your face, sure, but not losing," Philip teased, provoking a giggle from Mollie, who shook her head, exchanging a look with Lane.

"Ha, Ha." Harry shook his head playfully at Mollie and then snapped his fingers. "Oh! Will you still be able to Hattie-sit tomorrow? If not, I'm gonna need to find someone else or stay home." Harry, his voice low, leaned into Mollie. "Hattie loves Phil almost as much as she loves me."

At the mention of Miss Hattie, Lane recalled a conversation Philip had shared between himself and the old woman, convinced Hattie had almost omniscient powers of insight when it came to their fellow islanders.

Two things had stuck out to Lane.

"He seemed like a nice fella. Too bad he went that way,"

and *"Those kinds of people feel as if taking a life is worth the reward."*

Had Hattie known or guessed Bob was at a crossroad? He could have readily confessed to his brother how financially burdened he was and asked for help but had instead chosen to murder for money—something he'd done before and seemed to have no qualms about repeating.

"She loves me WAY more." Philip's jest broke Lane's concentration and she looked up to see him wink at Mollie before nodding at Harry. "Don't worry, Har. I've got you covered. You guys have fun tomorrow."

"See you two, Friday." Mollie lightly tapped Lane's shoulder and gave her a hurried wave, the couple leaving as the approaching Lacey arrived to take their order.

"Two surf and turf specials coming up!" Lacey gave them both a broad smile and hurried off to the kitchen.

"Those two are smitten with each other." Lane took a quick sip of water. "It's cute."

"She'll eventually come to her senses."

"Oh, stop it, Phil." Lane scolded with a smile as she shook out her napkin.

"Getting back to our original subject, did you ever find out the deal with the green Prius?" Philip copied her motions and set his elbows on the table. "Was Dub wrong about the color?"

"Nope, he was dead right." Lane leaned in and kept her voice at a whisper so the neighboring tables would not overhear. She then explained how when finding out Martha had forgotten to run the Canadian plates on the green Prius seen on the ferry video, Caleb had been the one to discover the vehicle, after all, had belonged to Emma Girard, Roger's live-in-housemaid. Her deputy had then made a mad dash to the mainland, convinced that Emma had purposely held back information, the poor man jaded by Bailee's deception. He quickly found out he'd simply asked the wrong question. As she had stated, Emma had driven to Canada, but not in her own car. She had chosen to rent a vehicle, one with a larger trunk, the car filled to the brim with presents for her new grandbaby.

Caleb concluded that Roger, not wanting to drive his own colorful car because it would stick out like a sore thumb on the island, especially parked in front of Kristen's house, had taken his maid's vehicle, the woman, none the wiser, upon her return.

"So, mystery solved? They killed Bob, packed him into the Prius, drove down to Dub's dock, threw the body into the rowboat, rowed out, where Roger stripped, bludgeoned, and tossed the body over the side. He then tried to sink the rowboat, and swam back to the dock, where Kristen was behind the wheel, ready to drive him back to her place."

Lane nodded, chipping in, "And then come morning, to cover her tracks, Kristen texted Bob's cell phone, doing her best to look the concerned and doting wife, who thinks her husband is still on the mainland when she knows his body is with the fishes."

"Must have been a hell of a shock when she got a text back."

"Courtesy of Bailee trying to cover Bob's butt."

"What a complicated mess." Philip sighed, his gaze softening. "And you figure it all out." He shook his head, as ever, in awe of her. "You know, you really are amazing, Lane. In fact, I think you're the most amazing—"

Philip's words of praise were interrupted by Lacey plunking down two cold beers as she skirted to the following table with her water pitcher.

The conversation stalled at her departure.

Philip cleared his throat.

"I've uh, I thought about what you said a while back, the last time we were here, and I want you to know, I'd go with you."

"What?" Lane shook her head, not following.

"If you were to leave the island, would I follow?" Philip reminded. He took a deep breath and reached across the table, his fingertips brushing Lane's wrist. "And I want you to know. I would. I'd go with you. If you wanted me to, that is."

"Phil." Lane eagerly snatched at his fingers and

gripped him tightly, pulling him closer. "I know I'm not the most emotional woman. It's hard for me to..." Lane glanced at the table beside them, Martha's curious eyes peeking over her husband's shoulders. "To be affectionate in public. But I do. I do truly care for you."

"There's no need to explain, Lane. I've already got you all figured out." A smile quirked Philip's mouth as Lane straightened, her eyes wide in surprise.

"Figured me out?" She let go of his hand and crossed her arms. "What's that supposed to mean?"

"I've told you before. You're just like a tootsie roll pop. Hard outside, soft and gooey with love on the inside." Philip lightly tapped her forearm, and Lane uncrossed her arms, allowing him to hold her hand. "I think I'll start calling you, Tootsie. Or maybe Toots. It'll be my little nickname for you."

"You wouldn't dare."

"Oh, come on, you have to admit. It fits you."

"You know, Phil. I love that you find yourself so funny."

Philip's eyes suddenly widened, and his mouth dropped open before slipping into a sly smile.

"Lane? Did you say I love you first?"

"NO."

"I think you did!"

"I said, I love THAT you... THAT!"

"No, no." Philip shook his head, his face aglow. "I

distinctly heard. I love you."

"That's not what I—"

Philip put a finger to her lips, halting Lane's speech, and leaned across the table, gently pressing his mouth against hers.

After a lingering moment of bliss, he pulled away, his smile devilish and his eyes intent on hers, his voice low and soft.

"I love you too, Toots."

The story isn't over!

Don't miss the next exciting and intriguing adventure with Lane and Philip in **Book IV**: *Within the Pines*.

WITHIN THE PINES

CHAPTER ONE

The dwindling campfire, neglected as much as she, struggled to fend off the encroaching darkness, the glow barely touching the surrounding pines, their spindly tops moving with the midnight breeze, towering in judgment, unpleased with the group of city slickers daring to venture among their midst.

"I'm cold. Can someone—"

A log was tossed onto the starving fire, and sparks cascaded, flirting upon the air with the laughter and conversation of the camp. Bits of flame mingled with the spiraling smoke, narrowly missing the swaying branches before extinguishing from a violent red to a fluttering ashen grey... much like her marriage.

She watched her spouse and their fellow campers, the group moving further away from the fire, laughing and cajoling, migrating to the mess tent, a shout for more whiskey and smores, the warrior cry.

Her gaze lingered on her husband's back as his hand slipped down and cupped the butt cheek of their young guide, who moved away from his touch a tad slower than expected. A heavy sigh of disappointment escaped her lips, and Nancy Scott, instead of joining the festivities or admonishing her husband, focused on the flames, her thoughts drawn to the charcoaled splinters fueling the small inferno, very much mimicking her internal turmoil.

"So much for your promises, Witt."

An unexpected crunch of needles and pine cones underfoot, a heavy step beyond the tree line, caught her ear, and her head jerked up, eyes darting past the firepit and out into the trees.

What was that?

The group, successful in their campaign, flowed from the mess tent, shouting their triumph, and made their way back to the firepit. She ignored their antics, her eyes searching the condensed darkness and the tall, crowded pines stark against the starlight bleak.

A scarlet glow, an ember at the end of a cigarette, suddenly inflamed and exposed an outline, a blotting black matching the denseness of the evergreens, standing still, reverent, like the trees, a silent observer.

Who is that?

She leaned forward, curiosity piqued. Her plastic red solo cup crackled under the pressure, her grip tightening as she strained, fearful of taking her eyes from the silhouette, unsure she'd be able to find it again, the outline barely noticeable.

A head, shoulders... definitely a person. What were they doing?

"Cami?" she called and then, realizing the shadow was more masculine in stature than her petite friend, tried, "Aaron? Or is that you, Nick?"

There was no given response, and she leaned forward, head cocked, eyes slit, wondering if she was seeing things. The day's fatigue, conjuring a figure, smoke and darkness tricking her eyes. She tried again. "Clint?... Witt? What are you doing? Watering the tree? We have a perfectly fine outhouse!"

The shadow shifted, sliding behind a vast pine and out of sight, her call unanswered.

"Nance..." A whispered hush against her ear caused her to start, the source stepping back and announcing loudly, "Looks to me like you need more "toddy" in your hot toddy, ya hottie!"

A glass bottleneck suddenly weighed heavy upon the rim of her plastic cup, the sharp smell of whiskey reaching her nose. She peered down, her solo cup dipping under the pressure, the pourer sloppily cascading Crown Royal all over. She quickly transferred the drink to her other hand and shook out her fingers, dispelling overcast droplets from her skin.

"Clint! Watch it!"

"Cheers!" Clint threw her a wink, along with one of his best disarming and charming smiles, before moving on to their fellow campers and heavily tipping his bottle into each of their cups, a double pour into Witt's. As if her husband needed more liquid courage.

She continued to follow his drunken path, all the while taking count. One... three... five... Seven. She leaned forward and peered into the mess tent, counting two more. Nine... nine people. Everyone accounted for... and drunk. Well, almost everyone.

Her frustration rose as the group arranged chairs and log stumps around the rock-bordered pit, tossing an additional log onto the fire and pulling out their pilfered goods: marshmallows, chocolate, and graham crackers.

"What is that smell?" Nancy's nose crinkled at the overwhelming aroma of weed, which suddenly outweighed the stench of campfire smoke, and muttered, "You've got to be kidding me." She gave a pointed glare in Clint's direction, knowing full well who supplied the additional merriment, and it suddenly occurred to her that it might be the explanation for the figure in the woods. She sat up, her voice dripping with disappointment. "You're all acting like this is a frat party. We have a ride in the morning!"

"Hey, now! Get that woman a smore!" Aaron Coletta bellowed loudly, his wife Sandi hanging on his plaid flannelled arm, an infectious laugh following his declaration, the outburst very unlike his usual uptight bank manager demeanor. The small group cheered the edict, and Nancy flopped back into her canvas chair, defeated.

This was supposed to be a corporate getaway, a reward for their top sellers, she and Witt, the gracious hosts.

Vita Mineralium, their small garage-headquartered business, within a year, was on the brink of becoming an empire, practically an overnight success! Between her enthusiasm and Witt's business savvy, they had enlisted an army of friends and family, who engaged and created a litany of internet resellers via various and numerous social media outlets, the enthusiastic militia, selling and promoting their vitamin products, the initial small group growing and reaching astronomical numbers.

The new members, all of whom continuously bragged about the benefits of their product, gave them free advertising and spread the word like wildfire across the nation, boosting their sales and expansion. Their foothold in the Pacific Northwest, home base, was just the beginning. Witt had set his eyes on the East Coast, hiring a publicist who arranged several small interview slots with the top morning news affiliates and minor talk shows, landing her husband a coveted five-minute stint on a financial segment of CNN.

That's when their progress with the business exploded. Though head twirling to Nancy, it wasn't fast enough for Witt. He was hungry for more, pushing for additional airtime and larger crowds, their P.R. agent insisting they needed to have patience, hinting that self-help books and seminars were the next step... that this was the beginning of a windfall of success, they simply needed to trust him. Frustrated with impatience, Witt was tempted to take things into his own hands... Much like he did in other aspects of their life. This trip, for instance.

Initially, Nancy had hoped for a few days away without the kids, an intimate adventure all their own. He saw it differently and turned the horseback riding-camping excursion into a tax-deduction opportunity, pushing her to arrange the gathering, transforming her romantic suggestion into a corporate gift trip. A formal celebration for their top sellers. As Witt put it, a jumping point of encouragement, a time and place for a serious discussion on how people could reinvest and expand on their platform of followers. A declaration that if Vita Mineralium was going to make it to the top of the health industry, it had to be a joint venture. Everyone had to carry their share of the load, everyone needed to be invested and... INVEST.

"Nancy? Can I get you anything?" Cami plopped

down her camp chair and inched closer, their knees touching, her puppy-dog eagerness instantly annoying. "Are you still cold? Should I grab a blanket from your tent? Here, I'll get one—"

"I'm fine, Cami." She looked at her self proclaimed assistant, in truth, her right arm, and smiled, the expression failing to reach her tired eyes. "I was trying to enjoy the fire and a bit of quiet." The hint went unnoticed.

"Oh, I don't blame you!" The spiky-haired blonde lowered her voice to just above a whisper, leaning further into Nancy's space, her hand lightly landing on her forearm. "Things are starting to get a bit rowdy. Don't you think?" Cami failed to acknowledge that it was her husband, Clint, who was hyping the party atmosphere. "Have you noticed how much Sandi has had to drink tonight?" She tilted her head toward the pretty brunette clinging to Aaron's arm, a thirty-something like them, and added, "Like she's upset about something? I don't know if you noticed, but Aaron and Maddie disappeared for a bit... TOGETHER. Wonder what they were up to?" She raised an eyebrow, giving a knowing nod with a lopsided smile, and cast her eyes sideways in the direction of Maddie and Nick Mason, the superstar sales couple of Vita Mineralium.

Nancy followed her gaze, her own attention instantly drawn to Nick, a smoldering cigarette in hand. She forgot he smoked when drinking. Possibly it was him she had seen, and he hadn't heard her call his name...

"How long ago was this, Cami?"

"Oh, forty minutes or so." Cami inched even closer, her voice rising in volume instead of lowering. "Both were gone for QUITE a while." She twisted toward the fire and caught Sandi's eye, giving her nemesis a mock cheer with her cup before turning back to Nancy with a wicked smile. "Look at the way Sandi is clinging to Aaron. She can barely stand!"

Nancy frowned at the observation and noted, despite Cami's claims, that Sandi was having no problem standing under her own power. However, the woman's eyes and ears were pinned on Witt, devouring his every move and syllable.

Did she need to worry about Sandi?

Cami's face bobbed into Nancy's line of sight, breaking her train of thought, Cami's eyes wide with curiosity, her voice dropping to a whisper, "Will you say something to Nick? I... I know you don't approve."

"Of course, I don't approve!" Nancy huffed and then smirked in triumph. "But it's no longer an issue. I had a little chat with Maddie this afternoon and told her to end the affair with Aaron. If not, I'd be forced to tell Nick. I also strongly suggested she keep the Vita Mineralium family in mind before jeopardizing her standing over a man... especially

THAT man." Nancy smugly sat back in her chair, a pleased smile on her lips. "I would imagine Maddie and Aaron disappearing for a bit was so that she could end things."

"Or squeeze in a quickie."

"Cami!" Nancy's eyes slit, and she twisted in her chair. "I really don't think you are in a position to throw rocks at a glass house."

At the rebuke, Cami leaned away, stung, and, feigning ignorance, gave a confused shake of her head with a weak smile.

"Ohhhh!" Nancy suddenly gave out a long sigh, her scowl morphing into shame. "I'm sorry, that was rude of me, Cami." She lightly patted the other woman's hand. "I'm on edge, but that's no excuse. You know the new accountants will be looking at our books come Tuesday?" She shifted in her chair. "You'll have everything in order, correct?"

"Oh, yes." Cami's head joggled up and down. "On your desk, Monday morning."

"And there won't be any discrepancies, like last time?" Nancy arched an eyebrow. "Because if there were, I think you know how disappointed I would be."

"There won't be, Nancy. Everything will be in order. I promise."

Worried she'd displeased her employer, Cami quickly added in a chipper, change the subject tone, "Everyone seems to be having a good time! We really should make this a yearly thing." She glanced toward the mess tent where Angie and Tanya, their guides, were putting away the chaos caused by the raid for midnight snacks. "Especially if you can get the same deal. How hard did you twist Angie's arm?"

"Twist her arm? I did nothing of the sort! If anything, I am helping her!" Nancy gave Cami a severe look and then leaned in herself, her tone lifting. "With my circle of friends and a raving review, Angie's business should quadruple. Besides, the poor girl has no business sense." She waved toward the rest of the camp. "If it hadn't been for me already.. Seriously, nylon tents? Who would pay the kind of money she wants to sleep in a nylon tent? I helped her elevate things. The price decrease in her quote was in gratitude."

Cami furiously nodded, as if she wouldn't dare to disagree, and turned in the direction of Nancy's wave, indicating the rest of the campsite, a "glamping" campsite, to be precise. Large Yurt-like tents were erected behind them, Italian solar-powered lights strung from one pole steeple to the other, enhancing the cream canvas flaps, pulled back, exposing sheer mosquito fabric allowing one to look in, revealing a full-size queen mattress piled high with blankets and fluffy pillows, accompanied by leather chairs and matching ottomans, trunks full of books and other merriment stationed in the corners – a far cry from camping if ever there was.

As if her ears were burning, Angie Bennett stepped within the circle, a tin bucket in hand, and cleared her throat, garnering the group's attention.

Nancy and Cami huddled in a conspirator's whisper directly in front of her, looked up, curious, while Maddie, drunkenly hovering marshmallows on a stick, did the same.

Witt ignored her entrance and continued speaking. Nick was seated to his right and Aaron, with Sandi still clinging to his arm, was seated on his left. Clint stood behind them, refilling their drinks after every sip.

Witt's brow was furrowed, his tone serious, the conversation ongoing, "Invest their college fund in Vita Mineralium now, instead of waiting, and in two years' time, rather than sending them to some community college, you'll be shipping them to one of the big four, the tuition fully paid. I'm telling you. Commitment is the driving force for a successful..." His words faded as Angie stepped closer, his bloodshot eyes following the lines of her leg, stopping on her Levi's back pockets.

Angie plastered on a patient smile and raised her voice, "Okay, folks! Time to call it a night. We've got the sunrise mimosa ride in the morning."

As if on cue, a loud whinny from the corral went up into the night, and everyone turned as Angie's assistant, Tanya, locked the makeshift pen gate, giving a final pat to the rear of a lingering dapple grey, encouraging the horse to move along, it pining for another apple.

"We'll need to leave by five-thirty a.m.," Angie continued, "And you'll want to dress warmly. The October mornings can be pretty chilly here on the island." She turned toward Tanya, the young girl making her way to the group. "We'll have muffins for breakfast at the sunrise point and then a full brunch waiting for you when we arrive back at camp."

"Ang? I don't know if I'll feel up to a ride," Maddie confessed, stumbling to the side, Sandi's arm jetting out, stopping her from taking a tumble. "I have a funny feeling I'm going to have one hell of a hangover tomorrow."

"And you're very welcome, Maddie!" Clint cheered, taking the final swig from the Crown Royal bottle, and tossing the empty over his shoulder with a self-congratulatory smile, as Tanya, shooting Angie an annoyed look, quietly circled behind him and retrieved the discarded item.

"Maddie, you'll be fine." Nancy's voice shot out, her tone authoritative, "All of you will. I suggest everyone drink a good amount of water before hitting the pillow, which is NOW."

"That's not a bad idea," Angie agreed lightly, "I'll have Tanya bring some water bottles to everyone's tent." She hurried, a chorus of grumbles igniting, "Besides, the view really is to die for. Not only do you have the gorgeous sunrise, but the ocean view is spectacular, and you can see a miniature Seattle in the background." She stepped forward and tilted the bucket in hand, sending water sloshing down upon the campfire, a hiss of hot steam rising with a large plume of white smoke. "You might even see some whales!"

The enthusiasm Angie had hoped for did not come as everyone rose from their spots and began heading for their designated tents.

Sandi quickly released Aaron's arm and made a straight beeline for their hostess.

"Um, Nance, one second." Sandi put a polite hand on Nancy's back, her other still gripping Maddie's arm, the latter teetering from side to side. "Sorry, hold on." She gave a pleading nod to Nick, who was taking the last drag from his cigarette before tossing it into the doused fire, and silently asked for him to take his drunken wife's arm. Releasing Maddie to her husband's care, she turned to Nancy with a concerned look.

"I don't know if you overheard, but Witt was pushing pretty hard on Aaron and Nick tonight."

"Pushing? About what?" Nancy gave a friendly wave and mouthed, "Sleep tight!" to Nick and Maddie, her eyes watching Witt over Sandi's shoulder, her husband still speaking to Clint and Aaron, his hooded stare focused on Angie's backside.

"Investing our savings. ALL of our savings, Nance. Listen, we don't have the kind of money that you and—"

"Oh, that's not pushing!" Nancy gave a light laugh, her full attention now resting on the anxious woman. "That's sound advice, Sandi! He's a financial adviser. I mean, that's what he did before we started our business and... Well, Sandi...You and Aaron, you're in the inner circle. You're practically family, and if you ask me, you'd be wise to heed any advice he gives."

"But he's advising we invest our kid's college funds! We're already sinking several thousand dollars in product monthly and—"

"And I've signed your commission checks!" Nancy's face suddenly blossomed into a proud smile. "Sandi, if you continue to do as well as you have, in six months, YOU will be the breadwinner of your home, NOT Aaron. That's an incredible accomplishment for a stay-at-home mom! And if Witt is recommending you invest more than just your time into Vita Mineralium, which..." She lowered her voice to a whisper. "Is on the verge of becoming a multi-million-dollar company..."

Sandi's eyebrows raised in surprise as Nancy gave her a subtle nod, stating it was true.

"Well, it's because we love you guys!" She suddenly leaned in and squeezed Sandi's shoulders in a half-hug. "Don't believe me? Ask Maddie and Nick. Each month they put eighty percent of their commission check BACK into the company, and EACH MONTH, they earn its return, plus twenty-five percent." Nancy patted Sandi's arms and stepped back, adding, "Aren't you tired of being in second place? You know, Sandi, if Aaron applied himself a bit more, you two could knock Maddie and Nick from the top."

Sandi shook her head, apparently still mystified by the figures.

"Eighty percent? Even with commission chargebacks? Our last check was far below—"

"Maddie does an excellent job of up-selling. She moves more Titan packages than anyone, and because of that, chargebacks on the lower items have no effect on her commission. They basically wash each other out, and she knows that investing in the product is investing in her and Nick's future. She has faith in the process, and you should too."

"I understand the concept, but Aaron doesn't make the money that—"

"You wait and see. The growth within this last year will be nothing compared to what is coming, and knowing Witt as I do, the few measly thousand you have sunk away for the kid's college will come back a thousandfold, if not more! Think hundreds of thousands. Now..." She patted Sandi's arm, her tone motherly. "Get some sleep. We've got an early ride in the morning!"

Thank You!

Thank you for reading the third book of the Rockfish Island Mysteries series, False Findings, A Rockfish Island Mystery:III. The soon to be released fourth book in the series, Within the Pines, will be available summer of 2023.

If you enjoyed False Findings, would you be so kind as to put a review on Amazon, Goodreads, and Bookbub? Thank you for your support!

ALSO BY J.C. FULLER

A ROCKFISH ISLAND MYSTERY SERIES

Black Bear Alibi

The Push

False Findings

Within the Pines - Available Summer 2023

www.ingramcontent.com/pod-product-compliance
Lightning Source LLC
Chambersburg PA
CBHW010650010826
48969CB00014B/2445